"Turner [is] one of the best writers in the Christian market."

—*Publishers Weekly*

"Turner [proves] that a faithful Christian witness can come packaged in a quality novel."

—*Publishers Weekly*

JAMIE LANGSTON TURNER

WINTER BIRDS

BETHANYHOUSE

MINNEAPOLIS, MINNESOTA

Published by Bethany House Publishers
11400 Hampshire Avenue South
Bloomington, Minnesota 55438

Bethany House Publishers is a division of
Baker Publishing Group, Grand Rapids, Michigan.

Printed in the United States of America

ISBN-13: 978-0-7642-0015-1
ISBN-10: 0-7642-0015-1

Library of Congress Cataloging-in-Publication Data

Turner, Jamie L.
    Winter birds / Jamie Langston Turner.
       p. cm.
    ISBN 978-0-7642-0015-1 (pbk.)
    ISBN 0-7642-0015-1 (pbk.)
    1. Older women—Fiction. 2. Widows—Fiction. 3. Domestic fiction.
I.Title.

    PS3570.U717W56   2006
    813'.54—dc22   2006017659

With gratitude and love

FOR IVA MAE PATTERSON TURNER
(May 11, 1921–January 6, 2004)

*Daily I see your tender heart, your ready
smile, your strong faith, your love of
music, your pleasure in a job well done,
your sense of humor.*

AND

FOR ALTYN JAMES TURNER
(b. November 27, 1918)

*Daily I see your standards of excellence,
your attention to detail, your reverence
for God's Word, your willingness to
sacrifice for those you love.*

*Daily I see you both in your son Daniel,
my husband, and for your great gift to
me, I thank you.*

JAMIE LANGSTON TURNER has been a teacher for thirty-five years at both the elementary and college levels and has written extensively for a variety of periodicals, including *Faith for the Family*, *Moody*, and *Christian Reader*. Her first novel, *Suncatchers*, was published in 1995. Born in Mississippi, Jamie has lived in the South all her life and currently resides with her husband and son in South Carolina, where she teaches creative writing and literature at Bob Jones University.

CONTENTS

After so long grief, such felicity!

— *THE COMEDY OF ERRORS*

CHAPTER 1

CONSCIENCE IS BUT A WORD THAT COWARDS USE

The pine warbler eats its neighbors in the pine tree—insects and spiders—as well as seeds and berries. As it creeps over the bark of the tree, the warbler's olive green and yellow plumage sometimes becomes stained with pine resin.

Rachel comes to take my dishes. I watch her move slowly and silently. I have cleaned my plate tonight, have used my biscuit to polish its surface. The dish is one Rachel makes from an old recipe card titled Irma's Beef Dinner. The card is worn around the edges and splattered with tomato sauce and onion soup. Rachel doesn't know who Irma is, she has told me, and she doesn't remember how she came by the recipe card. Rachel may be excused from remembering such details.

As for me, perhaps I may be excused from remembering details, also. I have been young, but now I am old. That is the usual course, though I have often dreamed of how it would be to say I have been old and now I am young, to implant my old mind into my youthful body of fifty or sixty years ago. I would even trim it to twenty or thirty if someone were granting favors. Or ten.

In matters of money I have been poor, and now I am rich. I have often considered how it might have been had my youth intersected at some point with my wealth. But I have no time for dreams now, nor for regrets. I have had plenty of both in my life, as any other man or woman, but I give my attention now to staying alive. It is an endeavor at which I continue to toil in spite of its many inscrutabilities, for to give it up would be to yield to nothingness, an enemy I am not eager to confront.

I am in the cold season of life, and the words that come to mind as I rise in the morning are these: "Now is the winter of our discontent." I borrow them from William Faulkner, a fellow Mississippian, who lifted them from Shakespeare, who put them into the mouth of the Duke of Gloucester, also known as Richard III. Though I am hardly the villain Richard III was, I am no saint. Though I have not murdered, I have used words to maim and destroy. Though I repudiate the notion of conscience, as did Richard, I do not rest easy at night. Often when I wake in the morning, it is after few hours of troubled sleep. I cannot sleep long for fear that I will let go of living. Rather a winter of discontent than no winter at all.

By day birds flock to my window. I watch them feed, sometimes companionably, two or three different species at the same feeder, and sometimes singly, pecking quickly, nervously, darting glances to yard and sky for unwelcome company. I monitor the feeder for squirrels, which devise crafty methods of mounting it. If tapping on my window fails to scare them off, I open the window. I also have a small-caliber handgun, which I know how to use. Squirrels, however, are not intimidated by the sight of a gun, and I would never fire it for risk of damage to the bird feeder.

Birds never interested me before this, the winter of our discontent. I was sometimes diverted by other things, but never birds. Even now I know little of them except what I observe through my window and what I read in my *Book of North American Birds*, a large but overly generalized collection of short summaries describing six hundred different species of birds, each page also boasting an artist's rendering, in color, of the featured bird. This worthy volume was compiled by the editors of *Reader's Digest*, a body of persons whose aim is knowledge rather than understanding. It was presented to me by my nephew Patrick, who, with his wife, Rachel, shares with me the winter of our discontent.

Because of Patrick and Rachel, I do not have to modify the phrase to make it singular: "the winter of my discontent." Truly, it is the winter of our collective discontent, though Patrick and Rachel try to hide it and though at the end of it they will receive a reward to compensate for the trouble of wintering me. It is a winter barely begun, for I have been here only four weeks. By the calendar, a week into November, it is shy of literal winter by six weeks. "Short winters" is a description misapplied to Mississippi by those who know nothing of the South. We natives know how long these short winters can be.

A cantankerous old woman is never so annoying as when she is in some way related to you, and if you are strapped with her, overseer of her care, recipient of her complaints, then she may be a burden past telling. I know this. Before I lived here, before I myself qualified as a burden, I knew this, for I was my mother's keeper for five months before she died of irritability, a condition that had started in her bowel years earlier but metastasized to her mind and behavior by the end. Throughout my life I have been told that I am like my mother in many ways except in looks. My mother was a great beauty in her youth.

A difficult old woman may be entertaining if you are not responsible for her upkeep. Such a termagant lived in my mother's boardinghouse when I was a child. I used to delight in Mrs. Beadle's nasty temper, the tactless things she said about the meals my mother prepared, the way she upbraided the postman, whom she accused of withholding letters from her and whom she regularly threatened to sue in a court of law.

One day I was hiding behind the spirea bush at the corner of the house, spying on Mrs. Beadle as she sat on the front porch. She was muttering to herself and working her jaw in a way I found both freakish and fascinating. Between mutterings she would pucker her mouth, then push her tongue out and let the tip of it move about slowly, like a mollusk venturing from its shell, testing the air for danger. I must have laughed, for she turned and saw me. Before I could flee, she had pronounced me an ugly, spiteful child with the look of a bow-legged, mangy dog, at which point I ceased to delight in her. It was Mrs. Beadle who first apprised me of the fact that I was not an attractive child. My parents and sisters had kept it from me. After that, whenever I looked into a mirror, I marveled that I had not seen it for myself, that it had taken a peculiar old woman like Mrs. Beadle to point it out.

This I also share with Richard III. As he was small of stature, ill-featured, distrustful, and fidgety, so am I. Though not truly a hunchback, I am crooked, one shoulder being higher than the other. This defect I saw for myself when I began to examine photographs after Mrs. Beadle's pronouncement of my ugliness. After this I could adjust my stance to correct the fault when I remembered. Now I do not care. The fact that I stand off-center is the least of my worries. That I limp when I walk is likewise of no concern.

Imagine two pretty, graceful hands shaping a mud pie. I am the mud pie, my sisters the hands. Or two flowering dogwood trees with a little stunted ginkgo growing between them. I am the ginkgo. Smell the fruit of a ginkgo sometime for a full appreciation of the analogy. Or a common field sparrow occupying a nest with two golden-winged warblers. I am the sparrow. But the hands have fallen silent and the dogwoods ceased flowering. The sparrow has outlived the warblers. My bird book tells me that the female field sparrow does not sing.

My care is a responsibility that Patrick has taken upon himself willingly, though, as in most duties, with insufficient understanding of what it will entail. Tall mountains always look surmountable from a distance, but once the arduous upward trek commences, the peak is nowhere to be seen. There are ruts and thorny weeds along the path, sometimes only sheer wall with no path at all.

Patrick was chosen, along with his wife, Rachel, from among five applicants to house me during the winter of our discontent. I interviewed each of the five—two nephews, two nieces, and one great-niece—and selected Patrick. I was honest with all five, to a point, stating the simple terms of the trade: my money for their food and shelter. The food and shelter would come now, the bulk of the money later. Perhaps I led them to believe there would be more money at the end than there will be. I suffer no distress of conscience because of this. "Conscience is but a word that cowards use," as King Richard put it. There will be money enough, certainly more than Patrick has ever had.

I had the foresight to arrange for my winter before autumn had ended, though the flutterings of my heart spoke urgently of leaves falling rapidly. My mother died at eighty-six, my sisters at seventy-nine and seventy-five. At eighty I knew I must not delay. The branches of the tree were nearly bare. My method: I sent letters to nine people, family and acquaintances, five of whom responded to apply as Providers of Winter Hospice for Sophia Marie Langham Hess.

In the letter I laid out the terms of my care. I stated my reasonable expectation to die within a year, two or three at the most. I did not state my intention to resist this expectation. Those reading the letter could have concluded that I had no fear of meeting my end, that I was ready to yield, that their part would be easy.

During the past summer I traveled from my home in Kentucky to visit each of the five respondents, ten days in each home, with a suitable interval for rest between each trip. This took the entire summer, after which I announced my decision. All travel arrangements were furnished by the applicants, as stipulated in the letter. I would not negotiate airports alone.

In each home I looked at the accommodations with an eye to light and privacy more than to space and luxury. I would not spend my winter in darkness nor in the hub of chaos. I wanted many windows but few doors, though I did not state these requirements in the letter.

As for privacy, I saw the necessity for interior access to my quarters, but I wanted a solid door with a bolt on my side. That is not to say that I wanted absolute quiet, however. I wanted to hear convincing evidence of living on the other side of my walls. One home I eliminated because, among other reasons, it was too quiet. My great-niece Adrienne offered me an entire apartment in what she called her "deluxe townhouse" in Jackson, in a private community with iron gates and a guardhouse, but for the ten days I was there, I felt as if I were in a vacuum-sealed vault. Adrienne was away all day in an office downtown. Her maid fed me breakfast and lunch, then left at one o'clock. I had a phone number and a television for the long afternoons and evenings.

I can tolerate a great deal of noise. I am not deaf, although because I sometimes choose not to reply, people often assume wrongly that I am. I do not take pains to relieve them of this misconception. I have learned to turn to my advantage such misconceptions. They may serve to gather useful information, as in the case of Adrienne.

"Oh, I'll get a system worked out," I heard her say to a man in her kitchen late one night, a man she called Roger. "The food part will be easy," she said. "I gave her a Lean Cuisine tonight—put it all on a plate, and she thought I'd made it."

Young people are forever overestimating their cleverness. I had seen the frozen dinners in her freezer. While she was at work that very day, I had explored her house.

Roger said something, and she laughed. "Don't worry, she'd never figure it out. She's deaf as a fencepost. Besides, she probably wouldn't care. She had plenty of boyfriends in her day." Obviously, Adrienne had mixed me up with my sisters. I had friends but never a boyfriend, not until a short, bearded man became charmed by my typing skills, which I faithfully exercised on his behalf through numerous lengthy articles for scholarly journals and papers to be presented at conferences. He rewarded me at last by marrying me.

I heard Roger's car leave Adrienne's driveway the next morning before eight. I wondered what attracted him to Adrienne, who was severely thin with a square jaw and a garish blond streak in her short black hair. I had also heard her say of me, "She's loaded." Maybe Roger was interested in sharing the profit. She left for work soon after he did, and I counted on my fingers the number of days I had been in her house, sorry that I still had four to go. When I heard the maid arrive, I turned up the volume on the television and waited for her to pound on my door.

"Dolly here to clean!" was how she announced herself. She always sounded angry. I wondered what Adrienne had told her about me, if anything. The routine was unvarying. First Dolly set a plate of food on the large ottoman, then a glass of orange juice on the table beside it. The menu was not creative—a single fried egg, a piece of toast, a slice of bacon. I was never consulted as to preferences. As I ate, Dolly moved about the apartment, never speaking, never glancing at me. She made no noise with her feather duster and Windex. She was short and round like me. Perhaps she avoided looking at me because she did not want to see how a short round woman looks when she gets old.

My only view through the windows of Adrienne's apartment revealed other luxury townhouses on every side. A patio and garden in the rear were enclosed by a high fence of bleached wood. Adrienne had filled a shelf in the guest apartment with books, had left a large volume of Shakespeare on the mahogany table beside the sofa. Like others in my family, she imagined I was an intellectual, had heard the rumor, which I do nothing to dispel, that I had lectured on Shakespeare in my days of university teaching. Many people do not realize how much information one can pick up secondhand and pass off as his own, how narrow his understanding may be of things he references with apparent ease. A person can feed the assumptions of others by affecting an aura.

Associations may heighten one's reputation, but they may also lower it. "Birds of a feather flock together," as the old saw goes. If the flock is predatory as a whole, each member will be judged a predator. If they are songbirds, bird watchers will expect each bird to sing. In a flock of crows, it will be assumed that each one is a messy squawker. One may stain himself by the company he keeps just as surely as he may catch the reflected shine. Because of my husband, I consorted with scholars. Though I was quiet, having many questions but few answers in matters of philosophy and literary criticism, I was considered one of the windbags by association. I have read that the pine warbler soils his feathers by living in the pine tree.

Patrick's house was my next visit after Adrienne's, and the last of the five. It was also the smallest and most modest of all the homes. Though I am in no way averse to luxury, perhaps I settled for this one since it was closest to my childhood home in Methuselah, Mississippi, or perhaps because I had taught school in this town for a few years in the sixties. Perhaps it was because of all the windows facing the backyard. From my vantage I could see a field where children played, birds at the bird feeder, a birdbath, pine and poplar trees, a gazebo with a weathervane on top, a neighbor's trampoline. Perhaps these images held more interest for me than those of the other four houses.

Or perhaps, weary of the interviewing process, I had lost my powers of concentration and my capacity and patience for comparison. It was easy to simply surrender and say, "This one—I'll take this one." Maybe it was that Patrick and his wife didn't act falsely eager for my company, as some of the others did. Or maybe there was some mysterious quality this house possessed. Who can tell? I have chosen it. Here I am, and here I shall stay.

I will admit to one certainty: Patrick's wife intrigued me during my ten-day visit. People, like the ginkgo fruit, may look small and harmless on the outside yet emit the vilest of smells when crushed. I know that Rachel cannot be as good as I imagine her to be. One does not live to be eighty and still harbor delusions about the fundamental goodness of humankind. Perhaps this in itself should have driven me to choose another home, one in which the inhabitants wore their imperfections like old clothing. But then, maybe I purposely sought the site of inevitable disillusion for the final act in my play, to confirm to the end what I have known life to be.

The first night of my visit with them, I watched Rachel slice red potatoes for supper. I pretended to be looking at a magazine Patrick had placed in my hands, telling me in his strident voice that I would be interested in the article on a certain page. I was not. It was an article about the unreliability of college entrance exams, especially the new writing component, but I read only the first sentence, which opened with the pedestrian words "Statistically, the likelihood of a quality education in the public schools today is lower than it has ever been." I was not interested in statistics or a quality education. I was interested in Rachel's slicing of the potatoes.

I sat at the kitchen table in view of the counter where she was working. She handled the potatoes as someone working her way through a delicate puzzle. She first sliced each potato into four segments, then studied each quarter, as if measuring it into equal parts before laying her knife against its red skin. She sliced each quarter into three parts, then gently scraped them to one side of the cutting board before beginning the next quarter.

After finishing the seventh potato, she looked at the small pile of neat wedges for several long moments before stooping to get a pan from the bottom drawer of the stove. This she filled with water and set on an eye of the stove. I thought it curious that she would slice the potatoes before setting the water to boil. Did this suggest a lack of intelligence, a habitual failure to plan ahead, or simply a reluctance to presume upon the future?

I remembered the pots of boiling water on the stove in my mother's boardinghouse kitchen, usually two or three of them churning furiously as my mother stood at the counter hacking vegetables into pieces so large that the boarders had to cut them down to size before they could eat them. At least they were always soft enough to cut easily. In fact, they often verged on mushy, since my mother's method was to let everything "cook down" until the liquid was nearly gone.

Rachel took up the saltshaker and gave it four deliberate shakes into the water before turning on the eye. When it grew red, she wiped her hands on the apron she was wearing over her blue jeans, then opened a cupboard door and stared inside before reaching up to remove a can of green peas. She cranked it open with a handheld opener, then emptied its contents into another pan, rinsed the can, and threw it into the garbage.

Hanging on the kitchen wall nearest where I sat were four matched prints in blue frames. The titles of the prints were *Granny Airs the Quilts*, *Grandpa Chops Wood*, *Aunty Hoes Cotton*, and *Mama Washes Clothes*. The scenes were of tidy shacks beside cotton fields, with happy, neat-looking, colorfully dressed Negroes doing their work under large shade trees. The prints were matted, but two were not centered properly. On the counter beside Rachel's canisters was a large ceramic cookie jar in the shape of a fat, jolly Negro mammy. Her big scarf-tied head was the lid, which lifted off at her broad shoulders so that she could be filled with cookies to make everybody else as fat and jolly as she was.

The pictures and the cookie jar are the kinds of things I hate about the South, even though I call it home. Perhaps these items should have provided further cause for me to eliminate Patrick from among the five applicants, but I think I knew, even as I was sitting in the same room with these things, that I would come here to live. I hate small, constricted minds, but I had seen Rachel slice potatoes and wipe her hands on her apron. I also saw her place a cube of butter in the pan of peas, open a can of biscuits, and take meat loaf out of the oven. It wasn't the food itself that drew me but the slow grace of her actions, as of moving against resistance, like someone under water, someone capable perhaps of surprising, like a large mermaid.

I do not spend my days wondering if I should have chosen differently. I live in a single large room, a former "rec room," as Patrick called it when I first arrived for his interview. I also have a walk-in closet and a small bathroom, which shares a wall with Rachel's laundry room off the kitchen. The proximity of the washing machine spares Rachel from having to transport my laundry a great distance. Laundering an old woman's clothes is no pleasant task. This I remember from the months that I was my mother's keeper.

I watch birds and television. Patrick pays for cable service, which provides me with fifty-one channels. I also eat, sleep, and bathe, though not in excess. I do these things alone, without help. I read sometimes, mostly my bird book and old issues of *Time* magazine, which Patrick has saved and stacked on the bottom shelf of the bookcase.

And I listen. Rachel rings a bell every night sometime between five-thirty and six. It is a small gold bell that sits on the windowsill above her sink. She rings it for Patrick, thinking I can't hear it. Then she comes to my door with a tray. She knocks and calls out, "Suppertime, Aunt Sophie."

I watched her ring the bell the first night I visited, the only night I ate at the kitchen table with them. First she stood at the stove and lifted the lids of the pans to check the potatoes and peas. Then she opened the oven and looked inside. Then she filled three glasses with tea. Then she reached for the bell on the windowsill. The table was not yet set when she rang it.

CHAPTER 2

THE WHIRLIGIG OF TIME BRINGS IN HIS REVENGES

The pileated woodpecker has demonstrated admirable resilience as its preferred habitat of mature woods has disappeared. It has been known to carry its eggs one by one in its beak to a new site when its nesting tree was destroyed.

Certain names of cities are quite popular, appearing on the maps of many states. Greenville is one such name. Besides the one where I now live with Patrick and Rachel in Mississippi, there are Greenvilles in Texas, Virginia, Pennsylvania, North Carolina, South Carolina, Michigan, Kentucky, and Alabama. Tennessee has a Greeneville. These are the ones I know of. No doubt there are others.

At the feeder in the backyard I see woodpeckers among the birds. I sometimes hear them jackhammer on a tree or gutter. These are the large speckled variety with bright red heads. The feeder sways when they light on it. My *Book of North American Birds* tells me that the woodpecker family, which includes seventeen species, is amazingly adaptable. Adaptability is often a pathetic thing, coming on the heels of calamity.

Patrick's house in Greenville, Mississippi, is on Edison Street. At one time strictly residential, the street is now an odd mixture of homes and various enterprises. Old homes have been torn down and new buildings erected so that there is no architectural unity. The concept of zoning appears not to have existed during the evolution of this street. At the north end a Taco Bell and a 7-11 convenience store stand side by side, and the south end is anchored by a coin laundry and what used to be the post office but has been turned into a pet grooming establishment called the Pooch Office. Between the north and south ends are two dozen more buildings, homes and otherwise, devoted to the business of living and dying.

Patrick's house was built in the late 1940s, a plain three-bedroom structure with gray shingled siding. It has a carport and a large backyard. A former owner added the rec room and extra bathroom before Patrick bought the house. In 1980 he carried Rachel across the threshold, a feat of no mean effort. Patrick is slight now, was even more so in 1980. Rachel is perhaps an inch taller and more substantial of frame, a sturdy big-boned woman. They had doubtless dreamed of occupying one bedroom and filling the other two with children, had in fact begun living out their dream when the stiff wind of reality snuffed out the candle.

If Patrick and Rachel's two children had reached school age, they would have attended Carrie Stern Elementary School in Greenville, Mississippi, at the corner of Moore and McAllister, the very school where I once taught before moving to Kentucky. But their children never attended school. Patrick and Rachel's children were kidnapped from them at the Memphis Zoo, and their bodies were found a month later at a little spot in the road called Golddust, along the Mississippi River north of Memphis. This was in 1986, and these babies were two and three years old, a boy and a girl.

I was still in Kentucky at this time, a widow by then, having taught Fundamentals of English Composition to uninspired college freshmen for fifteen years at two different colleges. My sister Regina, Patrick's mother, called me on the telephone and communicated the news of the kidnapping between long silences, then later sent me a newspaper clipping, which showed a picture of Patrick's family taken less than a month before the abduction, a picture that had recently appeared in their church directory.

Patrick and Rachel had received an eight by ten of the same pose from the photography studio, free to all participating families of the church. This eight by ten, Regina told me, was what Patrick had taken from an end table in the living room and lent to the *Delta Democrat Times* for the write-up. This was only one of the many random details Regina wove into her halting narrative. Another was that Rachel couldn't hold anything on her stomach, that she had been vomiting constantly since the children's disappearance. Others were that it had rained solid for twelve hours, that Patrick's roof was leaking right over the bed in the master bedroom, and that their church had held a prayer vigil through Saturday night and all day Sunday. No regular services, Regina had said, just people on their knees all over the sanctuary praying, many of them out loud.

Imagine hundreds of prayers floating up, hitting the ceiling, and vanishing just as the two children had. The case was never solved. Leads flooded in, but nothing turned up until four weeks had passed and a twelve-year-old boy saw his dog pawing at the ground along the riverbank in Golddust, Tennessee. Patrick and Rachel never had any more children. Regina never knew why, though I'm sure it wasn't for want of asking. My sisters were not timid, especially Regina, who was the oldest of us and who believed in a Woman's Right to Know Everything. Even as a child, when Regina sensed that information was being withheld, she would pester and snoop until she found out.

Eager to replace the gaps those two grandchildren had left in her life, she no doubt felt she was due an explanation as the years passed and Rachel bore no more children. As far as I know, however, her curiosity went unsatisfied. Because her other son never married, her obituary listed no grandchildren among her survivors. She died in her sleep at the same age our father had died of a heart aneurysm. Several years later our other sister, Virginia, likewise succumbed while stooping to water the African violets on her back porch. I have often thought I would prefer to go swiftly, as my father and sisters did, rather than linger as my mother, a curmudgeon and an inconvenience at the end.

But who can say? There is no good way to die. I cling to life, empty though it is. Soon the trees outside my window will shake in the cold wind, their leaves fallen, their branches "bare, ruined choirs, where late the sweet birds sang," as Shakespeare describes it in his seventy-third sonnet. Most of the birds have already flown farther south, but some will stay through the winter. Those that do will be intent on survival, and I mean to help them. The laws of the universe demand that someone help the weak. If not someone stronger, then let the weak help the weak.

The trip to the Memphis Zoo in 1986 had been a church outing. They had gone by bus, ten or twelve families, had taken their picnic baskets with them that hot summer day, had eaten together a little past noon, then separated for another two hours with plans to meet back at the bus at three o'clock to head back to Greenville. Since most of them had young children, they didn't want to be too late getting home, especially since the next day was Sunday and there were Sunday school ribbons to be earned for perfect attendance. The preacher of the church, with his wife and four daughters, was among the group that day.

The specifics of the actual abduction were few. I discarded the newspaper article after reading it. I saw no need to keep it. It was a great tragedy. Why should I want to review it? Though I had not seen Patrick since he was a child, I was touched by his loss. I had not met his wife at the time, had no blood ties with her, but their children were my great-niece and great-nephew. I felt enraged by the crime but powerless, as one always is in the face of evil. I did not go to the funeral.

The newspaper reported a disappearance so swift as to be beyond possibility, except that the facts spoke for themselves. The children were indeed gone. They were sitting on a bench one minute, with ice cream cones, and in the blink of an eye they had vanished. Both parents were within arm's length, one fetching napkins at the concession counter behind the bench, the other turned sideways on the end of the bench, loading the camera with a new roll of film. Imagine turning around to wipe a mouth or to snap a picture and finding your children gone.

I met Rachel for the first time at Regina's funeral, by which time she looked different from the picture in the church directory. Her face had lost its smooth roundness and its smile. At her mother-in-law's funeral I saw people treat her tenderly, as one who had suffered much. I saw them follow her every movement with their curious eyes. I heard the hiss of whispers as she and Patrick entered the chapel behind Regina's casket, and I imagined the words: "They're the ones whose babies were snatched."

I would like to state that curiosity played no part in my coming here to live, though many will not believe me. I am something of an anomaly among southern women, for I have no morbid urge to wallow in tragedies or feast on the grotesque. I am too old to ponder such darkness. I serve only myself. Old age is tragedy enough. Like the birds at my window, I am intent on surviving the winter.

Since coming to Patrick's house, I have never heard the children referred to, have certainly never spoken of them myself, have seen no evidence that they ever existed in this house. Their names were Toby and Mandy, I remember that, and they both had yellow-white hair, as did their father in his childhood. I imagine their mother to be a saint, martyred by grief and sanctified by pain. I have constructed for her a purified essence that I know to be false, for I know people. Yet it is easy to maintain my fantasy, as she rarely speaks. Fantasy may account in part for my survival thus far, as may silence for hers.

I have no fantasies about Patrick. He is a simple, literal-minded man concerned with office supplies, which are sold at a store called the Main Office, where he goes by the title of Manager. I hear him talk to Rachel at length about his employees, new products, late shipments, monthly profits, and the like. He reads aloud letters to the editor from the *Delta Democrat Times* and comments on each, sometimes angrily. He reads aloud from the Bible in a preacherly voice. He follows sports, though he was never an athlete himself.

Dugout brawls and slugfests on the basketball court interest him, as does boxing, the most primitive and brutal of sports.

He reads historical accounts of battles, explorations, and naval disasters, as well as biographies of inventors, presidents, and entre-preneurs. He also reads *Time* magazine and *Reader's Digest*. At the supper table he often speaks in great detail to Rachel about what he is currently reading. Patrick has high blood pressure and an abun-dance of nervous energy. He has an opinion about every subject and gives it unsolicited. Though he windily claims to be politically inde-pendent, it is clear that his bumper stickers in an election year bear the image of an elephant rather than a donkey.

Patrick and Rachel attend a church regularly. I do not know its name. Whether it is the same church that chartered the bus to the Memphis Zoo in 1986 I cannot say. Neither do I know whether the loss of their children reinforced the foundation of their religious beliefs or gnawed away at it. I do know, however, that they leave the house before ten o'clock every Sunday, dressed for church and carry-ing Bibles. During the first two weeks I lived here, they invited me to go with them. The second time I told them they needn't ask again. I believe I made it clear that my religion, or lack of it, was my own business. Another Sunday they invited me to go for an afternoon drive with them, but again I declined. I have no desire to see beyond Edison Street. I know what Greenville, Mississippi, looks like.

There is another view from Patrick's house besides the backyard view of field, gazebo, and the like, though to see this one I must go to some trouble. This I do. When I hear Rachel start her car and drive away for groceries or other errands during the day, or when she and Patrick leave for church on Sunday, I open my door and walk through their kitchen into the dining room and from there into the living room. I turn the rocking chair around to face the window, and then I sit down.

Across the street is a lawyer's office in what was formerly a neighbor's redbrick house. To the left of this is the parking lot of a funeral home, and to the left of that the funeral home itself, a two-story white Victorian-style house with gingerbread trim. A signboard, like a doctor's shingle, hangs above the top step: *WAGNER'S MORTUARY*. The clients here, however, have passed beyond a doctor's skill. I wonder if this was the same mortuary where the bodies of Toby and Mandy were taken. Imagine looking out your front window to the place where you chose caskets for your babies.

Were I a deep thinker, I would contemplate death from a philosophical perspective. Were I religious, I would have yet another vast cave to explore on the subject. But I am neither. I am a former teacher, a quarter Jewish and three-quarters Doubtful. Therefore, I sit in the rocking chair staring at the mortuary, often with my hand over my heart, feeling its quick shallow beats. I sit and wonder what it was like for all those people in their last breath, before they were brought through the back door covered by a sheet. This is the extent of my deep thinking. I try not to think of the moments after their last breath.

And did the proximity of Wagner's Mortuary influence my choice to live with Patrick? For some people a nearby mortuary would be a discouraging factor. For others, an attraction of sorts, considering man's inevitable end. For me—well, here I am. I knew the mortuary was across the street when I chose Patrick's house.

I have heard the term *prearrangement* as it relates to funerals. I have heard it described as a way "to spare your loved ones additional grief when the time comes." The word *death* is carefully avoided.

I knew a woman once, a colleague of my husband's named Helga Sedgeworth, an imposing spinster who taught university courses in ancient and medieval literature. At a department dinner party one evening Helga told us that she had recently flown to New Brunswick, Canada, to the town of her birth, where she had gone to a funeral home to choose her own casket and headstone. She had filled out a form concerning her choices for the funeral service itself, had even selected flowers for the casket spray. She had gone to the adjoining graveyard to view the location of her plot.

She spoke solemnly to the ten of us around the dinner table. One of the men, a professor of modern fiction and poetry, tried to lighten the moment by asking if she had climbed inside the various caskets to test them for size and comfort, but she seemed not to hear him. For her headstone, she told us, she had chosen the inscription "Perhaps my love, my lord, inhabits there," words she identified as those spoken by Psyche upon spying a distant temple on a mountaintop in her search for Cupid.

Helga had then written out a check for over eight thousand American dollars and left the funeral home. The same professor tried once more to make her smile. Had she gone dancing after that? he wanted to know. She turned to him and said, "No, I drove to a seafood restaurant and ate lobster." Much later, during coffee, after we had drifted to other subjects, Helga filled a pause: "If one dies in the winter in Canada, the body is kept in storage until late spring when the ground has thawed."

When my breathing comes faster, I force my eyes away from the funeral home. I look into the sky and try to think of rules that don't bend. I try to remember things I might have once said in a classroom: "The past participle of *lie* is *lain*," or "The pronoun must agree with its antecedent," or "Avoid the sentence fragment." I see these rules regularly broken in the things I read. I break some of them myself.

The page I seek out first in Patrick's *Time* magazines is called Milestones. In sentence fragments, it records the deaths of note-worthy people. "DIED. FANNY BLANKERS-KOEN, 85, Dutch homemaker who won four gold medals in track and field at the 1948 Olympics, the most ever in one Olympics by a woman." "DIED. UTA HAGEN, 84, revered stage actress and acting teacher best known for originating the role of Martha in Edward Albee's 1962 *Who's Afraid of Virginia Woolf?*; in New York City." Sometimes the cause of death is given: "of leukemia," "of pancreatic cancer," "a sui-cide by hanging," "of a pulmonary illness."

CEOs of companies, authors, actors, shipping magnates, gospel singers, museum curators—one by one they fall. "Some are born great, some achieve greatness, and some have greatness thrown upon them." Thus quotes the clown at the end of *Twelfth Night*. And then there are the masses, of whom I am one, who never taste greatness in any form, whose deaths go unrecorded in *Time* magazine.

Perhaps some would say that my wealth is a source of greatness, but I know what happens to money when one draws his last breath. It changes hands. Whatever man has done to get and keep it is, in the end, of no consequence. It is his no longer. Having lifted not a finger, fools may fall heir to a wise man's fortune. Or wise men may fall heir to a fool's fortune. Whatever the case, the "whirligig of time brings in his revenges." The clown in *Twelfth Night* was no fool. He knew that nothing very much matters after all.

CHAPTER 3

TO DIVE INTO THE FIRE, TO RIDE ON THE CURLED CLOUDS

Since it catches most of its food on the wing,

the barn swallow spends more time in the air

than almost any other land bird, perhaps as much

as ten hours a day. It has been estimated that

a swallow may travel close to two million

miles in its lifetime.

It is Thursday. Rachel is away but will soon return. She rarely leaves for more than an hour at a time. As I watch the funeral home, I see a moving van crawling down the street toward Patrick's house. It stops in front of the lawyer's office, then creeps forward to the next house, which has stood empty during the weeks I have lived here. On the side of the van I can make out the words *CARRIED AWAY* in large letters and beneath them the slightly smaller words *MOVING AND STORAGE COMPANY.*

The van slowly maneuvers its way backward into the driveway. A man climbs down from the driver's side and a woman from the passenger's. I watch the woman, who is dressed like a man, in work boots and overalls. She walks across the front yard with her head raised, as if studying the roofline, the gutters and eaves. Is this her job, I wonder—working for a moving company—or is she the new owner of this house? Perhaps the man is her husband and they are renting the van, which is full of their possessions. Perhaps the man is her husband, and together they own the moving company, including the van, which is full of other people's possessions. Perhaps he is not her husband but merely a co-worker, and the van is empty. The possibilities and combinations are limitless. Perhaps he is a wizard, she is a sorceress, and the van is full of genies in lanterns. Perhaps, like most other things, it doesn't matter.

The man comes to stand beside the woman and lays his hand on her shoulder. He is a big man, built like a football player. She moves closer to him in a way a co-worker wouldn't. A minivan pulls up at the front curb, and a teenager gets out. She slides open the back door and lifts a small child out of a car seat. The man meets her and takes the child. He points to the house. Maybe he's saying, "There it is, pumpkin. Our new home!" The teenager walks slowly toward the house, hands jammed in back pockets, head down. Maybe she's not so excited about the new home.

Rachel's car appears now, moving slowly past the mortuary, and I rise from the rocking chair, turn it around, and walk back through the dining room and kitchen, into my apartment. I close my door before I hear her key in the lock.

It occurs to me that I never see Patrick and Rachel touch, not even a hand on a shoulder. This means nothing, of course. There is no correlation between love and touching, at least the kind of touching done in front of others.

I sit down in my chair at the window by the bird feeder. I think about the woman across the street dressed as a man. I think of Rachel in her denim jeans and flannel shirts. Perhaps she and Patrick share shirts. Perhaps not. Perhaps his fit her a bit snugly. I turn to the *Time* magazine spread open on the table beside my chair. I think of all the women in the world who would never think of wearing men's clothing.

"DIED. GEORGETTE KLINGER, 88," I read. The woman pictured above the paragraph is dressed femininely, in something white, imprinted with a large flower across the bodice. A vase of roses stands on the table behind her. She wears a long strand of pearls around her neck and smiles openly toward the camera. She is described as a "fashionable skin-care pioneer of the 1940s," a woman who experimented with "European facial techniques" and "inspired a revolution in cosmetic skin care." I wonder if the mortician saw anything to distinguish her skin from that of all the other bodies he handled. I wonder what was hidden in the heart of this woman wearing white.

I think of how fragile a thing a heart is. Some hearts are broken early, some late, and some, I suppose, never at all. Considering the length of adulthood, my own heart was broken later than many. For this, perhaps, I should count myself fortunate, but I don't. *Fortunate* has lost its purest meaning. It is a word often used to describe incomplete victories, bad circumstances that could have been worse.

Having survived childhood with a heart intact, a woman's heart may be broken in so many ways. Men and children are common causes. The kinds of abuse a man may inflict are many, all of them involving a choice. Though a man may sometimes hurt a woman unwittingly, the pain is nevertheless a result of some choice made and carried out. He may not have meant to break her heart, but intention is irrelevant. Once a heart is broken, the words "I didn't mean to" afford little relief.

A woman's heart may also be broken by the absence of a man. I have known women, many of them buried now, whose lives were spent in quest of a man—*spent* in the sense of used up, depleted of emotional resources. Some of these women never found one man, yet some found too many, for "the absence of a man" does not mean the absence of a physical presence.

When speaking of children, however, absence is more literal. The physical presence of a child engages a woman's whole mind and heart, defines not only the perimeter of her life but occupies the total square footage. A child, though imperfect in any number of ways, can light up a woman's life. This I have observed. I have not experienced it firsthand. I speak now of a child of one's own, not merely a child placed in one's care for a time, for such children may delight a woman's heart only temporarily. At some point she must always give them back to their mothers.

I recall a child in the first class of third graders I taught. I was twenty-one years old, and she was eight. I remember only her first name—Starr. Her eyes were like polished onyx, and she could run faster than all the boys in the class. Starr's face is the picture I always carried with me of the daughter I might someday have. I carry it still, since I never had a daughter to take its place.

By simple arithmetic I know that Starr would be a woman of

sixty-seven now. She might have arthritis, the beginnings of osteo-porosis. Her black eyes could be clouded with glaucoma. In my pic-ture, however, she remains a child.

It is after school, and Starr has just drawn a square on the chalk-board, very neatly, using a yardstick for the sides. I am at my desk only a few feet from her, correcting spelling papers. "Look, Miss Langham," she says, and I do. I look at the square first and then at her face. "If I got in there," she says, placing her finger in the center of the square, "and pushed hard against the sides—" she stops to lift her arms and flatten her hands as if trying to move a wall—"I could bend the square into a circle."

I believe a child does this for a woman, changes the contours of her life, reshapes the square of each day into a circle, then expands it by another dimension into a sphere. The sphere is punctured when a woman loses a child. I think about Rachel and myself, inhabiting the same living space. We are a sad pair, a deflated balloon and a flat empty square.

I hear Rachel moving about in the kitchen on the other side of my door. I hear thumps, as if she is setting down heavy bags on the countertop. A bird alights at the feeder outside my window. I have seen his type before and have searched him out in my bird book, which identifies over thirty species of sparrows. This one, the chip-ping sparrow, has a chestnut crown and a white stripe above each eye. Described in my book as "pesky and tireless," it is also called the hairbird because of its obsession with hair, which it supposedly favors for the lining of its nest, horsehair being its first choice but other donors also accepted—dogs, raccoons, deer, even humans.

I imagine this bird darting about, making diving raids to nip strands of hairs from the tails of grazing horses or lazy dogs. I imagine hatless men feeling a sudden pinch and reaching up to rub their heads. I watch now as the chipping sparrow pecks seeds out of the feeder, then flutters down to eat them off the ground. He hops about briefly, then is off, a streak of brown and gray disappearing into the treetops.

I think of a bird's life, so much of it spent in the air, its nest only a place to lay and incubate its eggs, to house its fledglings until it can push them out. I think of the miles traveled by some birds in migration—a continual cycle of leaving their homes when the days grow cool, then returning in the warmth of spring.

I think of my husband. For thirteen years I marked the box for "married" when filling out forms. He sought me out, pursued me, won me, though with no appreciable resistance on my part. At forty-two I was not miserable with my unmarried state, for my sisters' husbands had not impressed upon me that marriage was an altogether fulfilling way to live one's life. Still, the prospect of marriage interested me.

I first found in Eliot a companion, an employer, and a teacher, and I was content with the arrangement. Later I found in him a husband, and I was more content—or I thought I was. Still later I discovered his fondness for flight, for the wide-open spaces of his imagination. I observed his sense of confinement in a nest, yet his habit of returning seasonally to the small comfortable pleasures of his domestic life.

When he was accessible, I was the one who flew. I fluttered about attending him. I ranged far and wide to bring home the things he requested. I plumped his pillows, brought his slippers, fetched his meals, typed his essays. I would have done anything he wanted. I came eagerly when he called. As in *The Tempest*, I was Ariel to his Prospero, ready "to fly, to swim, to dive into the fire, to ride on the curled clouds" for him.

I close my eyes and drift off into a confusion of squares and circles bumping against one another. I am in the air, and the shapes are soft and changeable as I fly through them. I have often flown in my dreams, an object of wonder to those on the ground. "Look, isn't that Sophie up there? How does she do that?"

"Suppertime, Aunt Sophie!" I hear a knock at the door. Looking at the clock, I am surprised to see that almost two hours have passed. Rachel enters with a tray. She sets it on the small round table next to the sofa. She removes the items one by one, first the napkin, then the silverware, which she places one utensil at a time on top of the napkin. Then the glass of water, then a saucer on which sits a muffin, and finally the plate of food. From my seat by the window I see brown, orange, green. I can tell it is too much food on one plate, but I say nothing. Rachel rearranges the silverware, moving the knife and spoon to the right side, then looks at me as she turns to leave with the empty tray.

"It'll taste better hot," she says. She doesn't raise her voice the way Patrick does when he talks to me. She seems to have realized already that the reports of my deafness have been greatly exaggerated.

She nods toward the table, as if to encourage me to leave my chair. Her eyes have the look of one who wants to say more but won't. No doubt she is thinking of yesterday, when I sat across the room looking at my plate of supper until it got cold. It was not from obstinacy nor lack of hunger. I was merely contemplating the fact that so much of daily life was measured by food, that each day had now reduced itself to three meals delivered on a tray. When Rachel came back an hour later, I was nibbling at the edges of the spaghetti. She halted by the door, looking embarrassed. "Is it too spicy?" she asked, and I shook my head no.

After she leaves, I get up and walk to the table. It would be easier for Rachel simply to set the tray down and let me eat from it. It would take me back to my years of eating in the cafeterias of various elementary schools. The fact that she takes care to set the table and remove the dishes from the tray should make an old woman grateful. Perhaps it is calculated to do so. And perhaps at some level it does. Or perhaps an old woman could see it as another useless expenditure of effort.

On the plate are a mound of lima beans, another of carrots, and another of beef and gravy over yellow noodles. I feel no hunger, yet I sit down and pick up the fork. I think of robots programmed to perform manual tasks. I read once of a factory with hundreds of the little metallic men moving about in perfect synchronization. Not one of them late for work. Not one complaining about the long hours, demanding higher wages, or calling in sick. No on-the-job chatting to undercut production. I fill my fork with beef and gravy and transfer it to my mouth. Down to the plate for more, up to my mouth. I imagine a factory in my stomach, hundreds of tiny robots wielding files, mashers, and power sprayers, pulverizing the food, pushing it along. This is a cartoon picture from a film I once showed a class of fourth graders: *Your Digestive System*.

The night I first ate meat loaf with Rachel and Patrick, when I came for my ten-day trial visit, Patrick said a blessing over the food. He placed his hands on the table, one on each side of his plate, and as he prayed, in his loud managerial voice, I studied his hands, which were not much larger than mine but surely stronger. His nails were bitten to the quick. We formed a V at the table, Patrick at the end, one hand extended toward Rachel and one toward me. I looked at Rachel's face when Patrick pronounced the amen, but her eyes were on the bowl of buttered potatoes, which she picked up and passed to me with a face as placid as a nun's.

I eat less than half of the beef and noodles Rachel has put on my plate tonight. I take a final bite of muffin, then a sip of water, and push the plate away. I know she will bring a dish of dessert with her when she returns. This is the routine. Whether she waits to prepare it after she has brought the tray or simply waits to deliver it, not trusting an old woman to eat her vegetables when dessert is at hand, I don't know.

Upon getting out of bed each morning, I find myself wondering what Rachel's offering of dessert will be at suppertime. It is a paltry existence when this is one's first thought upon waking. Sometimes the dessert is store-bought—a little round yellow sponge cake with canned peaches on top or a cake doughnut with a small dish of apple-sauce. Sometimes it is a scoop of ice cream with two vanilla wafers propped up on either side. Other times it is something I have smelled baking in her oven throughout the afternoon—a cherry pie or choc-olate cake, once a small and beautiful strawberry tart.

As I sit at the table now, waiting for dessert to be brought, I hear Patrick and Rachel on the other side of my door. They are eating their supper in the kitchen, a menu which I assume to be the same as mine. Often I can catch the gist of Patrick's supper monologue. Tonight he is discussing something he read in the newspaper today about the mayor's wife and her work with black adults in a literacy program held in the evenings at St. Joseph High School. Patrick believes this is a fine project. He imagines the mayor's wife, along with himself, to be a paragon of fair-mindedness, a kind and generous soul to whom racial discrimination is a foreign concept. Certainly a literacy program for blacks speaks for the magnanimous heart of the white mayor's wife.

One evening last week Patrick arrived home late for supper due to a flat tire. I heard him tell Rachel that "the nicest black man" had stopped to assist him. He makes frequent mention of black doctors, black businessmen, and black politicians, the subtext of such references being "Just imagine—black people *can* make something of themselves!" When the newspaper ran a picture recently of a local boy who achieved a perfect score on the SAT, Patrick said to Rachel, "Did you see this black boy in the paper? Why, we might have us a black valedictorian at Greenville High come spring." He spoke with great awe of the contestant on *Jeopardy* who won over $65,000 one week—"a black woman stock analyst!" he said to Rachel. A smart black woman—triple marvel! I imagined him drawing his chair up to the television, gaping wide-mouthed at the spectacle of a black woman rattling off correct answers. Patrick is not a stupid man; he simply cannot see or hear himself.

I sit at my table a few minutes before Rachel appears again with my dessert on the tray. Patrick stands at the doorway behind her. "Hello, Aunt Sophie," he says as Rachel sets a saucer on my table.

On the saucer are two frosted cookies sprinkled with small colored candies. "I guess Rachel told you the electrician is coming tomorrow to see about rewiring this end of the house," he says. I nod. "He'll have to get in here to work," Patrick adds, looking around. "Hope he doesn't disturb you too much."

"Is he a black electrician?" I ask. The irony is lost on Patrick, though Rachel pauses, a dish of orange Jell-O in one hand, and turns to look directly at me. Perhaps I only imagine that a faint smile gathers in the corners of her eyes. I turn and look toward the window. It is dark outside now.

"No, he isn't," Patrick says. "Duncan's folks used to run the taxi company. You probably remember them from when you used to live here—the Graves. They lived in that big stone house across from the library."

"Well, good," I say. If Patrick thinks I am relieved to learn that Duncan the electrician is a white man, I will leave it at that. I can't see what difference it makes. Let him think what he wishes.

I have long since understood that fairness is a dream. Black or white, man or woman, rich or poor, life will do to you what it will. "DIED. MARGE SCHOTT, 75, controversial philanthropist and former owner of the Cincinnati Reds; in Cincinnati, Ohio." This was reported in another issue of *Time*. As in Marge Schott's case, unfairness may be coupled with efficiency. It is said that she once settled a dispute within the Reds organization by the flip of a coin. This, I believe, was economical in every way. As in Marge Schott's case, also, unfairness may be coupled with generosity, for though she publicly made numerous offensive comments, her gifts to charity were well-known among the citizens of Cincinnati. Ask a dozen people in

Cincinnati about Marge Schott, and you will get a dozen different opinions.

After Patrick disappears from the doorway, Rachel moves about, setting my supper dishes back onto the tray. I look at the frosted cookies and the dish of orange Jell-O in front of me, considering briefly which to taste first. I imagine Marge Schott flipping a coin, and I reach for a cookie. For now sweetness fills my mouth.

CHAPTER 4

SOME METEOR THAT THE SUN EXHALES

From its home in the Canadian conifers and
high mountains of the West, the evening grosbeak
has migrated increasingly farther south and east
over the years. Perhaps its wanderlust was first
caused by a food shortage in its native regions,
and, flying south, it found well-stocked bird
feeders to supply its hunger.

Greenville, Mississippi, situated on the eastern banks of the great river, has an impressive heritage of literary talent. Shelby Foote grew up here, and Walker Percy spent a good part of his youth here with an older cousin, William Alexander Percy, who adopted him and who was also a published poet himself. Hodding Carter Jr., long-time editor of Greenville's *Delta Democrat Times*, won a Pulitzer Prize. Another of the town's award-winning writers is Josephine Haxton, novelist and storywriter, who uses the pen name of

Ellen Douglas in order to mollify her aunts, who appear as characters in her stories and who, for family honor, do not want to be recognized by the reading public.

More recently two Greenville women, Gayden Metcalfe and Charlotte Hays, have written a book titled *Being Dead Is No Excuse*, which claims to be the "Official Southern Ladies Guide to Hosting the Perfect Funeral." Without the trouble of opening the book, one can tell that it is meant for humor. It is not a book I care to read.

The library in Greenville has a special permanent display of the town's most well-known writers, close to twenty of them, while the local bookstore carries more than fifty books by Greenville authors. Greenville's residents, though proud of their writers, aren't greedy. They lay no claims to William Faulkner, Eudora Welty, or John Grisham, also Mississippians, though they might be quick to point out that Faulkner's literary agent, Ben Wasson, was one of their own. Wasson succeeded in getting Faulkner's first two books published, and it is said that Faulkner often visited him in Greenville and even did some of his best writing here.

Another of Greenville's distinguishing features, of which I am daily reminded, is its brown water. When I lived and taught here some forty years ago, it was a long time before I could bring myself to take a bath. I could shower without distress, but sitting in a tubful of amber liquid was not compatible with my idea of cleanliness. Besides its unusual color, it is very soft water, also. Rub your hands together under soft water, and they feel slippery. After shampooing, you may rinse the suds out of your hair yet never feel the sensation of "squeaky clean."

It is a joke in the state of Mississippi that the explanation for the high number of published authors per capita in Greenville has something to do with its soft brown water. Fewer new writers are coming along, they say, because too many youngsters these days are drinking bottled water.

Though I already knew some of these facts, I heard them rehearsed by Patrick during my visit last summer as he read an article to Rachel at the supper table one night. It was from a back issue of *Southern Living*. The page, called Southern Journal, is a regular feature of the magazine. All persons, places, or things southern are considered suitable topics for this page. It came to me as Patrick read the article aloud, this one concerning the brown water and the writers of Greenville, Mississippi, that he most likely had aspirations to be a writer himself. Since moving here, I am confident of this.

Patrick has written many letters to the editor of the *Delta Democrat Times*, several of which have been printed over the years. He has mounted them all in a scrapbook that sits on the coffee table in the living room. He often repeats stories his father told him about his paternal grandfather, who grew up in Southern California. "I'm going to write these all up in a book someday," he says. No doubt Patrick thinks the publishing world is eagerly waiting for the manager of an office supply store to burst on the scene with a collection of apocryphal stories about a deceased relative.

The stories, the ones I've heard, sound like folklore. A dead armadillo on the side of a road in New Mexico figures prominently in one of them and a one-legged ventriloquist in another. Most of them are silly stories with no point except to illustrate the many ways a man can waste his days on earth.

Patrick's grandfather was what his family called a character, a card, a pill. He was, at various times in his life, a minister, a barber, a bricklayer, a chauffeur for a judge in Lafayette, Louisiana, and a writer of advertising slogans, one of his best-known being for a brand of men's hair tonic in the thirties and forties called Magic: "Want a magic wave? Wave the Magic Wand!" The picture on the poster showed a man in a business suit, his hair neatly slicked and waved, with three admiring women gazing up at him. In the thought bubble above his head was a bottle of Magic Hair Tonic with a wand touching it and multicolored sparkles shooting away like fireworks. One of the framed posters hangs in the hallway in Patrick's house.

The white electrician arrives a little past eight in the morning. I have been awake since five. I am dressed, sitting at the window beside the bird feeder. Rachel has already come and gone with my bowl of oatmeal, slice of toast, and glass of orange juice. My television is on, but I glance at it only occasionally. It is tuned to a channel called TV Oldies, which carries programs such as *Gunsmoke*, *Bonanza*, *Green Acres*, *I Love Lucy*, and *The Waltons*. John-Boy Walton is on the screen now, talking to a man who is milking a cow. He says, "Aw, Daddy's not that way at all, Mr. Logan." Mr. Logan grunts and the cow shifts restlessly.

In the afternoon *Carol Burnett* comes on. I watch her every day, hoping to see the scene in which she wears the green velvet draperies as Scarlett O'Hara in *Gone With the Wind*. Hope has sunk to this— waiting for a television rerun.

The white electrician makes a few attempts at conversation. He speaks into the fuse box on the wall, however, so I feel no obligation to answer. Rachel stands in the doorway for a minute, then disappears. "Might get a little dusty in here," the electrician says. "That plaster dust, you know—no matter what you do, it'll find a way to get in." He knocks on the wall that separates my apartment from Rachel's kitchen. "Solid as a fort," he says. "Far piece from how they build 'em today." He moves around the room, counting electrical sockets. He writes something in a small notebook he takes out of his hip pocket. His boots are old, the leather crusty and cracked like a dirt yard in a drought.

He goes back into the kitchen, and I hear him tell Rachel that he'll start the job on Monday, that he wants to move the location of the fuse box while he's at it and change over to circuit breakers, that he'll bring a helper with him and it will be a three-day job. He'll try to be as neat as he can and will cover the floor with plastic.

After he leaves, Rachel stands in my doorway. John-Boy is back at home now, talking to his granny, who is pouring water from a bucket over the front porch steps and sweeping them. I can't make out the words John-Boy says to his grandmother, but I wonder why he doesn't pick up the bucket of water and help her, or take the broom out of her hands and tell her to go sit in the swing while he finishes up.

"Not as polite as they would like us to think he is," I say.

"Well, I thought he . . ." Rachel pauses, frowning. "I've heard he's good to clean up after himself."

I decide that nothing is to be gained by explaining that we are talking about two different people. Rachel starts to say something else but doesn't. She leaves, closing my door behind her.

Later *MacGyver* will come on and then *Love Boat*, followed by *Bewitched* and *The Cosby Show*. At one-thirty in the afternoon a court-room program called *Judge Jack* comes on another channel. People sue each other over various offenses—ruined wedding cakes, crooked driveways, faulty transmission repairs. The judge sees through people's lies and refuses to allow speculation as evidence. When somebody says something like "Well, if she'd of paid me on time," or "If he hadn't gone and busted my mailbox," or "If he coulda give me some warning," the judge replies with "Yes, and if frogs had wings, they wouldn't bump their rumps when they jump." This is one of his trademark witticisms. The judge is a large man with a mustache.

"DIED. PETER USTINOV, 82," who "earned his greatest movie renown as Agatha Christie's Hercule Poirot, as in the film *Death on the Nile*." *Time* magazine goes on to say that Mr. Ustinov spoke six real languages "and a few others of his own comic invention." His talents were many. He was a writer, a film director, and an actor, both on screen and stage, skilled in depicting both tragedy and comedy. Besides short stories and an autobiography, he wrote a hit play titled *Romanoff and Juliet*.

I have not read or seen Mr. Ustinov's play *Romanoff and Juliet*, but I take it to be a comedy, unlike the play on which its plot is based. To write a play, one needs a good ear for the spoken word. Without this, the playwright may inadvertently turn his tragedy into a comedy.

Romeo and Juliet is one of the few Shakespearean plays I have both read and seen. It is a story of ill-fated love. The last paper I typed for Eliot was to be read by him at a meeting of Shakespeare scholars in New York City. It was a tedious discourse comparing the five quartos of *Romeo and Juliet* with the first folio and pointing out the differences between Shakespeare's handling of time in his play and that of Arthur Brooke in his long-winded poem *The Tragical History of Romeus and Juliet*, on which Shakespeare built his play.

It was not Eliot's best writing, and we both knew it. But as Eliot said, neither was *Romeo and Juliet* Shakespeare's best writing, some of the lines so falsely poetic as to verge on the absurd. "A writer cannot produce his best and brightest with each new work," Eliot said. "The quality of a writer's output follows the same ebb and flow of the tides, the same rise and fall of the seasons. Sometimes there is lush new growth and other times only bare branches." At times Eliot could also wax poetic verging on absurdity.

Eliot was shot by his son with a gun two days before the Shakespeare conference and thus did not read his paper to the other scholars. I found it locked inside his rolltop desk after what was referred to as "the accident," though it was no accident. I found other things in his desk, also. Juliet claimed to be "past hope, past cure, past help" because of her thwarted love, and in the end she fell upon Romeo's dagger gratefully. I understand such despair.

Now everyone in the Walton family is saying good-night to one another on the television, signaling the end of today's episode. I wonder if John-Boy was ever in love with a girl, someone from a neighboring farm or some merchant's pretty daughter in the nearby town. I did not watch the program regularly when it first appeared on television, but no doubt the writers at some point included a romantic interest in the life of good-hearted John-Boy Walton. No screenwriter would overlook an opportunity for romance.

Perry Mason and *Hawaii Five-O* come on in the afternoon, after *Judge Jack*. Then *Gomer Pyle*, *Happy Days*, and *The Mary Tyler Moore Show*. *Leave It to Beaver* and *The Beverly Hillbillies* come on around suppertime. In the evenings, instead of watching *The Brady Bunch* and *The Munsters*, I often change to a nature program. Sometimes I turn to the History Channel, where I may watch the Wright Brothers at Kitty Hawk or the sinking of the *Edmund Fitzgerald* or resistance fighters in Germany during World War II.

"DIED. DOWAGER VISCOUNTESS DILHORNE, 93, who trained pigeons to carry secret communications during World War II; in Northamptonshire, England. Lady Dilhorne's carrier pigeons returned to her home west of London with coded messages strapped to their legs that had been sent by secret agents and resistance fighters in Germany." By watching television and reading *Time* magazine, I am reminded of the many connections between life and death. That the lives of men could ride on the wings of pigeons—this is something to think about.

If it's a long night, I know that *Sanford and Son* comes on at three in the morning, followed by *All in the Family*, then *Bob Newhart*. At times I turn the television off and listen to the radio. Sometimes I have them both on at the same time. One night *Mister Ed* was on television while a radio talk-show host was taking calls about something referred to as "road rage." Mister Ed performed better than the talk-show host. He also had a more pleasing voice.

I hear Rachel's doorbell, the short back-door chime instead of the longer one for the front door. A commercial about no-questions-asked life insurance is on, demonstrating that the network knows its morning audience. I turn down the volume of the television. Perhaps the white electrician has returned for something he left. I hear a voice at the door, the words rapid and high-pitched. I hear low words from Rachel; then the door closes, and all is silent.

I hear Rachel open and close a kitchen cupboard. She says

something, yet there is no reply. She says something else. It is not like Rachel to talk to herself.

I see a bird light on the feeder. I know this bird, for he has come before. I have sought him out in my *Book of North American Birds* and identified him as the evening grosbeak. This is a male, black wings with white patches, brownish head, yellow belly. My book tells me that the evening grosbeak has become a vagabond over time. Whatever the cause of the first migration, my book states that the evening grosbeak now "wanders widely in winter." I have known men to do this. One may also wander without leaving home.

I hear Rachel say something else in the kitchen. Maybe she is on the telephone. I turn the volume up again on the television. Mac-Gyver is in his old Chevrolet station wagon at a stop sign on a dark country road. It strikes me that he and Rachel have the same hairstyle—short around the ears, long in back, with a feathered crest on top. It is a style I have heard called a mullet.

MacGyver looks across the field and sees what looks like a spaceship. He blinks and shakes his head, then looks again. A glowing figure is walking toward his car. But MacGyver is not afraid. He has had much experience with thugs of all kinds. He gets out of his car and walks toward the figure, who is carrying something that looks like a floor lamp. The next frame shows MacGyver slumped unconscious on the ground.

I wake up when Rachel knocks at my door and brings my lunch. She is removing from the tray a bowl of something when the doorbell sounds again. "I'll be right back," she says to me, and she leaves the tray on the table. From my recliner I cannot see the back door, but I hear the same voice as before, then laughter. Though I've never heard her laugh, I know this laughter isn't Rachel's. "So it was just a false alarm," the voice says, "but I sure appreciate your help. I didn't know what else to do. Hope I didn't upset your plans for the day."

Rachel says no, her plans weren't upset, she had planned to be home all morning anyway. Before the woman leaves, she thanks Rachel again.

"You said her name is Veronica, right?" Rachel asks.

"It was my mother's name," the woman says.

"It's a pretty name," Rachel says. "She's sweet."

I wonder who Veronica is and where she is. Surely if she were a child there in the kitchen with Rachel and the visitor, I would hear her.

The other woman must have stepped out into the carport by now because I can't hear her reply. I hear Rachel, though, when she says, "Could you come over for some dessert tonight?"

In the weeks that I have lived here, only the white electrician and the mailman have come to Patrick and Rachel's house. An empty lot of weeds stands on one side of their house and an unoccupied house, surrounded by a tall hedge, on the other. I haven't thought of my nephew as having friends, but I have wondered if Rachel does, perhaps someone at their church or a neighbor down the street, though I have never heard nor seen her talking to another woman until today.

After my trial visit in the summer, I worried briefly that Rachel might have agreed to take me in part to ease her loneliness. I wondered if she wanted more from me than my money. I liked the fact that she was to be home all day, for I wanted to hear the sounds of living, but I had no desire for the door between my apartment and her kitchen to stand open. I made it clear that I wanted shelter, food, and privacy. I was to have no responsibilities beyond my modest monthly contribution to Patrick's household expenses. I had long since had my fill of talk. One does not want to spend her final days trying to follow someone's story or participate in the fruitless discussions most women seem to enjoy, the kind I myself once enjoyed. That time is past.

But Rachel has left me alone. She has told me no tales, has read me no rhymes, has sung me no songs. Nor have I imposed my words upon her. She is a riddle for which I need no answer. I am content with her silence. Watching her is sufficient.

But "Could you come over for dessert tonight?" This is a breaking of the silence. She steps out into the carport to talk. But what is a single word in a vast emptiness? What is a flicker of light in a dark night? Only a moment and then it is gone.

I think of the dangers of love. Romeo's line comes to my mind: "I must be gone and live, or stay and die." I hear Juliet as she tries to dissuade him, to make him believe that the light in the sky is not daylight but only "some meteor that the sun exhales." I think of the ill luck of Romeo and Juliet. If Tybalt hadn't been so quarrelsome. If Romeo hadn't avenged Mercutio's death. If old Capulet hadn't insisted on Juliet's marrying Paris. If the letter telling Romeo of the sleeping potion hadn't miscarried. If Romeo had patiently grieved long enough for Juliet to awake.

And if frogs had wings, they wouldn't bump their rumps when they jump.

Rachel reappears to finish laying out my lunch. She works quietly, her lips slightly parted as if a spring is loose, but no words come.

CHAPTER 5

THE WIDE WORLD
AND ALL HER
FADING SWEETS

The horned lark loves the open country and with
its mate builds its nest on the ground. The male,
the black tufts of his "horns" barely visible,
performs his courtship ritual by circling at great
heights while warbling sweetly, then closing his
wings and plummeting silently to the ground.

On Sunday morning it is raining. Patrick informs me after breakfast that it will be best if I move to the back bedroom for the three-day electrical project. He apologizes for the inconvenience. I do not ask if the rewiring is necessary. I know men and their home repairs. In their minds they are always necessary. If asked, Patrick would launch into a lengthy discourse about the dangers of old wiring and the advantages of new. He would talk about the age of the house, the demand for increased voltage capacity, and many other things that would give him great joy to explain. I will deny him the pleasure.

While Patrick and Rachel are at church, I take a few things to my assigned bedroom across the hall from theirs. Rachel has set several magazines on the table beside the single bed and has opened the blinds and curtains. I wonder if this is the room where Toby and Mandy once slept. There are two windows in the room—one of them facing the street, the other looking out on the tall hedge around the empty house next door. A small chair upholstered in pale green chintz sits between the bedside table and window. A pink towel and matching washcloth have been laid out on the foot of the bed.

A note, presumably from Rachel, is propped against a lamp on the dresser: "There's plenty of closet space. Patrick will move your radio back here. He will bring in the TV from his study." This does not surprise me that Rachel has written something she could have told me. Her handwriting is large and sensible, her style economical.

I go back to my apartment to get two dresses to hang in the new closet. I have five dresses, all alike except for color, which I wear in no particular order. They button in front and are of a crinkly fabric that requires no ironing. Over these I wear sweaters, often more than one at a time. I also wear heavy socks and slippers. My apartment has its own thermostat, set at 78 degrees. I have told Patrick that I will not suffer cold to save money on an electric bill. I have two pairs of pants with elastic waistbands, but I prefer the dresses. I also have three other dresses, nicer ones suitable for dining out and attending church, neither of which I intend to do, and three pairs of rubber-soled lace-up shoes, which I have not worn since coming here.

I sit in the pale green chair and find that it both swivels and rocks. I turn to face the window, from which I can see Wagner's Mortuary. It is the kind of cold, gray, wet day common to the months of November and February. A woman is getting out of her car in the parking lot of the mortuary and walking quickly toward the front door. She has no umbrella but has pulled her raincoat up over her head. Sunday is generally a slow day at Wagner's, at least at the front entrance. No doubt the deliveries at the rear continue unabated, as death observes no day of rest.

Though I will miss my bird feeder for the next few days, I will not object to staying in this room as much as I will pretend to. There is a bathroom separating it from Patrick's study, with doors on either side, like the shared bathrooms in old hospitals. I will sit in this chair and observe the small world of Edison Street in Greenville, Mississippi. Between meals I will watch television and read Rachel's magazines.

I look through the small stack on the table and find, among the issues of *Country Home* and *Country Chef*, an old copy of a magazine called *Writing Life*. The name on the address sticker is that of my nephew: Patrick Martin Felber. I have heard Patrick say he should not have quit college after two years, that he could be a tenured professor of history or literature by now if he had set his mind to it. I believe that the inflated value he places on universities has caused him to think more highly of me than I deserve. I notice that the magazine is two years old. I imagine Patrick eagerly opening it two years ago, drinking in its announcements of newly published writers, writers' retreats, fiction contests, and the like. No doubt he still dreams of seeing his own name someday on the page titled Recent Winners of Grants and Awards.

I thumb through the magazine now, taking note of the feature articles: "The Spirit and the Hand," "Time-Tested Words," "Benefits of Solitude," "Finding the Heart of a Story." Someone has high-lighted passages with a yellow marker: *I aim for a style that is pared down, with a rough-hewn elegance*, and *I insist on an artist's right to break the rules*, and *Look for an agent who is well connected, pushy, and vision-ary, with a little gypsy blood in his veins*.

I close the *Writing Life* magazine, feeling sorry that my nephew has an aspiration to write. I remember the way Eliot haunted our mailbox when he had a manuscript circulating among scholarly jour-nals. I remember his descent into silent gloom when an article was rejected. When an article was accepted, he exhibited only the brief-est joy before a grim resolve took over and he got back to work. He must publish again and yet again. My bird book tells me that the horned lark may sing sweetly at great heights, then suddenly and silently dive groundward. The pressure to publish was considerable in the English Department of South Wesleyan State College, where we taught, and even more intense in the larger academic circles in which Eliot was anxious to make a reputation.

I met him at a time when his song was often cheerful, when he saw in me the chance for improving his life, particularly in regard to his writing—an activity that necessitated a reliable proofreader and typist. I knew nothing of the black moods to which he was prone after his literary setbacks. Yet my life as Eliot's wife was not unpleas-ant. Between moods he could be considerate and jovial. I learned to read him, and it was a book I loved. I knew when to leave him alone, when to draw him out, when to serve quietly.

What time does to "the world and all her fading sweets" is a common theme in Shakespeare's sonnets. How time touches the body can be seen with the eye. What it does to the spirit may be hidden from sight but be more cruel by far. I have heard it said that a woman never really knows a man until she marries him. This much is true. Yet sometimes a woman may marry a man and live with him for many years, may learn many things about him during that time, yet still not truly know him.

As a teacher of freshman grammar and composition, and content to remain so, I felt none of Eliot's compulsion to be published but rather gave myself to helping him prepare his manuscripts and lecture notes. I had come to university teaching late, having spent almost twenty years in elementary school classrooms. It was Eliot who urged me to take summer courses in English Education, then apply for an entry-level position at the college where he taught Shakespeare and Seventeenth-Century Literature.

Teaching university students was not the grand, uplifting experience I had imagined. It was tedious and only rarely rewarding. In the areas of attention span and ability to follow directions, I found little difference between ten-year-olds and college freshmen, who saw no glory to be gained from learning rules of grammar and composing a research paper. To say that their efforts were halfhearted would be an exaggeration.

Yet I dutifully drilled the rules and graded their papers for ten years at South Wesleyan in Hillcrest, Kentucky, and another ten at Tri-Community College in Carlton, Kentucky, before retiring from teaching. During that time I often wished I had remained in the elementary classroom, but having already fallen into the habit of university teaching, meeting students only three hours a week instead of six or seven hours a day, I found it was a habit not easily broken. Recalling, furthermore, the great outlay of physical energy required to teach children, I never went back.

I want to tell Patrick that his job at the office supply store is eminently more interesting than grading workbook exercises on subject-verb agreement, marking comma splices and fused sentences in essays, checking sources in the library for plagiarism. I want to tell him of the emotional battering he will experience if he insists on trying to write for publication. I want to describe the lonely valleys of discouragement the writer must walk, the long hours of toiling in the field for only a handful of fruit. Sometimes there comes a drought and there is no crop at all.

Or I could take a different tack. I could tell him that writing in itself is harmless, may even be deeply, personally gratifying. I could encourage him to write reams of pages out of the abundance of his desire, to collect these treasures into large notebooks, to build bookshelves to house them all, to add a room onto his house if necessary. "Empty your heart," I could tell him. "Get it all out on paper." Then I could fix him with a stern gaze. "But don't expect an editor on the face of God's green earth to care in the least about what you have written. And don't expect to be paid a red cent for any of it. And don't pawn it off on friends and family to read."

From hearing Patrick's spoken words, I know what his writing would be like: bombastic, self-important soapboxing. I have read some of his letters to the editor printed in the *Delta Democrat Times*. The words *clear*, *direct*, and *understated* do not describe Patrick's style of communication.

I put the writing magazine at the bottom of the stack and see that

there are also a few old issues of *Time* magazine on the table. I find
the Milestones page in one of them. "DIED. SIDNEY JAMES, 97,
founding editor of *Sports Illustrated*." I wonder if Sidney James
included a swimsuit issue in the early years. Pictures flash into my
mind as I think of the different ways women try to please men and
of the degrading uses to which the human body can be put.

I look at my hands and think of the many hours I typed for Eliot,
of the suitcases I packed and the meals I cooked for him, the trips we
took together. I think of the thirteen years we spent as husband and
wife, years that I considered to be good until the very end. I think of
Eliot's son, locked away for life in a Kentucky prison, of his daughter,
living on a sheep farm in New Zealand, a woman I have never met.
I think of her two boys, Eliot's only grandchildren, whom he never
saw. Nor did he know their names.

The lawyer's office across the street is closed. The sign in the yard
reads *SAMUEL F. GRAHAM, ATTORNEY AT LAW*. I wonder
what kinds of cases Samuel F. Graham specializes in. Would he
accept the defense in a murder case? If the defendant were a shiftless
thirty-year-old who never called his father except to ask for money,
who never visited except to follow up on a phone call, would he
believe the claim that the gun had fired accidentally?

The two wicker rocking chairs on the wide front porch of the
lawyer's office are likely intended as a touch of domestic comfort, of
assurance that Samuel F. Graham is just one of the common towns-
folk: "Come on up and sit a spell. Tell me your troubles and we'll
talk it over." People in the South have a great fondness for front
porches. Surely no one with rocking chairs on his front porch would
fleece you of your life savings. Surely he just wants to help.

The house next to the lawyer's office has a discouraged look. Its high-pitched roof gives the effect of an old hat that is too large. The windows appear to have blankets or sheets over them, and rain is pouring from a misaligned gutter at the corner of the house. There are slats missing from one of the shutters, and the shrubs in front of the porch look beaten down, as if a large grazing animal has been tramping through them.

November can be a changeable month in the Mississippi Delta. Though it is forty-five degrees and raining today, two days ago it was a warm, sunny day in the sixties. On that day there was a great flurry of coming and going across the street as people arrived in shifts to help the family move in. The woman dressed as a man was in and out, doing a man's work. The man did his share, also.

At one point the man appeared on the front porch with cups on a tray, and a half dozen other people came out to take a break. The teenage girl was among them, hunched over, looking down into her cup. They sat on boxes and drank whatever was in the cups, then got up and went inside again. Later the man came back out carrying the little girl. He was talking to a man and woman, and when they got in a car and left, he waved good-bye from the front step. He lifted the little girl's hand to make her wave. All this I watched for an hour while Rachel was at the Department of Motor Vehicles renewing her driver's license.

It must have been the woman dressed as a man who came to Rachel's door on Friday, the one who spoke of a false alarm, whose mother's name was Veronica. She and the man came again that night for dessert. I didn't see either of them, but by muting the television I heard much of the conversation.

They sat at the kitchen table to eat Rachel's apple cobbler, and they patiently answered Patrick's questions, which he fired rapidly, interspersing the questions with bits of advice about landscaping, which he knew they were eager to start on considering the former owners' neglect, and repaving, which he likewise knew they had already thought about since the driveway was so badly cracked. He told them that one of his employees at the office supply store had a brother who did driveways and sidewalks, and he would be glad to give them his name and phone number; in fact, he would look it up and write it down right now while he was thinking about it.

The man, whose name is Steve, said he worked at the catfish processing plant. Teri, the woman, didn't work, he said, "except at home, and she does plenty of that." Teri interjected that it was a full-time job just keeping ahead of Steve's smelly work clothes. They had two girls, Mindy the teenager and Veronica, who was almost four. Steve volunteered the fact that they had lost a boy, Jody, eleven years ago when he was only a baby.

I wondered if the mention of the boy's death and the names Jody and Mindy, so close to Toby and Mandy, suddenly made Rachel feel that there was a noose around her neck. And did she feel that some-one had kicked the chair out from under her and left her hanging when Patrick said, "We lost two children ourselves, so we know what that's like"?

But Rachel's voice was low and calm. "How many days a week does Veronica have therapy?" she asked.

Teri answered in her quick, light way. "Mondays and Thursdays," she said. She laughed, a nickering sound such as a young horse might make, and said that Veronica had begun tracking bright objects with her eyes the week before, at which time I understood that Veronica wasn't like other children. I remembered how Steve had lifted her hand on the porch to make her wave.

Patrick, ever curious about any deviation from the norm, began at once to quiz Steve and Teri concerning Veronica's disabilities, asking if she could walk, talk, sit up, feed herself, and so forth. The answer to each question was no. Was the condition genetic, Patrick wanted to know. Yes. Though Mindy had been spared, the disorder had played a role in Jody's early death and had appeared full-blown in Veronica. She had seizures, sometimes a dozen a day, sometimes none. Doctors had advised them against having more children.

"We thought she was deaf for a long time," Teri said, "but last week she turned her head when I dropped a pan on the kitchen floor." She gave another whinnying laugh and added, "The doctor thinks she might eventually get back fifty percent of her hearing." Patrick didn't question how one could get back something she had never lost, that had simply been undetected.

Steve and Teri were glad to be relocating to Edison Street—"a real neighborhood," as they put it. They had left a trailer park out off Highway 82, a place nicknamed Honeymoon Hole. "Our honeymoon stretched out to almost twenty years," Steve said. He knew he had his work cut out for him, buying a fixer-upper like the one across the street, but it was the only way they could "swing the homeowner thing," he said. They had big plans to "spruce it up," but it would have to be "slow going because of time and money." No doubt he wanted to make it clear to Patrick that the landscaping and new driveway wouldn't be happening next week.

Before they left on Friday night, Teri thanked Rachel again for helping her out "in a pinch" earlier that day. What did she mean, Patrick wanted to know. "Oh, she didn't tell you?" Teri said. "She kept Veronica for me today when I had to run over to see about something at Mindy's school. That was nice enough, but then she turned around and asked us over for apple cobbler, too."

Perhaps the false alarm had related to Mindy somehow, but no further details were offered, and Steve and Teri left shortly after. Patrick closed the door behind them and said, "That Steve sure is a talker. Nice guy." I heard no reply from Rachel. I wondered if she knew how much Patrick talked before she married him. Or maybe he didn't always talk so much. Maybe when they were first married she had been the talker. Maybe he had begun filling the void when she fell silent.

She came to my door and knocked a few minutes after they had left. "Aunt Sophie? I forgot to come get your dessert dish. Are you still up?" She must have wondered why I was sitting in my chair staring at the television with the sound muted. Or maybe she didn't wonder. Maybe Rachel's thinking is consumed with surviving each day. Perhaps there is no surplus to expend on wondering about an old woman watching television with no sound.

The rain is falling more heavily now. Several more cars have pulled into the parking lot of Wagner's Mortuary. From the window where I sit, Edison Street looks like an old photograph, blurred by a photographer's shaky hand and faded over time.

CHAPTER 6

VOWING MORE THAN THE PERFECTION OF TEN

The feet of the fox sparrow are large,
with elongated toes and claws, allowing it
to dig longer and deeper. The male bird
prefers solitude when he sings, retreating
to a hidden perch in a dense thicket.

I t is not the front door of the mortuary that fills me with awe and horror but the back door. I have read about what goes on in the inner sanctum of a funeral home. When Eliot died, I was oblivious to the details of the funeral industry. It was years later that I read *The American Way of Death* by Jessica Mitford, a book that informed me of the procedures to which his body had been subjected—by that time, the same procedures already performed on my father, mother, and both of my sisters. Death American style is a gruesome prospect. In Eliot's case, however, it was no more than he deserved.

I did not know, when I was responsible for planning the funerals of my husband and, later, my mother, that embalming is a custom common only to North America, but that even in the United States and Canada no law dictates the practice. This curious tradition is routinely carried out for one purpose: to prepare the body for yet another curious tradition, that of placing it in an ornate box for the living to "view." At no time is the family consulted about whether they wish these procedures to be performed on the body of their loved one. The funeral director merely goes about his business, then collects from the family the standard fee. Apparently no one raises a protest.

The steps of "preparing the body" may be summarized briefly. First, it is interesting to know that a mortician learns the craft that is to earn him his fortune by attending an embalming school for a year at any point following high school graduation. Here the student, who may still be a teenager, handles the tools of his trade—the needles, scalpels, forceps, clamps, scissors, basins, pumps, tubes—and is instructed in the proper administering of the customary fluids, plasters, creams, oils, powders, pastes, paints, and waxes. As in medical school, the aspiring "doctor" practices on cadavers. Unlike genuine surgeons-in-training, however, he will never, thankfully, progress to performing his skills on living humans.

There is no way to be delicate about this. In the embalming room the mortician drains the body of blood, by means of a small incision in a major vein or artery, and injects a solution of formaldehyde, alcohol, borax, glycerin, phenol, and water. With needle and suture thread, the lips are literally sewn together and the eyes closed with small caps and a special cement. The body cavities are invaded by means of a long, hollow needle, then emptied with tube and pump and replaced with yet more chemical fluids.

To restore the body to a normal, restful appearance, the mortician, after allowing the body to lie undisturbed for ten to twelve hours, then reaches into his bag of cosmetic tricks. Whether the challenge is to reduce swollen features or plump up emaciated ones, the modern, well-trained mortuary scientist is equal to the task by way of various methods of surgical trimming, padding, injecting, and so forth. He may need to make creative use of splints, wires, drills, anchors, patches, masking creams, and parlor lighting to achieve the desired effect, but the ambitious mortician will go to almost any lengths in his efforts to make available to the family an open-casket funeral.

I sometimes wake during the night with visions of a dark shape hovering over me, something sharp and metallic in his hand. At times I have heard voices: "Let's push that left shoulder down a little; she's lying crooked," or "Hand me the suntan tint; this pink blush shade doesn't match her skin tone," or "She looks too glum. Can we stitch up the corners of the lips a little higher?" Once I heard, "Maybe we ought to dislocate the jaw to fix her mouth." This is a method sometimes employed to keep stubborn lips together. The mortician simply unhinges the jaw and then wires it shut. For less serious cases he may keep the mouth closed by pushing a straight pin through the inside of the lower lip and angling it upward through the two front teeth. I awake from these dreams trembling.

I have written down clear instructions concerning the disposal of my body and have left them in a sealed envelope with my lawyer, to be delivered to Patrick at the time of my death. I have told Patrick that there will be no transfer of money if the instructions are not followed. All of this depends, of course, upon the trustworthiness of my lawyer and of Patrick. Either could find ways to circumvent my wishes.

It is Friday, five days after my move to the back bedroom, and Rachel is in my apartment with a can of furniture polish and a dust-rag. She has been at work all day and is now finishing with the cleanup from the plaster removal. True to the white electrician's word, the plaster dust, also white, found its way into my apartment, a fine film over every exposed surface. Patrick had the foresight to cover my furniture with old bed sheets. True to his predictions, the rewiring project took longer than originally planned. Patrick prides himself on his ability to prophesy the difference between a person's stated intentions and reality.

I am sitting in my recliner watching Rachel dust the blinds of the four large windows. She has already polished the windowpanes and vacuumed the sills and the blinds, moving the wand slowly back and forth. Now she sprays her cloth and runs it over the length of each wooden slat, top and bottom. This takes time. She does not hurry.

To the casual observer watching her clean my apartment, she would appear to have no method, but I am not a casual observer. I believe there is a master plan behind her actions. This much I know: She has saved the windows for last. After the blinds she will be done. Then she will proceed to the other rooms of her house, I presume, and by the time she finishes, it will be time, as my mother used to say, to start the whole shebang over. Housework is a discouraging proposition. I have had my fill of it and have stipulated as one of the conditions of my winter hospice the privilege of watching someone else do it.

Except for her normal Friday laundry chore, Rachel has devoted today to my apartment. Her kitchen and dining room have remained untouched. Large sheets of plastic still hang over her cupboards. Patrick asked the white electrician to leave the plastic sheeting up. "We'll take it down after all the dust has had time to settle," he told the man. The electrician and his helper cleaned up their mess, after a fashion. They picked up all their tools and disposed of the loose pieces of debris. They vacuumed the floor with their own high-powered machine, which sounded like the landing of an aircraft in Rachel's kitchen. They plugged the appliances into their new sockets and moved them back into place.

I have walked back and forth between the spare bedroom and my apartment today, tracking Rachel's progress. The days have gone slowly in my temporary quarters, with much clatter at the other end of the house. I have found the major television networks to be poor substitutes for the TV Oldies channel, which the smaller television does not pick up. *Live with Regis and Kelly*, *The Price Is Right*, *As the World Turns*, *The 700 Club*—these are samples of the daytime offerings on the television brought in from Patrick's study. At night it's the news and *Wheel of Fortune* and the so-called reality shows.

I have an idea for a reality show. Set up a camera at the back door of a funeral home. Follow the journey of a corpse from its arrival to its installment inside a casket, all pickled, painted, and propped to receive guests. Then film the faces of all the people who come to "view the body" and record their platitudes as they extend comfort to the grieving family. Then set up a camera outside the same funeral home and watch the same people exit. Record their cheerful plans for the next meal, show their eyes scanning the sky to check the weather for tomorrow's golf game, observe them hurrying to their cars to get on with their lives.

Take care to film the family, also. Zoom in on their faces, amplify the sound to hear every word they speak to one another, follow them home to record private discussions concerning the disposition of money and goods. Note the difference between their public and private faces during these few days of official grieving. Look closely and you will see many dollar signs in their eyes. Finding a family to participate in the show would not pose a problem. Most people are willing to do almost anything for the right price.

The program would be what they call "a hit." The major problem would be getting a funeral home to cooperate, for if the public were to see the indignities performed in the embalming room and observe the cheap imitations of sorrow, the funeral industry would be out of business in short order. Family members would begin hurling the bodies of their dead relatives into canyons or dropping them into the ocean. Do not speak to me of desecrating the bodies of the deceased. It happens daily in funeral homes all over the continent of North America.

For the past five days my meals have continued on schedule. I assume they have been an inconvenience for Rachel, though I have heard no complaints. On Monday her stove and refrigerator were moved into the garage, where they were plugged into a 220 outlet. The meals have been simple and the desserts have suffered, but they have arrived on time, morning, noon, and night. A few have been purchased by Patrick elsewhere and brought home to be transferred to a plate, then onto the tray, and delivered to my bedroom by Rachel. I do not know where she and Patrick have taken their meals. I have not heard any part of their mealtime conversations—another small part missing from my daily routine, another reason for the week's slow passage.

Rachel has plodded through the week silently, doing her duty. I cannot imagine having to cook in one's garage. She is cleaning the last set of wooden blinds now, bending to reach the lowest slats. She is wearing a pair of denim jeans and a sweatshirt with OCTOBER BALLOON FESTIVAL printed on the front and a large colorful hot air balloon pictured on the back. This event was held last month, a few days after my arrival at Patrick's house. Patrick urged me to go with them to the festival, but hot air balloons in the sky and crowds of people on the ground were of no interest to me.

A week after the festival he brought the sweatshirt home to Rachel, telling her they had hundreds left over and were selling them for five dollars each. Perhaps it was because of the unpopular color, a bright orange, or perhaps because the order had been mixed up—the picture of the balloon intended for the front and the name of the event for the back. Patrick's generous impulses soared when he saw the bargain, and he bought one for his wife. Gaudy colors and reversed designs do not matter to Patrick, nor apparently to Rachel, for she wears the sweatshirt frequently.

She is finished now. She steps back and turns slowly, taking in the entire room, as if looking for areas she may have missed. It is nearing four o'clock. Danno has already successfully booked another criminal on *Hawaii Five-O*, and Gomer Pyle has been making a fool of himself for almost a half hour, cheerily countering every exasperated outburst from Sergeant Carter with his usual countrified simplicity. Gomer says, "Shazam, that shore is nass of you, Sergeant Carter!" and Rachel glances at the television.

"I'm sorry we've had to put you out this week," she says. "I sure didn't know Patrick was planning on having all this work done. Looks like we could've done it before you came."

This is a long speech for Rachel. I also realize it's as close to criticizing her husband as she is likely to come.

"There is no way to know what a man is going to do next," I say. "And there's no reasoning with them when they get something in their minds."

As if wishing to restore her husband's good standing, she says, "Patrick says he's bringing something home for supper. He told me not to cook."

"You've worked hard today," I say.

Again she looks around my apartment. "Well, it needed a good cleaning." She moves toward the door. "Shall I help you bring your things from the other room?" Her use of "shall I" sounds out of place. Rachel went to high school in Tupelo, Mississippi, then attended a two-year Bible college somewhere in Alabama, during which time she met Patrick at a Billy Graham crusade in Atlanta. In many ways she's a typical southerner, yet southerners rarely say, "Shall I help you?" They are more likely to say, "Want me to?" or "Can I?"

I tell her I've already returned everything to its place, even though this isn't entirely true. I still need to move the dresses hanging in the closet. The telephone rings in the kitchen, and she goes to answer it, leaving my door open. She says three words—"hello," "sure," and "yes"—and when she hangs up she comes back to my door and tells me she's going to "run across the street for a little bit." She closes my door, and I hear her leave through the kitchen door. I assume that "across the street" means Teri's house rather than the lawyer's office or the mortuary.

Gomer Pyle ends and a program called *Happy Days* comes on. Since I have never been much interested in the Cunningham family or Fonzie, I walk to the back bedroom to get my dresses. The door to Patrick's study is standing open. Throughout the past five days it has remained closed. In the evenings I could see Patrick's light shining beneath the bathroom door, but until now I have never looked inside the room.

And now I regret that I am looking, for I see something that gives me a sudden tightness of breath. I reach out and hold onto the doorjamb until the moment passes. I close my eyes briefly, then open them, taking care not to see what I already saw.

I proceed to the bedroom, open the closet and remove the dresses, then start back down the hallway to my apartment, glancing into Patrick and Rachel's bedroom across the hall. Their bed is only a double size, which must feel crowded. Here Patrick holds forth both before and after the lights are out, speaking his mind about all the pressing political and social issues of the day. I imagine Rachel staring up at the ceiling as she listens to the same opinions she must have heard many times already. Several nights during the past week I have heard the drone of his voice across the hall as I prepared for bed. Their bed is covered by a thin red-corded bedspread, such as the kind one would expect to see on children's bunk beds. I see the control for an electric blanket sitting on the nightstand beside the clock. I wonder if it is a dual control or if in this matter, as in most others

I have observed, Rachel defers to her husband's preferences.

I move down the hallway, keeping my eyes straight ahead as I pass Patrick's study. I can't erase the picture of what I saw, however, and after I return the dresses to my closet, I lie down on my sofa and close my eyes, forcing myself to breathe slowly and steadily. The image floats in the black space of my mind.

The rolltop desk isn't as large as Eliot's was, but I think of the heavy cargo so light a vessel may carry. The top was rolled back on Patrick's desk. I saw a great many papers scattered around. I saw many small cubbyholes and drawers. I can't help wondering if he keeps it open all the time, or if he, like Eliot, pulls down the top and locks it when he has things to hide. I wonder if Rachel goes into the study, if she moves Patrick's things around to dust.

Tidying Eliot's desk was verboten in our home. He found me in his study one day shortly after our marriage, straightening books and stacks of papers on a shelf, wielding a feather duster around the desk, which was closed and locked. From the doorway he fixed me with the kind of look a teacher reserves for an insolent student. "Do not bother my study, Sophia," he said. "Do not ever come in here when I am not here."

Another day, weeks later, I opened the door of his study and walked in to ask him if he wanted cucumbers on his salad. He closed a drawer and held up a hand to halt me at the door. Before I could ask my question, he said, "You must knock before coming in." I laid it to the account of his long years of living without a wife, of struggling to preserve a private place in the midst of raising a difficult son and daughter by himself. He was sixty and I forty-two when we married. I excused his sternness. Surely a man of his age, education, and background deserved a single refuge in his own home, a place where he could think, write, and read unmolested. My bird book tells me of a sparrow that can dig deeper than other birds, that sings its sweetest when hidden away in dense foliage.

The television is still on, and I hear a woman's voice say, "I'll believe that when a snowball melts in you-know-where," followed by canned laughter. I think of the man and woman who played the Cunninghams on *Happy Days*, pretending to be a typical married couple. I wonder what their real-life marriages were like. I think of my sister Regina and her first husband, who was a traveling salesman, then the second one, who invested all her money in a paving company that failed. At least by fathering her two sons, her third husband gave her something before she divorced him, too. I think of my sister Virginia raising her four children virtually by herself. Her husband was dismissed from his job with an accounting firm because of something she never divulged, after which he took sick and was in bed for almost ten years before he finally, mercifully died.

I think of my parents and the arguments I used to hear before my father died, in which each blamed the other for their financial failures. I had wanted to defend them each to the other, wanted to point out to Daddy that Mother had worked slavishly at keeping up the boardinghouse during all the years he tried to make a success of his small printing company, wanted to remind Mother of all the sacrifices Daddy had made to keep the business going, to publish articles that told the truth, that championed the causes of minorities. But I was timid when it came to standing up to adults. Even when I got to be a young adult myself, I never would have told my parents they were wrong about anything.

I think of the paper on *Troilus and Cressida* that Eliot presented at a national conference a few months after we were married. It was the paper I had been typing for him, in fact, when he slipped up behind me, placed his hands on my shoulders, and said, "I hope you will agree to marry me, Sophia. I believe that it would be a good arrangement for both of us." I continued typing, not knowing what to say. Thinking me reluctant, he went on at some length to list the many advantages of marriage, promising to make me happy. I cannot recall now what the advantages were or if the word *love* was ever mentioned.

I remember the great irony of the moment, for as he talked, I was typing a quoted passage from the play, in which Cressida scoffs at the things lovers promise when their ardor is new. They always "swear more performance" than they are capable of, she says, "vowing more than the perfection of ten," yet never delivering a tenth of one part. Though the highest level of mathematics I ever taught was to sixth graders, I can compute this output to be a mere one percent of the vow. If the promise is a dollar, the delivery is a penny. If the lover vows to run one hundred meters, he keels over after the first stride.

I open my eyes and look at my hands, wrinkled and spotted from the toil of eighty years of living. If all ten fingers represent the perfection vowed by a lover, the actual performance doesn't reach the first knuckle of the smallest finger. Promises are easy to make. I think of the many things two hands can do. They can sculpt something beautiful, then break it to pieces. The same hands that set words onto clean white paper can handle filth. They can touch the shoulders of a woman. They can push love away.

CHAPTER 7

A FOUL AND PESTILENT CONGREGATION OF VAPORS

Though the blue jay has earned the reputation

of a bully, it also has a kinder, gentler side.

Besides its noisy mocking cries, it has a low

musical song. While it is often a bossy, greedy

eater, it may also patiently labor to bring food

to its mate during nesting season.

I n spite of Eliot's failures, I mourned his loss. I had come to depend upon his companionship. Even during periods when he was unapproachable, I knew he would eventually return. I stored up bits of conversation to share with him, questions to ask. I allowed him to instruct me in all things, counting him stronger and wiser. He did not rule with a heavy hand, and it was my joy to order my days according to his wishes. I suppose some latecomers to marriage may rebel at the sudden restrictions. In my case I translated the restrictions into privileges, giving up what I considered to be little in order to enjoy much.

And I can say this: At least Eliot left me financially comfortable. He had accumulated a great deal more money in his lifetime than I could have guessed. Indeed, this was all I had to console me in the wake of his death, for in one five-minute span of time, thirteen years turned to rubble. After the shooting he lived two months—a dungeon of time, divided neatly into two cells: Before I Knew and After I Knew. Following those two months, there was his funeral, then later the trial of his son, my testimony playing a key role in convicting him.

Alonso and his sister, Portia, had hated me since my marriage to their father, for though they claimed fidelity to the tender memory of their mother, who had died twelve years before, I knew it was their father's money that fueled their resistance to the marriage. They did not want a widow in the picture when Eliot died. When I married their father, he was already, at sixty, an old man in their eyes. Though only teenagers at the time, they were champing for their inheritance money.

Portia steadfastly refused to "lay eyes on that woman"—that's what I heard her say one time when Eliot brought me home through the front door of his house and she exited, shrieking, through the back. She left home for Middlebury College in Vermont a week before we married, and she never returned. She studied French, lived in Paris after college, then moved with a Russian man named Slava to New Zealand, where she still lives and hates me from a distance of more than eight thousand miles. I feel no sorrow over her hatred. It is an abstraction. It does not touch me. The planet is round and revolves in an elliptical orbit around the sun. The stars shine. The rain falls. Portia hates me. Man breathes the air threescore years and ten, then dies. I have passed the mark by a decade.

Alonso, finishing high school the year we married, was rarely home. This was not an unhappy situation for me, and in many ways it was also a relief for Eliot, to whom his son was a mystery and an embarrassment. He didn't know where Alonso slept most of the time. Except for the shaved strip down the middle of his scalp, I would barely have recognized the boy had I passed him on the street. The only time I heard him acknowledge my existence was once when he screamed to Eliot, "She's a tub of lard! Why don't you just call her Fat-Soph?"

If Alonso had not been convicted and jailed for life, no doubt he would have threatened and hounded me for his father's money— money rightfully his, he would say. He surely would have contested the will, which awarded him only five thousand dollars and Portia only ten thousand. The remainder was mine.

Alonso would have stopped at nothing. I have seen and heard Alonso in action. Even now I sometimes imagine him breaking out of jail, tracking me down, and pointing a gun at me. I have awakened at night with his evil face floating above my bed, his small red-rimmed eyes glinting with greed and revenge. I keep my handgun in the drawer of the table beside my bed. I do not know if I could fire it in a crisis, but in its presence is a small measure of security.

I still see the spreading pool of blood on the rug in Eliot's study, where he fell. I hear the screech of tires as Alonso fled from the scene; I hear the sound of the siren minutes later; I see Eliot's form in the hospital bed, where he lay for two months in a coma before he died; I see him in the casket, wearing his best gray suit and a necktie for which he had paid eighty-five dollars. I feel the hatred radiating off Alonso's sinewy body as he stared me down in the courtroom, straining forward as if he'd like to climb over the table and come at my throat. Sometimes in my dreams Alonso is a monkey, nimble and hairy, screeching and gnashing his teeth.

Eliot's children were named after characters in Shakespearean plays. Growing up, they must have wished for normal names like Bob and Susan. I've often wondered if they were somehow set on the path of their hostile behaviors by the names they were given. I have envisioned Alonso slugging Bills and Davids when teased. I have seen Portia kicking and scratching at Janes and Lindas.

I suppose Eliot felt entirely justified in pinning literary names on his children, perhaps even compelled to do so for the sake of family tradition. Eliot himself had been named after George Eliot, whom his father had considered the finest of all English novelists, though Eliot preferred to think of himself as having more in common with T. S. Eliot, the poet and critic. T. S., however, had not yet made his mark in the literary world by the time Eliot was born in 1908. Eliot's two older brothers were Hugo and Dickens. His father's first name had been Hawthorne and his grandfather's Marlowe.

In Eliot's case, he liked the name Eliot well enough and didn't object to the fact that George Eliot was actually a woman. He declared her *Middlemarch* to be a masterpiece. As for T. S. Eliot, Eliot ranked "The Love Song of J. Alfred Prufrock" just below Shakespeare's sonnets. He nevertheless felt it was an unfortunate pairing with his last name, Hess, calling to mind Elliot Ness, a name well known in the United States during the first half of the twentieth century. At his first teaching job in Indiana, he and a student named Al Caponi were the subject of much teasing.

But concerning Alonso, regardless of any possible role his name could have played in the shaping of his character, the facts of the incident that sent him to prison were inarguable, though he did attempt to argue them. Alonso claimed that Eliot was cleaning the gun, a .22-caliber, when he came to see him that day in his study. The truth was that Alonso took the gun from the bookcase, where he knew his father kept it. I saw this.

He said that his father got angry at his request for money, that he pointed the gun at him and threatened him. Instead, it was Alonso who pointed the gun and shouted—his customary mode of communication with his father—that Eliot give him money, "or else." This I also witnessed.

From here the story proceeded along predictable lines: When in self-defense Alonso wrenched the gun from Eliot's hand, a scuffle purportedly ensued, during which the trigger was accidentally pulled. In truth, after he aimed the gun and pulled the trigger himself, Alonso pressed the weapon into Eliot's hands, then ran from the room. He did not know I was at home, that I had been watching from the doorway behind him. He did not see me flattened against the wall beside the door as he dashed out of the house. If he had, Fat-Soph certainly would not have been alive to testify against him in the courtroom.

The bullet's trajectory in what Alonso called "the accident" led straight to Eliot's head, where it lodged against his brain. As he lay unmoving in a hospital bed for two months, the doctors gave me little hope of his recovery. Alonso was held without bond, and when Eliot died, the charge became capital murder. Because I had been standing outside Eliot's study during the altercation, I was called to the witness stand to tell what I had seen and heard. The jury found no cause for reasonable doubt and judged Alonso guilty after only an hour of deliberation. As he was led out of the courtroom, he flailed and cursed like the wild man that he was.

It is a wonder that I held up under the close scrutiny of cross-examination, for between the shooting and Alonso's trial, I had walked through a chamber of horrors. By the time of the trial, I was in a daze of compounded grief. But I recalled every detail of the incident and reported it boldly and truthfully, knowing that my life depended on the jury's belief in my account, knowing that if Alonso were not convicted, another gun would go off, this time directed at my head.

The chamber of horrors of which I speak was located in Eliot's rolltop desk. Since then the horrors have been transferred to my mind, a large and commodious black screen upon which they are constantly replayed.

I went to Eliot's study the day after the shooting to look for certain insurance papers in his desk, but it was locked, and I couldn't find the key. It wasn't on Eliot's key ring or in his bureau drawer or any of the other places I looked. The key wasn't a matter of greatest urgency at first, however, and by means of several telephone calls I was able to provide the proper information to the hospital without producing the actual papers.

For the first several weeks, I was at the hospital every waking hour, hoping against all reason that a miracle would occur, that Eliot would open his eyes, sit up, and say, "Have you got the suitcases packed, Sophia? Did you finish typing the paper? Bring it to me quickly! We need to be on our way to the conference." I would have to urge him to lie back down, tell him gently there was a bullet in his head. After the excitement of his waking from the coma subsided, I could ask him at some point where the desk key was in case I ever needed it again.

In spite of the doctors' evasive answers to my questions, those early days were full of hope. I sat by Eliot's bed for hours on end, my eyes fixed on his face. I wanted to be the first to see him when he awoke. I fed on stories of hope I had heard, of coma victims suddenly waking and talking. Sometimes I sat on the edge of his bed and leaned down close to his face, thinking how happy I would be afterward to hear him tell people, "And when I opened my eyes, there was Sophia's face not six inches away from mine. She was faithful. She never gave up. It was her courage and hope that snatched me from death."

And I talked to him. I read sonnets and entire plays. I had never had a good singing voice, but I sang to him. He had always liked Broadway tunes. I sang songs from *South Pacific* and *Camelot*, two of his favorites. If I didn't know all the words, I made them up. Eliot had always been quick to correct an error. My hope was that he would hear the mistake and wake up to fix it.

Many days passed before it began to sink into my consciousness that Eliot very likely would never come out of the coma. Early one morning, after I had fallen asleep in the chair next to his bed, I woke up, looked at him, and thought, *He will never come home.* He was as pale as a corpse, as my mother was known to say. This is a simile no longer used by the younger generation of funeral goers, those who have grown accustomed to the cosmetic wonders achieved by the modern mortician's expert application of "peach glow" or "velvet rose."

That day I rose from beside his hospital bed and went home. I showered, took the phone off the hook, and slept for ten straight hours. I returned to the hospital late that afternoon and sat beside my husband for two hours, during which time I looked at him and thought, *I must start planning a funeral.* He had lost flesh around his face and neck in only a few weeks, the intravenous fluids a poor compensation for the diet of steaks, potatoes, and bread he had always preferred.

I knew that Eliot would never teach again. It was the middle of September now. School had already started, and other professors had been hastily called in to teach our courses. The academic dean had already contacted me about the search for a new professor of Shakespeare. He felt that two or three of the graduate students could cover my freshman grammar and composition classes. "For now" is how he put it, but I heard it for what it was: "From now on."

That night—now some four weeks after the shooting—I went home and searched in earnest for the key to Eliot's desk. He had purchased burial plots within recent years at a new cemetery on the outskirts of town, less than ten miles from South Wesleyan, where he had taught for the past twenty-five years. I knew the papers would be in a file folder somewhere in his desk. Eliot had always placed a high priority on organization. I also knew he had a life insurance policy, though I didn't know the exact amount. In many ways Eliot was a frugal man, yet he could be extravagant when it came to his own comforts. I had a sudden vague worry that the insurance policy, relating only to the comfort of someone besides himself, might not be as generous as a prospective widow might hope.

As I walked from my car into my house that night and then through each room, I felt as if I were walking on a plane elevated slightly above the floor. My thoughts were strangely focused and uncluttered: *I must find the papers in Eliot's desk, but first I must find the key to open the desk.* The logical room in which to hide the key was the study itself. I went to the door, opened it, and turned on the light. If I were hiding a key in this room, where would I hide it? This was the question I asked myself as I stood in the doorway. The hardwood floor had a naked look. The large oval rug upon which Eliot had bled had been removed and taken away to be burned.

"A foul and pestilent congregation of vapors"—thus Hamlet described the sky that had once seemed so clear and beautiful to his senses before his disposition was afflicted with distrust and melancholy. These words came to me now as I stood at the door of Eliot's study. It smelled of death. This was a place I used to consider a scholar's haven, a retreat from the ordinary cares of life, a quiet forbidden garden.

Because I was not welcome here, it held a certain mystery, and now that I was free to enter I did so timidly. With each advancing step I felt misgivings I could not explain. Perhaps, like Hamlet, I had by now "lost all my mirth" so that I expected only trouble at every turn. In many ways my husband had been two different men—one a benevolent friend, the other an exacting master. It was the frown of the master that I felt upon me now. I have read of birds that have two natures. Most often it is the less desirable one that dominates.

Having been closed up for weeks, the room did indeed seem to hold within its four walls its own collection of foul vapors. I walked over to one of the large windows and raised it. It was a mild night in September, with the faintest hint of the autumn to come to south-western Kentucky. The heavy draperies moved slightly as the air flowed in. I walked back to the doorway and turned on the overhead fan, then walked to the far side of the room to open another window.

This is when I found the key. It was on the top ledge of the bottom panel of the window. I actually felt it before I saw it. As I pushed back the drapery and then released the latch that secured the window, my hand brushed against something small and metallic, something that moved. I knew it was the key to Eliot's desk as soon as I felt it.

Eliot was obsessively neat. Sharing personal secrets did not come easily for him. I had attributed this characteristic to his background, for he had told me that his father had praised him only once in his entire life, when he had successfully defended his doctoral disserta-tion. Though the compliment was significantly diluted—"Finally, one of my sons has earned a doctorate"—Eliot felt gratified to know that he had succeeded in his father's eyes where his brothers had not.

Nor did he receive much praise from his mother, who suffered from ill health during most of his childhood. Nor from his first wife, whose attention was likewise distracted by poor health. Never rebounding from the stress of childbirth, she died while Portia and Alonso were in first grade and kindergarten. Growing up thus in an ungenerous home, then losing his wife when he most needed her help with the children had taught him, I reasoned, to keep to himself, to guard his resources, to give in small amounts.

The fact that he would keep his desk locked, then, didn't surprise me as much as that he would have hidden the key in such an unimaginative place. If I hadn't run across it accidentally, I couldn't help wondering how long it would have taken for me to find it. Perhaps that was the rationale behind the hiding place, however. Perhaps Eliot was quite sure no one would think to look in an obvious place like a window ledge.

As I stood before his desk with the key in my hand, I could not explain the foreboding in my heart. I knew, of course, that Eliot would not want me looking through his things. Even though I felt quite sure that he would never wake up again, would never know what I was about to do, I still feared doing something of which I knew he would disapprove. Generally mild-mannered and courteous, he had not rebuked me often, but those times were branded on my heart.

Also branded on my heart are the five minutes of time following my unlocking of the desk.

There were six drawers in his desk, one of them a larger bottom drawer filled with folders, all neatly labeled with a black fine-tip fountain pen, the only kind Eliot ever used. This is the drawer I went to first as the most likely to hold important documents.

And this is where I found his treasury of filth. The labels on these folders were no doubt intended to discourage meddlers, for they were dry, innocuous things such as "Houghton Contract," "San Diego Proposal," "Othello Outline," "ENG 503 Syllabus." The pictures themselves were organized into categories and bore evidence of much handling. I sat in his chair and looked through the twelve folders, one time through each. I didn't skip a single picture.

I saw pictures of unspeakable, unthinkable perversion, things I had never dreamed of, image after image of vile human pollution. My senses were stunned, not only by the pictures themselves but also by trying to follow the steps that led to their being here in my husband's desk. Someone had thought of these scenes, then had planned their execution. Someone had stood behind a camera and taken the pictures with the express purpose of distributing them. Human beings had been used. Compared to the women in these pictures, those in the swimsuit issue of *Sports Illustrated* were Victorian ladies.

And how many other men besides my husband, I wondered, had received copies of these pictures, had prepared a sanctuary for them in the very homes they shared with wives and innocent children? And how had they been received? By mail? Had they exchanged hands in some clandestine meeting place? Had they been purchased in some den of evil? Did they come in sets? Did one look through catalogs and place an order? And how many other women had stumbled upon them as I had? Had they sat as I now sat, stupefied and past all grieving at such documentation of their husbands' secret lives? There are no words to tell what such knowledge does to a woman.

This was the old-fashioned way of viewing such images. Today he could have concealed his vice by the use of a computer. But for all of his brilliance, Eliot had shunned electronic advances. He had often said he preferred doing his writing the way Shakespeare had—with paper and ink. He left to me the transcribing of his handwritten pages into typed form, which I did on a typewriter, first a Remington manual and later a Smith-Corona electric. After he died, I learned to use a computer.

And my intellectual, scholarly husband—had he never considered the likelihood that I would find these? Had he never realized that someone besides himself would someday be sorting through his personal papers in his absence? Had he never considered destroying them?

And then it hit me: I was holding in my hands undeniable evidence not only of a corruption I had never suspected but also of a selfishness of the greatest magnitude. No doubt he must have known that someone would discover his cache someday, that very likely I— eighteen years his junior—would be the one. But he was counting on being gone in a permanent sense whenever this happened, and, as the consequences of the truth couldn't touch him then, he had refused to surrender his immediate pleasures for a mere eventuality.

CHAPTER 8

AS THE GENTLE RAIN FROM HEAVEN

The yellow-billed cuckoo, an unoriginal songster,
emits a continuous call of kuk-kuk-kuk-kuk with
no variation of pitch or rhythm. Though often
heard, the bird is seldom seen. It likes to
conceal itself among sheltering foliage
to gorge on hairy caterpillars.

And so it was twenty-five years ago that I sat in Eliot's study and learned why he kept his desk locked. At the age of fifty-five I was educated concerning the depths of man's depravity. I had lived among good and evil people for all of those years, had heard profane language, had seen cruelty enacted firsthand on playgrounds, in classrooms, in homes, on street corners. I had witnessed the telling of lies, had participated in the act myself, had seen hundreds of murders and adulteries portrayed on television and movie screens, had read true and fictional accounts of theft, conspiracy, drunkenness, betrayal, brutality, shameful conduct of every stripe.

Yet that night in Eliot's study I felt as if a veil had parted between innocence and knowledge, as if every foul deed I had ever known before that time would have filled no more than a teacup compared to the flood that had now swept over me. I felt as a child must feel who suddenly wakes in the nighttime to sounds of his door splintering from the weight of a monster. Before the child can cry out, the door is down and the creature has leapt onto his bed and is mauling him. Overcome with fear, the child looks into the monster's eyes and knows that death is better than living with the memory of this moment.

But I am not a child. I would choose the monster's eyes, the mauling, the black memories any day over death. I would fight to the end. I can sometimes keep the memories at bay by looking around me, setting my eyes on specific things far removed from Eliot's study, remembering that many years have passed, that it is now instead of then, that I am here instead of there. I sit up now and let my eyes travel around my newly cleaned apartment, taking in the wooden blinds, the round table where Rachel serves my meals, the television, my recliner, my bed in the far corner. I see other things: a bookcase filled with books I have not read, a lamp with a red shade, an artificial fern in a yellow ceramic pot, a framed picture of a soldier saluting the American flag. They are only things. They stir nothing within my heart. They were here before I came. They will be here after I go. They have nothing to do with me.

I see the door between my apartment and Rachel's kitchen, the door through which I hear many things. Last night I heard Patrick read from the Bible again. It was a story about a boy's lunch of bread and fish that multiplied itself to feed a crowd of five thousand.

I look toward the window I have come to think of as my bird

window. No sign of activity there. I look at the other three windows and see that dusk is already beginning to sink into the trees in the backyard, filling in the spaces between them. A small table stands beside the recliner at my bird window, the *Book of North American Birds* sitting within easy reach. In addition to this table and the round one where I take my meals, there are two others in my apartment: the nightstand beside my bed and an end table beside the sofa where I now sit. I see several issues of *Time* magazine on this table. They are random back issues, but this is of no concern to me. I have come to view time as a circle that repeats itself. One can skip a lap of the circle without missing anything of importance. Or as waves of the ocean. One more or fewer makes no difference in the rolling expanse of the water. Today's news is not to be prized over last week's or last year's. It has all happened before and will happen again.

I reach forward and pick up the magazine on top. "DIED: JULIUS DIXON, 90, rock-'n'-roll songwriter; in New York City." When no cause of death is given, as in the case of Julius Dixon, I assume that the person's time on earth exceeded man's normal life span and he expired, simply put, of old age. Or "of natural causes," as is often said.

I try to imagine what a ninety-year-old former rock-'n'-roll songwriter would be like. While spooning Metamucil over his All-Bran every morning, would he hum snatches of his biggest hits from the 1950s? Would he tap out the rhythms with the end of his cane? *Time* magazine reports that Julius Dixon's first hit was "Dim, Dim the Lights (I Want Some Atmosphere)." Did he think of those words as he lay dying? Did he think the atmosphere was appropriate for a death scene? His most popular song was "Lollipop," performed by a group called the Chordettes. *Time* describes it as a "buoyant" song. I wonder what Julius Dixon thought of his life's work as he drew his last breath. I wonder if the memory of his song "Lollipop" played through his mind and gave him a feeling of buoyancy as he stepped from the shores of life into the waters of death.

When one is eighty years old, as I am, the handling of time is her greatest challenge. There is no place to rest comfortably. The present is an empty waiting room. The past is a narrow corridor, along which doors open into examining rooms too brightly lit, full of frightening instruments to inflict pain. The future is a black closet at the end of the corridor. No one knows what is inside this dark cubicle. The possibility of nothingness is a terror. If present, past, and future seem out of order in this analogy, it is no wonder. There is no tidy sequence of time when one is eighty and waiting to die.

One keeps wandering into the corridor without meaning to, then stumbling back to the waiting room, then later somehow finding herself stretched out in one of the examining rooms, stopping her ears with her hands to block out the echoes of time, starting up and groping for the door to get back to the waiting room, where there are windows, stacks of old magazines, and a television to fill the deadly silence. And always, always as one flees back to the present, she carries with her the knowledge that at the end of the long corridor is the black closet. It is unlocked, and the hinges of its door are oiled. They swing easily.

But it is November, I remind myself now, and a quarter of a century has passed since the night in Eliot's study. I look at the telephone on the small table beside my bed. I have used it one time since my arrival to call the automated bank service, to verify that my money was transferred successfully from the bank in Kentucky to the one here in Greenville, Mississippi. I look at the wall beside the doorway into Rachel's kitchen, and I see the electric clock made to resemble the face of the sun, with yellow plastic spikes representing rays around the circumference. The cord, half of it concealed by a straight-back chair, snakes down the wall to the outlet. The numbers and sturdy black hands of the clock are large and easily seen from every vantage within my apartment. At any time during the day I can lift my eyes to see how many minutes have passed since I last checked. I notice that Rachel has already reset the sun clock, which was disabled during the rewiring project.

I look over at the smaller windup clock beside the telephone by my bed. This is the clock I can see when I turn the lights out at bedtime. Its numbers and hands glow pale green in the dark, and I have grown accustomed to its loud tick-tock throughout the night. Sometimes when I wake from a troubling dream, I hear it and am calmed. I am still here, I tell myself. I recall a puppy we had in my childhood that howled and whimpered through the first two nights. Someone told us to put a clock in his doghouse to simulate the heart-beat of his mother. We did it, and on the third night the puppy was quiet. I think of how easily duped living things are.

I see my silver hairbrush on the dresser and a small photograph of my parents in a pewter frame. These things—the windup clock, the hairbrush, and the photograph—are my own, yet like the other things, they stir nothing within me. They are only things.

There is a blue clothes hamper beside the bathroom door, into which I deposit anything I want Rachel to wash for me. A white plastic wastebasket sits on the floor next to it. More than once I have had to pause and look at what is in my hand: Into which receptacle do I want to drop it? Once I accidentally threw two pieces of unopened junk mail into the clothes hamper. I left them there, and Rachel removed them later. Another trash can sits beside my recliner, and yet another sits beside the nightstand. A fourth is stationed under the sink in my bathroom. There is no need for so many trash cans. I don't know what Patrick and Rachel were expecting from me. All four are checked and emptied regularly.

So I am in an apartment with four trash cans and four tables, I tell myself, not in Eliot's study in Kentucky. I am at my nephew's house on Edison Street in Greenville, Mississippi. Patrick will soon be home from the Main Office. He will have supper of some kind in a sack. Rachel is across the street. Perhaps she is helping Teri "in a pinch" again. She will be home soon, also, and will take my supper from the sack, arrange it on a plate, and bring it to me on a tray. Maybe she will bring me ice cream later for dessert.

The television is still on. Lou Grant is in the newsroom giving Ted Baxter a dressing down for some violation of good sense, and Georgette is in the background looking sympathetic. Murray and Mary are at their desks, heads lowered, trying to act busy. This was one of the few programs I used to watch regularly some thirty years ago. I liked the fact that Mary, Rhoda, Georgette, and Sue Ann, though they all seemed to have a high regard for marriage, nevertheless led happy, interesting lives in different ways as single women.

Since I was married by then, I could afford to admire their pluck in the adversities of singleness. Had I still been single, I might not have enjoyed the program so much, perhaps would have resented the attempts to depict the single life as a series of funny misadventures. For though I had not been struck with the blessedness of the married state in my sisters' and parents' lives, I had always harbored the dream that it could be so. I was not unhappy as a single woman, but feeling that I was missing out on something important, neither can I say I was especially happy. One's marital status is not relative, though in many ways happiness is.

Too much knowledge is not a good thing. I have seen people ruined in various ways by knowing more than they need to. My five minutes of knowledge knocked away the foundation on which I stood. I could have remained steady, I believe, had I not discovered Eliot's secret. I could have borne the shooting, the hospitalization, the death and funeral, Alonso's trial, and all the adjustments that accompanied the sudden change from wife to widow. I was used to working hard. I would have set my face to the rising sun every morning and gone about the task of survival. I would have valiantly forged ahead as the Widow Hess, dispatching my duties and asking for no special favors. If there had been no pictures to find, I would likely have remained in Eliot's house, would have continued to teach freshman composition at South Wesleyan, would have maintained my contacts with Eliot's acquaintances.

But the ground had fallen away from my feet. The thirteen years of our marriage disappeared in a puff of smoke, as a magician's trick. I knew in an instant that it had been a sham. Perhaps someone would argue with me, would say Eliot's flaw was a sickness that had no bearing on his love for me. I would argue back. His flaw was a sickness, certainly, one that engulfed his whole heart and soul and mind, one that left no room for love. Only for the briefest second was I tempted to invent some other explanation for the pictures in his desk, to deny his behavior, to rationalize the denial by remembering how timid and uncertain he seemed to be during lovemaking, how lacking in imagination. Surely this same man couldn't enslave himself to such baseness.

But the truth settled upon me as a sure thing. Eliot had no idea how to love a real woman. He had forfeited reality for warped fantasies. His pictures had had the same effect as an addiction to mind-altering drugs. Was I merely being prudish? I wrestled with the question. But then the pictures would rise again, and again I knew that no one with a soul could love such things.

For a man like this, a thing so dull and mundane as a wife could hold no pleasure. For thirteen years I had competed with a mistress of unparalleled power, one whom I didn't even know. But I was no rival against the seduction of twelve folders in a desk drawer. I wondered for the flash of a moment if he had shut himself away from his first wife the same way, by retreating to his private collection, and then the thought vanished as quickly as it had come. What did it matter when the perversion had begun or who else had suffered from it? It had emptied my heart. I had no strength to care.

Since the day of Mrs. Beadle's declaration that I was an ugly child, I had lived with the knowledge that I had no power to attract in a physical sense. Short and homely, with no compensating grace of movement or admirable talent, I became stout as the years drew on. Throughout my school years, however, I was not without friends. I had three dates in high school, all arranged by my sisters. If not as pretty, at least I was as smart as my sisters, though mine was a quieter kind of intelligence, one that seldom gained notice. I used to have a sense of humor and a quick eye for detail. In school I could sit in the back of a classroom and provide diversion for those around me by means of clever comments, whispered or written on slips of paper.

The teacher would move other students to the front of the class in an effort to quell the undercurrent of mischief in the back, never suspecting I was the cause.

After high school I attended a teachers' college in Mississippi. It was serious business for me, my father having announced that I would take over my mother's work at the boardinghouse if I did not succeed in college. He led me to believe that college was a much more challenging proposition than high school had been.

Daddy had plans to use my mother in his printing business. Regina had already escaped from home by marriage, and Virginia had launched a plan whereby she acted deliberately clumsy and incompetent in our father's presence, having no intention, she told me, of "being a drudge for a bunch of transigent boarders the rest of my life." I knew she meant *transient* instead of *transigent*. Though smart, Virginia often misused words. She endured countless scoldings for spilled food, botched cleaning tasks, and broken dishes, as she systematically shaped our father's opinion of her as "useless around the house."

Mother may have suspected Virginia's ruse, but she never let on. I believe she preferred staying in her familiar world, at the helm of the boardinghouse, rather than serving under Daddy at the printing shop. When he was at home, Daddy operated according to the "king of the castle" philosophy popular in that day. No doubt Mother looked forward to the mornings, when the king left his castle for nine or ten hours and gave her some peace.

I succeeded in college, as my father no doubt knew I would, secured a teaching position immediately upon graduation, and thereby escaped the boardinghouse. I took my teaching as seriously as I had taken my college studies and was good with children of all ages. As the years wore on and no prince presented himself, I frequently reminded myself of the benefits of a woman's running her own castle, citing the many disappointments I had witnessed among the marriages of others. Still, a woman hopes. When I moved from Mississippi to Kentucky in 1965, I took a job that summer in one of the offices on the campus of South Wesleyan. I had started a fund for a special trip I was planning in honor of my fortieth birthday the following July. If I was to be a single woman, I meant to be as happy a single woman as possible.

At some point during the summer of 1965, I saw an advertisement on a bulletin board in the Academic Records Building requesting the services of a typist for "several scholarly papers of considerable length." The card was handwritten, neatly printed in all capital letters, with the name Dr. Eliot Hess and a phone number at the bottom. This is how I met Eliot. The "several scholarly papers" were reworkings of both his master's thesis and his doctoral dissertation, as well as three new articles for academic journals.

I believe I am correct in stating that Eliot's brand of perfectionism was unusual even in academia. He never considered a paper truly finished. Even after multiple revisions, even after publication, even after a degree was conferred on the basis of a paper, even after presentation at a conference, he continued to tinker with every moving part within it, striving for a flawless machine, a product he never achieved, judging from the repeated modifications. I doubt that anyone other than Eliot has ever continued to revise his doctoral dissertation for years after successfully defending it, simply to make it better.

This was my husband. After Eliot married me, I allowed myself for thirteen years to believe that he saw in me a kind of beauty that surpassed shallow commercial standards. As a gentleman and scholar of the highest caliber, he was one of the few men, I thought, who could recognize true beauty when he saw it, the kind of beauty that doesn't fade with time. How he must pity men with pretty-faced wives, I told myself, for when they lost their prettiness, what was left?

He used to smile at my gentle parodies of our colleagues in the English Department. On the way home from receptions or dinners, I would repeat to him various remarks I had overheard during the course of the evening, complete with mannerisms and inflections, and have him identify the speaker. It was easy work for both of us, for I possessed the gift of mimicry. These were private performances, however. I would never have agreed to repeat them in public if, say, Eliot had pressed me to do so for entertainment at some department function. In the English Department at South Wesleyan, I was the intellectual runt of the litter, and I knew it. I sat, observed, and listened but seldom participated in a discussion, fearful lest someone should say, "What does she know? She used to teach elementary school!"

I fashioned a romance for my life with Eliot: I imagined that he looked at me and saw a rare woodland flower, one that bloomed in deep shade and could be discovered only by someone with patience and keen vision. I imagined that he looked into my soul and saw a shining jewel, that whenever he withdrew from me, it was the steady glow of my jewel-like soul that always brought him back.

At the age of fifty-five this romance was shattered. I knew the truth now. Eliot had looked at me and seen someone who would make his life easier. He had tolerated my presence because of the work I did for him. I was not a rare woodland flower. I was a common weed, rooted up and thrown aside. I was merely ground cover that filled up space and provided a little greenery in his life. I was field vegetation—cowbane, milkweed, henbit, burdock, thistle, ragweed. I was not a shining jewel. I was a piece of gravel, a clod of dirt, a crooked stick.

He had not loved me. He had looked at impurity for too long. He had locked himself in a room of white noise, had turned up the volume so loud that he could no longer hear music. He had so feasted on abominations that he could not taste wholesome food. A man cannot keep company with twelve folders such as the ones in his drawer and love the good and simple things of life.

Until now I had thought myself to be an adequate judge of character. I had not known that a man could construct such secret and impenetrable compartments within his soul. There are certain birds that conceal themselves in thickets to gorge on grubs. One night many years ago I learned in an instant that there are such men, also.

And here is what the knowledge did to me. Do not speak to me of one's choosing his own responses, of taking the moral high road regardless of provocation, of one's character only being revealed by hardship, not shaped by it. Here is what happened to me in five minutes that night in Eliot's study. I had laughed easily before that time, had sometimes cried, though not often. From that time on I saw little to laugh or cry about. When one suffers a violent blow, he is often stunned past feeling. In the face of unbearable pain, one may go into shock and lose consciousness. These things can happen to the mind as well as to the body.

And yet I did feel one emotion: anger. I felt it intensely and aggressively. I had been deceived, and the culprit had gotten away. It wasn't hard to track him down, but he was beyond the judgment bar. I could pronounce him guilty but had no power to sentence him, to see him pay for his crime. Yet while there was time, I would do what I could.

I went to the hospital that very night. The nurses knew me, disregarded the posted visiting hours, and allowed me to come and go as I pleased. They must have known that Eliot would never leave his room alive. They would permit a grieving widow-to-be unlimited access to her beloved.

When I bent to Eliot's face that night, I spoke as softly "as the gentle rain from heaven," but unlike the unstrained mercy spoken of in *The Merchant of Venice*, my words were curses rather than blessings. This rain was hot acid rising from the pit of hell. As mercy is "twice blest" to both giver and receiver, I suppose it is also true that hatred is twice cursed. As I cursed Eliot with my soft words that night, I was cursing myself. A day earlier I could not have believed myself capable of the things I said that night.

I longed to see some sign to show me that he heard my words— the flicker of an eyelid or the twitch of a muscle—but he lay in his bed as still as a wax dummy. I went to the hospital every day during the next four weeks, and every day I repeated my curses in his ear, revising them each time, expanding on the theme, striving for higher excellence. He died at two o'clock one morning, and I was both sorrowful and glad when I received the phone call. Sorrowful because all hope of revenge had ended and glad because the waiting was over and he had died alone in the darkest part of night.

CHAPTER 9

AGAINST THE STORMY GUSTS OF WINTER'S DAY

A "shy and hidden bird," the hermit thrush sings
"the carol of death" in Walt Whitman's poem
When Lilacs Last in the Dooryard Bloom'd. *In a*
nest close to the ground, the thrush incubates its
eggs for thirteen days, and thirteen days after
hatching the young birds fly away.

Supper tonight is from a place called Steak in a Shake. This is the name stamped on the paper napkin folded beside my plate. Rachel comes to my apartment at six-fifteen, apologizing as she carries the tray in. "I'm sorry we're running a little late tonight. Hope you're not starving." I say nothing. I am by no means starving.

It is not a typical fast-food meal. There are small bits of steak, which Rachel identifies as sirloin tips, a baked potato, a plump roll, a tossed salad, and a glass of tea. I have not eaten steak in months.

As soon as Rachel empties the tray and leaves, I walk to the round table and sit down. I hear Patrick in the kitchen on the other side of the door. He is talking loudly, as always, this time about someone named Potts at work. I spear a cube of steak and put it into my mouth. I chew it slowly, savoring the taste.

I piece together the information Patrick relates to Rachel. Potts is evidently a new employee at the Main Office Supply. Today was Potts' "orientation day," which consisted of his filling out paperwork, viewing two safety videos, and listening to the standard new employees' lecture, delivered by Patrick. I pity Potts for having to sit through this. His first regular day of work will be Monday. In my opinion, any new employee who reports for work after orientation day with Patrick has already earned his first week's salary.

I can hear in his voice that Patrick is proud of himself for hiring Potts, who is a black man in his thirties "with a record." He pauses to allow Rachel to ask about the record, but when she doesn't, he proceeds to tell her about it. Potts has served time in jail twice, once on burglary and drug charges when he was nineteen and five years later for kidnapping. It was his own little boy he had kidnapped, Patrick tells Rachel, and he did it because he heard the boy's mother was going off and leaving him unattended all night while she went out. Still, he had broken the law, for he had been ordered by the court not to come near the house where they lived and to stay away from the child. He took the boy from school on a Friday afternoon and kept him for a week until the boy was spotted buying milk at a convenience store in Jackson. An off-duty policeman recognized him from the picture that was circulating all over the Southeast by then. This happened seven years ago.

I wonder how such a story affects Rachel. I wonder if she is standing in the kitchen with her eyes shut tight, remembering her two babies who were kidnapped but were never spotted by a policeman or anyone else until they were dead.

I hear Patrick's voice move toward the kitchen table. I hear sounds of the chairs against the floor, then a hearty prayer recited by Patrick, followed by clinks and scrapes of silverware against plates. Patrick resumes his report on Potts, each word resonating with virtuous pride over his being such a fair-minded white man—to hire someone on parole, to hire a *black* man on parole. Potts will work in the stock room, he tells Rachel. He will unload and unpack shipments, and when a customer wants a large item such as a file cabinet or desk, he will get it from the back and roll it to the customer's car on a dolly.

Patrick goes on to declare his belief that Potts is smart, telling Rachel that he speaks remarkably well, that he used the words *prerogative*, *apportion*, and *equitable* during their conversation three days ago. Potts used his most recent jail time to improve himself by reading, Patrick says. "And guess what he said when I asked him what his favorite book was!" Rachel doesn't guess, but Patrick tells her anyway. "The Bible! He said he reads it cover to cover once a year!

"Hey, this steak is good," he breaks off to say. "Chip says the chicken is good, too, but he said try the steak first. I think the place is going to make a go of it. You should have seen the line waiting to pick up orders, and the phone was ringing off the hook the whole time. Of course, it's not cheap." Silence for a few seconds, then, "You like it?"

Rachel says something, brief and indistinguishable, then

something else. I hear the name Veronica.

"Oh yeah?" Patrick says. "Did Teri say why?"

Evidently Teri hadn't said why because Rachel says nothing else. Patrick takes up the reins of the conversation again and gallops off in a different direction, this time relating the details of an evening course he is hoping to take at Mississippi Delta Community College starting in January. It is a course called Elements of Literature. He describes it as an introductory course. I wonder if such a course will open up the cramped quarters of his mind or if it will only make him more insufferable. I feel no pleasure in the thought of hearing him expound upon works of literature at the supper table.

Though my knowledge of literature is spotty compared to that of my former colleagues at South Wesleyan State College, and vastly inferior to Eliot's, I am quite certain that I will not be enlightened by any literary interpretations and applications trotted forth by my nephew. I can imagine arguing with him through the door: "Listen to what the piece is saying! Stop imposing your silly religion and conservative politics on everything you read!"

I understand by what he says now that this course is the beginning of a journey he has set for himself. He will take a few literature courses "to get a foundation," he tells Rachel, and then he will take a writing course. Or possibly he will try taking a writing course concurrent with the first literature course. This is the word he uses—*concurrent*. It is Patrick's delight to use big words whenever possible. He will see how the first writing course goes, he says. He may take another one if he feels that the professor of the first has "something to offer." No mention of his own capability, only that of the professor.

And then—though he doesn't say this, his intention is clear—he will appear on the horizon as a messiah in the heathen world of publishing. I can see his hopes like a banner unfurling in a stiff wind: *BEST-SELLING AUTHOR!* He no doubt dreams of large posters in the windows of major bookstores: *PATRICK MARTIN FELBER'S NEWEST BOOK!* Perhaps he imagines jaunty little airplanes skywriting their way across the continent: *READ FELBER!*

Patrick's ambitions will fail, surely. He will work no miracle to feed the masses. His writing will amount to only a few broken loaves, if that. Ten years from now he will still be working as manager of the Main Office Supply. He will have spent untold hours laboring over his writing to no avail, with no book to show for his effort, unless he finally, in desperation, spends his own money to publish his work. I feel no sympathy for Patrick, only for Rachel, having to put up with him. But then, perhaps she needs no sympathy. Perhaps she hears Patrick's words as the ceaseless tides beating against the shores of her life, coming in and going out into the forgotten sea of all his past words. Perhaps after each surge she knows that this, too, will pass.

I look at my plate and see that half of the sirloin tips are gone. One does not expect such succulence from food that comes in a sack. I cut open the baked potato. Packets of salt and pepper, salad dressing, sour cream, and butter are sitting beside my plate. Steak in a Shake has thought of everything—even a dinner mint. I butter the roll and potato, then open the salad dressing.

On the other side of the door Patrick has evidently circled back to the subject of his new employee, Potts. "He hasn't laid eyes on his kid in over five years. The mother picked up and moved to Little Rock while he was in jail. The boy is thirteen now."

Suddenly I find myself out of the waiting room and in the corridor again. One night Eliot brought home a piece of steak and grilled it over charcoal for our supper. In the months since we were married, I had typed new copies of all his lecture notes in addition to three lengthy papers, two of them revised from former manuscripts. One paper concerned the subject of money in Shakespeare's day, another the disqualification of *Romeo and Juliet* as a true tragedy in the classic sense, and the third the concept of fatherhood in Shakespeare's sonnets.

From typing the first paper, I learned the names of coins: the angel, noble, groat, and half-groat. I have forgotten the comparative values of these coins. The mark, I learned, was a sum referred to in business dealings but not an actual coin. For some reason I remember this bit of useless information: The mark equaled thirteen shillings.

From the second paper I learned that Juliet was thirteen years old. Having read very little Shakespeare before I married Eliot, I had always assumed Romeo and Juliet to be star-crossed lovers in their teens or early twenties. I had made the common man's mistake of seeing all things in light of what he has experienced in his little bubble of time and space. I broke off typing the paper, I recall, to ask Eliot if the phrase "a girl of thirteen" was in error. He must have thought me foolish, though he merely smiled, opened a book at hand, and showed me the opening lines of the third scene of act 1, in which it is affirmed four times that Juliet has not yet turned fourteen.

In typing the third paper, I learned that Shakespeare was a father himself, that he apparently thought a great deal about one's leaving himself behind, so to speak, in the lives of his children. I cannot explain why I remember so clearly Eliot's reference to sonnet 13. Children, Shakespeare says in this sonnet, will keep a man's house from falling to decay, will uphold him "against the stormy gusts of winter's day," will buy the most reliable form of life insurance.

I wanted to talk with Eliot this particular night about a matter close to my heart. He had not known this when he brought the steak home, but I saw it as a friendly sign that he would listen to me and understand my wishes. It was my hope, of course, that he would agree with my request. I recall my nervousness as I prepared the other food to be served with the steak that night.

I marvel at the power of something as neutral as a numeral to call up disturbing associations. Why does the mention of Potts' thirteen-year-old son, whom I have never met, call to mind a certain night almost forty years ago? I cannot answer this. Thirteen is spoken of as an unlucky number, but I do not hold to suspicions, hexes, jinxes, magic tricks, rabbits' feet, and such. What happens happens, regardless of our feeble attempts to influence chance.

Thirteen—it is one greater than twelve, one fewer than fourteen. That is all. It is a baker's dozen, the number of stripes on the American flag, the number of letters in Steak in a Shake. It is a curious fact that the incubation time for many of the smaller woodland birds is thirteen days. "DIED: ROOSEVELT BROWN, 71, Hall of Fame offensive tackle," who played for the New York Giants for thirteen years. This was most likely a good thirteen years for Roosevelt Brown. "DIED: FRANCES SCHREUDER, 65, onetime New York City socialite who served thirteen years in prison" for pressuring her teenaged son to kill her wealthy father before he disinherited her. These thirteen years could not have been good ones in the life of

Frances Schreuder. I was married thirteen years. I cannot call them good years or bad years. They were both good and bad. Good at first, or so I thought, but bad at last.

The number thirteen means nothing except to send me back in time. Or perhaps the steak on my plate is more responsible for triggering the memory of that night. Who can tell? Why I am remembering that night is of no consequence. Nor is the memory itself of any consequence. For an old woman whose life has very nearly played itself out, what is to be gained from looking back?

Though not at home in the kitchen, Eliot fancied himself skilled in outdoor grilling. I allowed him this misconception. Concerning doneness, "rare" hardly describes his preference. He was never happier at the dinner table than when he sat before a large slab of bloody beef. As he preferred to eat his meat straight off the grill, he had no patience for cooking mine longer. When he began eating, I was generally waiting for my portion to finish cooking in the oven. He chided me, gently but insistently, for "robbing the meat of its flavor."

My own gifts in the kitchen were limited, though from childhood I had helped my mother with meals at the boardinghouse. On the night in question I prepared a potato dish Eliot liked, a tossed green salad, and a loaf of yeast bread that I had set to rise that afternoon. He never liked a great variety of food. He had his favorites and could be most pleased by repetitions of those.

I permitted him to eat before speaking of what was on my mind. From my father I had learned not to trouble a man at the dinner table. In my father's case, he was most approachable after he had eaten his evening meal and retired to his chair in the living room. It was necessary, however, to catch him quickly, before he drifted off to sleep.

In Eliot's case it was necessary to catch him before he retired to his study, for by this time I had already learned that when his door was closed, he was the only one who should open it. Like the hermit thrush in my bird book, Eliot sought privacy. As I have said, he was not a harsh man. He could be kind and gentle when he chose. Others perceived him as shy. I don't know what he saw when he looked in the mirror, how he lived with himself, but he managed in his own way to give the impression of a contemplative serenity, a peaceful distance from the everyday business of life.

I struck at what I considered the right moment. It was late June at the time, and peaches were ripening in an orchard at the edge of town. I had bought a small basket of them and made a peach pie that afternoon. With the bread, potato dish, and pie, it had been a busy afternoon, but I knew that the occasion called for unusual measures. And it was almost as if fate was on my side, I had told myself when lifting the pie from the oven two hours earlier. It was a beautiful pie, one that could have been pictured in a cookbook. The crust was perfect, and the juice bubbling up through the slits on top appeared to be nicely thickened.

When I removed Eliot's empty plate and set the slice of pie in front of him, his eyes flickered upward for an instant, as if searching my face for the cause of this unexpected addendum to an already fine meal. We were both still timid in our roles as husband and wife. Perhaps Eliot was having to remind himself of how it was done. In my case I was simply afraid of not performing well. I couldn't help thinking Eliot must be comparing me to his first wife, though he had never even told me her name.

As Eliot ate his pie, I began my speech. I had planned and rehearsed it that afternoon as I did my kitchen work, but it had sounded better then than now. He listened but kept his eyes on his pie. I don't recall my exact words, but I must have begun with something like "You must know that motherhood is the natural desire of most women." I thought I detected an instant crease of worry on his brow, but I pressed on. Perhaps he was only wishing the pie were sweeter. I had started my speech and couldn't undo it.

I was almost forty-three years old, I reminded him. He had turned sixty-one a week earlier. My desire to have children would not always coincide with the physical ability to do so. In fact, time was short. It was clear that he understood my meaning. He set his fork down, as if to answer, but I was not finished with what I had to say. I knew that he had already experienced parenthood, I said. Though his children, I thought, had hardly made the experience an agreeable one. I wanted very much to have a child of my own, I said, and I hoped that he would see this as a reasonable desire and a happy prospect for himself, too. I assured him that the care of the child would not be his burden, that I would see to its needs, that it would not be permitted to interrupt his work. I rushed on, abandoning the prepared script and stumbling over my words, repeating myself. During the whole of my speech, I saw before me a vision from twenty years earlier of my third grader Starr, whose shining black eyes met every day as if it were a present wrapped especially for her. I wanted a child like her. I wanted a star for the evening of my life.

I felt a thickness in the air when I stopped. The vision of Starr vanished. Eliot's face showed a mixture of disapproval, awkwardness, and fear. Your work in the kitchen this afternoon has been for nothing, I said to myself during the long silence.

He spoke at last, with what sounded like great tenderness and sorrow. We should have discussed this before we married, he said. Had he known of my desire, he never would have given me false hope. He had not meant to mislead me. Children were not—this was accompanied by frequent pauses, sighs, clearings of the throat— something he felt he could . . . accommodate at this point in his life. Though he knew he had been remiss in not broaching the subject earlier, before I had formed and fed my dreams, he had hoped that I would find joy and fulfillment in helping him "nurture Portia and Alonso to adulthood."

I knew he was straining for excuses. The word *nurture* had a hard, grating sound like a rusty plow. When one has a part in planting the seed, I wanted to tell him, his interest in the yield is greater. A hired hand may labor diligently, but his heart doesn't yearn after the harvest with the same fervor as that of the farmer himself. Besides, from what I had observed of Eliot's young plants, they were wild and stunted, the time for nurturing them long past.

He took his last bite of pie, then pushed his chair back. I rose to clear the table. I walked to the sink and stood there to hide my eyes. Before leaving the kitchen, he came up behind me and placed a hand on my shoulder. "I'm sorry, Sophia," he said. "I didn't know." He stood there a few moments, the weight of his hand as light as a breath of air. Then he turned and walked to his study. I heard the door close.

I had set a slice of pie at my own place but had not yet taken a bite. I scraped it off the saucer into the garbage can.

I didn't cry. Even then I knew that life would do to me what it wanted. Tears couldn't change the course laid out for me. I knew at that moment that my night would be a starless one. I comforted myself with the thought that at least I had a husband, a moon that was good and steady, though it sometimes waned to a mere sliver of light and many chilly nights was hidden behind clouds.

CHAPTER 10

HONOR IS A MERE SCUTCHEON

A member of the duck family, the lesser scaup is ready at birth to take on the challenges of life. Hatched with its eyes wide open and a downy coat for insulation, the lesser scaup learns within the first three days how to dive to food, anticipate and escape danger, and make its own home.

I cannot say why I mourned Eliot's absence. I have often wondered if anything I said during those last four weeks found its way into his consciousness. If so, he must have known, as my father used to say, that there was more where that came from. He must have longed for death's release. Perhaps some vague realization of what his life would be like if he survived snuffed out any desire for recovery. To live in the same house with the woman who had said the things I had said, to sit at the table with her, ride in a car with her, lie in the bed with her would have been a horrible confinement, enough to make any man let hold of life. Perhaps in reality I struck the blow that killed Eliot.

After his death I looked ahead to the years stretched out before me and knew it would not be easy. I had grown accustomed to his presence in my life. For thirteen years I had thrived as a wife, believing that I was finally like other women—desired, sought, and provided for by a man. I had given myself to married life, settled down deep into it as into a comfortable armchair.

Eliot had given me suggestions for improving myself—returning to college for graduate work, teaching freshman composition in the university, cutting my hair, buying a few new dresses, reading great works of literature such as *Paradise Lost* and *Beowulf*, joining a group of faculty wives in a water aerobics class, and so forth. It was my joy to take his suggestions, always spoken softly and tactfully yet always with assurance, as if he knew I would obey. I imagined myself as a new plant flourishing in the sunshine of his love. I felt fortunate to be his wife and fancied that other women, including Eliot's college students, envied me.

When he died, I knew it was no more than he deserved for his evil heart and for his treachery against me, but I felt he had gotten off easily. Compared to my own injury, which I must now carry with me for the rest of my days, his one-time payment of death for the crime he had committed seemed a pittance. Still, he had suffered. What he loved had been taken away—his private sins and his public honor as the revered, reclusive college professor—and for this my sense of justice was somewhat satisfied.

And yet I missed him. There is no accounting for this. My days seemed long and hollow, the nights even worse. How a woman can miss a man and despise him at the same time is a mystery past all understanding.

The nights were often a cave where the dreadful images I had seen in Eliot's study were drawn on the walls. I heard voices in distress calling out words I couldn't understand. If I drifted off to sleep, it was only for minutes and never restful. I hated Eliot for destroying my peace, for his consummate selfishness. And I hated my own weakness in feeling lonely, in still remembering his gentle nature, in knowing that if I were offered the chance to wipe the slate clean, to erase what I knew now and restart my thirteen years of wedded ignorance, I very possibly would accept it. In ignorance there is indeed a bliss of sorts. In loneliness the mind is not rational.

Somehow I pulled myself up and resumed my life. After Alonso's trial I resigned from South Wesleyan in Hillcrest and moved sixty miles away to Carlton, Kentucky, where I began teaching at Tri-City Community College. I found that I was properly equipped to take up single life again, for I could change fuses, tighten faucet washers, and balance a checkbook. Like certain birds I have read about, I had been born with an independent streak. By the time I left home for college, I was well acquainted with hammer, wrench, and screwdriver.

Setting up a new home, then, posed no great difficulty. Physically, I was the same person as before. Emotionally, I was transfigured. A mind that has been shocked with corruption has new eyes. The world is suddenly a different place.

Even today I see the pictures. Though I had laid a fire and burned them to ashes, they yet rise again and again. It is said that a picture is worth a thousand words, but there are no words for such human degradation.

Right before he died, according to a nurse who saw it, Eliot's eyes suddenly flew open, a look of overwhelming fear contorting his face. He stared wildly, as if at a hungry beast bearing down upon him, then closed his eyes and was instantly dead. What had he seen? What did death look like? This is what I ask myself in the nighttime, when Eliot's terrified face rises before me in his last moment of knowing, and I press both hands over my thudding heart, fearful that my own moment has come, that I am about to see whatever it was Eliot saw. I place no confidence in deathbed stories of shining lights and angel choruses. I know that a great many things emit light—volcanic eruptions, chemical explosions, fiery collisions—and that swearing can sound like singing to someone who is not in his right mind.

The suddenness of death frightens me as much as the finality of it. Sometimes I wake at night and hear a voice that says, "You have only ten minutes left to live." I look at the clock beside my bed, its steady ticks a slow cadence compared to that of my heart, and start the countdown. Now I have only nine minutes, now only eight, now seven. When I get to zero and am still breathing, I know that the voice was only mocking me, that my time has not come. Not yet. Maybe later tonight. Maybe tomorrow. Maybe next week. I feel certain I will die in the nighttime. This waiting for death is no way to live, but it is the only life I have. I am not eager to give it up.

Many theories are tossed about concerning the nature of heaven and hell, assuming there are such places, which I do not assume yet in my idle moments cannot help considering. I have time to consider many things. I would accept this heaven: the perpetual repetition of pleasant memories from the years before I knew what I know now. I do not let myself imagine a better heaven than this, for I know I don't deserve one. I would also accept limbo, a region of oblivion, in which all memories, good and bad, are forgotten.

"DIED. ULRICH INDERBINEN, 103, Swiss mountain guide known as the King of the Alps; in Zermatt, Switzerland." Between the ages of twenty and ninety-five, *Time* magazine reports, Mr. Inderbinen climbed the Matterhorn 370 times. I wonder if by the age of 103 Ulrich Inderbinen was ready to exchange his memories of mountain climbing for the chance of heaven or hell. I wonder what his idea of heaven might have been. Perhaps a daily trek up the Matterhorn. Perhaps his concept of hell was a flat plain with no mountains to climb.

As for hell, my imagination is rife with potentialities. I have heard of the mythical king Sisyphus, who was punished in the afterworld by having to push an enormous rock uphill only to have it roll down again each time. This would seem like playtime compared to some of my ideas.

Could my mother have meant it when she cried out, "Oh, let me die"? This I heard from her bedroom in the middle of the night two weeks before she died, nearly five months after she had come to live at my house, or, more accurately, to die at my house.

Endlessly repeating the five months of my mother's dying could qualify as a worthy hell by anyone's definition. Expand it by three years—beginning with Alonso's shooting of Eliot and extending through my mother's funeral—and it would be a misery past enduring. Or distill all my sorrow to one five-minute segment in Eliot's study, running the pictures over and over on a large color screen for eternity, and words like *misery* and *hell* are so weak as to be meaningless. With such possibilities of hell, no amount of suffering on earth could drive me to cry out, "Oh, let me die!"

But before all this—the shooting, my discovery of Eliot's secret, my transformation into the woman I am now, Eliot's death and my return to loneliness, Alonso's murder trial, my mother's final illness and death—before all this, I was not unhappy.

Many rooms of my past were filled with laughter. I was not always a fearful woman or a disillusioned one—certainly not an angry one. Though not gullible, neither was I cynical. As a young woman, I cried when I read sad books or watched sad movies, and these were the kinds of books and movies I preferred. I loved sentimental stories, and even though Eliot eventually coaxed my literary tastes to a level closer to his own, introducing me to many classics I had never read, I still considered *Anne of Green Gables* and *Little Women* the two best books ever written.

This is no longer true. I know that Anne Shirley could never have existed, nor could Meg, Jo, Beth, and Amy March. Lucy Montgomery and Louisa May Alcott, grown women both of them when they wrote their books, could not have been portraying the world they saw but rather the world they wished for. I want to say to them what my mother often said: "Shame on you." But then I remember how many times I read both books, delighting in those alternate worlds, and I cannot help feeling grateful for them, false pictures though they were. I cannot help wondering if I would still be rereading those books, living contentedly among their romantic ideals, their scenes of sweet domestic tranquility, had I never unlocked Eliot's desk and opened the bottom drawer.

But I did unlock the desk. I did open the drawer. Life molds a person. Once fashioned and fired in the kiln, he cannot go back and redesign the mold. Life is not a freshman composition that can be rewritten and turned in for a better grade. If I had not found the twelve folders, would I still be a happy woman today? This is a question without an answer. A student once asked me, "If it weren't for the ten spelling errors, would I have made an A on my paper?" This, too, was a question without an answer. If I had not been so distracted by the poor spelling, I told him, perhaps I would have seen and marked other kinds of errors. Or perhaps not. As Judge Jack says, "If frogs had wings, they wouldn't bump their rumps when they jump." In eighty years of living, I have learned it a waste of time to imagine how things could have been.

Before the five minutes of truth in Eliot's study, however, before life had molded me and baked me in its hot oven, I knew happiness. I had my own allotment of regrets, as any woman, but if allowed twenty or thirty pleasant days to repeat for the heaven of my preference, I would have a wide store of memories from which to choose.

My sister Regina, nine years older than I, read to me as a child. We had one book I especially loved called *Easy to Read Stories*, a large blue book with a picture on the cover of three little girls dressed in coats and fur muffs, standing on a snowy hillside. I liked to imagine that the three little girls were Regina, Virginia, and me, though the snowy hillside was obviously in a distant land far from our home in the flat delta of Mississippi. This is the only book I have kept in my possession throughout the years. It is in the top drawer of my dresser. The flyleaf bears the inscription "To Sophia and Virginia, From Grandma, Christmas 1930." We would have been four and three years old. Regina was thirteen, too old for such a book.

All the words in the storybook were divided into syllables. I suppose this technique justified the book's claim to be "easy to read." "The twen-ty-fifth of June was El-sie's birth-day," one story starts. "When the lit-tle girl came down to break-fast on that day, she found six beau-ti-ful ros-es with long stems and pret-ty green leaves ly-ing on the white ta-ble-cloth, placed so that they formed a wreath a-round her plate. There were six su-gar kiss-es in a new hand-some chi-na dish up-on which sis-ter Mar-jo-rie had paint-ed some pink rose-buds."

Curled up beside each other in bed, Virginia and I would listen to these stories as many times as Regina would read them. We would pore over the pictures, dark, richly detailed engravings with captions such as "Nell and the Ma-gic Lan-tern" and "Babs and Her Kit-tens." Snug in bed, we could hear our mother in the kitchen of our boardinghouse, preparing for the next morning's breakfast. These would be among the happy scenes I would choose for my heaven.

When I started school, my teacher was Miss Reynolds. She was a young woman, engaged to be married, and I adored her. Watching her every move, I vowed in my childish heart that someday I would be like her. I would have beautiful dark hair, fair skin, and a diamond ring upon my white hand. I would stand before children and make them love me as I loved her. I would teach them to read and write, would print in straight lines on the chalkboard, would wave my arms gracefully as I led them in singing "Camptown Races" and "Oh! Susanna." For my heaven of happy scenes, I would choose any day of my first year in Miss Reynolds' classroom.

I would also choose my high school graduation day. Our school in Methuselah, Mississippi, was small, with a graduating class of only thirty-two, of which I was valedictorian. My father was inordinately proud of this achievement. Though I was only seventeen at the time, I knew that mine was merely a small-town victory, that I would have been overshadowed by brighter minds in the academic competition of a larger school.

Still, I would like to follow my father that day, to hear him greet others about town and know that I was responsible for the note of good cheer in his voice. For one day his spirits were lifted from his worries over the dismal future of his printshop, and when I saw his happy face as I stood at the head of my classmates that day to give my valedictory address, I felt the deep satisfaction of having won the approval of a respected authority, of having lightened his countenance for a moment.

After the ceremony my father, not a demonstrative man, took both of my hands in his, kissed my forehead, and said, "You have brought me great honor today, Sophia." I have often thought upon his words. That I remember them more than sixty years later attests to the fact that they were rare words and that they touched me deeply. Yet what is honor? Is it not relative? Good marks on a report card, a string of platitudes spoken from the mouth of a seventeen-year-old—are these truly honorable?

I believe many words could bear reexamination. My knowledge of Shakespeare is sketchy compared to that of a scholar like Eliot, but I gleaned more than a little from typing his papers. It was Sir John Falstaff, I believe, who spoke of honor in *Henry IV*. Honor is only a word, he says, only empty air, only a painted decoration signifying nothing of substance. *Scutcheon* is the word Falstaff used. "Honour is a mere scutcheon," he says. A scutcheon is an ornamental shield—something pretty to hide behind. And yet, for all my doubts, I would like to relive the day my father said to me, "You have brought me great honor, Sophia."

I would add to these scenes any number of days from my twenty years of teaching children. I would disqualify a few, such as the day ten of my thirty pupils came down with stomach flu in a continuous wave within the space of six hours, or the day a fifteen-year-old sixth grader, hauled to school by the truant officer, assaulted the principal, or the day one of my fifth graders was hit by a car and thrown from his bicycle on his way home from school.

The boy's name was Dewey Flint, and it happened a week before summer vacation. He was high-strung, a tall boy with flaming red hair, quick in every subject and always laughing. I'll never forget how much smaller and sadder he looked in the casket. No one could tell looking at him so still and somber in death that in life he could multiply large numbers in his head. He was the only child of his parents. His mother, whose hair was as red as Dewey's, sobbed hysterically at the funeral, collapsed in the aisle on the way out, and was borne away in the arms of her husband. Dewey's death left a gaping hole in our classroom that last week of school. I would not want to repeat any of those days.

But others, so many others, were full of the joy of watching children learn, of laughing with them, of supervising their play, of hearing them read and sing. At Carrie Stern Elementary School in Greenville, Mississippi, where I taught fifth grade for five years, we sang the state song and "The Star-Spangled Banner" at the end of every school assembly.

The state song started out "Way down south in Mississippi, / Cotton blossoms white in the sun. / We all love our Mississippi, / Here we'll stay where livin' is fun." It was a cheery song, and the children sang it with abandon. In 1962, after I had moved to Kentucky, the state of Mississippi adopted a new state song with the unimaginative title of "Go, Mississippi"—an inferior ditty in every way. My new principal in Kentucky never closed school assemblies with the state song, the familiar "My Old Kentucky Home," perhaps because of the troublesome line " 'Tis summer, the darkies are gay."

For my heaven I would go back to Carrie Stern Elementary School and choose one of the school assemblies—perhaps the one when the magician asked Miss Parks, our principal, to come to the stage. I would watch the children's faces as Mario the Magnificent pulled a yellow canary out of Miss Parks' nest of hair. I would close my eyes and listen to them sing "Way down south in Mississippi" and "Oh, say, can you see," their voices full throttle, their eyes shining, their hearts too innocent to know that something can never come out of nothing.

In the heaven I am contemplating, one would see the scenes of yesterday with the eyes of age. Therefore, I would not relive my wedding day. Though I thought it was a happy day at the time, it bore within it the seeds of deep sorrow. In my white dress coming down the narrow aisle of the small chapel, I was a blind child walking toward a cliff.

No more of this. The effort has wearied me. Happy memories can make one as fretful as sad ones. The last lines of the old state song of Mississippi were these: "The evening star shines brighter, / And glad is every dewy morn, / For way down south in Mississippi, / Folks are happy they have been born." I could not sing this song today. There is ultimately nothing bright, glad, or happy about being born, either way down south in Mississippi or anywhere else.

So I close the day with my own easy-to-read story: "Soph-ie will sit qui-et-ly now and wait for Rach-el to bring her des-sert on a tray. Per-haps she will bring sher-bet in a pret-ty crys-tal dish. This is heav-en e-nough for an old wo-man in the win-ter of life."

CHAPTER 11

SO STRONG A PROP
TO SUPPORT SO
WEAK A BURDEN

*When food is at stake, the loggerhead shrike is
ruthless, catching and gulping insects on the wing,
knocking smaller birds out of the air, and biting
the necks of mice with their toothlike bills. Before
eating it, the shrike often impales its prey on a
thorny bush or barbed-wire fence.*

Three weeks pass. Midway between Thanksgiving and Christmas, I am served a piece of Rachel's pumpkin pie. She has made it "from scratch," Patrick tells me when he brings it to my apartment. He does not carry it on a tray. Rachel is in bed, he says. After baking the pie, preparing supper, and delivering my meal an hour ago, she sat at the table with him but did not eat anything. "I sent her to bed and told her I'd clean up the kitchen," he tells me in a brisk, efficient manner. He is speaking much louder than he needs to. I wonder how closely Patrick's idea of cleaning up the kitchen matches Rachel's.

"She says it's only another headache," he tells me, "but I told her to go to the doctor if it's not better tomorrow." His tone tells me that he will make an appointment for her if she fails to. He sets the pie on the round table and starts to pick up my plate. "Are you done with this?" he says. "Weren't you hungry?"

No, I tell him, I wasn't. Don't I like turkey, he wants to know. Yes, turkey is fine, I say. Is it because it was left over from Thanksgiving, he asks. No, I say, I am not opposed to leftovers. Am I feeling okay, he asks. I sigh. It is hard to imagine how Rachel tolerates this man. Yes, I tell him, I am feeling well enough.

The sight of the pie has kindled my appetite. It wouldn't surprise me if Patrick were to take it back and say, "Well, no dessert for you if you're only going to pick at your supper that way," but he doesn't. To my dismay, however, he takes my supper plate into the kitchen, leaving my door open, and then returns with another serving of pumpkin pie, which he places on the round table, also. He sits down at the table across from me. Apparently he means to eat dessert with me.

He has forgotten forks and must return to the kitchen for them. Before sitting down again, he glances at my half-empty glass of tea and asks if I want something more to drink. No, I tell him. But he decides that he does. He returns to the kitchen and comes back holding the lid of the Thermos he takes to work every day. He's glad he didn't throw his coffee out yet, he tells me, and he takes a noisy sip.

By this time, I have already eaten two bites of the pie. It is still slightly warm. He remembers the can of whipped cream in the refrigerator, and when he returns with it I have eaten two more bites. Before he can ask, I tell him I don't care for any whipped cream. Still standing, he shakes the can vigorously and depresses the nozzle, ejecting a mound of topping on his slice of pie. White flecks spray out messily and dot the surface of the table. He wipes them off with his index finger, then realizes he has no napkin. Another trip to the kitchen and he sits down again.

I can eat quickly when I need to. By now I have only a few bites left near the thin fluted wall of crust. Assuming I am interested, Patrick proceeds to tell me how he selected a pumpkin before Thanksgiving, describing to me the difference between a regular pumpkin and a pie pumpkin, as if he is the only one who knows this secret. He then takes me through the process of cutting up the pumpkin, removing the seeds and stringy insides, then slow-cooking the pieces of rind in the Crockpot until soft enough to mash and store in freezer containers.

"I always do this for Rachel every Thanksgiving," he says, as if he is to be commended for such difficult work, and as if it takes a man to do it. "You do this for Patrick every Thanksgiving," I want to tell him as I watch him take a large bite of pie. The whipped cream appears to be somewhat runny, perhaps because the pie is still warm. He will be wanting a spoon before it is over, I predict, so that he can clean the saucer. Or perhaps he will lick the saucer like a kitten.

He goes on to declare the superiority of pumpkin pie made "from a real pumpkin," expressing scorn for "that stuff from a can." He lifts a forkful and examines it appreciatively before opening his mouth. He likes a pumpkin pie with some substance to it, he says, a little bit of pulp, something to bite down on.

In a tone of disrespect he speaks of the pumpkin pie Teri made a couple of weeks ago, the one she served when she issued Patrick and Rachel a reciprocal invitation to come across the street for dessert a few days after Thanksgiving. "Way too smooth and bland," he says. "Rachel's recipe calls for six different spices, I think it is." He begins trying to name them all.

Rachel's crust isn't always perfect, but tonight it is. Lard gives the flakiest texture, but Rachel's crust, made with plain shortening, is nevertheless light and delicate. Piecrusts are one of the few kitchen arts I mastered in our boardinghouse. Because Mother disliked making them and because the boarders complained about Regina's, the task fell to me. My mother had an aversion to measuring cups and spoons, preferring to use a method she referred to as "eyeballing it." Regina followed my mother's example but had the added disadvantage of inexperience, so her eyeballing produced one failure after another.

I tried a method rarely used by my mother in the kitchen: I read the instructions in a cookbook. Though it took several tries, I eventually turned out beautiful piecrusts, my success due to precision and patience. I measured the flour and salt carefully and took my time cutting in the lard. I added the cold water one tablespoon at a time, stirring with a fork until the dough cleaned the sides of the porcelain bowl. I gathered the dough into a ball and then rolled it out on a flour-coated surface instead of simply flattening it with my hands and mashing it directly into the pie tin the way I had seen Mother and Regina do it.

I followed the instructions in the cookbook to turn the empty pie tin upside down on top of the circle of dough and neatly cut a larger circle around it, then peel away the surplus dough, fold the piecrust over, and ease it into the tin. I experimented with various edgings pictured in the cookbook under the heading Handsome Pastry Rims: fork press, spoon scallop, circle cutouts, ruffle, rope twist, zigzag pinch, and pretty petal. I developed no great skill in filling the piecrusts, but the crusts themselves were things to be admired.

Patrick has stopped talking and is now holding his dessert saucer in one hand and his fork in the other to decrease the distance between the pie and his mouth. As he eats, he looks around my apartment, his eyes settling on the television, which is on but muted. Vanna White is touching blank panels that light up into letters. It is the final jackpot challenge, and the contestant is a pudgy woman with two short stiff wings of blond hair flaring out on either side of her cheerful, round face and another ragged tuft standing erect above her forehead. I think of birds in my bird book with similar crests: certain woodpeckers and jays, the snowy egret, the ruffed grouse. I think of MacGyver's hairstyle and of Rachel's, both of them sporting the same crown.

The category is "living thing," and Vanna has revealed only two letters for the woman: __ A __ __ __ N. Pat Sajak looks sympathetic, but I can imagine what he is saying: "Not much to go on, but, hey, talk it out and see what happens."

Patrick attempts to guess the word, coming up with *jargon, gallon,* and *happen,* none of which qualifies as a living thing. My mind still on my bird book, I can think only of *martin* and *falcon.* The answer, however, is *baboon.* The woman has not won the jackpot prize, but she looks comforted by the reminder that she is taking home all the cash she has earned. The total that flashes onto the screen is $14,600. Members of the woman's family come forward to give her hugs, all of them as pudgy and merry as she is.

I finish the last bite of my pie and leave the table. I sit in my recliner and turn up the volume of the television. There was no clause in my agreement with Patrick when I came to live here that I would socialize with him over dessert. He has begun talking again as if he has not noticed my absence from the table. He shouts that he hopes I'm comfortable here, that he's afraid he has a "little bad news to pass along"—the furnace is "playing out" and will need to be replaced soon, maybe before the end of winter. If I had the energy to carry on a conversation with my nephew, I would like to ask him if the furnace hadn't given signs of age last winter, if a prudent home-owner wouldn't have taken steps to remedy the problem during the spring or summer, long before the next winter arrived.

I say nothing but switch to the Nature Channel. As if the pro-gramming directors of *Wheel of Fortune* and *Animal Wonders* have gotten together, tonight's feature is about a chimpanzee named Oli-ver, who became a minor celebrity in his day, proclaimed by some to be the "missing link" between man and ape. It was reported that Oliver had forty-seven chromosomes, compared to the forty-six of humans and the forty-eight of common chimpanzees.

At this Patrick snorts dismissively and asks if I have any Christ-mas shopping to do. If so, he says that Rachel can take me to the mall, or if I'd rather, she can buy whatever I ask her to and get it in the mail for me. I can't help wondering to whom Patrick thinks I would send a gift. Perhaps he thinks I want to give tokens of conso-lation to Adrienne and the others who entered the contest to provide shelter and food for me while awaiting my death. Perhaps he is hinting for me to buy gifts for Rachel and him since they were the chosen ones.

The truth is I have not bought gifts for many years. It was one of the themes in my mother's frequent harangues during the short time between Eliot's death and her own: "You need to quit thinking about yourself! Lots of other women have lost their husbands! You need to snap out of your depression! Go out and do something for somebody else! Buy somebody a present and write them a nice note of appreciation!"

The somebody to whom she was referring was herself. After Mother's Day, Christmas, or her birthday, she would say to me, "Well, I heard from Regina and Virginia both—right on time, too." The weighty pause that followed completed the meaning: "But you, my ungrateful self-absorbed middle daughter, couldn't spare the little bit of time it would take to buy me a gift and write a few words on a card."

She continued such speeches even after coming to live with me during her last few months of life. "Regina called me twice yesterday," she might say, or "Look at all these cards Virginia has sent me." Evidently the fact that I was caring for her—feeding her with a spoon, dressing her, washing her soiled underwear—escaped her. I was the dutiful daughter. In her way of thinking, phone calls and cards were acts of love; bathing her and changing her sheets did not qualify.

And my mother was right. After Eliot's death I had become self-absorbed. I couldn't spare the time for anyone else. It took all of my emotional and rational resources merely to make it through a day. I began doing whatever seemed necessary for survival, dispensing with the niceties of social interaction. Whereas I had once been friendly and courteous, I was now glum, even gruff. Don't tell me such a change cannot happen overnight. It can and it did. I know the kinds of things others must have been saying behind my back: "She just walked away right in the middle of something I was saying! She didn't even answer when I called to her, just kept walking!"

But people love sentimental explanations for bad behavior. I was thought to be emotionally prostrate over the loss of my husband. I was an object of pity. I was excused by virtue of my great love and of the great empty hole in my heart. I let the assumption stand. I learned that silence is the best refuge from responsibility. No need to tell lies. Say nothing and let the merciful and the ignorant think what they will.

The act of teaching, which in earlier years had been my purpose for living, was now only a framework to hold my days together. Though I taught for almost ten more years after Eliot's death, my students were like walk-ons in a play—necessary for the illusion of reality but not memorable. I could have been a cardboard cutout standing at the front of the classroom for all the warmth that passed between us.

I think of how many worthy institutions become nothing more than props for mankind: education, art, religion, law, marriage. "So strong a prop to support so weak a burden." These words from the dedication of Shakespeare's poem *Venus and Adonis* come to mind. The prop in this case was the Earl of Southampton, to whom the poem was dedicated, and the burden was the poem itself. A self-deprecating declaration by the bard. But again, my logic fails. The

Earl of Southampton would still have existed without the poem. Without humans, however, the institutions of man could not exist. It is men, weak though they are, who create the props on which they lean. In their ideal form, institutions may possess a strength that is almost holy. Ideal forms are an extinct breed, however, if indeed they ever existed at all.

The television describes the "holiday atmosphere" that surrounded Oliver and his owner during the three weeks of their Japanese tour in 1976. I am reminded that the word *holiday* was originally "holy day." Pictures are shown of Oliver wearing a tuxedo at a banquet, drinking beer, smoking a cigar, dressed for bed in a kimono. I am reminded of the many ways man corrupts the institutions that support him, that give his life meaning.

I tell Patrick that I have no Christmas gifts to buy, that holidays are nothing more than props. He is momentarily silenced. I hear him scraping his plate with his fork.

Oliver displays extraordinary behavior for a chimpanzee, the television reports. Though he is now old by chimp standards—in his midforties—he once distinguished himself by walking on two legs all the time, by doing simple house chores for his trainer, by pouring himself a drink and watching television at night. Shunned by other chimps, he has always preferred the company of humans, especially women.

Patrick gets up from the table. He takes a few steps toward my recliner, then clears his throat. "Well, Aunt Sophie, I guess I'll go now," he says, and I nod but don't look at him. If I had the energy, I might remind him that I never invited him to stay in the first place. But I say nothing. Rudeness often requires energy. On the television screen Oliver is hugging people and shaking hands. He is in a large crowd. In another shot he is eating a jelly sandwich and drinking a cup of coffee.

"I see the book there beside you," Patrick says, taking another sip of his own coffee. "Do you ever look at it?"

I nod again. I have never thanked him for the bird book, but neither has he ever thanked me for the wealth that is to be his upon my death. Nor is he likely to. When it is his, I will be beyond thanking. Thanking is another of man's conventions worn out from overuse. I recall reading in my book about certain birds that show no gratitude, that fall upon their food cruelly, sometimes impaling it on a spike until they feel like eating it.

Patrick takes another slurp of coffee, then moves toward the door, stopping first to stack his dessert saucer on top of mine. He drops one of the forks on his way out and bends to retrieve it. He then returns to get my glass and the used napkins from the table. When he finally closes the door, he has not thought to wipe off the round table. I want to call after him, to tell him to check on Rachel and bring me a report, but I say nothing. His checking would include too much talking, first to Rachel and then to me.

I wonder what Patrick's Christmas gift to Rachel will be. I wonder if he buys her things that he wants. One of the English teachers at South Wesleyan used to tell us about the gifts her husband bought for her: fishing rods, circular saws, hunting knives. She started playing his game by buying him pearl necklaces, leather purses, and silk lingerie. The arrangement worked quite well, she said. Once opened, the gift was simply handed over to the buyer. Each looked forward to the other one's birthday more than his own. On anniversaries and at

Christmas, they were always assured of receiving gifts they knew they would like and use.

I wonder what Rachel would request from Patrick if asked for a gift list. Would she ask for clothing? I can't imagine that she spends time wishing for a new pair of denim jeans or a new flannel shirt. She wears a dress only on Sunday. One dress worn once a week would last a long time. Her only jewelry is a wedding band and an engagement ring with a diamond not much bigger than a sesame seed.

Perhaps Rachel would put books and bath powder on her gift list. While staying in the back bedroom during the rewiring project, I went into Patrick and Rachel's bedroom one day while Rachel was out grocery shopping. I saw two books on the table beside their bed: a Bible and a book titled *Old-Fashioned Grace for Modern Times*. In their bathroom I saw a pair of men's pajamas on a hook. Something told me they were Rachel's, not Patrick's. I saw bath powder in a round pink box beside the sink and another book, titled *Looking to Heaven*, on top of the commode.

Folded inside my book of *Easy to Read Stories* is an old letter written in my own hand in the year 1936. I was ten years old and still believed in Santa Claus, to whom the letter was addressed. "Dear Santa Claus," the letter reads, "I am going to write you and tell you what I want. I want a blackboard that has a seat to it, and it has a felt eraser. One side is black and the other side is white. You can use it as a desk. There are three pieces of chalk for the black side and four colored pieces for the white side. I want a yo-yo in my stocking. I want a house set. I want six Shirley Temple books. I want a watch that costs $1.98. It is in the Sears Roebuck book. And ten pounds of hard candy and all kind of nuts and fruit. The candy is not stick candy. Your friend, Sophia Langham."

I am quite certain that I didn't receive any of these items that Christmas, except perhaps the candy and fruit. I keep the letter, however, as a relic of hope and innocence, as well as a reminder of broken promises. My mother had told me she would mail my letter to Santa Claus. I found it in her drawer, folded inside her box of handkerchiefs, the next summer.

And what would I request today if asked for a Christmas list? The things an old woman wants can't be purchased with money. My list would be blank.

A picture of Oliver, taken a year ago, fills the television screen. He is hunched in the corner of what appears to be a wooden cage, wearing his age with no trace of dignity—shaggy fur, pot belly, leathery hands, milky eyes. No celebrity now. No grinning poses in tuxedo or kimono. No cigar or jelly sandwich. No holiday atmosphere.

CHAPTER 12

MEN MUST ENDURE THEIR GOING HENCE

Carolina wrens are stay-at-home birds, weathering all kinds of winters to increase their population in a region until a severe cold spell kills them off in large numbers. But the process of repopulating begins again, and new nesting sites soon appear in mailboxes, baskets, even pockets of old coats.

Before she died, my mother said to me numbers of times, "Getting old is no fun, Sophie. Just wait. Your turn is coming." I was almost fifty-eight when she came to live out her last few months at my house in Carlton, Kentucky. I drove to Mississippi to get her in May, and she timed her death conveniently so that I was free again by the end of September. I speak amiss. There was nothing convenient about the last five months of my mother's life. Instead of five months, it seemed like five decades. After she died, I had three months, from October through December, to try to rid my house of the smell of death before returning to the classroom in January.

The business one must see to when undertaking the care of a deathbed patient is enormous. It fell to me to clear out my mother's apartment, where she had lived after selling the boardinghouse in Methuselah, Mississippi, and to sort through her papers and personal effects. She was unable to help in any way, and my sisters, both of whom lived in Vicksburg, less than two hundred miles away, claimed to have family conflicts or health issues that prevented them from driving to Methuselah to lend a hand.

The small towns of Mississippi, like those of any state, have colorful names. Methuselah was only one of many. Hard Cash, Whynot, Increase, Picayune, Errata, Pentecost, and Soso—these are a few others I recall. But every state has its share. In Kentucky you will find Rabbit Hash, Dwarf, Monkeys Eyebrow, Top Most, and Hell for Sure. Arkansas has Need More, Blue Eye, and Ink, and on your way through Louisiana you might pass through Jigger, Plain Dealing, and Many. Georgia has a Lax, Tax, and Wax, as well as a Social Circle, Newborn, Between, and Poetry. Unusual names of towns used to give me pleasure for reasons I no longer remember.

My mother's apartment was a shambles. She shouldn't have been living alone. Since Eliot's death I had not been to see her, and my phone calls had been distracted and infrequent. In my widowhood I hadn't realized she had become an old woman. Three years before Eliot died, when she was eighty, she had ridden a bus to Bean Station, Tennessee—a state that also boasts the towns of Belt Buckle, Difficult, and Frog Jump—to visit her youngest brother, had found him sick in bed with pneumonia, and had stayed two months to see him back on his feet.

This was before my world changed, when I still thought life was a good and simple proposition, when the idea of nursing a relative to health seemed a decent and reasonable thing to do. I am now the same age my mother was when she spent those two months in Bean Station, Tennessee, emptying bedpans, preparing meals, and keeping nighttime vigils. The thought of my doing such a thing now, possessing either the ability or the impulse to do so, is beyond my powers of imagination.

Sometime during the five years following my mother's trip to see Uncle Abe, both her mind and body began to break down. My sisters detected it before I did, both of them having more stamina than I for telephone conversations and both of them driving over together for short visits twice a year. When I entered my time of trouble, beginning with the firing of the gun in Alonso's hand, I had no room in my heart and mind for my mother's well-being. This sounds hard, but it is true. I suffered her phone calls, her admonitions to "get over" my grief, her accusations about my selfishness in the absence of birthday and Christmas gifts, hearing it all as from a great distance, muffled and garbled.

I soon discovered that her words were indeed muffled and garbled, not because of distance but because she was a sick woman. For three years following Eliot's death, I knew I had a mother, yes, and that she was living in an apartment in Methuselah, Mississippi. If asked her age, I would have known she was in her eighties, could have figured it to the exact year if necessary. I would not have known, however, that she was inventing and diagnosing illnesses for herself, ingesting large quantities of medications, some of it outdated leftover prescriptions of my father's and a great deal of it taken off drugstore shelves and slipped into her pocketbook.

And suddenly, it seemed, everyone was alarmed. Within the space of two days, I received four phone calls—one each from Regina and Virginia, one from Uncle Abe, and one from my mother's land-lady, all apprising me that my mother's condition was extremely pre-carious. I received the first one on a Saturday morning in early May as I was grading the last of a set of freshman research papers on a topic of my choosing: "The Death of John F. Kennedy—Lone Assas-sin or Conspiracy?" By Sunday evening I knew that there was a con-spiracy against me, to relieve everyone of the burden caused by my mother's physical and mental deterioration.

I was unattached, with no husband or children. In spite of my weight I was in moderately good health. I had money, one of my primary qualifications. I had a house with an extra bedroom. I had time, at least imminently, with the summer ahead of me, and if need be, a rich single woman could take as much time as she needed to attend to the urgent task of nursing her mother. This was the think-ing of my sisters and uncle. And there was no loophole in the argu-ment. I fell victim to the lone assassin of logic.

It could be asserted that my life suddenly had purpose. It was a purpose I was not eager to embrace, yet one I could not escape. I knew Regina and Virginia felt, as my mother had, that it was time for me to become involved with life again, specifically with my mother's life. The word *involved* is a frightening thing, encompassing such extremes as minimal, polite contact at the one end and absolute immersion at the other. I knew toward which end I was headed. I had the sense of one about to be tortured, who sees his persecutor standing over him, the glint of a blade in one hand, a black hood in the other. This is a grim metaphor for the care of a loved one, yet I speak the truth. I could feel the sensation of too little air to breathe.

And so I gave myself to duty. I finished grading my papers, arranged for a colleague to cover my remaining classes and proctor my exams, received permission to take an early leave, and drove to Methuselah. Never having had children of my own to tend, I felt ill-equipped in a physical sense. Though I had performed basic first-aid skills in my years of teaching elementary school, I knew my mother's illness would require more than the application of Band-Aids, Mer-curochrome, and ice packs.

There was no talk of nursing homes or other facilities. My mother had always said she wouldn't submit to a "dumping place," as she put it, and not one of us was willing to test her. My mother had developed a formidable temper in her old age. My sisters and I had heard her say many times since our father's death, "I will not die in a hos-pital or a nursing home. I will kill myself, or someone else, if you ever take me to one. If you try it, my spirit will haunt you for the rest of your lives." I have no doubt that she would have kept her word.

She had not been to a doctor for a checkup in over thirty years, ever since a certain Dr. Halliday, a new doctor in Methuselah, had recommended a hysterectomy, which she considered "mighty pre-sumptuous of a young doctor." She ignored his recommendation and began ordering herbal medicines to treat her symptoms.

During my father's illness several years later, she had become fur-ther convinced that the medical profession as a whole was not only untrustworthy but also aggressively venal, seeking opportunities to defraud patients of their money by what she called their "hobby of waving their knives around," by which she meant unnecessary sur-geries. When Daddy died, she claimed grounds for numerous potential malpractice lawsuits against various doctors who had overlooked obvious red flags, misprescribed medications, botched simple office procedures, and in general failed to cure him, as if a heart aneurysm was something you could fix with the right pill.

"Step foot inside a doctor's office," she would say, "and you'll never be well again." She delivered the speech regularly: First you have the checkup, she said, at which time the problem is first brought to light, then another checkup to verify the first one, then a pre-operation visit, then the surgery, then the post-surgery checkup, then the post-post-surgery checkup, by which time "They've gone and found something else wrong with you that starts the whole cycle over again." It was her belief that they "had their hand inside your pocketbook from day one" and "weren't about to take it out." They knew where their fancy cars and expensive vacations came from. Further, she suspected many male doctors of having gone into the business simply so they could see naked women.

This was the woman I took home with me to Carlton, Kentucky. I did not know the exact nature or extent of her ailments, except for a few general self-diagnoses she offered from articles she had read in medical magazines, one of which was irritable bowel syndrome. "I've had it for years," she said, "but it's gotten worse. Lots worse. And this is bad, too," she said, showing me her stomach. "That's where it's growing." This was no mere irritability. It was a raging distemper.

I had no false notions that this would be a mild illness or that she would be an easy invalid to nurse. Disbelieve me, if you wish, that I did not have the courage to force my mother, almost eighty-six years old by this time, to go to a doctor, that I dared not call an ambulance to take her to the emergency room and thus admit her to a hospital. Tell me, if you know, how to force a fiercely determined old woman to do anything. She may have been losing her mind, but one look into her eyes told me that her will was intact. It was her belief that she was dying, and I knew she was right. She wasn't afraid of pain, she told me. She was convinced that if she went to a doctor, he would knock her unconscious and operate on her. It was the surgeon's knife that scared her.

Her apartment, as I said, was in a state of disarray, and, to borrow one of her expressions, it stank to high heaven. Before I moved her to Kentucky, I spent over two weeks throwing things away—stashes of empty plastic milk cartons, bottles of old medication, spoiled food, catalogs and sale circulars, stacks of used wrapping paper, hundreds of brown grocery sacks, old magazines and paperbacks, drawerfuls of receipts, cardboard boxes, and all manner of shabby clothing stained past repair. To see to what depths my mother's standards had fallen was heartbreaking. She had been a beautiful woman in her prime— very particular and well groomed.

At times she was lucid. One day she said to me, "My arteries are hardening, Sophie. There is no healing for that." At other times she was lost in the labyrinth of the past. In the back of her closet I found a garbage bag full of strips of fabric. When asked about them, she said, "I was saving them for bandages. The soldiers will need them." She had four hatboxes in the top of her closet filled with old socks rolled up into balls. "I was darning them while Ivy fixed the buggy wheel," she told me. Ivy was her youngest stepbrother, who had been killed in a hunting accident over sixty years earlier.

I found an old pair of my father's high work boots in the same closet, filled to the top laces with coins of all denominations. These

I took to the bank, where they poured the coins into a counting machine. When I told my mother that she had collected a little over six hundred dollars in coins, she looked at me sadly and said, "Many's the time the tramps came to the back door asking for a plate of supper."

She and my father had never trusted banks but had always kept their money hidden in the house. This was how my father had come to own the printshop. When the original owner had gone bankrupt at the beginning of the Great Depression, my father had paid him cash for the business—"purchased it for a song," my mother liked to say. My father was not a businessman, however, and the song turned into a sad one. Wary of banks, he had the misfortune of placing his trust in certain individuals who betrayed him.

I discovered that at some point in her widowhood my mother had opened a checking account, into which she deposited her monthly social security check. Her records of deposits and checks were haphazard, however, and the account balance was only a few cents over four hundred dollars.

I found cash in my mother's apartment, though not much, certainly not the savings of a lifetime. "Where is your money, Mother?" I asked her repeatedly. Once she looked at me calmly and replied, "No one is good, Sophie. No one." Another time she began crying and said, "They promised it would come, but it never did." When asked to identify "they" and "it," she had no information to give. There was nothing in her papers to tell me what had become of her money. The official bank records showed check after check written out to "Cash," but there was no sign of the cash anywhere.

Regina and Virginia were beside themselves. Both had hoped for at least a modest inheritance, their husbands having proven less than financially stable. They urged me not to discard anything without searching it thoroughly. After I had been there a week, they arrived together one morning and set about combing the apartment for possible hiding places, going through boxes of trash I had set aside. They left late that afternoon, desperately disappointed that their efforts had yielded nothing except two nickels in the bottom of a vase. When Mother saw the nickels, she smiled and said, "And he bought a new radio that Christmas."

Regina presented the possibility that perhaps Mother had opened a savings account. But there was no record, I said. No book, no statements, no deposit slips. "Did you have another account at the bank?" I asked Mother, but she began crying again and said, "He would have been so angry." To satisfy my sisters, however, I called the bank the next day and asked if there was a savings account in our mother's name, but, as I already knew, there wasn't. There was only the checking account, with its balance of four hundred dollars.

The three of us divided what money I had found in small stashes around the house, some two thousand dollars in bills and the six hundred dollars from the coins, and a week later I took Mother in my car to Kentucky. For the next five months I attended her night and day. I do not care to think about the sights, sounds, and smells of that time, about the bitter taste in my mouth, the feel of cold fingers raking my flesh as I accompanied my mother to the threshold of death.

I have heard the phrase "a labor of love." In the strictest sense I suppose I can claim it. Of a certainty I did labor. And I did love my mother—I was not beyond that. It was a strange love, however, that lacked certain characteristics usually associated with the word—heat, spontaneity, steadiness, joy. At times it felt like an instinct, an unthinking reflex, and at other times like an ancient law one had no choice but to obey. I often meant to sit and ponder this kind of love, to determine its validity, but the days passed, and now it is too late. If one does one's duty, is his motivation of any importance?

I dream that my mother calls her three daughters before her, as King Lear did, and asks them, "Which of you loves me most?" We answer, not by age as in Shakespeare's play, but in order of height and beauty: Virginia first, Regina second, and I last. Virginia replies prettily, declaring that words are inadequate to express her love for our mother, though she expends a great many of them in her effort to do so. Regina follows with more of the same, pronouncing Virginia's love tender and well-meaning yet coming up short when compared to her own.

And then it is my turn. "What do you have to say?" my mother asks me. And like Cordelia, I reply, "Nothing." Oh, but "nothing will come of nothing," my mother sternly reproves, indicating that I will receive no deathbed blessing if I remain silent. I will be consigned to my small dark house with its stench of death. She admonishes me to mend my words, to plump up my chances by speaking. I cannot.

And in my dream, as in life, she dies at last. I receive no blessing, no parting words of encouragement. But I have weathered the storms of her going and am content to remain in my small dark house, mercifully alone.

I called Purtles Funeral Home in Carlton, Kentucky. They informed me that I must acquire a death certificate before they could "accept the body." Who was her doctor, the man wanted to know. She had no doctor, I replied. Had she been in the hospital recently, he asked. No, I said. What had she died of, he asked. I heard suspicion in his voice. I didn't know, I told him. I knew what he wanted to ask: "What do you have to say for yourself—a daughter who would not even take her own mother to a doctor?" And if he had asked, I would have given Cordelia's answer, as in my dream: "Nothing."

And now, in another time and place, in a corner of someone else's house, I await my own ferry to cross the river from this life to the next. As Edgar, the Earl of Gloucester, says later in *King Lear*, "Men must endure their going hence." Death is not a negotiable proposition. If the ferry doesn't come now, it will come later. Eventually every man and woman must take his or her trip across.

I stored away my mother's dying words to think about later, perhaps to smile about someday. But many years have passed, and I still have not smiled over them. Though my mother was not a religious woman, neither was she a blasphemer. The closest to a curse word we ever heard from her mouth was the mild epithet *durn*, which she used sparingly for times of greatest provocation. She was of the opinion that southerners were generally guilty of lazy talking, which, she said, inevitably led to unladylike speech. She once washed Virginia's mouth out with soap when she heard her call a teacher a "jackass from hell." It was with some surprise, then, that during her final months at my house, I heard her speech peppered with *durns*, as well as a few other words I had never before heard her say.

She died on a bright September morning, one of those days poised between summer and fall. I sensed that the end was near. Her breath was coming slowly, faintly. The air outside was clear and dry, the sky a brilliant blue. The sun streamed through the window beside her bed, where I sat. Suddenly she strained forward from her pillows, pointed to the window, and cried out, "Turn off the durn light!" Then she fell back, dead. Perhaps Julius Dixon would have suggested to her another way to put it: "Dim, dim the durn lights. I want some atmosphere."

My mother was right. Getting old is no fun. And, as she told me it would, my time has indeed come. This is a winter that will not turn to spring. No new nesting sites for old birds when the snow melts. I am reminded of the names of other towns I have seen on the map: Death Valley, Tombstone, Last Stop, Edge of Nowhere.

CHAPTER 13

WIPE OFF THE DUST THAT HIDES OUR SCEPTER'S GILT

When robins return north from their wintering
grounds in the South, they start out in an
enormous flock, which steadily breaks into
smaller groupings as the birds seek out the
regions where they were hatched and fledged.
By midsummer robins may be spotted in
the northernmost regions of Canada.

I take careful note of the ages of the people whose deaths are recorded in *Time* magazine. In some issues my own age of eighty falls in the middle, sometimes near the end. Out of the six or seven people listed, there are sometimes as many as four who were older than eighty when they died. I feel the smallest spark of gladness when I see such an issue. "DIED. PRINCESS JULIANA, 94, revered Queen of the Netherlands for 32 years." See, I tell myself, you may live another fourteen years. Other times, however, I am not encouraged. Once the oldest out of seven entries was only seventy-eight.

The deaths on the Milestones page are recorded in order of age, youngest to oldest. I always read the page backward. In one issue the first entry I read was "DIED. TIMOTHY THE TORTOISE, approximately 160, British navy mascot that in 1854 witnessed the bombing of Sevastopol during the Crimean War aboard the HMS *Queen* and later served in the East Indies and China." To what extent, I wonder, did a tortoise "witness" a historical event?

I felt it was frivolous of *Time* magazine to include Timothy on the same page with inventors, musicians, political figures, entrepreneurs, shapers of society. Timothy's obituary continued its inappropriate humor by recording that the "veteran" had spent his "retirement" in an earl's garden and that "an ill-fated mating attempt in 1926" had brought to light the fact that Timothy was a actually a female. Ending with the fact that "Timothy will be buried with full honors on the castle grounds," *Time* completed its demonstration of tastelessness in the matter of life and death.

Since coming to Patrick's house, these are some of the younger victims I have read about in *Time:* Jason Raize, 28; Marco Pantani, 34; Paul Klebnikov, 41; Olivia Goldsmith, 54. An actor, a champion cyclist, a journalist, a novelist. These are some of the older victims: Robert Lees, 91; Joseph Zimmerman, 92; Frances Dee, 96; Morris Schappes, 97. A screenwriter, an inventor, a movie star, a scholar.

As noted earlier, causes of death are seldom reported for people of advanced age. No reason is necessary to explain the sudden absence of those who have already occupied space on earth for more than the average lifespan. There are exceptions, however, as in the case of Robert Lees. *Time* reveals that Lees, 91, "was beheaded by a transient in his home." The suspect "was charged with capital murder." I should hope so.

Each of these deaths is the end of a story, none of them a happy ending. Suicide, drug overdose, gunshot wounds, heart attack, decapitation, old age—no "happily ever after" for these people. But then, I ask myself, what kind of death would qualify as a happy ending—for the person most directly affected, that is? For others in his family it may be a happy ending, of course.

When I taught elementary school, a fellow teacher received word one day while we were on recess duty together that her father had died after a lingering illness at a private nursing home in Missouri. The two of us were standing by the fence near the swings. Millie was not one for pretense. After the secretary had given her the message and left the playground, Millie turned and placed her hands on the top rail of the fence. She looked out across the parking lot for a long, silent moment. I spoke at last, expressing my sympathy for her loss, for the thoughtless way the news had been delivered, and asked what I could do to help.

The secretary had already called a substitute to take her class for the afternoon and for the next several days, but I offered to come to her house and do whatever she needed. I could cook, I could clean, I could pack her suitcase, feed her cat, get her mail, whatever she needed. Millie turned to me and said, "I thought this day would never come, Sophie. I've dreamed of it for years." She squeezed my hand and said, "Thanks for your sympathy, but save it for someone who deserves it. I don't." When she came back to school a week later, she was driving a new black Mercedes.

I wonder what Patrick and Rachel will do with my money when it is theirs. I wonder if they have already made plans. I wonder if they talk about my health: Do you think she looks as well as when she came here in October? Did you notice how distracted she seemed tonight? I wonder if it's some form of dementia? What did her parents die of? How old were they when they died? Do you see how she puts her hand over her heart? Do you suppose she has a heart condition?

I know about heart conditions. The human heart is a deep well, and its waters are never pure. I know that the contamination of one heart can spoil the heart of another, like a polluted stream flowing into a clean one. I know that a betrayed heart can never again be a soft heart, for the knowledge and pain of deception calcifies into stone, which, ironically, becomes a breeding ground—for anger and hatred. Yes, I have a heart condition. It is called an understanding of reality.

————

It is a Thursday morning, a week before Christmas. Rachel has risen from her sick bed and wrapped gifts to put under the tree. She had a doctor's appointment three days ago, but I have not heard it discussed, nor have I asked the outcome. I observe the gifts now from across the room, twelve in all. They are wrapped in two different patterns of paper—one with snowmen imprinted on it and the other with red and green holly.

Rachel is presently away from home, for what she called a "prayer vigil" at church, and I am at my post at the front window. Someone has decorated the entrance of Wagner's Mortuary with two festive wreaths. Funerals have continued at regular intervals during the holiday season. Even now a hearse is pulling out from under the side portico, a line of cars forming behind it, all with their headlights on, heading north on Edison toward the cemetery at the edge of Greenville.

I think of the prayer vigil Rachel is attending. She offered only one detail before she left: it is for a woman with cancer. How does a woman like Rachel pray? Does she pray for life, which is merely a prolonging of the illness, or for death, to ease the woman's suffering? I wish I could see and hear her at the prayer vigil. I wonder if she prays aloud. I can't imagine that hers would be a lengthy prayer. Perhaps she prays for the miracle of healing, though Rachel has seen little enough evidence of miracles in her lifetime.

The cars continue to join the funeral procession snaking solemnly down Edison Street. One of them, a streamlined red convertible, looks out of place, like Timothy the tortoise on the Milestones page. I have considered asking Patrick to give me his copy of the *Delta Democrat Times* each day after he has read it. This way I could read the local obituaries and keep track of the funerals across the street. I would know which ones are for important people. I would be reminded of the fact that the corpses of former mayors and school superintendents are transported in the same hearse as those of waitresses and janitors. And of the fact that death visits itself upon young and old alike. It has no sense of time.

Many years ago Eliot prepared a speech on "Problems of Time" in Shakespeare's plays, which he delivered at a conference in Cincinnati, Ohio. I typed the manuscript for him, of course, and also attended the conference with him. Because Eliot's accommodations were covered by the conference, we stayed in a Holiday Inn rather than a budget motel, which was his usual choice if he was paying. I sat in the audience for Eliot's speech and looked at him proudly. *That is my husband,* I said to myself. This was early in our marriage, when I was newly smitten with my status as wife.

I suppose Shakespeare scholars are familiar with the bard's warpings of time that allow such unlikely events as the separate sightings and dockings of three different ships in a single harbor within the space of fifteen minutes and such inconsistencies as that of Desdemona's having no opportunity to be alone with Cassio, with whom she is accused of having an adulterous relationship. Months, even years, are passed over without comment during many of Shakespeare's plays. In his speech Eliot cited these and many other instances of liberties taken concerning the passage of time. I recall the sense of awe I felt that my brilliant husband could stand before other brilliant minds and comment on the weaknesses of William Shakespeare.

I also recall his pointing out the lapse in logic that occurs somewhere in *Richard II*, when Northumberland announces an impending invasion of England, which could hardly have been planned and executed in the available time. In the rush of drama, however, such problems go unnoticed. Impressions, the sweep of emotions, striking characterization, significant and well-motivated action—these were of more concern to Shakespeare than literal precision of time. This was the theme Eliot reserved for the conclusion of his speech.

When he stopped abruptly, then nodded primly at the smattering of applause that followed, this was the thought that came to me: *Thus by altering realism, a writer may actually enhance realism.* In my mind, this would have provided a fitting summary for his speech, though I never would have dared to suggest a revision of anything Eliot wrote or said. What did I—a former elementary school teacher, a mere typist—know about Shakespeare? When he asked me how I liked his speech, I told him it was perfect. He smiled complacently, as if he knew it already but was pleased at my discernment. I, too, had learned a good deal about enhancing realism by altering it.

Like Shakespeare's plays, every man has his own problems of time. In my life I, too, have sighted remarkable things within mere minutes of time, things that have changed the course of my life. In addition, entire years of time have been lost in my memory. At times I have set logic aside and acted prematurely; too often, though, I have done nothing. So often there is nothing that can be done.

Were I a character in *Richard II*, I would have hung back when Northumberland urged the rising up and going forth to fight. To his request to "wipe off the dust that hides our scepter's gilt," my reply would have been, "Not I, I pray thee. Let me stay behind / I am content with dusty scepter, lord." From Eliot I learned the art of writing in blank verse. From life I have learned that the effort required for most endeavors is generally too great for the small glint of gold dust that might be uncovered. I prefer to let sleeping dust lie.

The funeral procession is ending. I wonder how many people in the cars following the hearse are fretting over their own problems of time. The last car in the line is an old Chevrolet, turquoise and white—a car that has overstayed its time. I see only a driver inside, no passenger. I lean forward until the turquoise Chevrolet creeps out of sight. From the opposite direction a florist's van pulls up in front of the mortuary. A man gets out and removes a large spray of red flowers, which he carries inside. He comes out only seconds later, skipping down the front steps like a schoolboy.

I think of the only flowers Eliot ever gave me, a bouquet he had picked himself from his own backyard and brought to my house when he came to tell me that the most recent paper I had typed for him, an expanded version of a formerly unpublished paper, had been accepted by the *Yale Review*. He was particularly happy that night, and his happiness spilled over into generosity. Besides the flowers, he brought a small cheesecake, which we shared at my kitchen table.

Eliot's last three manuscripts had been rejected by various literary magazines, and for several weeks he had brooded over his failures. I was to discover later, after our marriage, the depths to which he descended during times of gloom, but for now I could only rejoice with him that the cloud had lifted. The letter of acceptance from the *Yale Review*, which he brought for me to read, was salve to his bruised ego. I served the cheesecake on white china dessert plates and put on a record of waltzes to play in the background. I loved him already, had loved him for months now, but he had shown no interest in me beyond my typing skills. The bouquet of flowers and the cheesecake gave me hope.

It was many more months before he spoke to me of marriage. The flowers—a mix of irises in every color and size, from dwarf to queen—wilted within a week. But I recall the way they held on, new blooms unfolding one at a time along the stems as the old ones shriveled. I was over forty years old and had never before observed the wonder of irises. Each day I clipped off the dying blooms and marveled as new ones opened. At last there was only a single bloom left, a deep inky purple. I left it in the vase a day too long, for the next morning I saw that its head had drooped, bleeding a purple stain on my best tablecloth. When I emptied the water in the sink, a horrible smell arose.

My mother had been far too busy at our boardinghouse to pick bouquets of flowers. I was presented a corsage by one of the boys who took me to a dance in high school, but it wilted quietly, without the fanfare of Eliot's live bouquet. During my years of teaching, children had occasionally brought me flowers, mostly late summer roses and early spring daffodils, but they, too, had died gently. It was after four decades of living, therefore, that I first saw the mingling of beauty and ugliness—in a bouquet of irises on my kitchen table.

For all those years I had viewed life as a child, seeing good and evil as separate kingdoms. I had secluded myself among children, had read them sweet stories, had taught simple unbendable rules of arithmetic and behavior, had directed them in plays such as *Tom Sawyer*, which depicted naughtiness as humorously cute and good as ultimately triumphant. I had ordered my days neatly and safely, lived peaceably with my neighbors and colleagues. I had pushed to the back of my memory the small deprivations of my own childhood, the failures of Santa Claus to answer my letters, the quarrels over money between my parents.

And then one day I observed cut irises in a vase, saw them continue to bloom as if unaware that they were separated from their native soil, saw them turn translucent as they collapsed inward like pale shriveled fists, saw them leak in their dying, smelled the foulness of their death. For weeks thereafter I argued with myself. Relinquish your hope of marriage now, I said, before its inevitable demise. And then I answered myself: No, hold fast to love, for nothing else matters.

I saw Eliot's imperfections—his melancholic nature, his excessive frugality, his regimentation, his aloofness, his prudish public persona, his disagreeable children. Yet I loved him. Whenever I heard the voice warning me of his faults, I defended him: Love is its own reward, I said staunchly. I will behold the marvel of this flower; I will take it to myself; I will not forfeit beauty for the dread of disappointment. I will hope for marriage, this wondrous thing that has been the cornerstone of life on earth for untold centuries. I closed my eyes and saw Anne Shirley and Gilbert Blythe strolling hand in hand along fragrant lilac-bordered lanes, riding in a wagon beneath a canopy of flowering apple trees, sitting on a dark hillside under a full yellow moon, bending over their firstborn child. I saw Jo March and Professor Bhaer sheltered under the umbrella, gazing into each other's eyes. I wrote down a list of Eliot's virtues—his intelligence, his quietness, his politeness, his neatness.

Later, after I had received and accepted his offer of marriage, I learned of the extremes of his neatness—his reluctance, for instance, to entertain the thought of romance except on specified days and immediately after bathing, his unvarying methodology, his inordinate haste to rise from our bed afterward to bathe again. I fell into the habit of examining the faces and gestures of other married couples in public, wondering whether impulsiveness played any role in their love. I looked into the eyes of other wives and wondered whether their husbands ever coaxed them into the bedroom in the middle of a Sunday afternoon, a day Eliot always spent in his study with the door closed. And yet, I tell you, I felt myself to be happily married. If there were small troubling questions, I knew the fault must lie with me.

No one appears to be home at Steve and Teri's house across the street. I recall that Teri takes Veronica to therapy on Thursdays. I remember the lilt in Teri's voice when she reported to Patrick and Rachel that Veronica was starting to hold her head more erect. I try to imagine what Veronica does in her therapy sessions. Perhaps the therapist rolls balls toward her on the floor and moves her arms to music. Perhaps Veronica lies on a mat while the therapist exercises her legs. Perhaps puppies lick her face. I think of her small fair face, her blond hair, her hand waving good-bye. I am reminded that from a distance uncommon things may look normal.

I think of Steve at work now at the catfish processing plant. I wonder if he ever comes up behind Teri in the kitchen and places his hands on her body, if she ever lays her knife or spatula down and turns to him. I wonder if fancy and passion ever prevail in the house where I now sit. I wonder if Patrick ever approaches Rachel at unexpected times for the purpose of love, if she sets down her dustrag, turns the vacuum cleaner off, or leaves her cake batter unmixed to follow him. Imagine an old woman thinking thoughts like these.

I hear the telephone ring in the kitchen, but I do not get up to answer it. Patrick owns an answering machine, which is seldom put to use since Rachel is home most of the time. I hear Patrick's voice: "Hey there, I wanted to remind you that I'm bringing Potts home for supper tonight, but you probably remember already. You must be gone. Or maybe you've just stepped outside." He goes on at some length about where she may or may not be. I wonder if Rachel has ever placed her hand over Patrick's mouth to stop his words.

All the other cars have left the parking lot at the mortuary—the ones that opted not to join the procession to the cemetery, those done with death for now, with missions of life to accomplish. I think of the casket on its way to its hole in the ground. I think of Timothy the tortoise, who outlived all the other veterans of the Crimean War. My bird book reports that when robins fly north after winter they take leave of the flock one by one as the others continue on their way. Others in my family have dropped off along the way, but if I were a robin, I would be well into Canada by now.

CHAPTER 14

SECOND CHILDISHNESS AND MERE OBLIVION

Birdwatchers disagree on the sound made
by the rufous-sided towhee. Some hear its name
in its call—"chip towhee." Others hear
"chewink," and others "shrenk." In the
South, watchers claim to hear "Louise!" Other
transcriptions of the towhee's call are "drink
your tea" and "chip chup chup zeeeeeee."

The voice I hear at Patrick's supper table tonight is deep and well modulated, a radio voice. It is easily distinguished from Patrick's rapid tenor. I move from the round table to the chair beneath the wall clock to hear the new voice better. I have already eaten what I want of my supper—pot roast with potatoes and carrots that are bronzed from having been cooked with the meat. It is a good meal, but I have eaten my fill and left the rest. At the age of eighty I am at last able to walk away from food. All my life I have carried with me my father's voice saying, "Clean your plate!"

I am following other instructions of my father's now to "leave room for dessert." I heard these words every night as a child from my place at the foot of the table, beside my mother: "Help yourselves to the food, but be sure to leave room for dessert!" He tended to put on an air of cheerful magnanimity in front of the boarders. Out of their presence he was most often weighed down with the thought of long columns of figures that he knew would never balance at the end of the month.

More than once, late at night, I overheard Daddy telling Mother that he would have to keep back part of her grocery money for the week because of some other expense that had come up, usually something relating to the printshop. And more than once I heard Mother protest, "But I hardly have enough as it is to put a decent meal on the table!" As the argument escalated, I would wait for Mother to fire her strongest weapon, the one that gave her the best chance of prying the full amount of grocery money out of Daddy's tight grasp. "Well, all right," she might say eventually, with a tone of resignation, "I'll just have to cut out the desserts for this week. I'll let you explain it to our renters."

I have heard much scraping of silverware against plates in Rachel's kitchen tonight, more than usual. I have heard the man's deep voice telling of his family—a sister who works at a bakery in Greenwood; two younger brothers who have ended up on opposite sides of the country, in Los Angeles and New York City, which, he says, "speaks of their animosity toward each other"; an older brother who lives here in Greenville; and his mother, who lives in Pearl, Mississippi, and works in the lunchroom of the same school where a boy went on a shooting rampage several years ago.

I have heard Patrick talk about the proliferation of daycare centers as a result of so many working mothers, about his own older brother who left home as a seventeen-year-old, and about the number of murders committed in the United States by minors. I have heard Rachel ask Potts if he would like more tea. I have heard Patrick's laughter when Potts asks if he gets good food like this every night. "Sure do, except when the truck is late," Patrick says—an inane reply.

I have heard Potts talk at length of his son. Even through a wall I can hear his love for the boy. Tyler plays baseball, Potts says. He wants to be a major league pitcher someday. He plays basketball, too, but baseball is dearest to his heart. These are the very words he uses—"dearest to his heart."

Patrick doesn't exactly interrupt people, but he follows close on their bumper, then speeds around and slides in front of them. The mention of baseball reminds him of an article he has recently read about a black baseball player who is deaf. He begins to relate the entire story, an inspirational feature from Reader's Digest, a story which I also read during the wiring project in November when I stayed in the back bedroom. Patrick keeps back issues of Reader's Digest in a basket on the floor of the bathroom between his office and the spare bedroom. I believe Reader's Digest to be the source of much of Patrick's discourse.

He talks now of the deaf baseball player's discouragement, the taunting he suffered as a youngster, his parents' unfailing support, his work with disabled children, his experiences on farm clubs, his break into the majors.

"Do you know his name?" Patrick asks, as if he is a quiz show host and the category is "Noteworthy Black Americans."

"Was it Curtis Pride?" Potts asks. "He played for the Expos back in the nineties sometime, didn't he? Had a .444 average his first season, I believe."

Potts is a smart man. He knows the wisdom of cushioning his knowledge—"Was it?" "Didn't he?" "I believe"—so as not to upstage his white boss.

"You're right!" Patrick says. I wonder if he is staring at Potts in open disbelief. Imagine, a black ex-con working at an office supply store knowing so much! Patrick recovers from his shock and goes on to talk about a specific game between Montreal and Philadelphia in which Pride was called in as a pinch hitter in the seventh inning with one out. Montreal was trailing by three, with two runners on base. To quote the article, Pride's "bat exploded," and the two runners scored off the double he hit.

I wonder if Patrick will point out what I considered to be a glaring deficiency in the story as reported. For without telling the outcome of the game, the article stopped there, with Pride on second base looking up at the stands where the forty-five thousand fans were on their feet, cheering for him. It closed in typical *Reader's Digest* fashion, with a tear in the eye and a catch in the voice: Curtis Pride, the deaf but plucky black baseball player, feels within his soul a vibrating warmth as he realizes he is at last truly connected to the vast sea of mankind from whom his disability has always separated him.

I have little patience with such stories. I suspect *Reader's Digest* of blurring the edges of reality. What I wanted to know, but wasn't told, was whether Montreal won the game. Since the information was omitted, I assume that they didn't. Perhaps the next batter struck out, and Curtis Pride was thrown out trying to steal third. Perhaps the Phillies went ahead by ten runs during the last two innings and Curtis Pride cried bitterly in the locker room. But no matter, *Reader's Digest*, the "World's Most Widely Read Magazine," found in an otherwise uneventful game one little beam of light to flash to all the readers of its "more than twenty-five million copies in nineteen languages."

There is a sudden whirring sound, as of an electric mixer. I wonder if Rachel has suddenly thought of a part of the meal she forgot to prepare. The sound temporarily, mercifully, blocks out Patrick's voice just as he has moved on to talk about yet another baseball player he has read about recently, Cal Ripken Jr., who broke Lou Gehrig's Iron Man record in 1995. Perhaps Patrick is thinking that he will stump Potts now, that surely he will be less likely to know about white baseball players than black. I also read this article in Patrick's bathroom collection of *Reader's Digest* magazines, another story with the standard sentimental ending in which young Cal Ripken pays tribute to his father's shining example on the baseball field and in life.

When the mixer finally stops, there is silence for a moment, and then I hear Patrick: "Nor of a bramble bush gather they grapes. A good man out of the good treasure of his heart bringeth forth that which is good; and an evil man out of the evil treasure of his heart bringeth forth that which is evil: for of the abundance of the heart his mouth speaketh." I wonder what has elicited these words. How has the conversation pivoted from baseball to the treasure of a man's heart? These words were not part of the *Reader's Digest* articles about Curtis Pride or Cal Ripken.

When Patrick pauses, the new voice says, "And why call ye me, Lord, Lord, and do not the things which I say? Whosoever cometh to me, and heareth my sayings, and doeth them, I will show you to whom he is like: He is like a man which built an house, and digged deep, and laid the foundation on a rock." And now I understand. It takes no powers of clairvoyance to realize that they are reading from the Bible. An old woman, even one with Jewish blood in her veins, has heard enough in her lifetime of the King James New Testament to recognize it for what it is. She may never have attended church or synagogue, yet the tune and cadence of the language are as familiar as an old folk song. Perhaps my nephew and Potts are looking at the page together. This would make Patrick feel very expansive and liberal of soul—to share a holy book with a black man.

And then I hear Rachel's voice, at a volume I rarely hear from her: "And when the flood arose, the stream beat vehemently upon that house, and could not shake it: for it was founded upon a rock."

The new voice picks up again, but I lose the first words as I think of Rachel's acquaintance with vehement storms. Then I hear Potts say, "And immediately it fell; and the ruin of that house was great." The reading appears to be over.

And then, strangely, after a pause Patrick lifts his voice in prayer. I am mystified by the turn the conversation has taken. I am further mystified by Patrick's prayer. Though shot through with pompous word choices, it somehow rings of sincerity. He prays for Potts by name, expressing thanks for his "dear brother in salvation, whose path has divinely intersected my own." He prays for Potts' son, Tyler, that the "ways of this young man would be ordered according to your holy will" and that "he would be preserved from the evil one" and "sheltered in the hollow of your almighty hand."

When he finishes, I hear the sound of weeping. Potts' deep voice is broken. He thanks Patrick for his prayer. He speaks of things such as the sinner's unworthiness, Satan's stranglehold, the dark valleys of life, and God's grace. He speaks of his burden for Tyler and the temptations he has to face as a teenager, of his regret that he "can't be there for him every day." There is a rhythmic eloquence in Potts' rolling tones that reminds me of Martin Luther King's "I Have a Dream" speech, which my father drove to Washington, D.C., to hear in 1963 when it was first delivered, and which I have heard from a library recording. Rachel speaks to Potts softly. I can't hear her words.

Patrick keeps repeating himself, using less formal language now, telling Potts that "God is in control," that "God's not going to let the devil get at Tyler," that "the Lord is always on duty," and so forth. Patrick supplies no documentation for such knowledge, and Potts lets his empty assertions go unchallenged, saying over and over, "Yes, yes, I've got to keep looking up. I've got to keep my eyes fixed on Jesus."

You'd best keep your eyes on the solid ground beneath your feet, I want to tell him. I've seen people stumble and fall flat on their faces while craning their necks to look at something in the sky.

The sound of breaking glass interrupts their conversation. It seems that Patrick has overturned his glass, which shatters on the hardwood floor, for he is the one who says, "Well, good. I'm getting rid of these old glasses one by one." He laughs and tells Potts that he never has liked these glasses because they're too tall and too narrow at the base, making them easy to tip over. "Case in point," he says, no doubt thinking he is witty.

I hear the opening and closing of the broom closet and Patrick's cheerful talk as he sweeps up the pieces. I will say this for Patrick: He is not afraid of housework. Last Saturday Rachel went to bed in the middle of the afternoon. Shortly thereafter Patrick appeared at my apartment door with the vacuum cleaner. "Rachel says she didn't get around to vacuuming in here," he said. I watched him from my recliner as he moved about briskly. The sound of the machine didn't stop him from talking. "This has been a good little vacuum!" he shouted. "We got it at Montgomery Ward, must have been twenty years ago!" He was not as thorough and methodical as Rachel, but at least he was done quickly. It was a mercy when he finished and left my apartment, taking his flow of words with him.

I can't help wondering what Potts thinks about Patrick and Rachel, who have invited him into their home but whose kitchen walls are decorated with pictures of happy Negroes beside their shanties in the cotton field. Is he accustomed to the blindness of white men who imagine themselves free of prejudice yet who are taken aback by any sign of intelligence in other races?

Rachel must have brought dessert to the table, for Potts makes appreciative sounds and says, "I certainly don't get anything to compare to this at my house." Patrick tells him that the "whipped cream is the real McCoy, not that processed abomination." This explains the sound of the mixer earlier. I hear the stacking of dishes as Rachel clears the table. Most hostesses would clear the table before serving dessert.

"Here, let me take those," Patrick says to Rachel. "You sit down." I wonder if Patrick is showing off in front of Potts, trying to display a superior level of servanthood to confirm that he is a Christian Man. I wonder if the doctor has told Rachel to take things slowly until she regains her strength.

Back at the table Patrick tells Potts he should write a book some-time about his life. "I'd buy a copy!" he says, as if all a writer needs is the assurance of one reader. I suspect Patrick of considering a col-laborative effort. Potts could tell him the details, and Patrick could write the book for him. What a story it would make: *Black Drug Dealer Turns Religious* by Patrick Martin Felber. Patrick would not be above embellishing the facts.

Potts deflects Patrick's suggestion about the book. He tells Patrick that he is grateful for the job at the office supply store. He says that job offers in Greenville, Mississippi, are limited, especially to black men on parole. He likes the work at the Main Office, he says, and hopes to repay Patrick by being an "exemplary employee." Patrick takes this as an opportunity to educate Potts as to how he got his own start at the Main Office, first as a cashier, then stock clerk, then stock supervisor, then floor manager, then general manager. The unstated message is this: See, if you are diligent, you too can work your way up the ladder until you are as successful as I am.

Potts asks Patrick to explain the new system of inventory at the store, a system I have heard Patrick expounding upon recently to Rachel. He eagerly begins detailing the modifications he has devised. This is further evidence of Potts' intelligence: Always appear to be in awe of your boss's methods.

Suddenly there is a knock at my door and Rachel opens it. "Aunt

Sophie, here's your—" She stops when she sees me sitting in the chair beside the door.

I bend over as if scanning the floor. "I'm looking for a button," I say. "It came off my dress."

"Let me set this down, and I'll help you," Rachel says. As she carries the tray to the round table, I wrench a button off my dress and drop it onto the floor. She comes back and kneels down. She moves heavily as if kneeling is a great effort. She bends forward on all fours and runs one hand lightly over the carpet. "Did you see it roll over here?" she says, and I answer yes. I glance toward the round table and see a mound of whipped cream on top of a piece of yellow cake, with something red between the cake and whipped cream. Strawberries, cherries, raspberries—I have no preference. I like them all.

"Here it is," Rachel says, holding the button up for me to see. I nod.

"I'll sew it back on for you after I wash your dress," she says, and I nod again. She hoists herself from the floor.

You have made unnecessary work for this woman, I tell myself, then push the thought aside. She will be paid for her work when I die.

"Aunt Sophie, I'd like you to meet our guest," Patrick calls from the kitchen. He comes to stand in the open doorway, and Potts appears behind him. Still seated in my chair beside the door, I look up at them. Potts is a big man. Patrick looks like a child next to him. Potts is exceedingly dark-skinned, with a round face and very large smile. Sir, you have no reason to smile, I want to tell him. You have been in prison twice, you are prohibited by law from seeing your own son, and you are working for a tedious, small-minded man.

He steps around Patrick, beaming, to take my hand and declare himself pleased to make my acquaintance. His grandmother, he tells me, lived with his family when he was a child, and he has always had "a healthy respect for women of your generation." I say nothing but allow him to pump my hand briefly before pulling it away. I wonder if his grandmother was still living when he started dealing drugs and went to prison.

I am not offended by his reference to my age. I am an old woman of eighty. Anyone would be an idiot not to recognize the fact. I think of the man who bought my house before I moved from Kentucky to Greenville, Mississippi, the man who called me "young lady" in the lawyer's office. If I had thought him capable of improvement, I may have offered a word of instruction. As one does not try to reason with a retarded child, however, I turned away and refused to converse with him except through my lawyer.

Patrick is now speaking again, telling me things I have already heard through the door. I think of Jaques' famous "All the world's a stage" speech in Shakespeare's *As You Like It*. I want to tell Patrick to hush his "childish treble" so I can hear Potts' voice. I think of the four of us in my apartment right now, whose ages span many years: Potts in his thirties, Patrick and Rachel in their fifties, and Sophie the octogenarian. I think of Jaques' lines that all men have "their exits and their entrances." It struck me when typing it in one of Eliot's papers that he must have accidentally reversed the two words. Surely the entrances should come before the exits.

But, no. I looked up the reference and saw that Eliot had quoted it right. Perhaps the order was dictated by the metrical pulse, but I believe there is a statement there: One's life is over before it begins. I think of what a sad speech it is. In thirty lines the sum of life is told, from infanthood to "second childishness and mere oblivion." I think of the depressing closing line: "sans teeth, sans eyes, sans taste, sans everything." Granted, Jaques is a moody moralizer who takes himself too seriously, and as such he is a comical character. Yet for all his affectations, he sees the truth that life is not the grand enterprise young men like to think it is. Rather, it is ultimately a pathetic thing.

I think of all the ways men and women like to justify their existence on earth as important and worthy. I think of all the words spoken in the history of mankind, of all the ones spoken in the course of a day, of those I have overheard tonight through the kitchen wall. I hear Patrick now, his words like the endless piping of a bird.

I have read that bird watchers cannot agree on the towhee's call. They hear the same thing but interpret it differently. People may also disagree on what a man says. They may hear the same words but interpret them differently. Throughout my eighty years, I have heard many regional accents, dialects, foreign tongues. I have listened carefully and have found that most of the words spoken may be reduced to a few: I, me, my, mine.

"You'll like the dessert," Potts says, gesturing toward the tray on the table. I rise and go toward it. Though life is a pathetic thing, I cling to its small joys. And, I remind myself, I have not yet lost everything in this "last scene of all." I still have my teeth, my eyes, and my taste. I sit at the round table and prepare to eat.

CHAPTER 15

A TATTERED WEED, OF SMALL WORTH HELD

The nest of the great crested flycatcher may be constructed of an odd assortment of materials: leaves, sticks, roots, bark, even cellophane and plastic. According to bird lore, the flycatcher sometimes discourages predators by weaving a discarded snake skin into its nest.

I sit in my recliner through Christmas Eve, unwilling to go to bed and wake up disappointed. Disappointment is easier to take if one slowly steeps himself in it than if he is suddenly plunged in head first. If given a choice of one day to eliminate from the year, I would choose December 25—a day that brings to mind empty dreams.

My father, having grown up with people who had conflicting feelings about Christmas, was never one for holiday merriment. His Jewish mother had met his father in New York City and had believed him when he said he was interested in converting to Judaism. After she married him, his interest in Judaism was revealed for the lie that it was. Within a year he was interested in agnosticism. Having been disowned for marrying outside her faith, his mother threw over all her Jewish heritage. I have often wondered if, as time wore on, my grandmother ever regretted the trade—her Jewish family for Gentile freedom.

Daddy's father went from agnostic to atheist and after ten years left his wife, the Jewish girl he had liberated from her strict religion, with three little gaping mouths in the nest.

These were shadowy grandparents I never knew, born and bred in New York City, over a thousand miles from the delta of Mississippi, where my father eventually settled with my mother, a native daughter of Methuselah, Mississippi.

My father, afflicted with wanderlust as a young man, had left his mother in New York City in the year 1914 and over the next two years made his way southward to Atlanta, taking whatever odd jobs he could find to earn his keep. In the summer of 1916 he decided to seek his fortune in the West. He didn't make it very far, however. He hitched rides on the backs of wagons through Alabama and Mississippi, and when the last driver, a drunk farmer, passed out and turned his wagon over in a ditch somewhere near Kosciusko, Daddy got out and walked, arriving early the next morning in the little town of Methuselah, so named because the first family of settlers were supposedly very long-lived.

The first house Daddy came to, on the edge of town, bore a hand-painted wooden sign on the front gate that read *Wiggins' Boarding House*. Hungry and exhausted, Daddy turned in. Fatigue won out. He paid for a room, washed up, and slept for ten straight hours. When he woke up, he heard a bell and went downstairs to find supper on the table and an empty chair beside a girl with two dark brown braids tightly wound and pinned around her ears—"curled up like skinny rattlesnakes" is how Daddy described it the only time I heard him talk about first meeting my mother.

She was only sixteen, and her name was Penelope Wiggins. Saul Langham, weary sojourner and man of the world at twenty-two, sat beside Penelope Wiggins, only daughter and youngest child of the owners of the Wiggins' Boarding House, and asked her to pass the platters of stewed chicken and fried squash.

According to the story, she was so shy she wouldn't even look at him, and when he asked her a question, she bit her lip and looked the other direction. Her father first scowled at her from the head of the table, then tried a lighter approach by leaning down to ask the family cat, which was lying in his usual post under the table, what he had done with Penelope's tongue, and then finally rebuked her outright for displaying to a guest a "shameful want of southern hospitality."

Daddy, who wasn't used to shy girls, thought Penelope Wiggins' southern hospitality was just fine the way it was. He stayed on in Methuselah, lodging at the boardinghouse and working at a new enterprise in town, a small printshop, until Penelope was finally able to look at him when he asked her a question. After he asked the big question and she said yes, they were married, and when Grandpa Wiggins died suddenly a year later after being kicked in the head by a horse, Saul and Penelope moved from the room in the rear of the printshop back to the boardinghouse as the proprietors.

Daddy, whose penmanship looked like Thomas Jefferson's, painted a new sign for the front gate: *Langhams' Boarding House.* Grandma Wiggins took the big room off the kitchen for hers and gave the rest of the house to my parents. She was done with cooking and washing and collecting rent, she said. She was ready for a rest now that she was a widow.

Mother's four brothers all scattered to other parts of the state, evidently wanting no share in the running of the family business. Two of them went off to fight in World War I, but only one came home. The boardinghouse was a huge edifice with two wrap-around porches—one for each floor. My parents, and eventually my two sisters and I, occupied most of the first floor except for Grandma's room and another small bedroom rented for many years to Mrs. Beadle, whom my father referred to as "Methuselah's grandmother." As mentioned earlier, it was from Mrs. Beadle that I learned I was not a pretty child. She and Grandma Wiggins didn't like each other. They called each other names not befitting their status as southern ladies.

It is early Christmas morning now. Grandma Wiggins and Mrs. Beadle are long dead. Saul and Penelope have likewise recited their lines and exited life's stage, along with two of their daughters. Their middle daughter is now an old woman sitting alone in the dark on Christmas Day.

In many ways we were strangers in Methuselah. Though the bloodline was diluted and the religious beliefs held in contempt, we were labeled Jews. Daddy spoke out for equality of the races in a day when it never occurred to most white men to do so. He printed flyers expressing his beliefs and exposing certain outrages conducted by organizations such as the Ku Klux Klan. Daddy's was a well-known name in Mississippi but not a popular one among those in high places.

My father's Jewish mother and atheist father left Daddy with troubled memories of Christmas, which he recycled and passed on to his three daughters. The Methodist church in Methuselah staged an outdoor nativity play each Christmas, but Daddy forbade us to go. "Silly theatrics," he called it. It didn't matter that the whole town turned out for it; in Daddy's opinion, this was only more reason for the Langhams to stay home. Daddy never argued against Christmas on religious grounds, however. It was simply a mindless tradition and a waste of good money—this is what he told us over and over.

My mother eventually found it easier to be silent than to argue with him. Besides, by the time Christmas rolled around each year, the last thing she wanted to do was take on anything extra in the way of baking or decorating. Any charms to be found in housewifery lose their luster quickly for women who run boardinghouses. Holidays mean very little for those whose daily duties never cease.

Not being in the habit of celebrating Christmas, I continued to pass the season quietly after I left home and began teaching. My students gave me small gifts, of course—a benefit of teaching I had not expected. These were a great joy to me. I would arrange them on a table at home and marvel over the sight: all these gifts for me! I recall a green velvet pincushion and a red sachet pouch among my favorites. Though I allowed my students to decorate the classroom and sing carols, and though I presented each child with a candy cane the day school let out for Christmas vacation, this was the extent of my festivity.

Aside from the candy canes, I had never bought a Christmas gift for anyone until I married Eliot at the age of forty-two. And having received only one that I could remember, I looked forward to what the season might hold. As I had happily embraced marriage, so was I ready to embrace Christmas, especially the tradition of exchanging gifts.

Though Eliot and I had not talked about how we would spend our Christmas break that year, I began laying my plans in early December. I bought a charcoal gray cardigan sweater and a pair of leather gloves for Eliot, wrapped them up, and hid them in my closet. We had no tree, a fact I laid to Eliot's preoccupation that December with a new Shakespeare textbook for which he was serving as a contributing editor.

On Christmas morning I served cinnamon rolls and gave the gifts to him at the breakfast table. He opened them with polite surprise, then went to his study and came back with a small box that might have held a necklace. It didn't. I opened it and found a pen and pencil set. Taped to the underside of the lid was a card he must have overlooked: "To Eliot Hess, For Ten Years of Service at South Wesleyan College." Evidently the box had been in his study for some time, for the ink in the pen had dried up.

Too intellectual to be religious, Eliot at last voiced his opinion, very gently in hopes that I would not be offended, that Christmas was a commercial trap he preferred to avoid. He did appreciate the gifts, he said, but I needn't think I had to do this each year. He didn't expect personal gifts. If I liked, he said, we could use the holiday in years to come as an excuse to buy some small item for the house. And so on our second Christmas together we bought a new coffeepot, a suggestion that Eliot put forth with his usual courtesy. Perhaps he had forgotten that I rarely drank coffee.

I suppose it should seem highly unlikely that the two most influential men in my life, my father and my husband, both scorned the most important American holiday. I had learned, however, that one takes whatever he is given. Never having celebrated Christmas before my marriage, it was no sacrifice, I told myself, to forgo it after my marriage. And yet the next time December 25 arrived, I felt a tightness in my throat.

As the years passed, the sensation gradually subsided to only a general restlessness to have the season over and done. Gifts are not practical, I often reminded myself. The gray sweater I had given Eliot, for instance—it remained folded in his drawer, unworn. The gloves were too large and had to be exchanged. Then one was dropped in a muddy puddle, after which both were laid aside and finally discarded.

I have heard other old people, their minds afflicted with the fog of sentimentality, speak about the Christmases of their childhood. "We didn't get much," I have heard them say, "but we were happy!" They go on to talk of stringing popcorn and berries to decorate a tree, of finding oranges and stick candy in old socks hung by the chimney, of homemade toys and shiny pennies. As for me, I have a single memory: the storybook I received from my grandmother Wiggins when I was four, the year before she had a stroke and lost all concept of time and place. Lit-tle Soph-ie had no pa-per dolls, no pep-per-mint sticks, no black-board with chalk, no yo-yo in her stock-ing.

Nevertheless, my sisters and I spent hours with the Sears catalog, dreaming of the gifts we would find under the tree on Christmas morning. We made lists of our dreams, wrote letters to Santa that went nowhere. Not only were there no gifts under the tree, there was no tree. My father claimed to be allergic to evergreens of all kinds. His allergy spared him the effort of cutting, hauling, setting up, and decorating a tree, along with the troublesome hopes that would be raised once a tree was installed in the front parlor.

I have no warm, inspiring stories to tell of weathering the

deprivations of the Depression. It was a dark time of wishing. I was only three years old in December of 1929 when, in a daring moment, Daddy, possessor of liquid cash, took advantage of his employer's despair and offered to buy the shop where he worked. The offer was readily accepted, his employer being eager to leave Methuselah and move to Tennessee, where his wife's family lived.

So at the age of thirty-five, Daddy sank all his cash into the printshop, which left him the last four decades of his life to regret his purchase. He would have sold the shop hundreds of times, even at a loss, had anyone wanted to buy such an albatross during a time when newspapers were folding and printed advertisements were considered a luxury. With no head for business, Daddy hired a young assistant named Woodrow Carper and gave him more liberty than the man's character could sustain. When Woodrow left town in the middle of the night two years later with all the cash Daddy had hidden in a metal box behind the coal bin, Daddy's view of mankind, which had never been very high anyway, hit rock bottom.

The boardinghouse revenue became the flimsiest of shields between the Langham family and poverty. Most of the work fell to Mother, of course, since Daddy continued to spend his days at the printshop trying to "drum up business," as he said. From what I could tell, Mother worked harder than Daddy. This gave Daddy ample time to be the family complainer and worrier, a role which he perfected.

Even when the printshop business picked up during the 1940s, my mother's workday always began earlier and ended later than my father's. She was remarkably efficient around the house, inside and out. She could wield a hammer as well as a mixing spoon, a garden hoe as well as a broom, a paintbrush as well as a feather duster. My sisters and I were regularly called upon to help my mother. When I was five, I was setting the dining room table three times a day for a dozen people.

It is quiet in my apartment. The television is off. I have no desire to see the Christmas specials and commercials that are on every channel this time of year. I hear the ticking of the clock as the day comes on, the marching feet and beating drums of time. I sit by my window waiting for the first light, wondering which species of bird will be the first to visit my feeder on Christmas morning. One day I tried to keep a tally of the birds that came to the feeder, but after the tenth mark on my paper I realized the stupidity of the endeavor. How could I keep from counting the same birds twice? And even if my count could be accurate, of what benefit was such a tally?

One's days are made up of a little of this and a little of that, all of it best forgotten. I have read that certain birds are known for the odd things they weave into their nests, some of them bright and shiny, some not. It is said that the great crested flycatcher sometimes weaves an old snakeskin into its nest. At the end of eighty years, I find no scavenged scraps of brightness in my nest. It is dull, dry, unadorned.

Memories are often touted among the aged as rescuers from loneliness, but the effort of recalling the good ones is too great. The best ones are elusive. The ones I remember offer no affirmation that my life has justified itself. So much of my eighty years is unaccounted for. The ivy of time has covered the neglected little house of my life. At no time of year is this more evident than on Christmas Day.

I knew a woman once, a fellow teacher at the last elementary school I taught in, who kept a record of her days in leather-bound diaries. I have observed that it is often not enough for such people to keep their accounts quietly; they must instead talk about their diaries constantly, citing the benefits of "living life thrice," as this woman was fond of saying—once in real time, once in writing it down, and again in reading it. She frequently referred to earlier events recorded in her diaries from past months and years, as if to demonstrate that her life was richer and fuller than anyone else's because she had *written proof* that she had lived and breathed. See here, she could say, pointing to her diary, the record says that I have gone to the supermarket, planted tomatoes, and baked cookies. I have painted my porch railing, wept over the Holocaust, and watched Neil Armstrong's one small step for man and one giant leap for mankind on my television set.

And this teacher's diaries—where are they now, I wonder? No doubt some younger relative has already come across them, pronounced them redundant for the purposes of modern living, and relegated them to their final resting place in the great trash heaps of mankind.

"DIED. FAY WRAY, 96, shriektacular heroine of the original *King Kong* and other thrillers of the early talkie era." "DIED. WIL-LIAM MITCHELL, 92, food scientist who accidentally invented Pop Rocks, the exploding candy that burst onto the market in 1975." "DIED. RODGER WARD, 83, one of auto racing's most prominent figures during the glory days of the Indianapolis Motor Speedway." "DIED. JAN MINER, 86, stage and film actress best known for her role as Madge, the manicurist in Palmolive commercials from 1966 to 1992."

How light the weight of what man leaves behind. How pitiful that a person's life may come down to so little—a scream, a candy, a speeding car, a television commercial. And these are the people judged to be famous enough for *Time* magazine.

The sky begins to lighten in the east. I am wearing a dress I have worn for four straight days. It is blue with dark spots where I have spilled my food on it. Shakespeare's second sonnet speaks of the wrinkled brow and sunken eyes of a loved one besieged by "forty winters." My winters are twice as many, the garment of my youth now "a tattered weed, of small worth held."

But enough of this, I tell myself. "Get a plan"—this was something I often heard my father say, though his own plans were most often thwarted. Rise from your chair on Christmas morning, I tell myself. Put your stained dress in the clothes hamper, from which Rachel will take it and return it spotless. Draw a bath before your breakfast arrives. These are things you can do. Then set your teeth and see the day through.

I lay my fingers to the buttons of my dress. The top one is more securely fastened than the others, the result of my recent deception and Rachel's needle and thread. It strikes me that Patrick and Rachel have taken me in as one would a stray cat, except for the fact that stray cats have no monthly social security checks to share, no inheritance to promise in return for food and shelter. They are also, I must remember, less bother than an old woman who soils her clothes and pulls off buttons.

CHAPTER 16

LIKE A RICH ARMOR, WORN IN HEAT OF DAY

The Brewer's blackbird is not easily intimidated.
It has been known to light among farmyard
chickens and drive them off, then eat their grain.
Flying in flocks of thousands, they appear to flow
through the air like a shimmering black river,
dipping and turning in unison.

With the aid of a safety bar and with the traction provided by adhesive strips, I have managed to ease myself into a tubful of brown bath water. Looking down at herself in the bathtub, an old woman's view does nothing to lift her spirits. From one extremity to the other, it is a depressing sight. However, the water is warm, the hum of the exhaust fan is low and steady, and my thoughts are singularly clear. I will get through another Christmas Day. I will bathe and dress in clean clothes; I will eat; I will watch my birds; I will breathe in and out. I will try to stay in the waiting room today. No trips to the corridor with its many uncertain cubicles.

I fix my eyes on my feet. They are not a pretty sight, yet they have served me for eighty years. One cannot demand more than dependability from servants. I keep them protected by thick socks and soft-soled slippers. Still, there is something that hurts when I walk. Perhaps it is a wart. I cannot see it. The second toe on both feet is longer than the first and overlaps it—a condition known as hammertoe. I have heard of people undergoing surgery to correct the defect, but having inherited my mother's aversion to doctors, I have never been tempted to do so.

Finding comfortable shoes has been a lifelong challenge. Had I wanted to wear fashionable shoes, I couldn't have. As I did not, I suffered no great disappointment. I left it to my sisters to wear fashionable shoes. I chose comfort instead. But my days of buying shoes are over. Morticians ask family members to bring in clothing for the burial of loved ones, including stockings and undergarments. They do not, however, request shoes. And when one is cremated, he needs no special clothes at all.

My legs have the wasted look of an invalid's. No larger than the shanks of a colt, they belie the burden they have supported through the years. Though I cannot see them now, great networks of spidery purple veins spread themselves down the backs of my legs, not from carrying children but from bearing my own weight. My eyes skim upward, passing over withered, sagging parts too sad to behold.

I move quickly over stretches of nakedness totally devoid of the appeal usually associated with the female form and come at last to the only part of my body I once thought a man could love, now simply two hugely empty bowls. When I married Eliot almost forty years ago, I imagined that he would feel great joy over such bounty. If he did, he concealed his joy. Alarm was the look in his eyes on our wedding night, as if such immoderation were a thing to be shunned.

My arms, unlike my legs, are large. When I lift them, I feel the great loose weight of flesh that has fallen away from bone. The skin of my forearms is finely wrinkled and strangely pigmented, a coat of many colors, from the palest patches of white to the dark brown spots of age. This is the body of Sophia Hess. Observe it and be instructed that time is an invincible foe.

My face I cannot see, but I know it well enough. Time has had its way there, also, though with faces it is different. Time levels facial beauty. A woman called beautiful in her youth will not be so when she is old. Put an ugly child and a pretty child side by side, add seventy or eighty years, and you will see no appreciable difference in their faces. One may have fewer wrinkles, brighter eyes, or a nicer smile, but the same adjective will be applied to both: old. My face is a map of time, many small roads crossing its planes, all leading downward. A cluster of broken blood vessels, like a tiny burst of fireworks, blooms beneath my left eye.

"DIED. ELISABETH KUBLER-ROSS, 78, Swiss-born psychiatrist whose incisive research in the 1960s demolished medical taboos against discussing death with the dying and helped establish hospice care in the U.S." In her book *On Death and Dying*, Dr. Kubler-Ross "gave permission," according to *Time* magazine, for us to "speak openly about our greatest fear." Her book described the "wondrous capacity" of the human mind "to prepare itself for dying" by progressing through five stages, beginning with denial and ending with acceptance, leading finally to "a peaceful resolution." No details of Dr. Kubler-Ross's own death are given except for the fact that she died in Scottsdale, Arizona. One must wonder if she talked candidly about her own death, if she coached herself through the five stages she identified for the world, if at the end she closed her eyes in peaceful resolution.

I think of the centenarians featured on the Discovery Channel one day last week. There are pockets of such people scattered around the globe, but the ones on this program lived in Nova Scotia. Medical researchers have studied them, trying to determine the factors contributing to their longevity. A lifetime of eating healthful foods hardly seems to be the answer, for most of the Nova Scotians supplement their seafood, a staple common to any coastal location, with traditional favorites such as buttermilk, curds, cream, bread, butter, and fried foods.

One of the men interviewed in the program had spent his life building fishing boats. This man, who was 103, looked right into the camera and said, "I've always worked hard and eaten plenty of sweets." I took heart from his words. If hard work and consumption of sweets are qualifications for living a century, I am eligible.

After almost an hour of interviews with a number of the centenarians, who routinely engaged in pastimes such as reading, piano playing, cooking, computer games, and crossword puzzles, the program concluded with this fact: Researchers are still mystified by the causes of the advanced years achieved by so many of the Nova Scotia elderly. Except for its sensationalism, therefore, the program was of little value. It was tantamount to an ogling of freaks.

The final word was "One thing is sure. Out of all the folks we talked to in this little corner of the world, there didn't seem to be an ill-tempered one in the lot. The centenarians of Nova Scotia are a contented and optimistic people, ready to share a kind word and a laugh with anyone, friend or stranger, who happens along." I did not take heart from these words. Besides the folksy, condescending tone in which they were offered, the implication was troubling. If contentment and optimism are qualifications for reaching the age of one hundred, I am not eligible. To the question "Why would anyone want to live to one hundred?" I counter with "Why would anyone want to die?"

I pick up the bar of Dove soap, with which Rachel keeps me supplied, and lather my washcloth. I take stock of my ailments on Christmas morning. I have arthritis. My shoulders and back ache. My knees are stiff. This is nothing out of the ordinary for one my age. Because of whatever is on the bottom of my foot, I limp slightly when I walk. I forget more easily than I once did. I once had a mind for names, but today I can recall the names of only a handful of my elementary students and none from my years of university teaching.

I am weak and slow. To say that I am overweight would be a kindness.

In my youth I was quite strong. When I married Eliot and moved my things to his house, he reproved me for carrying a heavy box of books by myself. "You will hurt yourself, Sophia," he said. Having carried my own boxes many times in the past, I found his remark humorous, but I obeyed when he instructed me to set the box down, then take up one end of it while he took the other. Such an arrangement of carrying was awkward and slow, but I was touched by his solicitousness. It did not occur to me at the time that he could have offered to carry the box by himself.

I have other ailments common with age, things related to stomach, bowel, and bladder that one does not like to talk about. I frequently hear a ringing in my ears. My heart often beats too fast. I sometimes must lie on my bed and breathe deeply to slow it down. When I get up, I often feel dizzy and must hold myself very still until the sensation passes. Some days I feel dizzy most of the day. My left arm throbs on cold, rainy days, perhaps a phantom pain from a shattered elbow as a child. I sometimes burp or break wind suddenly, with no warning.

Occasionally I find it hard to swallow. My vision blurs when I read for long periods of time. My hair is thin and wispy, like the underplumage of birds. From time to time patches of eczema erupt on my arms and hands. I have poor circulation in my legs and feet. My fingers are not reliable in following simple instructions. When instructed on a package to "Tear here," it is often beyond my ability.

On the other hand, I can walk, dress and feed myself, speak intelligently when I choose. I can hear reasonably well. I chew with my own teeth. I have food, shelter, and clothing. I have a thermostat by which I can keep my apartment as warm as I like. I have windows. I have a great amount of money in store.

I take my time with soap and water on Christmas morning, slowly washing my body inch by inch, for I know several days may pass before I undertake another bath. I do not set such a store on cleanliness as I once did. It comes to me that it must be getting light outdoors by now, but because I have taken myself away from my post by the bird feeder, I cannot see which bird comes first. And yet, I remind myself, this is no great loss. I would be no better off knowing such a fact than not knowing.

I wash the backs of my hands carefully. I close my eyes and feel the large ropy veins through the washcloth. Even in their youth, these were not hands that Madge the manicurist could have improved with Palmolive dish soap. Short and broad to match the rest of me, they are hands that have not shirked hard work. They are hands that wear no jewels. Though I once wore a wedding band, I had no engagement ring. I would not have been opposed to one, but Eliot neither produced one nor ever mentioned such a possibility. The wedding band he presented to me was plain but beautiful in my eyes. It was not shiny but rather a flat, scrubbed-looking gold. At some point during our marriage, it crossed my mind briefly to wonder whether this was the ring Eliot's first wife wore. I had no way of knowing, and I would never have asked.

In spite of my determination to remain in the present today, my thoughts flash, before I can retrieve them, to my second Christmas with Eliot. This is the trouble with Christmas Day. I can scrape together a few pleasant thoughts of past Thanksgivings, July Fourths, and birthdays, but not of Christmases.

Neither Portia nor Alonso made an appearance at home that second Christmas. Eliot stated that Alonso had possibly hitchhiked to Vermont to visit Portia at Middlebury, but I doubted it. Though only a year apart in age, they were not close siblings. The only interchange I had ever witnessed between the two of them took place on the back porch of their house a month before Eliot and I married. Out of my sight but not my hearing, they quarreled heatedly about who would take the car that night. It was a used car their father had bought for them to share, though the concept of sharing was one neither of them had ever learned. All manner of underhanded behavior occurred in the securing of the car keys from day to day.

On this particular night I heard sounds from the porch indicating more than just the exchange of words. I heard Alonso curse his sister with language I had never heard at his age. I heard the rip of clothing, the slap of flesh on flesh, the grunt of deeper blows received. I heard the clatter of garbage cans knocked over as the winner fled the driveway in the car. The loser, whoever it was, must have left on foot, for the porch screen slammed, and all was quiet.

This had happened some sixteen or seventeen months before my second Christmas as Mrs. Eliot Hess, however, and served only to stir my doubt that Alonso had gone to Vermont. I believed he was spending Christmas in Hillcrest, the same town where we lived, ingesting large quantities of drugs and alcohol with other young derelicts unacquainted with the words *work*, *study*, or *respect*.

School had been out for the midyear break for several days. Eliot had used those days to rework an article he was submitting to the *Michigan Quarterly Review*, a literary magazine established a few years earlier and one in which he had already published one article. This second article dealt with Shakespeare's breadth of knowledge concerning the life of a soldier in Elizabethan times. It was a brisk and sprightly manuscript, I recall, and one of which he was extremely proud upon its acceptance and subsequent publication. Though I never read *Henry V*, a quotation from the play struck me as I was typing it, for it spoke of a knowledge of more than soldiers. It spoke of a knowledge of life. "Like a rich armor, worn in heat of day, that scalds with safety." One often pays for safety with considerable discomfort. The quotation has stayed with me.

On the day I completed the retyping of the manuscript, Eliot gently took the last page from my machine and placed it with the others. Eager to get it in the mail, he addressed a large envelope and affixed the proper postage. "Come with me, Sophie, to the post office," he said, bringing my coat. When Eliot was cheerful and serene, he most often addressed me as Sophie. In his darker moods, I was Sophia. As we drove away, I tried not to look at the houses all around ours that were decorated for the holidays. Eliot didn't like to leave lights on when we were gone, even if he knew it would be dark when we returned.

We drove to the post office, after which Eliot pulled into the parking lot of a shopping center. "Shall we shop for a gift for ourselves?" he said. This was the first mention of Christmas gifts since my unsuccessful attempts of the previous year. This was the year of the coffeepot, though Eliot had not yet announced his choice to me. He was humming as we walked toward the entrance of the department store. Not a Christmas song but a favorite tune of his: "A Little Bit of Luck."

All manner of Christmas decorations were hung about the store—red and green bows, large plastic bells, gold stars, candy canes, stockings, reindeer with large red noses, and such. An enormous artificial tree stood on a pedestal inside the entrance, brightly wrapped boxes heaped beneath it. A long line of parents with small children waited for a turn with the portly man dressed as Santa Claus, who sat enthroned on a dais in the center of the store. We passed a mother stooped before her son, holding his face between her hands. "Don't be afraid, sweetheart," she said to the boy. "Just tell him what you told me. Tell him you want the bicycle so you can ride with your big sister. Santa's a nice man."

By the time we arrived in the housewares section, I felt lightheaded and heavyhearted. I found it hard to breathe. A Christmas song was playing over the sound system: "Chestnuts roasting on an open fire, / Jack Frost nipping at your nose." It was an appropriate song, I suppose, for I felt hot and cold at the same time.

Eliot chose a coffeepot he liked, and I followed numbly as he carried it to the cashier. Perhaps he asked if I liked it, too. I don't remember. I was intent on getting out of the store. As a child, I had briefly dreamed of sitting on Santa Claus's lap to tell him what I wanted. When I gave up believing in him, I had imagined that I would one day take a child of my own to visit him in a department store, then buy the requested gifts, wrap them, put them under the tree, and on Christmas morning watch my child's face as he opened them.

You are an adult woman, I told myself as Eliot paid for his coffeepot. You know that dreams are slippery things. They wriggle off the hook and disappear. And even when you are lucky enough to land one, it is usually blemished in some way. The salesclerk put the coffeepot in a bag and handed it to Eliot. As we walked back through the store, past the line of children waiting to see Santa, past the Christmas tree, I heard a new song on the intercom. It was Elvis Presley. "I'll have a blue Christmas without you, / I'll be so blue thinking about you."

I return to the world of my bathtub. The water is not so warm anymore. I hear sounds in Rachel's kitchen. Someone is up on Christmas Day earlier than usual.

I think of the dreams that are taken from women and the ones that are simply never offered. Rachel's dream was taken, mine never given. I think of the blackbirds I have read about in my book, assertive creatures that take what they want, even to the point of driving away chickens in a farmyard to eat their grain. I sympathize with the chickens, one minute contentedly pecking and the next shoved aside, watching from a distance as a flock of blackbirds takes the food meant for them. I imagine them returning to the feeding ground after the flock has lifted like a mist and flown away. I see them pecking at the hard dirt, coming up with nothing.

I release the drain of the bathtub and watch as the water slowly recedes. Soon I am sitting in an empty tub. I raise myself slowly, with great effort, and step onto the mat. As I take up my towel, I hear a knock on my apartment door. "Aunt Sophie." It is Rachel's voice. "Are you awake yet?" From farther away I hear Patrick's voice. "Merry Christmas, Aunt Sophie!" He speaks in the tone of a command, yet one cheerfully given, as if the commander is assured of ready compliance from the troops.

CHAPTER 17

O TIGER'S HEART WRAPPED IN A WOMAN'S HIDE

Whereas the woodpecker typically hops up the
trunk of a tree, the white-breasted nuthatch
moves downward, headfirst, scouring the bark
for overlooked insects and larvae. With its long
toes and hooked claws, the nuthatch always
maintains a secure hold as it probes into
crevices with its upturned bill.

At two o'clock on Christmas Day I sit at Rachel's dining room table. I am one of ten people at a table intended for eight. I have not been in such a company of people for many months. Only two hours ago Rachel informed me of the plans for Christmas dinner and requested my presence at the table. Had Patrick been the informer, I would have flatly refused. With Rachel, however, I found myself agreeing to participate in something I had no desire to do. I did not trust myself to speak after the events of the morning, and so I merely nodded stupidly and turned away from Rachel's hopeful eyes. Thus, at the appointed hour, only minutes ago, she tapped on my door again and said, "It's time for dinner, Aunt Sophie. Are you still willing to come? Shall I show you your place?"

I allowed myself to be escorted to the dining room, a room I have only walked through until now, and am seated to the left of Patrick, who occupies the head of the table. I would prefer being at the foot, next to Rachel, but I say nothing. When I arrive, everyone else is seated except Rachel, who pulls my chair out. She then walks to her own chair and nods to Patrick. There is no food on the table, but each place is set with pink and white china I have never seen. No one is talking. I avoid the eyes of the other guests, but one quick glance tells me that this is as mismatched a group of ten as has ever convened around one table.

I will start with the youngest. Veronica is sitting between her parents, Steve and Teri, on the opposite side of the table. She is in a special chair that appears to be a hybrid model. Not exactly a wheelchair and not a high chair, for it is not high. The chair is pushed back slightly from the table, and a tray is fitted to the front of it. A strap similar to a seatbelt holds Veronica in place. A neck brace keeps her head erect. She has hair like corn silk, and her eyes are wide and blue yet focus on nothing. Her mouth is open, but she makes no sound. She has the face of an angel. I imagine all the things she could have been had she been born unimpaired.

On the other side of Teri sits Mindy, the teenaged daughter. Like Veronica, she is beautiful. It is a wonder to me that such beauty has sprung from two ordinary-looking people like Steve and Teri. I suppose this is no more a cause for wonder, however, than the fact that two handsome parents like mine produced a homely child like me. Unlike Veronica, Mindy appears to be normal in every way.

Like most teenagers, she looks as if she would prefer other company than that presently gathered around this table. No doubt she is eager to get this over with. She is wearing something black. It is snug and stretchy, with only cap sleeves, but she gives no sign of being cold. Her blond hair is pulled back in a ponytail. Certainly not "gussied up," as my mother used to say. As only one other person is gussied up, however, she is in the majority at this table. She appears to be lost in thought, perhaps musing over what she will do with more interesting companions after this required activity is over.

Potts is probably a few years younger than Steve and Teri. This is the second time I have seen him. Though I may not have recognized him outside Patrick's home, I would have known his voice anywhere. He is seated on the side of the table where I am, but two people separate us. Perhaps Patrick, remembering my question about the white electrician, believes I would dislike bumping elbows with a black man over Christmas dinner. Potts is wearing a maroon sport coat and a green necktie. Perhaps Patrick failed to tell him this was a casual affair.

"That is one of the prettiest sweaters you're wearing," the woman to my left says to me. I lift my eyes to hers for a brief moment. I have never seen her before today. She and the woman next to her are closer to my age, though I estimate them to be younger by at least a decade, perhaps more. "Did Santa Claus bring it to you?" she asks. Her head is cocked toward me, and she is smiling in a childlike way. Her hair is gray—in a style my mother would have called "flyaway."

Perhaps I am staring, for she lifts a hand to pat her hair. "My hair must look a fright," she says. "The wind is sure blowing today, isn't it?" She continues patting. "I don't ever remember a windier Christmas Day."

"Yes," I say.

"I thought it was going to blow us off the road on the way over here this morning," she says. "Helena was driving, and I was wondering how she could keep the car in check, the wind was so gusty." She lays a hand across her breast and laughs. "I kept saying, 'I'm sure glad it's you driving and not me!'" She laughs again breathlessly as if she has told a funny story. This woman is wearing a red plaid flannel shirt with a blue scarf tied at the neck. Perhaps this is a new fashion, to wear flannel and silk together.

Patrick taps his glass with his fork, unnecessarily, as if there is a great hubbub at the table instead of a single dithery woman talking about the wind. "For the sake of Aunt Sophie," he says importantly, "let's introduce everyone again." I want to tell him to skip this part, but I remain silent, knowing that Patrick cannot be deterred once he has an idea. As could be expected, he makes a production out of it, announcing that he will begin with Steve and "proceed counterclockwise." He is clearly pleased with his use of the term *counterclockwise* and pauses briefly, as if hoping someone will ask what it means so that he can have the joy of explaining the way the hands of a clock move. I have observed that Patrick often believes himself the only one possessed of the simplest knowledge.

He labors through the introductions of Steve, Veronica, Teri, and Mindy, using the words *neighborliness, congenial,* and *reciprocal* in the process. When he comes to Potts, he says, "And my amiable colleague from the Main Office, Cicero Potts."

There is a sudden intake of breath from the woman on my left. "Cicero?" she says, leaning forward to look at Potts. "Is your name really Cicero? Why, I had an uncle named Cicero, but I've never met another person with that name! He was my favorite uncle when I was a girl, but he died young, of a bad case of ptomaine poisoning. It took him fast. He left a wife and four little children." She laughs as if catching herself. "But *you* look healthy as can be."

Patrick opens his mouth to resume.

"Cicero Cork, that was his name," the woman adds. "He had a little produce stand in Yazoo City, and, oh, the prettiest fruits and vegetables you ever saw!"

Patrick tries to start again. "And—"

"His wife remarried after only a few months, which at the time might have seemed hasty to some people."

Patrick clears his throat.

"But four children and no man around the house would be awfully hard for a woman. I stood up for her when people started talking. She was a real soft-spoken little thing, frail as a flower."

There is a moment of silence, and she seems to be done at last.

"And we're delighted to have Teri's aunt Helena joining us today," Patrick says. "She drove over today from Yazoo City with her friend Miss Biddle, who is seated here next to my aunt Sophie on my left." He beams at me. "What good fortune is ours to have *two* aunts at the table!"

"Oh, it's Della Boyd, please, not Miss Biddle," says the woman on my left. "I will have to insist on that."

Patrick laughs a jolly Christmas laugh. "All right then, we'll dispense with the formalities. Della Boyd it is." He gives her a little nod as if conferring a great honor.

"And then, of course, my aunt Sophie is seated here on my left," Patrick says, apparently unaware that he is repeating himself. "So now we all know each other," he says cheerfully, as if to know a person one must simply know his name. He stands up now and puts on a pair of reading glasses. "With your permission, I would like to read a few verses from the book of Luke." He does not wait for anyone's permission but picks up the Bible from beside his plate and begins reading: "'And it came to pass in those days, that there went out a decree from Caesar Augustus that all the world should be taxed. . . .'"

It is more than a few verses. He reads about Bethlehem and swaddling clothes and a manger. He reads about shepherds and hosts of angels and good tidings. He reads about Mary pondering things in her heart.

It was wise of Rachel not to have the food on the table yet. No doubt she knew it would have been stone cold by the time Patrick finished with the preliminaries. When Patrick stops and closes the Bible, Cicero Potts says, "Thank you, brother. I never grow tired of hearing that passage from God's Word."

"Oh, isn't that the truth?" Della Boyd says.

Still standing, Patrick announces his intention to "offer a word of thanksgiving for this happy occasion." He proceeds to do so in a lofty voice, calling each person at the table by name and expressing gratitude for "the incomparable blessing of these, my family and friends" and for "the repast of which we are about to partake." He has very likely rehearsed this prayer. I watch Veronica across the table. Her head is turned in Patrick's direction, yet her eyes sweep back and forth. She cannot comprehend the unbearable tediousness of the man whose voice she hears. I think of the small world in which she lives, a world she has not chosen. But who among us has chosen his world?

When Patrick at last finishes, Della Boyd says, "Well, wasn't that nice?" to no one in particular, and then, as if conversing with herself, "Yes, that was sure a nice blessing." Rachel rises and goes to the kitchen, presumably to get the food. I hope there are no further delays, for I am hungry.

Teri is fastening a plastic bib around Veronica's neck. Steve is rubbing Veronica's arm as if stroking a cat. I think of the number of hours Steve and Teri give to this child, who will never be able to give anything back. I think of the morning two weeks ago when Teri sped to the hospital with Veronica, who had gone into sudden convulsions after breakfast. I recall the great display of joy when Teri came over to tell Rachel that evening that the doctors had once again been "able to get things under control," that Veronica was back home asleep in her crib. I marvel at a love so deep that a woman whose life could only be simplified by the absence of such permanent dependence cannot bear the thought of losing her child.

I feel a hand on my arm and look down to see Della Boyd patting the sleeve of my sweater. "That is the softest, prettiest shade of gray," she says. "It's almost a blue, isn't it? Did you say you got it for Christmas?"

"No," I say, not meaning that it wasn't a Christmas gift, only that I had not identified it as such.

For it was indeed a gift. When Rachel came to my apartment this morning with my bowl of oatmeal, a cinnamon roll, and a peeled tangerine on her tray, Patrick accompanied her, bearing in front of him a present wrapped in silver foil paper with a gold bow on top. Another smaller gift, wrapped in red-and-green plaid paper with a sprig of evergreen tied on top, was sitting on the tray next to the silverware and napkin.

"Merry Christmas!" Patrick said loudly. He set the larger present on the round table.

As Rachel removed the things from the tray, setting them on the round table, also, Patrick walked over to my recliner, as if to help me up. I stood before he could do so.

He pointed to the bird feeder outside my window. "What kind is that, Aunt Sophie? Do you know?"

Though I did know, I shook my head. It was a white-breasted nuthatch. The sight of the presents had muddled my thoughts and bound my tongue. I have read of the nuthatch in my bird book. It copes skillfully in difficult circumstances. It gleans for its food in places already foraged by larger birds, finding nourishment where it can. It is used to leftovers in life. It hangs onto branches and tree trunks tightly with its curved claws and bill. I wonder what a starving nuthatch would do if it encountered a great spread of insect larvae laid out for the taking instead of hidden in the usual crevices. Out of context, would the bird recognize its favorite food for what it was?

Sometimes one is so accustomed to the mere necessities of life that he cannot comprehend liberality. Sometimes when confronted with a dream come true, one cannot take it in. Sometimes he turns from it, as from a stranger. He may even fear it.

It was Patrick who pressed me to open the presents. After I sat down at the round table, he thrust them into my hands, first the small one and then the large one. The small one was a pin, as one might wear on the collar of a blouse or the lapel of a jacket, two articles of clothing I do not own. It was a cloisonné bird with its wings outspread. No bird I can name, in a pattern of bright enamel colors. No bird in my bird book sports such plumage.

The larger gift was a sweater—coincidentally, the blue-gray of a nuthatch—with silver buttons and small pink flowers embroidered around the neck and cuffs. I had never owned such a sweater, certainly never received one as a gift. I was filled with consternation. How does one respond to such gifts? I could think of nothing to say. Perhaps Patrick and Rachel took my silence as ingratitude.

I was staring down at the sweater, and I must have been shaking my head, for Patrick said, "Is it the wrong color? Wrong size?" Turning to Rachel, he asked, "How did you decide what size to get? Can you take it back?" Then, "I don't think she likes it." He reached to take the box from me, but I clasped it to myself.

"Oh, well now, maybe she does," he said. This is something people often do around old people, talk as if they are not present, or as if they are babies or dimwits. Rachel, standing a few steps away holding the empty tray by her side, said to me, "I thought you'd look pretty in that color." Though the thought of my looking pretty in any color was laughable, her words did not sound empty. Rachel is not one for mindless talk. Perhaps she has her own definition for a common word like *pretty*.

The woman next to me is talking again. "Well, my stars, I've been so busy admiring your sweater I didn't even see *that*!" She has twisted her head around farther and is gaping openmouthed at the cloisonné bird pinned near the right shoulder of my sweater. "Why, that is so beautiful it takes my breath away! Look, Helena, can you see it? Can you see Sophie's pin? It's a work of art!" Now Helena is leaning forward trying to see the pin, and Steve and Teri are nodding and murmuring in agreement from the other side of the table. Patrick is smiling with satisfaction, proud that his gift has inspired such admiration. Potts observes that such a wonder should be passed around the table for closer inspection.

Mindy is eyeing the pin, frowning slightly, as if wondering how such a small thing, something she would never be caught wearing, can evoke such emotion from adults. Perhaps she will tell her friends about it later: "And this fat old woman was wearing this weird-looking bird pin that everybody was having a cow over!" Veronica's eyes have landed on the light fixture above the table—an imitation chandelier, though most of the people at this table would likely think of it as the real thing. One of its six bulbs has burned out.

Rachel returns with a serving platter in one hand and a bowl of gelatin salad in the other. On the platter are slices of the turkey and ham I have smelled baking in her oven since early morning. The gelatin salad is red with pieces of fruit and nuts mixed in. She hands the platter to Patrick and sets the salad on the table next to me. "Why don't we start with Aunt Sophie?" she says to him, but he has already speared a piece of turkey with the meat fork and is reaching toward my plate.

"I just love birds!" Della Boyd says. "Don't I, Helena? Don't I love birds?"

"She loves birds," Helena says dryly.

"Especially little hummingbirds. They're my special favorites. Last summer there must have been an explosion in the hummingbird population because we had them by the hundreds!" I wonder how Della Boyd has ascertained this, but I say nothing.

Steve volunteers that he has seen an owl in his backyard. Patrick shares the fact that both long-eared and short-eared owls spend winters in the Southeast.

"Why, I didn't know owls had ears," Della Boyd says. "Did you, Helena?"

No one replies to this. Mindy opens her eyes wide and stares hard at her plate, as if thinking, Is anyone at this table going to say something *normal*?

Rachel returns with two more dishes, one of mashed sweet potatoes, another of green beans.

"But then, I suppose birds have to have some kind of mechanism for hearing," Della Boyd says. "What I meant was . . ." She trails off.

Patrick explains that the owls' ears are actually only tufts of feathers that have nothing to do with their hearing.

"Well, now, *that* is certainly interesting," Della Boyd says, looking at Patrick with great awe.

And thus, seated between a great innocent and a tiresome pedant, I am served my Christmas dinner. I think of what Samuel Johnson once observed, that one does not have to travel widely to see all there is to see of humanity.

I think of the unfulfilled dreams represented in this small dining room: of children like Veronica born defective, of children like Rachel's babies born healthy but crushed in the bud, of children like Potts' son removed by distance from those who love them.

I think of the women at this table. I think of us all—of Teri and Mindy, Della Boyd and Helena, Rachel and myself. I think of the things women will do for those they love. I think of the things they suffer because of love. I think of what becomes of women who are deprived of love. I remember a line from a play. It was one of Shakespeare's Henry plays, perhaps *Henry VI*: "O tiger's heart, wrapped in a woman's hide." I wonder what the three men at this table would say were I to quote the line now. No doubt Patrick would have something educational to offer about the tiger's circulatory system.

CHAPTER 18

NOW, MUSIC, SOUND, AND SING YOUR SOLEMN HYMN

A native American legend explains the many vivid colors of the painted bunting's coat this way: The Great Spirit, when assigning colors to all the birds, failed to save enough of a single color for the last bird in line—the painted bunting. He had to make do, therefore, by using all the leftover dyes from the other birds.

D IED. YANG HUANYI, late 90s, believed to be the last writer and speaker of a rare language used exclusively by women; in Jiangyong, China." *Time* magazine calls the language Nushu, which is Mandarin for "women's script." The language, it says, was reserved for expressing the deepest woes of a woman's heart, especially in matters of love and marriage. I find this of great interest. I agree with Shakespeare that words are weak props. For so heavy a load as the heartache of women betrayed in marriage, everyday language is inadequate. Though I have never spoken of my private sorrows, like Mary I have pondered them in my heart.

Two days after Christmas I rise from my round table, having finished my midday meal—a bowl of turkey-rice soup and a ham sandwich. I recognize the turkey and ham from Christmas dinner. I have just heard Rachel on the telephone with Teri. She has called to me, telling me she will be back in an hour, that Teri needs her help.

I open my apartment door and step into the kitchen. Rachel has left the countertop cluttered with things. A small mound of potato peels sits beside a cutting board. I see something else in the kitchen that gives me pause. The wall beside the dinette table is bare. This is the wall where the four pictures of the happy darkies once hung. The cookie jar is still on the counter beside Rachel's canisters, but the pictures are nowhere to be seen. Perhaps their removal is only temporary. Maybe Patrick wants to straighten the mats and reframe them. I look in the laundry nook off the kitchen, thinking they may be leaning against the wall or stacked on the folding table, but I don't see them. But enough of snooping. I turn back to the kitchen. Perhaps Patrick has made a gift of the pictures to Potts. Patrick would be perfectly capable of such a thing.

I walk through the dining room into the living room. Patrick and Rachel's Christmas tree is still up, elevated on a table in front of the window where I like to sit. It is not much of a tree. A small artificial facsimile, it is nevertheless abundantly decorated, laden gaudily with its bells, angels, candy canes, and whatnot. A glittery plastic star is fitted onto the top. I wonder if Patrick and Rachel decorated this same tree when their children were alive, if presents for Toby and Mandy were placed beneath it.

I pull the rocking chair over and sit next to the tree. Perhaps an eighty-year-old woman sitting by a Christmas tree should be filled with a warm glow. I am not. Like most things in life, Christmas trees—to quote my father—don't amount to a hill of beans. The time for gaping in wonder over such a trifle, though a trifle I once longed for, has long since passed. How often in life we wish for things, and then, once attaining them, we have no use for them.

By moving closer to the window, I can see the funeral home with its two wreaths on the double doors. I wonder if there is a Christmas tree inside somewhere. I wonder if the staff wishes people a Merry Christmas as they come through the front door during the holiday season. I wonder if the families of the deceased ask for Christmas carols at December funerals, for red and green bows to mark the family pews.

I see a brown United Parcel Service truck pull up in front of the mortuary. A deliveryman walks to the door empty-handed and emerges, carrying a box the size of a cement block. I muse briefly over the various contents of a parcel picked up by UPS from a mortuary. Perhaps it is an urn of ashes. I would suppose most of the traffic of such an end-of-the-line business to be incoming, except of course for the very large boxes carried out by a hearse and put into the ground. I can think of no reason Wagner's Mortuary would need to package something up for shipping.

Unless perhaps a body being transported to another place for burial. My mother once told me of a woman she had known in Methuselah, Mississippi, whose burial plot was in Alabama. When she died at home, her husband put her body into her cedar hope chest, loaded it onto his pickup truck, and drove to Alabama in the middle of the night. He told no one. In the early hours of dawn, he dug the grave himself in the family plot and buried his wife. Inside the hope chest, according to the story, the woman was wearing a pink flannel night-gown and robe set. The man then drove home and called his five children, who were scattered throughout the Southeast, and told them their mother was dead and buried. "We take care of our own dead," he said when the matter came to light, when he was called into question about the legality of transporting a dead body across a state line.

The UPS deliveryman disappears into his truck and pulls away. A blue station wagon, an older model with wood-grained panels on the side, pulls into the parking lot, and a man and woman get out. The man assists the woman, who creeps along with the aid of a walker. Perhaps the old woman has cajoled her husband into coming to Wagner's to prearrange her funeral. Or perhaps the husband has done the cajoling. Perhaps they plan to prearrange both of their funerals. They use the ramp instead of the steps, and at the front door they pause briefly to study the wreaths before the man takes hold of the doorknob with both hands and opens it slowly. He cups one hand under the woman's elbow and guides her across the thresh-old.

Seconds later a portly woman in a bright blue coat comes out carrying a large red poinsettia in a green pot. She descends the steps and waddles to a yellow sports car in the parking lot and opens the door. This will be a tight fit, I tell myself. She folds the front passen-ger seat down and places the poinsettia on the floor of the back seat, then walks around to get in on the other side. The car rocks as she sits down and slowly swivels herself inside. She rummages in her purse for several seconds before finally closing the door and fastening her seat belt. When at last she starts the car and drives away, I see her hubcaps blinking with multicolored Christmas lights. Someone has gone to a lot of trouble for this effect.

I think of the way mankind uses colors to hide the emptiness of life. I place a hand over the cloisonné bird pin on my sweater. I was once especially fond of the color blue. I think now of the picture of the painted bunting in my bird book. Some of its colors, the book says, result from a kind of optical illusion rather than genuine pigmentation. The book talks of light reflecting off microscopic particles in the feathers. I think of the optical illusions in life, of the many things we think are real or important that are only imaginary, of the ways we have perfected the art of disguise. I think of the painted buntings I have known in my life, their bright colors fading as the light fell and shadows deepened. I think of how time changes all things. I close my eyes and imagine a junkyard full of the rusted hulks of yellow sports cars.

Christmas is over, but the holiday has given me much to think about. For two days now I have replayed the Christmas dinner in my mind. Over and over I hear Della Boyd's breathless exclamations and Potts' sonorous courtesies. I see Mindy's eyes imploring her mother to do something about the Meal Without End. I see Steve and Teri feeding Veronica by turns. I see them wipe her mouth and chin after each bite.

I smell the smells of Christmas dinner and taste the flavors. I feel the stiffness of the pink napkin in my lap, the lace edge of the white tablecloth. I see Rachel's soft eyes scanning the guests, intent on their needs. I hear her announcing dessert, taking orders for the two pies she has made: chocolate and coconut cream. I hear myself requesting a small slice of each. I hear Potts say, "I like Aunt Sophie's idea—I'll have the same." Though I have never had a black man refer to me as Aunt Sophie, I feel no displeasure over Potts' words. Something radiates from this man.

Rachel serves dessert with Patrick's help. She rises after everyone has finished. As she starts clearing the table, Potts joins her, quickly stacking plates and collecting silverware, as if from long experience. I hear Teri tease Steve, telling him to pay attention to how Patrick and Potts have pitched in to help.

And I hear Patrick's words after the table has been cleared.

He stood again and here is what he said: "Rachel and I want to extend our heartfelt thanks to all of you for gathering around our table today. You are each a testimony to us of God's answer to a very specific prayer of ours." I glanced at Mindy, whose lips tightened. Again she gave her mother a quick worried look. It was a look that said, *Get me out of here.*

Teri appeared not to notice, however, and Patrick sailed on. "For some time Rachel and I have felt a need to be more connected with people on a personal level. Several months ago we began talking and praying about it. We were convicted by our unhealthy isolation and our failure to obey the Great Commission." He gave no explanation of this reference to the "Great Commission," and no one asked. Della Boyd gave a sympathetic murmur at this point, the kind one gives to encourage a timid speaker to continue.

But Patrick needed no encouragement. "Last summer we began

praying," he said, "that God would open our eyes to those around us and would allow us opportunities of ministry. Our prayer was twofold: that he would direct us to people and that he would direct people to us." He paused, obviously pleased with this description of his twofold prayer, then continued. "It was less than a week later that we received a letter from my aunt Sophie concerning her need for retirement accommodations."

I refused to look at Patrick, to see the self-congratulatory beam in his eyes. Hearing his voice was enough. He went on to tell of the "honor of housing such a quiet, dignified, intelligent woman" as I, his "mother's favorite sister." I wondered if Virginia had known that I was Regina's favorite. I wondered if Regina herself had known it. I wanted to kick Patrick under the table to show what I thought of such oratorical claptrap. Again Della Boyd made an approving sound, as if tasting something warm and soothing.

Patrick moved on to describe the need he felt "to have a more compassionate outreach" with his fellow employees at the Main Office, to "view them as people with needs instead of mere workers." He expressed great joy over the fact that "God guided the footsteps of Cicero Potts right to my office door" and that "the two of us enjoy a wonderful spiritual kinship." He then exulted over the arrival of "our new neighbors across the street, the Lowes, who have allowed us the privilege of developing a friendship with them." And it was his "earnest hope," he said, that the house next door would soon sell and that God would "allow us the privilege of ministering in yet other lives." And then the other two guests—Della Boyd and Teri's aunt Helena—had to be mentioned as further proof of God's "direct answer to our prayers."

He and Rachel had wanted to have such a dinner at Thanksgiving, he said, but Rachel had taken sick and had spent Thanksgiving Day in bed. And he couldn't miss the opportunity, of course, to give himself credit for stepping in to fill the gap by bringing home takeout turkey dinners from the L & K Cafeteria. He failed to say, however, that the Thanksgiving dinner from the L & K Cafeteria was a pathetic affair, consisting of pale, undercooked turkey, a spoonful of gummy dressing, hard green peas, and a dollop of institutional-style mashed potatoes with a small craterful of congealed gravy. Dessert had been mincemeat pie. If I were to make a list of all the desserts I have ever eaten, from best to worst, that slice of mincemeat pie would be the last entry on the list.

Somehow Patrick had finally wrapped up the speech and had ended the dinner by inviting us all to "join our voices" in singing one of his favorite Christmas carols, "O Come, All Ye Faithful." Mindy shot him a look of disbelief, as if he had suggested that we all play Bingo or try yodeling.

"Why, that is such a *nice* idea," Della Boyd said eagerly. "I just love Christmas carols, don't I, Helena?"

"She starts listening to them in October," Helena said.

Della Boyd laughed. "That I do! That I do!"

Patrick was nothing if not prepared. He had printed off copies of the carol, three stanzas and the refrain, which he now distributed around the table. Rachel rose and moved to the piano, an old upright model in the living room. I had never heard the sound of the piano since coming to live here. I didn't know Rachel could play it.

And as it turned out, she didn't play well, though her playing was no worse than our singing. Except for Potts and Steve—they outshone the rest of us. After the first stanza they began to harmonize. It was clear that they both had an ear for music. Della Boyd sang the melody in a high, light voice that could have been pretty at one time. Before the last refrain I stopped singing, ashamed that I had allowed myself to be coerced into participating. What was I thinking? It was the height of hypocrisy to sing "O come let us adore Him" when I had so long ago given up adoring anyone or anything, mortal or divine.

As the others finished the song, I said to myself, *My father was right. Christmas is much ado about nothing.* I thought of the play by that name, a play that Shakespeare did not intend to be taken too seriously, and of a song near the end of it. Claudio introduces the song thus: "Now, music, sound," he says, "and sing your solemn hymn." I remembered some of the words of the song: "Midnight, assist our moan, / Help us to sigh and groan, / Heavily, heavily. / Graves, yawn and yield your dead, / Till death be uttered, / Heavily, heavily." Scholars agree that it is a song that makes no sense.

Much like "O come, all ye faithful, joyful and triumphant," an entreaty that would yield a pitifully small turnout if the truth were known. As Patrick offered a "prayer in closing," I looked around the dinner table. Who besides my nephew, I wondered, would dare to call himself "faithful"? Or "joyful and triumphant"? I looked at Veronica across the table. She appeared to be enchanted by the lingering echoes of the singing, her head thrown back and her mouth open as if she thought the music was something she might like to catch on her tongue and taste.

After Patrick's prayer, Della Boyd said, "What a nice way to end our dinner, with a Christmas carol and a prayer. I'll never forget the time I sang that same song at one of our school programs in Yazoo City. We teachers were putting on a little play for the pupils, and I had to dress up like a fairy godmother and walk across the stage singing that song." No one spoke for a moment. Perhaps everyone was trying to imagine what kind of play would have a fairy godmother singing "O Come, All Ye Faithful." Perhaps someone would have asked the question if Mindy had not suddenly risen from her chair and bolted through the living room and out the front door.

"Well, my stars," Della Boyd said. "Is she all right? Did I say something?"

Steve and Teri looked at each other. Both of them started to speak, then both stopped. Teri started to get up, but Steve reached over Veronica and touched her hand. "No, don't run after her," he said. "Give her some time. She'll be okay."

It surprised me that Patrick had nothing to say at this juncture, no word of advice, no passage of Scripture to offer. Again no one spoke for several long seconds. And then Veronica suddenly made a quiet gagging noise and promptly deposited most of her Christmas dinner onto the tray of her chair.

"Oh no!" Teri cried. Steve jumped up and pulled Veronica's chair away from the table. Teri bent over Veronica and spoke to her. "There, sweetie, it's all right." She brushed Veronica's hair away from her face. The child seemed not in the least distressed. She looked vaguely at the tray before her but appeared to see nothing. Nor did she respond in any way to her mother's words of comfort. I wonder if the ancient Mandarin language of Nushu was ever used for expressing the woes of a mother's heart whose child was beyond her reach.

"I'm so sorry," Teri said to everyone in general. "She usually only does this in the mornings. We thought she'd . . ."

Rachel stood. "Hand me the tray," she said.

"Oh no, no. I'll clean it up," Teri said. "I don't want . . ."

But Rachel stepped forward and took it out of her hands.

I see a hearse now approaching the funeral home. It pulls into the parking lot and around to the back entrance.

Patrick's words come back to me: "It was less than a week later that we received a letter from my aunt Sophie concerning her need for retirement accommodations." I turn around to look at the living room of my retirement accommodations. What a grandiose term for such a house. I take in the old piano, the faded pink sofa, the large framed print of a lighthouse, the worn braided rug, the small tacky Christmas tree. Yet I prefer the retirement accommodations here at Patrick's house over those in what they call a "home" or a "facility." Certainly I prefer them to the place across the street.

I turn back to look at Wagner's Mortuary, its wreathed doors and gingerbread trim masking the horrors that go on inside. I wonder if the old couple who went inside are touring the casket showroom yet, listening to someone describe the various features of each model. Surely not yet. Surely they save that part until last.

Suddenly a movement catches my eye. The door of Steve and Teri's house flies open, and Rachel emerges, holding Veronica. She takes the steps quickly and heads toward the street. She is walking faster than she normally walks. In spite of the burden she carries, she is in fact almost running. I realize that I am caught. At the rate she is coming, I cannot make it back to my apartment before she will arrive at the kitchen door.

I rise from the rocking chair and move it back to its place, then

stand for a moment considering what to do. Perhaps I should meet
her head on. Perhaps a plausible excuse will come to me. Or I could
stay in the living room and hope for an opportunity to slip through
the kitchen to my apartment if she should take Veronica back to the
bedrooms.

But she opens the kitchen door and calls at once, "Aunt Sophie!
We need your help!" I hear her go to my apartment door and knock,
repeating her words: "Aunt Sophie! We need you. Can you help?"

I walk into the kitchen behind her. I see her shift Veronica in her
arms, then knock again. "Aunt Sophie, are you busy?" She turns the
knob and opens the door.

"Here I am," I say.

She wheels around. She looks relieved. "We need you," she says
again. "Can you help?" She does not ask what I'm doing in the
kitchen instead of in my apartment. Something far more important
is on her mind.

I nod. "Yes, what is it?"

I hear the honk of a horn in the driveway.

"That's Teri," Rachel says. "We have to take care of Mindy. Can
you watch Veronica?"

I don't remember answering, but seconds later Rachel is gone and
Veronica is lying on my bed. She makes no sound, but her eyes rake
the ceiling. There is no sign of fear in them, however, and her lips
are parted as if preparing to comment on the wonders of a new ceiling, one she hasn't seen before.

CHAPTER 19

LIKE A FAIR HOUSE BUILT ON ANOTHER MAN'S GROUND

Bird watchers are often disappointed when they
finally see their first glimpse of the elusive
warbling vireo. Though known for possessing one
of the most beautiful songs in the bird kingdom,
the vireo has little else to distinguish it—no bright
plumage, no unusual markings, no unique habits.

I t is New Year's Eve. A time for reflecting on the past year. A time
for establishing grand and noble intentions for the coming year.
In Patrick and Rachel's case, a time for going to church for a special
prayer service. For Sophie, a time for sitting in her recliner as she
does every night. Time for watching the images on her television.
Waiting for something she cannot name. Wondering what is on the
other side of now.

I have never been to New England, but tonight I learn from *Time* magazine that there is a place in Boston called Heartbreak Hill. "DIED. JOHN KELLEY, 97, Massachusetts native who ran the Boston Marathon a record sixty-one times from 1928 to 1992." He won the race two times, once at the age of twenty-eight and again at thirty-eight. Seven times he came in second. *Time* magazine reports that the city of Boston erected a statue in John Kelley's honor in 1993 at the base of Heartbreak Hill. The obituary also tells that John Kelley carried with him a "lucky handkerchief" when he ran. I think about the irony of a statue on Heartbreak Hill in memory of a champion who carried a lucky handkerchief.

I wonder if the statue depicts John Kelley as young or old. Chances are, the sculptor aimed for middle ground. Strangely, sculpture often comes closer to depicting reality than photography. Sometimes I see a photograph beside a newspaper obituary and say to myself, "And who is this youngster? Surely this beauty is not the same ninety-year-old woman whose death is being reported." I wonder about the implication of such a picture: "This is how we want her to be remembered." If this is truly the family's sentiment, does it not seem to suggest that they want to forget all the years between then and now, which in most cases would comprise the larger portion of the person's life? Is a person in the prime of life of more value than when he is old? This is a question with a ready answer: Yes. I envision all the old people of the world gathered in one place, all of them holding signs: Dead Weight, Burden, Has-Been, Drain on Society, Albatross, Millstone, and so forth.

"DIED. RODNEY DANGERFIELD, 82, stand-up comic whose old-fashioned style of one-liners thrived in an era of hip young satirists." His signature line, "I don't get no respect," will long be remembered, according to *Time* magazine. I think of all the comedians who have used old people as the target of their humor. At least Rodney Dangerfield, an old man himself, knew what he was talking about.

But as my mother used to tell me regularly, getting old is not funny. With her frequent reminders, I began to brood over my own advancing years. Having no children, I began to wonder who would take care of me when I got old and sick. Marrying Eliot distracted me somewhat from these concerns; however, since he was older than I by many years, occasionally I imagined the grim possibility of nursing an aging mother and a husband at the same time.

I think of the way people look past an old person, as if seeking someone younger and therefore more interesting to talk to. I think of how they smirk or yawn when an old person speaks, of how they discount the plain truth when it comes from the mouth of someone whose body is feeble, as if body and mind are one. I recall how my college students used to pass me on campus without a word of greeting. In their eyes I ceased to exist outside the classroom. I think of store clerks speaking their words loudly and slowly as if dealing with an imbecile or lapsing into a bored, mechanical delivery of their standard lines. I think of Mindy on Christmas Day, sitting at the dinner table with a look on her face that said, "Don't talk to me and don't expect me to talk to you."

Mindy's trip to the emergency room of King's Daughters Hospital four days ago resulted in this: Her stomach was pumped. This Rachel told me when she returned three hours later. Mindy's emotional distress of late is due to more than teenage moodiness, I have learned. It is due to a boy. A boy of whom her parents do not approve—a condition, I have noticed, that almost always leads to greater attraction between a boy and girl. Forbidden desire always burns hotter.

Steve and Teri have told Mindy she must give up the boy. They have told her she may not be with him, a difficult prohibition to enforce since the two of them attend the same school. Steve and Teri have requested the aid of the high school personnel to keep them separated, have asked to be called whenever Mindy does not report to her classes on time. The holidays have been full of turmoil for Mindy, being "stuck at home" and "watched like a hawk," as she puts it.

All of this was reported to me by Rachel when she came to my apartment to get Veronica and take her back home. For over three hours Veronica had lain silently on my bed, drooling onto a large bib around her neck. Part of the time I sat beside her and stroked her arm, though she gave no sign that she was aware of my presence. She finally fell asleep. She continued to drool in her sleep and several times jerked and grimaced. I wondered if a child like Veronica ever dreamed. What would she dream about? I have read that dreams are necessary for life.

I have not seen Mindy for a week, not since Christmas Day. I think of the trouble she is going through. I know what she thinks: that if she could have this boy, life would be a glorious thing. I want to tell her to listen to what grown-ups have to say about the false hope of young love and the speed with which "bright things come to confusion," as Shakespeare described it. I want to tell her that even in Shakespeare's time romance without the blessing of one's parents was never portrayed as happy. These words would fall on deaf ears, however. Even if she were to hear them, Mindy would consider the sources—an old woman and a dead playwright—and count them of no merit.

The house is quiet. It is almost eight o'clock. I take the *Time* magazine from my lap and drop it in the trash can, then turn up the volume on the television. I will see what my fifty-one channels have to offer on New Year's Eve. Patrick has given me a recommendation. I want to ignore it because of the imperious way in which it was given, but I suspect I shall look into it, out of curiosity if nothing else.

Patrick came in with Rachel earlier tonight, when she brought my supper tray. "Aunt Sophie," he said briskly, "we want you to come with us tonight. We don't like to think of you sitting at home alone on New Year's Eve."

"Then don't think of it," I said.

"Go with us," he urged. "It won't be a long service, and then there will be sandwiches and desserts and games. You'd enjoy it."

The idea of Patrick's presuming to tell me what I would enjoy rankled me. "I am well accustomed to sitting at home alone," I said. "That is what I enjoy. It suits me. New Year's Eve is no different from any other day. It is only a day on the calendar."

Rachel set a plate of meat loaf, black-eyed peas, and collard greens on the round table. I was pleased with the prospects, as my father used to say when Mother served collard greens at dinnertime. Though a native of New York, Daddy had taken to southern food with gusto, collard greens, corn bread, and black-eyed peas being three of his favorites.

"Well, then," Patrick said, "if you insist on staying home, you need to watch something at eight o'clock. It's a movie you'll like. It's on channel 35." I told him I did not watch movies, but he brushed me off. "This is one you need to see," he said. "It reminds me of Mother every time I see it. You'll see. You'll like the story." I instantly made up my mind not to watch it, or at least not to like it.

At precisely eight o'clock I turn to channel 35 to see what it is that reminded my nephew of his mother—my sister Regina.

Driving Miss Daisy is the name of the movie. Miss Daisy is Daisy Werthan, an elderly Jewish woman who lives in the South. I see at once why she would have reminded Patrick of his mother. Miss Daisy is a fine-boned woman with aristocratic carriage and strict standards of propriety. Though Patrick didn't mention this, I see also that Daisy's son, Boolie, and Patrick are alike in certain ways. Boolie speaks loudly and likes to take over. Like Daisy Werthan, Regina, though only a quarter Jewish, also employed a Negro man for many years, a man everybody in Vicksburg called Lingo.

Lingo drove Regina to the grocery store, to the meetings of her various clubs, to the doctor, to the library, and to Monk's Department Store, where she worked four hours a day on the lingerie floor. Lingo also took Regina to both of her divorce hearings and waited for her out in the hall, then escorted her to the car and drove her home by way of the Dee-Lish Drive-in, where she ordered a chocolate malt both times. When Regina reported this fact to me after the second divorce, she said, "I think I'll get a regular milkshake next time. I'm losing my taste for malt." Her third husband died before she could divorce him, however, and by that time she had lost her taste for marriage, also. She lived as a widow for the remainder of her life.

Though Miss Daisy's story is a good one, I keep losing track of the plot as I think about Regina. She was "unlucky in love"—this is how my mother referred to her and her three marriages. There was a time when I had no patience for Regina and her marital failures. This was before I married Eliot. Now I know how easy it is to misplace one's affections. I am reminded of the answer to Falstaff's question in *The Merry Wives of Windsor*: "Of what quality was your love, then?" The reply: "Like a fair house built on another man's ground; so that I have lost my edifice by mistaking the place where I erected it." So much is lost for all time when one mistakes the placement of his love.

Regina had two children, both sons, but she never understood either of them. One didn't graduate from high school, and the other one turned religious on her. It was Lingo who found her dead on the floor of her kitchen when he arrived one morning to take her to the department store. After her death Patrick discovered a drawerful of unpaid bills. He learned that she had not paid Lingo for over a year. At her funeral Lingo was a pallbearer. Lingo and five white men. I believe out of all the men in Regina's life, Lingo was perhaps the one who loved her most.

Before I know it, Miss Daisy and Hoke are very old in the movie. The world has changed around them, but they are still together. When Hoke comes to her house one morning, Miss Daisy has lost touch with reality. She believes she is a young schoolteacher with papers to be graded. The final scene shows Hoke visiting Miss Daisy in a nursing home, feeding her a piece of pie. The pleasures in Miss Daisy's life have diminished themselves to Hoke and pie.

The movie ends and an advertisement for Hardee's hamburgers comes on. So much of life comes back to food. I turn down the volume. I think of something I heard my small-minded nephew say recently through the kitchen wall. He was talking to Rachel at supper. "Just think!" he said. "God didn't have to give us all these different things to eat—all the different flavors and textures and colors. He could have made it so that we just had to eat a brown pill every day or a fistful of grass to stay alive. Or he could have dispensed with the idea of food altogether and made our sustenance dependent on something else—like a special beam of light or dipping your finger in water or rubbing a stone over your forehead."

"Or nothing at all," Rachel said.

"Well, yes, exactly!" Patrick said. "God being God, he could have just made these mortal bodies to keep on ticking without needing any fuel at all! But he didn't. He gave us the pleasures of taste and all this wonderful *variety*!"

And Patrick being Patrick, I thought, he will keep expanding upon this subject for the rest of the meal. He proceeded at once to prove my prediction true as he moved on to remark upon the marvels of variety in every food group, starting with the carbohydrates. He used the principle of variety to prove the existence not only of "a divine intelligence so vast as to defy the most brilliant human mind" but also of "a broad imagination and a profound capacity for fun." If there is a God in heaven, I am sure he must be honored to know that Patrick Felber admires his intelligence, his imagination, and his capacity for fun.

The television screen suddenly fills with images of faces, too many to number, superimposed upon one another in continuous succession. A title finally appears: *THE YEAR IN REVIEW.* I can only suppose that channel 35 means to rehash the old year on the eve of the new one. It is a merry-go-round I do not care to ride tonight. The faces continue fading in and out. It is a wonder that Patrick's recent speech, instead of stopping with food, did not proceed to Part Two: The Amazing Variety of People. Perhaps it would have if Rachel hadn't suddenly begun coughing, if he hadn't broken off with "Is something wrong? Are you all right? Here, take a drink of your tea."

I can hear him now: "Just think! God didn't have to populate the world with such a variety of heights and weights and hair and eyes— and *races*! He could have made us all exactly alike, with a different number stamped on everybody's hand! But he didn't. He made you and me and Steve and Teri and Aunt Sophie and Potts and billions of others, all of us different from each other!"

I think of Eliot and Toby and Mandy and Veronica and Mindy. Yes, his divine intelligence and broad imagination made it all. He made perverted men and kidnappers, he made deformed children, he made teenagers so heartsick they mix rat poison into a cola and drink it.

I change the channel to the TV Oldies and find that tonight there is a marathon of *Gilligan's Island* episodes. I find no more plea- sure in the thought of watching Gilligan and the Skipper on New Year's Eve than of sitting through a review of the past year. I turn to the Nature Channel and find a program already in progress concern- ing the emperor penguin. An Antarctic bird, it is not featured among the six hundred species in my bird book. This is not a bird I will see at my feeder.

"In temperatures of forty degrees below zero, the father penguin balances the egg on his feet and keeps it warm with a flap of belly skin." This is what I hear on the television. Imagine this, a father incubating his young. A picture of nesting penguins, apparently males, appears on the screen. They are huddled together over a field of ice—hundreds of black and white roly-polys peering out of masked faces, sitting patient and motionless.

"Meanwhile," the voice continues, "the mother penguin is away for two months, feeding in the ocean." I smile at the thought of the mother penguins frolicking on the beach while the men stay home to mind the eggs.

The program goes on to describe the different species of penguins besides the emperor penguin: names such as the rock hopper, the yellow-eyed, and the jackass. I am struck again with the connected-ness of life as Patrick's voice, unbidden, fills my mind: "All this wonderful variety!" it says. "What divine intelligence! What an imagination! What capacity for fun!"

As much as I want to dismiss Patrick's words as so much blather, I feel the weight of their truth sinking into my heart. More than once I have leafed through the last section of my bird book, some thirty pages titled "Special Collection," filled with pictures of birds described as "rarities with restricted ranges and specialized habitats," whose "very elusiveness only adds to the pleasures of encountering them." The elegant trogon, the mangrove cuckoo, the brown noddy, the wandering tattler, the hoary redpoll. So many different kinds.

Had I not heard Patrick's speech to Rachel, perhaps I would never have thought to ask the question that comes to me now: Why? Why would a designer make so many variations of a single thing? Did he simply get carried away? He could have made all birds small, plain, and timid and stopped at that. But even among the small, plain, and timid, there is remarkable variety. My book shows thirty-two species of sparrows. It shows a bird called the warbling vireo—a rarely sighted grayish olive bird with no special markings, no wing bars, no vivid colors, no wattle or crest, its sweet melodious song its sole distinguishing feature. I used to think that I, though lacking physical charms, possessed a beautiful song. That time is past.

The voice on the television says, "The dense feathers on a penguin's body, around eighty per square inch, insulate it from the extreme Antarctic temperatures." I hear the pop of firecrackers nearby and turn my eyes to the darkened window. As New Year's Eve approaches the midnight hour, I sit in my recliner staring out into the black night, watching the burst of colors in the sky and thinking about the designer of the universe, who gave his smallest creatures claws and beaks, feathers and camouflage colors, and wings to fly from trouble. I think about the ways man tries to insulate himself against the extremes of life. And I think about death, the ultimate extreme of life, against which there is no insulation.

CHAPTER 20

AND THEREFORE IS WINGED CUPID PAINTED BLIND

———

Few people have seen the brown creeper and still
fewer have identified it. A small bird with a
curved beak, the creeper searches for food by
spiraling upward on a tree trunk and then
fluttering, leaflike, down to the base of the next
tree. Though it can be a sociable bird, it
most often feeds alone.

Patrick's earlier warnings concerning the malfunction of the furnace have materialized into reality. In the middle of January it is clear that the unit will no longer hobble along until spring. It must be replaced. That this is an inconvenience goes without saying. At eighty, I have no pioneering spirit. I desire heat, a great deal of it, especially in midwinter. Patrick and Rachel have apologized profusely. Rachel I instantly forgave. Patrick I hold responsible for the lack of foresight that impinges on my comfort.

It is early morning, but I have been awake for over an hour. I am sitting in my recliner with an electric blanket draped over me. The radio announces the temperature to be thirty-seven degrees. The thermostat in my apartment shows it to be sixty-eight. Patrick knocks on my door and calls out, "I have heaters, Aunt Sophie! May I come in?" He brings two portable electric heaters into my apartment, plugs them in, and turns them to high. "There now," he says, rubbing his hands together, "these will keep you toasty for the next three days until we're up and running." Because of the ailing furnace, I have not felt toasty for weeks.

Men are coming today to begin the project. Today they will tear out the old ductwork, tomorrow they will install the new, and the next they will get the furnace in place and turn it on. This is the plan. We shall see. I know all about the schedules of workmen, which must almost always be multiplied by three concerning time and by even more concerning disruption and untidiness. As for cost, I have heard Patrick tell Rachel they will take out a home equity loan.

In addition to the portable heaters he has borrowed, Patrick now sets about laying a fire in the wood stove in the kitchen before he leaves for work. He tells me that the wood stove has a powerful blower that "puts out heat like you won't believe"—heat that I will feel if I leave my door open. I can see him through my apartment door, which stands open. The wood stove, which is a fireplace insert, has never been put to use since I have been here, though Patrick tells me that it was one of the features of which he was most fond when he bought the house.

"We quit using it six or seven years ago," he says, his back toward me. As always, he is talking more loudly than necessary. "I got to thinking maybe it was one cause for Rachel's having such respiratory problems every winter. Somebody suggested maybe she was allergic to woodsmoke, so we decided to give it a try." He pauses. "I can't say it changed much," he says, "but we just never got back in the habit. Besides, we ran out of wood, and I never did get it restocked." All this he tells me as he squats in front of the wood stove, arranging oak logs donated by Steve and kindling in the form of wadded newspaper.

Rachel comes to my door in her brown flannel bathrobe. She is carrying the tray with my breakfast on it. At the round table she removes the dishes one by one—a bowl of cream of wheat, a large biscuit on a saucer, a poached egg on another saucer, and a mug of hot cocoa. She sets a small pitcher of milk beside the bowl and a jar of red jelly next to that, then neatly lays my silverware and napkin side by side. From across the room she lifts her eyes to mine for a moment before she takes the tray and leaves. Rachel never says, "Good morning," for which I am thankful, but when she brings my breakfast she always looks at me with what appears to be kindness in her eyes.

Perhaps it is Patrick's mention of Rachel's past respiratory problems that triggers a thought. It now comes to me that Rachel may be seriously ill. She has taken to her bed off and on since I came to live here, more frequently of late. Though she always gets up again and resumes her duties, I realize now that she never fully recovers from whatever it is that weakens her. I try to remember how she looked when I visited last summer and then when I first arrived last fall. I study her now and try to compare the Rachel of mid-January with those other ones. Too many days have passed, however, and I cannot remember the other ones.

"There," says Patrick in the kitchen, "I've got it going now." He raises his voice even more. "We'll leave your door open, Aunt Sophie, so you can feel the heat, too." He has already told me this. To Rachel he says, "You can put another log on whenever these burn down some. I'll leave some right here in this bucket." I hear several heavy clunks, then the clicking on of the blower. Patrick runs water at the sink, tells Rachel it will be a busy day at the Main Office because of a computer sale. "Well, let me put it this way," he says. "I *hope* it will be a busy day!" He tells her about several good buys— "deep discounts," he calls them. At last he goes to the door to leave. "I'll call later to check on things," he says to Rachel. "We'll need to eat early tonight, remember. I have my first class." I imagine Rachel nodding mutely to her husband. I think of the long patience of her life, a life as devoid of real pleasure as a woman's life can be.

And still Patrick does not leave. "I sure wish I could stay till they get started under the house," he says at the door. "I was hoping they'd already be here by now." Another pause. "At least it's not as cold as they'd predicted for today. You should stay plenty warm." No response from Rachel. These also are things Patrick has already said this morning. "Well, okay, I guess I'm going now," he says, then adds, "If you talk to Teri today, tell her the wood is great, okay? Hard and dry—the best kind. Tell her I'll get Steve some more." He pauses again, then thinks of something else. "You all right? Did you sleep last night?" Then, "I won't go tonight if you're not feeling good. I can stay here and get something together for supper if you need me to."

"No, no. You go on now," Rachel says mildly. "I'm fine. I can take a nap later."

"Why don't you go back to bed now?" he says. "The furnace men will be under the house. They won't need to talk to you. I made sure of that yesterday. I covered all the bases with them."

"I've got a few things to do," Rachel says. "I'm making a cake for tomorrow night."

"Can't it wait till tomorrow?" Patrick says.

"I'm helping Teri tomorrow," she says.

"What kind of cake?" he asks. I wonder if Rachel ever imagines doing harm to this man. I picture her throwing the bucket of logs at him now, shouting, "Leave the house right this minute! Quit hanging around repeating yourself and asking stupid questions!"

"It's just a Bundt cake," she says. "Chocolate sour cream. It won't take long."

Finally the door closes, and Rachel is left in peace.

Only days ago I read this in one of Patrick's discarded issues of *Time* magazine: "DIED. H. DAVID DALQUIST, 86, inventor of the Bundt pan, the world's top-selling baking pan." Again I am struck with the many connections between the world at large and my small one on Edison Street. I wonder if this perception speaks of the broadening of my mind or, rather, of its constriction. At the age of eighty, is it possible for one to enlarge the landscape in his mind, or does he merely keep cluttering it with more details until at last they all overlap? Who can answer such a question? I rise from my recliner. At this moment my world is a still life: a small breakfast on a round table.

I feel the heat from the wood stove wafting through my apartment door. I smell it, too. It is a pungent smell, not unpleasant, yet one I have not missed. Both my father and Eliot considered the keeping of a fire to be a messy business, more trouble than it was worth. Having never gotten used to a fire and having no nostalgic associations with one, I have never felt its absence. I laid only one fire in my life, in Eliot's study after his accident. It was a brisk, hot fire, soon burned down to only the smallest scattering of ashes. A paper fire burns briefly, without the spice and elegance of a wood fire.

At the table I press my fork against the poached egg until the yolk breaks. Rachel has once again achieved the right doneness. The yolk must not run but neither must it be hard. As I lift the fork to my mouth, I allow myself to imagine what would happen, specifically what would happen to me, if Rachel were to be critically ill. In choosing family members almost thirty years my junior with whom to spend the winter of my life, I never thought of their falling sick or becoming disabled.

But I should have. I should have made backup plans, for I know how speedily things may change. I turn to look toward the window that frames my bird feeder. This is my picture of the world. The trees in the backyard, so full of color when I came in the fall, are now only dry skeletons, their leaves like loose scraps of music swept away by the winter wind. I think again of the words of the sonnet: "Bare ruined choirs where late the sweet birds sang."

And yet I hear Rachel moving about in the kitchen, humming. I cannot name the song. It is something plaintive, meditative. Or perhaps it is not meditative at all. Perhaps it is the opposite, the kind of tuneless noise one makes to fill up silence. It is unlike Rachel, however, to fill up silence. I hear stacking and clinking sounds. She is unloading the dishwasher. I try to decide whether she is moving more slowly than she used to, but I cannot say. Perhaps she wears her brown bathrobe later into the day than she used to, but again I can't be certain. I think she may lie down during the afternoons, for sometimes I don't hear her for long hours at a time. Yet perhaps she has always done this, and I am only now noticing it.

On the other hand she talks to Teri every day and often walks across the street to see her in the early afternoon. I heard her on the telephone just yesterday saying to someone, "We can have it here next week. Okay. I'll tell Patrick." If she is seriously ill, she isn't surrendering. I have read of a bird called the brown creeper, a bird which most often keeps to itself, though it is capable of socializing.

Rachel coughs. Perhaps the smell of the woodsmoke will not be good for her. I am finishing my egg when she appears at my door with the laundry basket on her hip.

"I have a few white clothes to do. May I check your hamper?" she asks.

I nod. Perhaps I should laugh at her politeness. Perhaps I should gently mock her: "Yes, Rachel, I grant you permission to check my hamper for soiled underwear and then to wash it in hot, soapy water."

She opens the lid of the hamper and gazes inside for a moment, then bends to retrieve what is there. No doubt she realizes that I take care to soak and rinse out the worst things. These I hang in the bathroom to dry before placing them in the hamper. Sometimes they are still damp when I transfer them.

I am spreading jelly on my biscuit as she passes the table on her way out. An impulse seizes me, and words come out of my mouth: "Did you know that the man who invented the Bundt pan died?"

She stops and looks at me as if doubly surprised—at the question itself and at my asking it.

More words flow from my mouth: "*Time* magazine says that the pan became popular in 1966, when a woman in Texas used one for her second-place entry in a Pillsbury contest."

I can't remember hearing Rachel laugh, but she does so now. It is a hesitant, low-pitched laugh, as if venturing out from cramped quarters. She glances over to the bookcase shelf where the issues of *Time* are stacked. "I was going to ask you if you wanted me to throw those out," she says, "but then I didn't. I thought you might be reading them."

I nod and take a bite of my biscuit, which is still warm. She has no doubt seen copies in the trash can and others folded back beside my chair.

"What kind was it?" Rachel says. "The cake that won the contest."

"It looked chocolate in the picture," I say. "But it didn't win. It was second."

Suddenly we hear men's voices. "They got electric down there?" one of them yells.

"Yeah, guy said look right by the crawl space door." Through one of my windows we see two men appear around the corner of the house, scruffy and unshaven, exactly the types you'd expect to make a living crawling under houses. They come to a stop in the backyard, and one of them spits something dark onto the ground. A third follows, wearing a ball cap and sweatshirt. He is a giant of a man, built better for standing upright than for crawling around in close quarters. His belly sags over the top of his pants, and he walks with a ponderous, stiff-legged waddle. It is not hard to imagine this man sitting on a barstool for hours at a time over a succession of cheap beers.

The fat man points to the crawl space door and talks to the other two with a supervisory air. One of them disappears through the crawl space door and calls out, "Yeah, it's here."

Rachel sighs. "I'll sure be glad when all of this is over," she says. At the door she stops and turns back to me. "I hope you don't mind about leaving your door open. Maybe with the two heaters you wouldn't need to, but . . ."

I shake my head. "We shall see how it goes." By this I could mean many things, but what I do mean is this: Nothing is easy. We must do what is necessary. I, too, will be happy when it is done. In the meantime my first consideration is my own comfort. If that means leaving the door open, I will tolerate it.

Both workmen are under the house now, and the fat man calls down through the crawl space door. "I'll be back in a coupla hours! Y'all got the cell if you need me." He stands for a moment, digging at a back tooth with a hooked finger, then lumbers off around the corner of the house.

"These men gave us the best bid," Rachel says, as if to explain the ragtag look of the three.

"I hope they will do the best work," I say. "Patrick's first concern should not always be the cost."

She leaps to her husband's defense. "Oh, Patrick asked a lot of questions about them," she says. "People gave real good recommendations. Patrick wouldn't go for something just because it was the best price." Her eyes cloud as if she might cry. I have no idea why she should cry.

I look away quickly and take another bite of my biscuit. Another connection comes to me: "DIED. JANE MUSKIE, 77, widow of Edmund Muskie, whose 1972 presidential campaign derailed after he appeared to cry in defending her against a newspaper editorial; in Bethesda, Md." According to *Time*, when the editor of a newspaper claimed that Mrs. Muskie smoked and told dirty jokes, her husband choked up at a news conference and called the editor a "gutless cow-ard." People seemed to lose interest in Edmund Muskie becoming president after that.

Though so many things have fallen from my mind, I clearly remember the incident, which I read about in the newspaper. I was forty-six, a bride of four years. I recall being embarrassed for Edmund Muskie but at the same time envying his wife, for surely his tears spoke of a love I did not know. Only days earlier I had approached Eliot's office at South Wesleyan in time to hear him say over the telephone, "Oh no, no, certainly not. Sophia is a good woman, but she is no scholar. She could never teach above the freshman level. Her mind runs in very small, simple circles." I never knew to whom he was speaking, but I had no doubt that the words were spoken of me. I knew of no other Sophia in Eliot's life.

When I read of Edmund Muskie's defense of his wife, I tried to imagine what Eliot would have said had someone accused me of lik-ing cigarettes and dirty jokes. Perhaps this: "Well, frankly, I'm not surprised. Such things are to be expected of simpleminded women like my wife." He would have been dry-eyed, disapproving, regretful that my low behavior reflected poorly on him.

I said nothing to him about what I had overheard. When he fell ill one day the next week, he gave me his class notes and kindly instructed me to deliver his lecture in an upper-level seminar on the Lyrical Plays of Shakespeare. By this time I had served as his substi-tute on more than one occasion. I was tempted to say to him that day, "Why don't you get a scholar to teach your class, someone who is qualified to teach above the freshman level?" But I did not. I took his notes and conducted his class. For an hour his students listened to me and took notes, not recognizing the small, simple circles of my mind.

Though so much of my teaching is lost in the fog of the forgotten, this I recall as if it happened yesterday: When a girl stood that day and read aloud Helena's speech in act 1 of A *Midsummer Night's Dream*, my heart twisted at the lines "Love looks not with the eyes, but with the mind; / And therefore is winged Cupid painted blind." It was a hard thing to suspect that my husband had never felt the arrow of winged Cupid, that his mind did not reshape and color the deficiencies his eyes saw, that he looked at me through his small round glasses and knew me exactly as I was—short, stout, homely, simpleminded, serviceable.

When the girl finished reading the speech, I stared at the page until the shuffling of feet reminded me there were others in the room. At last I found my place again in Eliot's notes and continued his lecture. At some point I broke off abruptly and interjected, quite heatedly, a thought of my own: "Some may think that Helena was a fool to continue to love Demetrius. He had already proved himself false by transferring his affection to Hermia." I then continued with Eliot's lecture.

"And therefore is Love said to be a child, / Because in choice he is so oft beguiled." These words are spoken by Helena, also. In love I was a child. Throughout our marriage I found ways to excuse my husband's failings. I looked at Eliot and saw a great intellect, a truthful soul, a noble heart, a gentle spirit. And then at the end of my service, I saw that he was none of these things, that I had loved blindly. Like the story of Pyramus and Thisbe, a most lamentable comedy.

"Would you like me to wash your sweater, Aunt Sophie?" Rachel asks. She is standing at the doorway still, the laundry basket in her hands. She is looking at the gray sweater I am wearing, the same one I have worn almost daily for three weeks, the bird pin still affixed to it.

"No," I say quickly.

"I could have it back in just a little while," she says.

"No," I say. "It gives me a little happiness and tranquility."

Rachel smiles a puzzled smile, unaware that I have stolen the words of a dead artist. "DIED. AGNES MARTIN, 92, reclusive abstract painter whose spare yet soulful geometric grids strove to induce nothing grander than, in her words, 'a little happiness [and] tranquility.'" *Time* magazine says that Agnes Martin was fond of the color gray. She lived in the desert regions of New Mexico.

"Okay, another day then," Rachel says. "I wouldn't want to take away your happiness and tranquility." She smiles again and leaves. Moments later I hear her start the washing machine. I think of Rachel and her silent walk through life. I think of my own solitude. I look at the open door between the two of us. I take up my cup of hot cocoa and find it has cooled sufficiently. I drink it slowly, imagining a mirage in the desert—a lush green oasis with a sign: Welcome to Happiness and Tranquility.

CHAPTER 21

AND WHEN HE FALLS, HE FALLS LIKE LUCIFER

The eastern kingbird perches boldly in the open, surveying its domain and squawking strident challenges to the world at large. During nesting season it is especially watchful and contentious, attacking squirrels and other birds that come too close to its young. Appropriately, its Latin name, tyrannus tyrannus, means "tyrant of tyrants."

I lie in my bed at daybreak watching the walls of my apartment emerge from the shadows. One day follows another, all of them alike. On the wall beside my bird window is a calendar featuring pictures of wildlife, but I cannot see it from my bed. It would not matter if I could. Looking at the calendar would not tell me what day it is. Nor do I care. I know it is still January, and I have a vague sense that it is approximately midway between Sundays. I know that the green tips of daffodils are pushing through the earth in the backyard.

The calendar was given to me by Patrick, who also hung it on my wall. It is an advertising tool for his place of employment, with the words MAIN OFFICE SUPPLY prominently printed on each page. It is the kind of calendar a man of narrow perceptions like Patrick would select, for each animal is linked with a human characteristic, which the animal supposedly illustrates. The linkages, neatly summarized in captions, are proof of man's ignorance in general and Patrick's in particular. For January I am informed by means of the calendar that the eastern hognose snake demonstrates "Quick Thinking in Times of Danger," and I have already looked ahead to see that February's caption praises the wolverine for "Concentrating on the Work at Hand."

A bird is cheeping outside my window. It is one I have heard and seen often, though I have not yet identified it in my bird book. It is in the sparrow family, of that I am quite certain, yet it is fatter than the chipping sparrow, more like the Savannah sparrow though lacking the streaked pattern on its underside.

It sits on a branch calling tirelessly: Cheep, cheep, cheep, cheep! Its cries cannot be driven by hunger or thirst, for Patrick has refilled the seed in the feeder, and there is water in the drainpipes and hollows where ice has lately melted. It is an ambiguous call. One could interpret it as a cheerful greeting of dawn, I suppose, an eagerness to get the business of the day underway. On Patrick's calendar, perhaps it could illustrate "Looking Ahead to the Bright Unknown."

Or perhaps the bird is an alarmist, worried over some small imagined danger. Or perhaps he is the equivalent in the feathered kingdom of the person who seeks attention: "Here I am! Look at me!

Listen to me!" Perhaps he is a complainer: "It's too cold! It's too quiet! It's too dark!"

One could amuse himself by imagining that the sparrow is mischievous, that perhaps he understands man's penchant for asking why and the compulsion of a small mind—like that which conceived the calendar—to interpret all things in relation to itself. Perhaps the bird cheeps only as a prank, providing one more unknowable for foolish men to pursue.

Perhaps the bird is this, perhaps that—more evidence of small-mindedness, this time my own, in trying to ascribe a humanly comprehensible motive to a bird's cry. My nephew is rubbing off on me, as they say. The sparrow cheeps, I tell myself, because he is made to cheep. He does not feel anxiety or alarm. He does not tease or reason. He flies through the air, lands on a branch, and opens his bill. Streams flow into rivers, seeds sprout into plants, and birds cheep.

A light comes on in the kitchen, and I hear Patrick running water to make coffee. The wood stove door squeaks as he opens it to make a new fire. The old fire has burned down during the night. Though the wood stove and two electric blankets on my bed have supplemented the portable heaters in my apartment, they have not been enough to ward off the cold for the past four days. Perhaps the sparrow outside my window is urging optimism: It could be worse! Be patient! Things will get better! As I suspected, the furnace project has extended beyond three days. As the fifth day begins, perhaps the sparrow is reminding Patrick that the lowest price does not translate into the best job: Cheap! Cheap! Cheap!

And how long, I ask myself, do you mean to lie in bed projecting your thoughts into the mind of a bird? I rise and sit on the edge of my bed for a moment, allowing the dizziness to pass before I stand slowly. I look toward the open door and marvel that such a simple thing—an empty space, really—can touch all of one's senses. I think of the things besides heat that have come through it since the latest episode at Patrick's house began: the one titled The Three Stooges Install a Furnace.

Through the open door I have heard about Patrick's first evening class at the community college. The word *summary* is meaningless to Patrick, who must have repeated every word the professor said that night as well as a great many he didn't. When he began explaining to Rachel the location of the classroom and the style of desks within it, I went into my bathroom, turned on the fan, and ran water into the tub to block out the sound of his voice. The exertion of taking a bath is to be preferred over that of listening to Patrick.

Patrick has decided to take two night courses at the college: one called Introduction to Literature—though he has expressed reservations about needing to be "introduced to something I am already acquainted with"—and another called Creative Writing 101. The prospect of hearing his pontifications on literature for months to come is a grim one, but not as grim as the thought of his reading aloud his compositions. I long for the completion of the furnace project so that I may shut the door of my apartment again. I imagine my nephew's words as truckloads of Styrofoam peanuts used as filler. I see myself packed inside a cardboard box, surrounded by his words, all of them lightweight, uniform, disposable, suffocating.

Through the open door I have witnessed, also unwillingly, the proceedings of what was referred to as a "cottage prayer meeting" held in Patrick and Rachel's kitchen three nights ago. The concept of the small-group meetings, Patrick informed me, is a new one for their church. He has been appointed "shepherd" of his group, a fact that he reported to me with a great show of humility.

On the evening of the cottage prayer meeting, Patrick the Shepherd moved the kitchen table against the wall and drew up chairs, eight of them, in front of the wood stove. I muted my television and turned off my lights to observe the spectacle that followed. Though there were seven other people in the prayer meeting, I was interested only in Rachel and positioned myself in the dark so that I could see her.

Through the open door I saw and heard her read from the Bible, her eyes taking in and her mouth giving out words past comprehending. I saw her kneel beside her chair, clasp her large hands, and close her eyes in prayer. I heard her say these words: "Not our will, Lord, but thine be done." Afterward I saw her stand again, then slice her chocolate Bundt cake and transfer the slices onto white saucers, which Patrick, in his customary officious way, distributed among the guests.

And the morning after the prayer meeting I saw Rachel in front of the wood stove once more, kneeling again but also dipping her hands into a bucket of water. I watched her hands make slow wide circles on the floor as she cleaned up another of Veronica's accidents. I heard her speak gentle words to Veronica and sing a song to her. "Winky blinky, niddy nod, / Father is fishing off Cape Cod," the song went. I wondered if it was a song Rachel had sung to her babies. "Winky blinky, sleepy eyes, / Mother is making apple pies," she sang.

Through the open door I have smelled the strong smell of disinfectant. I have also smelled woodsmoke. I have smelled bread baking, chicken frying, apples stewing. When a sweet potato burst in the oven, it came to me that all burned food smells alike.

Besides heat, I have felt something else through the open door, something unfamiliar yet not altogether disagreeable, something I would be afraid to give a name to. And I have tasted. Do you know that distrust and longing have a bitter taste?

Standing beside my bed at daybreak, these are the words that come to me now. They are high-sounding words that Rachel read from the Bible at the cottage prayer meeting: "Now faith is the substance of things hoped for, the evidence of things not seen. For by it the elders obtained a good report. Through faith we understand that the worlds were framed by the word of God, so that things which are seen were not made of things which do appear."

As when I heard her read them, the words disappoint. Though seeming at first to offer a pleasant view, they prove flat and useless, like a window painted onto a blank wall. The invisible can bear no weight, I wanted to call to her that night. And no good report, not the merest shred of understanding, may be gained from such silent sources as hope and faith. But I said nothing. Men will believe what they want to believe.

I had never before heard the words that Rachel read. Though a child of the South, I never held a Bible in my hand until the morning after the cottage prayer meeting. It was a red Bible I took off the bottom shelf of the bookcase in my apartment. From its unstitched binding, I knew it was old, much older than the outdated issues of Time magazine on the same shelf. Its cover, "Hand-grained Morocco" according to a faded gold inscription, was limp, its edges split. The first nine chapters of the book of Genesis had separated from the rest, exposing a web of interlaced silver white threads.

With the help of a reference guide in the back of the Bible and the table of contents, I located the verses within minutes in what is called the Epistle to the Hebrews. The verses Rachel read, I discovered, were followed by other verses listing Old Testament names I had heard of—Cain and Abel, Noah, Abraham, Isaac, Jacob, Joseph, Moses—all of whom purportedly triumphed "by faith." In the margin someone had boldly printed in blue ink *Heroes of the Faith.*

But all were not glorious victors among these so-called heroes. The writer was at least honest enough to include the defeats: the tortures, the mockings and scourgings, the imprisonments, the stonings. The language has an old-fashioned extravagance: some were "sawn asunder," others were "slain with the sword," and still others "wandered about in sheepskins and goatskins; being destitute, afflicted, tormented." The conclusion of this depressing record contains, as I have heard it said, good news and bad news. The good news is the reminder that these unlucky souls "obtained a good report." The bad news is that they did not receive "the promise."

I imagine the heroes of the faith as schoolchildren presented with a choice between a good report card or extra recess time. Stern and dutiful pupils that they were, they chose the report card, though no doubt my nephew and others would argue that in the end they received both. But such arguments rest on the flimsy, elusive, unprovable commodity known as faith—a commodity in even shorter supply than hard cash in the home where I grew up.

As children, Regina, Virginia, and I were not "churched," as I have heard it called. Our names were not on the Sunday school roll of any of the four churches in Methuselah, Mississippi. I have at times wondered how it might have been if my father had been embraced by his Jewish grandparents, if he had been taught the law and the prophets, if he in turn had instructed my sisters and me in the pillars of the Jewish faith. But against the word *if*, the facts stand immutable: My father wasn't embraced, he wasn't taught, and he didn't instruct.

One may be irreligious, however, and still hold to many of the same principles as religious people—that of divine judgment, for instance. "Chickens come home to roost" was something Daddy often said. He threw open the door to impending disaster, acknowledging its likelihood long before it arrived, eyeing it with certainty as it took shape, stepping out of the way so it could enter. It was not that he welcomed disaster but rather that he knew it was inevitable, that if he did not stand back and let it in, it would break the door down and flatten him. In this sense, I suppose he did have faith of a sort—faith that he was doomed.

Once I heard Daddy tell Mother during one of their nighttime debates over finances that he was destined to fail in matters of money because of God's wrath. Imagine this from the son of an atheist. As he explained it, he was paying for the sins of his parents—of his father, who said there was no God, and of his mother, who had left God's chosen people to marry such a man. This God would confiscate every cent of Daddy's money for so great a debt. There was no hope for him nor, because she had cast her lot with him, for my mother. I do not recall what my mother replied, if anything. Perhaps she wondered why he couldn't have informed her of his hopeless state before she had agreed to marry him.

Oppressed with thoughts of faithlessness, I stand at my open door now and watch my nephew strike a match to light the new fire. Leaning forward in his red flannel pajamas, he looks small and vulnerable. I could span his back with my two hands. I think about the hope and faith of a man like Patrick. "In my Father's house are many mansions," and "I go to prepare a place for you," and "I will come again, and receive you unto myself; that where I am, there ye may be also"—these are words I have heard him read aloud at the supper table, words he could not have heard at the supper table of his childhood, for his mother, my sister, knew as little of the Bible as I, and his father spent most of his time before he died on the gambling boats along the Mississippi River.

Patrick's hopes, I think, are few and simple. He hopes to turn a profit at the Main Office each month, to become a writer, and to have a mansion in a place called heaven. More immediately, he hopes to light a fire. The matches appear to be giving him trouble. They are the kind one tears out of a small cardboard book, the kind with a flat head that bend too easily when scratched against the emery strip. He tries several, discards them into the wood stove. I wonder what it would take for Patrick to fly into a rage, to shout, curse, and stamp his feet. As a child, he had a temper. Regina told me stories about him over the telephone. As a teenager, he battered another boy's car with a baseball bat. Then something happened, Regina said, and he went to that religious crusade and turned into a fanatic, a development over which she fretted more than she had over his tantrums.

Just as Patrick finally succeeds with a match, Rachel enters the kitchen. Brown-robed and solemn, she needs only a hood to look like a monk. She does not see me in the doorway. She opens the drawer at the bottom of her stove and takes out a pan. She stands for a moment looking into it as if wondering what to put in it. She moves beyond my view, and I hear her running water at the sink. And what, I wonder, are the hopes of a woman like Rachel? Can she put a name to them? I imagine her hopes, like Patrick's, to be simple: an eternity in which she will have her babies again, where she will wake for happy days without end to hear their laughter, to hold them and sing them to sleep.

Here is another verse I read in the eleventh chapter of the Epistle to the Hebrews: "Women received their dead raised to life again." This, according to the reference in the margin, speaks of a widow whose son was raised from the dead after the prophet Elijah stretched himself out over the child's body and said, "O Lord my God, I pray thee, let this child's soul come into him again." And how does a woman like Rachel remain faithful in the face of such preferential treatment? How does she reconcile the God of Elijah, who chose to return one woman's child alive, with the one who let her own children die?

Is not such a God a tyrant? Is he not like the kingbird, which sits on a high branch scolding the world? Yet even the kingbird has a soft spot for its young, swooping down to attack any threat, great or small. I think of the lullaby Rachel sang to Veronica. *Winky blinky, niddy nod, / Birds watch their babies, Why can't God?* Maybe he needs to take a look through Patrick's calendar sometime for a few tips on Resourceful Thinking in Times of Danger or Concentrating on the Task at Hand.

Patrick has already begun talking to Rachel, telling her animatedly of a dream he had during the night in which he was locked inside a giant freezer with slabs of meat hanging from hooks. "Everywhere I turned," he says, "I ran into a side of beef or a whole skinned hog!" He cuts a ridiculous figure in the kitchen, shuffling about in his red flannel, pretending to spar against phantom meat slabs, a little featherweight boxer of a man. I think of such a man battling the forces of life, sure to be knocked out. I cannot see Rachel's reaction to him. Does she look at him now, I wonder, and despair at the thought of having to live out the rest of her life with a man who dreams of boxing with meat in a freezer?

He stops springing about abruptly and says, "And when I woke up, I was completely uncovered. So that must have been why I was dreaming about being in a freezer!" I have noticed that Patrick is never so pleased as when he trots forth the explanation for some difficulty.

I think of the difficulty of his children's deaths. I see a sudden picture of the daffodils in the backyard, today putting out "tender leaves of hope, tomorrow blossoms," as Cardinal Wolsey says in *Henry VIII*, Shakespeare's last play. It was one of Eliot's least favorites. "The third day comes a frost, a killing frost," says Cardinal Wolsey. Just when man thinks his greatness is ripening, he says, the frost of fate "nips his root, and then he falls." Gone are his hopes. "And when he falls, he falls like Lucifer, never to hope again."

I would argue the last phrase. Though unschooled in the Bible, I know who Lucifer is, that according to legend he was thrown out of heaven and now prowls the earth, having appropriated it as his kingdom. Thus, "never to hope again" is puzzling, for surely Lucifer harbors many hopes and with good reason. If one believes the myth that his intent is to do evil, surely the fallen angel should have much cause for rejoicing in his kingdom on earth.

With a sigh I retreat from the doorway to make up my bed. You have started another day, I tell myself, this time with thoughts of murdered children, Lucifer, and dashed hopes. The sparrow is still busy at his cheeping. I move to the window, but I cannot see him anywhere. Yet I know he is there, for I hear his cry plainly, the evidence of things not seen. *Cheep! Cheep! Cheep!*

CHAPTER 22

A TIDE IN THE AFFAIRS OF MEN

A highly intelligent bird, the American crow squawks out news of food sources or approaching danger. It can be silent and furtive near its nest, however. Though slaughtered in large numbers by humans, the crow flourishes, its audacious caws heard throughout every mainland state.

I sit in my recliner waiting for two o'clock to arrive, a book in my lap. It appears that the rain has stopped for today. The daffodils in the backyard hang their heads. Buds swell on the spindly branches of the plum tree. Low bushes beneath the plum tree bear early flowers called passion roses, some white and some pink. "A wet February"— this is what the weatherman in Greenville, Mississippi, has said of the month. He could have said "miserable" to include both cold and wet, but weathermen do not editorialize. They deal in absolutes: "2.5 inches of rain in four hours," "seven inches above last year's rainfall for the month," "measurable rainfall for twenty of the twenty-six days thus far," "a high temperature of forty-two, a low of thirty-four."

Remarkably, the new furnace installed by the low-bid trio operates efficiently so that the cold and wet do not touch me. Because the human body and mind operate inefficiently, on the other hand, February has touched me in unexpected ways, ways not of my own choosing. I speak not of my own body and mind but of Rachel's body and Mindy's mind. If the two of them could trade body and mind, one of them could be whole. As it is, both are broken. Time has drawn its sword upon both. Both may wish to die, but those who love them take up the shield in their defense. That I should be enlisted to help is a strange matter—I, who came to Patrick's house to be served.

Were Rachel to die, hers would be called an early death. Were Mindy to die, hers would be called a tragic and untimely death. My intuition tells me, however, that neither Rachel nor Mindy will die, not yet and not of their present illnesses. For Rachel, time has wounded her but will sheathe its sword and retreat briefly, for hers, I have discovered, is a malady common to women of her age. I recall my own time many years ago and its deep silent sorrow. Before, I had sorrowed because Eliot had declared there would be no children, but now I sorrowed because nature had seen to it that there could be none. Perhaps Rachel does not sorrow as I did. Perhaps she is thankful at last to be ensured of an empty womb to match her empty heart.

While Eliot, preoccupied with his own concerns, appeared to take no note of my physical or emotional discomfort, Patrick has attended to Rachel's needs perhaps more than she would like. With Patrick there is very little moderation. He has researched on the Internet and checked books out of the library. Imagine a man of fifty-four bringing a stack of books on this subject to the circulation desk.

And he did not intend the books to be for Rachel alone. He has read them, discussed them, quoted from them at the supper table. Rachel has suffered him to do so, listening silently unless asked a direct question.

To his credit, Patrick has not only talked but has also acted, taking on certain housekeeping chores to lighten Rachel's work. He has often brought home meals for supper, emptied the dishwasher, folded clothes. He sometimes goes to the grocery store on his way home from work or on evenings when he doesn't have a class. I believe he sees this time in Rachel's life as a project to be completed, along the order of cleaning out a garage, finishing a basement, insulating an attic, and like many men whose mental scope is not broad, Patrick enjoys a project, especially one that he is supervising.

"I feel so slow," Rachel said to him one night in the kitchen, at which he launched into a description of the changes a woman's metabolism undergoes due to fluctuating levels of thyroxin. I did not listen to all he said. I was wondering if there had ever been a time when Rachel moved briskly, nimbly. Her slowness was such a part of the woman I knew as Rachel that I found myself unable to imagine a different Rachel, one who was a paragon of efficiency, whipping around the house, breezing in and out of my apartment with her tray, stirring up little whirlwinds as she set the table and sorted laundry.

The house has settled into its afternoon quiet now. Because Rachel's nights are not restful, she routinely naps after lunch, at Patrick's suggestion. Over the past week I have taken my own lunch dishes to the kitchen, rinsed them, and put them into the dishwasher. "Go to your bed and lie down," I told Rachel one day as she was setting a bowl of potato soup on my round table. "Leave the tray here, and I will clear the dishes after I eat." She turned and looked at me, then opened her mouth as if to say something. "I want you to lie down," I repeated. "I want you to do it now." She looked at me another long moment, then closed her mouth, turned, and left, the ham biscuit and dish of applesauce still on the tray.

I hear her at times in the kitchen in the dead of night. She resists taking pills to make her sleep, though the doctor has given her a prescription. Patrick has told her that hot milk may help her sleep. She makes cocoa and takes it into the living room. I have looked into the living room, have seen her sitting on the sofa with her Bible in her lap, talking aloud with her eyes closed. Some nights she cuts old clothing into small squares with which she plans to make a quilt someday. She clips articles and recipes out of magazines and writes in a diary. She dusted the furniture one night and polished Patrick's shoes another. She often sees the sunrise.

For Mindy, I believe hers to be a brief skirmish. For her, time will be put to flight, vanquished from the field for many years. To Mindy I wish to say, however, that "many years" is but an illusion. Perhaps I will tell her this today, for our lives now intersect in a way neither of us could have predicted. We sit together at my round table every weekday for a purpose other than eating.

Steve and Teri have taken a bold step, perhaps a foolish one, certainly a desperate one. They have withdrawn Mindy from high school. They mean for her to complete twelfth grade as what they call a "homeschooler." I have been persuaded to sign on as her instructor in English grammar and literature. Teri is, in her words, "giving geometry and economics a shot," and Steve has undertaken history and chemistry at night. Patrick has confidently offered to provide additional help as needed with either English or history, two subjects in which he is "especially gifted," a claim supported, first of all, by the spelling bee he won in eighth grade with the word *kohlrabi* and, second, by the medal he was awarded in tenth grade for his essay on Thomas Paine in the Sons of Liberty Essay Contest. It is amazing how often he can work these high points of his schooldays into a conversation.

Today I will sit with Mindy again, as I have for three weeks, from two to three o'clock. A strange pair we make. If costumed, we might pass for Juliet and her old nurse, though in appearance only. We meet purely for instruction. We have no bond of affection. Were Mindy casting me, she would likely assign me the role of one of the witches in *Macbeth*.

In three weeks we have concluded a unit of grammar: phrases and clauses. She has filled in blanks on workbook pages, demonstrating that she knows the difference between a gerund and an infinitive, between a dependent and independent clause. She has a keen mind when she chooses to put it to use. She can identify a participle, an appositive, an elliptical clause.

We have also read a story titled "The Destructors" by Graham Greene, and Mindy has written a two-page paper on "Trevor's Motivation for Destruction," for which she received the grade of C-, having attributed the boy's destructiveness to his environment instead of its true source: his black heart. Though her eyes registered surprise at the grade, she shrugged and stuffed the paper inside her spiral notebook. Perhaps she never took the trouble to read my comments accompanying her grade.

Today we will begin the next selection in her literature book:

Julius Caesar, another study of the motivations behind destructive actions, this time murder. Perhaps she will write another paper: "The Motives of Caesar's Murderers." This is one of the essay topics suggested in the teacher's manual. *Julius Caesar* is a play I have never read in its entirety before today, though I once typed a paper for Eliot titled "History Reconstructed in *Julius Caesar*."

I have made up a quiz for Mindy today to test her reading of the first two acts. I will read the questions aloud, and she will speak her answers. I do not trouble her to write them down. It is understood that I will award her a grade at the end of four months, after we have completed the course of study. She has behaved as though she does not care what this grade will be. To her these months must stretch like an endless road, though in reality they are but a few short steps in her lifetime.

When one lives to be eighty, he understands that the drawing out of man's days is a fleeting affair. "That we shall die, we know." Thus says Brutus after the murder of Julius Caesar. And Cassius, in response, justifies the murder by declaring that he who "cuts off twenty years" of a man's life "cuts off so many years of fearing death," by which he means this: We have done him a favor by killing him! We have relieved his mind! We have spared him many years of dreading the specter of death!

One may speak facetiously of death when it is that of another. When one is close to his own death, however, he sees life as a circle far too small: "Where I did begin, there shall I end." So says Cassius before he dies, no longer speaking lightly.

These are some of the things I may say to Mindy. But though I will speak, it is not likely that she will hear me. Certainly she will not heed me. While the old often cannot hear, even more often the young will not.

Why man does the things that he does—this is the concern of the unit in Mindy's literature textbook, the book I now hold in my lap. I run a finger over the title on the front cover: *LITERATURE: INVESTIGATING THE WORLD.* The title of the unit we are studying is simply "Why," its subtitle "Character Motivations."

The book is ambitious. It assumes, for instance, that teenagers care about the motivation of a murder committed over two thousand years ago, fictionalized and depicted in a play written over four hundred years ago. Already I can imagine the empty well of Mindy's eyes when I tell her today that Shakespeare took liberties with the actual historical events surrounding the murder, that the play titled *Julius Caesar* is more about Brutus and Cassius than Caesar, that the work marks a turning point in Shakespeare's development as a playwright. Before, he was more concerned with plot weaving, but now he turns his attention to the minds and motives of his characters. So says today's lesson in the teacher's manual.

The textbook writers were thinking deep adult thoughts, for motivation is something that interests grown-ups, not teenagers. What concerns teenagers is the act itself, not the motivation behind it. "Because I want to"—this is the motivation of the young. "Because I love"—though it may be claimed, it is not to be allowed, for love darts in and out of shadows, invisible to the eyes of the young. It delights in binding heart and mind with cords. When he finally wakes up, Gulliver finds himself incapacitated.

Through my apartment door, which has sometimes remained open since the installation of the new furnace, I have heard that

Steve and Teri mean to keep Mindy separated from the boy she imagines herself to love. She has no car keys, she has no telephone, she has no computer. Teri guards her like a warden during the day. At night Steve takes over. He has told Mindy that if she chooses to sneak out of the house at any time, she will not be allowed back for the rest of her life. This is extreme talk. I try to imagine the fear in a father's heart when speaking such words. He must rise every morning to wonder if she is still in her bed.

Furthermore, Steve has bought a dog, a young bulldog with a face and a bark that mean business. Steve has named him Stonewall after one of his Civil War heroes. Teri has observed that a stone wall is "what he looks like he ran into." Teri's nerves have been affected. She puts on a resolute face, but she talks and eats to excess. She has told Rachel that she feels "like a balloon ready to pop."

Rachel has seen the boy driving up and down Edison Street. And we have all heard him. Whether the rumble of his car is due to age or to deliberate sound enhancement, I do not know. He comes at all hours, the black hulk of his car moving slowly, growling ominously. He has come in the dark of night, honking his horn and throwing glass bottles. He has done all the standard things. Once he splattered Steve's truck with eggs. Another time he punctured a tire. Perhaps I should use the passive voice: A horn has been honked, bottles and eggs have been thrown, a tire has been punctured. These acts are laid by us to the boy's account. According to Teri, Stonewall has barked wildly and clawed at the front door during these nighttime raids.

Through my open door I have also heard Teri's reports of what Steve, built somewhat like a bulldog himself, has told the boy: In short, if he catches him on his property, the boy must be prepared to deal with drastic and permanent consequences. These are my words, not the ones Steve used. I cannot think that the boy cares to test his sincerity. I have also learned the boy's name: Prince Cook. I have learned that he has no father. I try to imagine what kind of mother the boy has, if when she named him she had visions of a noble and handsome son. I have heard Teri describe him in unflattering terms: "mean as sin," "scarecrow skinny," "eyes like a snake."

There is a tap on the side door, and I hear it open, hear footsteps in the kitchen, then see Teri and Mindy standing at the door of my apartment. "We're here," Teri says. She is wearing denim overalls and a yellow ball cap with the word *Umbro* stitched on it. She is carrying Veronica. Teri is not a tall woman. She won't always be able to carry the child, but for now she holds her securely and possessively, as if born to do nothing else but bear such a weight. Veronica's head lolls to one side, her mouth gaping. Teri walks toward me, saying to Veronica, "Look, sweetie, let's see if Aunt Sophie's feeder has any birds today."

The sun appears to be attempting a brief showing after the hard morning rain, and though the feeder has no visitors, a large crow, lighting on a nearby tree branch, caws weakly and shakes its feathers. I have read that crows are smart birds, thriving by their wits, their toughness, their strong sense of community. I think of Steve and Teri calling upon all their resources to save their daughter and defeat a boy named Prince.

Mindy seats herself at the round table, props her elbow on her textbook, and rests her chin on her fist in the attitude of one prepared to be bored. She gazes stone-faced toward the clock on the wall. She wears a dark brown jacket over a white T-shirt, tight pink pants, and slip-on shoes with thick heels. From her behavior over the past three weeks, I know that she will not remove her jacket and will not look at me during our hour together, thus giving every indication that she cares nothing about English grammar and literature nor for any ancient specimen associated with the teaching of it. Yet she is not insolent; rather, she seems completely indifferent, as if insolence would require more effort than she is willing to exert. Perhaps, at some level, she is too polite to be overtly rude. I do not know her well enough to say.

At the window Teri points to the crow and says, "He's a big old fellow, isn't he? See him, sweetie?" Veronica gazes vacantly toward the sky.

I rise from my chair, book in hand, and walk to the round table. Folded back on the tabletop is an old copy of *Time* magazine. "DIED. PETER FOY, 79, go-to man for flying actors on Broadway and beyond; of a heart attack; in Las Vegas." I have never heard of a go-to man, but *Time* magazine tells me that Peter Foy took out patents on odd contrivances made of "wire, pulleys and harnesses" by which he sent people soaring above the stage in movies and television. I think of Peter Pan, of Sally Field in *The Flying Nun*, of Superman. I think of a man who could invent ingenious ways to keep actors aloft but who could do nothing for himself when death came.

"Well, we'll be back in an hour," Teri says, moving from the window. At the round table she lays a hand on Mindy's shoulder. Mindy stiffens. Clearly she does not welcome the touch, but something keeps her from pulling away. Teri removes her hand, then says to me, "Will you be okay for an hour?" Yes, I almost say, I can endure unpleasantness as well as your daughter can. I only nod, however, and she leaves. In the kitchen she croons to Veronica, "You want a little nap, baby?"

I turn in the literature book to *Julius Caesar*. It falls open to act 4, and I see the words I underlined in pencil earlier today: "Our cause is ripe, the enemy increaseth every day." Without knowing why, I read these words aloud now. Mindy gives no sign of having heard me. For no good reason I continue reading: "There is a tide in the affairs of men which taken at the flood leads on to fortune; omitted, all the voyage of their life is bound in shallows and in miseries." These are well-known words. Mindy glances quickly toward me, then as quickly away. "On such a full sea are we now afloat," I add, "and we must take the current when it serves."

Except for the slightest pursing of her mouth, Mindy could be a statue.

"Do you know what the passage means?" I ask her.

She shakes her head. "It wasn't in the part for today," she says tightly.

"You're right," I say. "We'll get to it later." I turn back to the beginning of the play. "Here is the first question for today's quiz," I tell her. "Of what does the soothsayer in act 1 warn Caesar?"

And without hesitation she answers: "The ides of March."

"And we shall see," I say, nodding, "whether Caesar sails through the ides of March like Peter Pan and Superman. Or whether the wires break and he plummets to his death."

For the briefest instant Mindy's eyes flicker to mine. Surely, she must think, this old woman is losing her mind. And perhaps she is right.

CHAPTER 23

WHAT'S GONE AND WHAT'S PAST HELP

Cardinals hold the standard for monogamy among
birds. Mates for life, they stay together year
round, feeding and nesting up to four broods
each season. They are known for the harmony of
their singing, one bird trilling a melody
which the other picks up and completes.

More than two weeks pass, and the calendar tells me that the real ides of March has arrived. It is late afternoon, but I have been awake since a troubling dream in the early hours of morning. In my dream Mindy tried to wrestle the sword away from Brutus in the senate house of Rome in order to save the life of Julius Caesar. She was gravely wounded and borne away, apparently dead, by an old man in a long white robe who called out over and over, "The argument of Time! The argument of Time! The argument of Time!" I slept no more but sat in my recliner and watched the sky grow light.

I turned on the television and watched two episodes of *All in the Family*. I heard Archie Bunker and Meathead exchange many insults as the day dawned.

It takes no prophet to unravel my dream, for I looked at the calendar on my wall before going to bed last night, taking note of the fact that the next day, today, would be the ides of March. In my sleep I revised the death scene of Julius Caesar to include my pupil, and then, unable to let her die, fused the play with another, *The Winter's Tale*, in which Hermione is thought to be dead for sixteen years but is revealed in the end to be alive. The old man, designated as Time in the play, is a curious character among Shakespeare's colorful troupe, for he is meant to be symbolic.

It is my hope that Time will revive Mindy well before sixteen years have passed. She has already come and gone for her lesson today. We have now finished the study of *Julius Caesar*, have read Frost's "The Death of a Hired Man," and today concluded the discussion of two stories from the literature book: James Thurber's "The Catbird Seat" and "That Evening Sun" by William Faulkner, the first exploring the element of humor, the second dealing with terror. Though I still hold to my opinion that the book is overreaching its audience of high school students, I believe Mindy has understood more than she pretends.

I believe, for example, that she came close to smiling today when she read aloud a paragraph from the end of "The Catbird Seat" in which Mrs. Ulgine Barrows raves like a madwoman and tries to tackle the mild-mannered Mr. Martin, who has devised the perfect foil for her plan to reorganize his department at work. "If you weren't such a drab, ordinary little man," Mrs. Barrows bellows, "I'd think you'd planned it all." One thing I said to Mindy after she read the paragraph was this: "Never underestimate what drab, ordinary little men are capable of." To this she gave no response; indeed, I cannot explain why I said it. It is over now. Mindy came and Mindy left.

It has been a quiet day, the ides of March, a day as warm as June, though it is not yet spring. The children who live in the house behind Patrick's are jumping on their trampoline. March is a fickle month in Mississippi, rain and wind appearing alone or together in varying quantities within a forty-degree span of temperature. Today there is wind but no rain. The children, three of them, squeal and tumble together on the trampoline.

For a while the smallest one, a girl wearing a bright red cap, does a jumping jack with each upward leap until one of the boys upsets her balance. She scrambles back to her feet and begins again. A ball appears on the trampoline, and they begin kicking it to one another, and then at one another, both games necessitating many trips to the ground to retrieve it. I think of the amount of energy being expended on the trampoline. I try to imagine what it would feel like to be so small and to bounce so high.

A strange coincidence: One of the boys grabs his sister's red cap from her head and throws it high into the air. She looks up and reaches with both hands to catch it as it comes back down. And then I hear faint music on the television and someone singing. It is a song I have heard many times: "Who can light the world up with her smile?" I look at the screen and see a swift succession of vignettes: Mary Tyler Moore walking beside a lake, Mary Tyler Moore shopping for meat in a grocery store, Mary Tyler Moore on a crowded city side-walk spinning around and tossing her hat into the air, then reaching up to catch it. "You're gonna make it after all." With these words the song ends.

I look at the clock. It is half past four o'clock, and on the television screen Mary Tyler Moore is walking into the newsroom in her short skirt, her long dark hair as springy as the children on the neighbor's trampoline. She is about to encounter some small problem in her orderly world, and at the end of the program, before the kitten meows from the MGM logo, the problem will have been humorously solved. This is the way things happen on television.

I wonder how old Mary Tyler Moore is now, if she could still fit into such a skirt. I wonder if at the end of this day, today, she will feel that she has taken a nothing day and turned it into a worthwhile one. I wonder if she feels, looking back over her life, that she has "made it after all." I wonder if she ever watches herself on television and marvels that she used to smile so much. I wonder if she laughs at how insignificant her television problems were compared to the real ones she has. For this is a certainty of life: If Mary Tyler Moore is still alive, she has problems.

I think of what my own life would have been like on the day this program first aired. I would have been a married woman at the time, a teacher by day, a typist for my husband by night. I would have imagined myself happy. I wouldn't have known at the time, though all the clues were there, that my husband thought of me not as a wife but as a housekeeper and secretary. I would not have known what the drab, ordinary little man who was my husband was doing in his study at night, perhaps at the very moment this program was on television. I may have been in the kitchen clearing the table after cooking and serving a late supper, which was his preference. I may have been hoping that his desire would be turned toward me later in the night, that he would sleep in the bed with me instead of in the guest bedroom, where he claimed the mattress was more comfortable.

How foolish the little dreams of Sophie Hess now seem to me, an old woman gaining on eighty-one, sitting in a house that is not my own, passing my days in a recliner, entertaining no illusions concerning happiness. I try to think of what I have accomplished in fourscore years, and a favorite phrase of my father's comes to mind: "A great big zero with the ring rubbed out." This I often heard him say when he and Mother were talking about money.

I cannot claim the hundreds of students I taught as accomplishments. Only a few faces come into focus. I see my third-grade pupil Starr, her black eyes shining. But I know the truth: Neither Starr nor any other student I taught remembers my name today or spares me a thought. I accomplished no more in the classroom than I do in my recliner. If I had not taught my pupils arithmetic and verb conjugations, someone else would have. And later, in college classrooms, all those hours of instructing against vague pronoun reference, comma splices, murky topic sentences—they were but an echo in a canyon, an uncertain sound fading to silence.

So what worthy achievement would I choose if it were in my power? I can think of only one: A child of my own. Again I see Starr, her face upturned and laughing. Some other woman's achievement, not mine. But what of it? I say sternly. I will not give in to regrets. Life is what it is, not a thing to be shaped by desire. "What's gone and what's past help should be past grief." These are Paulina's sensible words in *The Winter's Tale*. How unlike the play is my life, however—no grieving husband, no surprise reunion with a lost daughter, no joyous blessing at the end: "Go together, you precious winners all."

I turn up the volume to see what obstacle Mary Tyler Moore is facing this time. It seems that she has been given the task of writing obituaries for prominent local figures. In the event that they die, Mr. Grant tells her, the station will already have something on file. I watch the entire episode, in which a local celebrity named Chuckles the Clown does in fact die. I take note of the fact that much humor is derived from the subject of death.

I suddenly remember something: While on the back side of Patrick's house children are jumping on a trampoline, on the front side cars are no doubt pulling into the parking lot at Wagner's Mortuary. Tonight there will be a visitation from five until seven, with the funeral to follow tomorrow.

Three days ago I heard Patrick read the account of the woman's accident from the newspaper, and then the next day, after she died, he read the obituary aloud. Tillie Flower was a woman my own age. Oddly, it was a name I felt I already knew when Patrick first spoke it, though I could not say why. The woman suffered a mishap in her car at a stop sign on Arnold Street; rather, that was the point of initiation. She was quite a distance from the stop sign at the moment of impact. According to her husband, who was in the passenger seat and sustained only a broken foot and cracked ribs, Tillie Flower had stopped the car, unfastened her seat belt, and reached into the back seat to get a tissue from her pocketbook to wipe a smudge off the rearview mirror. Such details the man reported.

"She was bad to take her foot off the brake," her husband also told the newspaper reporter, and when he "let her know the car was rolling forward," she accidentally "stepped on the gas instead of the brake" and "couldn't manage to get her foot up off of it." At some point in the article, he was quoted as saying, "She always did have a real heavy foot," a fact that a better reporter would have omitted.

Though her husband didn't relate this part of it, I can guess that his shouting only served to rattle her further. Witnesses spoke of the car jumping curbs, hurtling across lawns, and finally colliding head on with a mail truck idling down the street. The mailman, fortunately, was not in the truck, having walked up to hand deliver a package to someone's door. This is the kind of accident I can imagine young people making jokes about. The day will come when they will know the fear of being unable to control their own bodies. But for now they laugh as if growing old is a television comedy show and they are the audience.

There is a flash of red at my window, and a male cardinal lights on the bird feeder. From what I have read about cardinals, I know the female is not far away. And then I see her, sitting patiently on a branch of a nearby forsythia, cocking her head this way and that while her mate feeds. My bird book tells me that part of the cardinals' springtime courtship ritual includes feeding, the male presenting the female with morsels of food, which she takes from his bill as if they are kissing.

A picture fills my mind: Last week I saw Patrick lead Rachel by the hand to the kitchen table, where he seated her and then set before her a plate and a large paper cup. On the plate was a hamburger, wrapped in paper, also a handful of French fries. In the cup was a vanilla milkshake. I saw Patrick pick up a French fry and raise it to Rachel's lips. I saw her open her mouth and accept it.

On the television screen I see June Cleaver at the front door of her big white house, wearing high heels and a dress. I see her waving to Ward as he leaves for work. I know that Patrick will soon be coming home from work and that Rachel will be wearing blue jeans and a shirt, not high heels and a dress. Patrick will take off his jacket, hang it by the door, and wash his hands. Then he will say to Rachel, "What do you need me to do?"

I hear Rachel in the kitchen now. She is running water at the sink. I hear the thump of a cupboard door and the whir of the new can opener that Patrick presented to her last week to replace the one she held by hand. Helping in the kitchen has enlightened Patrick in certain ways.

I do not want to hear more laughter. Perhaps the History or Nature channel will treat life and death with more respect than the TV Oldies channel. Reaching for the remote control, I accidentally knock it off the table and into the trash can. I pull the trash can over and lift it to my lap. It takes some effort to retrieve the remote control, for the trash can is quite full, Rachel's cleaning schedule having been irregular of late. As I sift through it to find the remote control, I see the last issue of *Time* magazine I threw away, and it is suddenly clear to me why Tillie Flower's name sounded familiar.

"DIED. TILLIE FOWLER, 62, once the highest-ranking woman in Congress; of a brain hemorrhage." Tillie Flower and Tillie Fowler. Two dead women, both southerners with almost identical names, both of whom must have awakened on the day of their deaths with no intention of dying. *Time* magazine reports that Tillie Fowler was often called the "steel magnolia" in Congress, steel referring to her toughness, magnolia to her southern charm. Perhaps the U. S.

Congress and *Time* magazine do not know that steel magnolias are nothing remarkable in the South. I grew up among them. Women able to stand by themselves but allowing men to assist them.

I have just closed my hand around the remote control and pulled it out of the trash can when I hear a shout in the kitchen: "Where is she?" There is a loud clang as of a lid being slammed onto a pot. Then, "I know she's here! Where is she?" The voice has a maniacal pitch. I feel the onset of a nightmare.

I set the trash can down and move to the door of my apartment. A boy with low-slung pants stands two feet away from Rachel, who is backed against the stove. I can see the tip of the gun he is waving. Rachel's face is white and round, her eyes fixed on his. She is holding a wooden spoon in one hand, a stick of butter in the other.

"I know she comes here! I know she's here now!" the boy says. Rachel's eyes leave the boy's face for a moment and follow the gun. I used to wonder if I would be capable of heroics if threatened with violence, but I learned long ago that I would not. I cannot think of a single thing to do. I have a handgun in a drawer of my dresser, but I stand rooted in the doorway, the same feeling of numb horror flooding through me now as on the day I stood in another doorway behind another boy with a gun.

Rachel speaks. "You're Prince, aren't you?" Her eyes have returned to his face.

He utters a profanity. "Mindy!" he shouts. "Come here! We're going!" He swings his head around, sees me standing in the doorway, and grabs Rachel's wrist. The wooden spoon falls to the floor. He yanks her away from the stove and puts the gun to her neck. He has her in a choke hold now, facing me. "Girl! We gotta go! Come on!"

He is shrieking. "Make a move, old woman, and I'll blow her wide open," he says to me. I feel something large inside my chest, something slowly inflating, filling up my breathing space. My heart is racing. Somebody's foot is stuck on the accelerator.

"Mindy's not here," Rachel says. She is still holding the stick of butter in one hand. "You've got your information wrong. She comes earlier than this. She's already had her lesson. She's gone." I hear her clearly though she barely opens her mouth. The barrel of the gun is jammed into her neck. The boy glares at me with his mean snake eyes.

"Drop that!" he screams. I look down to see the remote control still in my hand. I drop it at once, at the same moment Rachel drops the stick of butter.

He curses again, a long vile stream of words. Then, "I know she's here! You're lying! Both of you, you're lying!" This, even though I haven't spoken a word. Again he bellows, "Girl! Get out here *now!*"

"You need to leave," Rachel says. "They could put you in jail for doing this. You don't want to go to jail."

"Don't tell me what I want to do!"

"Okay, okay," she says. "I just want you to think about what you're doing."

Here's what I want: I want her to stop talking. The gun is deadly, and the one holding it is young, wild, and angry. A question leaps to my mind, one I asked Mindy today in our discussion of Faulkner's "That Evening Sun." It was printed in the teacher's manual: "Is Nancy's terror rational or irrational?" Mindy's answer was brief but perceptive. "Both," she said. "When you're afraid, there's always a reason, but you don't stop to think about it."

And then there's a noise at the kitchen door, and suddenly Patrick is standing there, frozen in place, looking as if something is lodged in his throat. All I can think of is the gun against Rachel's neck, the boy's demonic eyes, his quick finger on the trigger. I think also of Patrick's gift for doing and saying the wrong things.

"Get in and close the door!" the boy screams.

Patrick does. He stands facing Prince across the room, his hands hanging limply by his side, his mouth open as if, for once, he can think of nothing to say. I want him to be quiet, but I know Patrick. For now his eyes are riveted on the boy and Rachel.

I want to tell him the boy is insane, that the least provocation will end Rachel's life, but the words will not come. I feel the room starting a slow twirl; I see the edges filling with black around the white spotlight of Rachel and the boy. Perhaps this is how I will die. No, I tell myself, the boy told you not to move. You will not fall to the floor; you will not die. I think of life without Rachel, and my vision clears. The room settles.

And then Patrick speaks, raising one palm in entreaty as if about to humble himself. But here is what my nephew says to the crazed boy holding a gun to his wife's throat: "Turn your weapon on me. If you have to kill, then kill me, because if you don't, and if you harm a single hair of her head, I'll hunt you down and make you beg to be put out of your misery if it takes the rest of my life."

This is uttered in an absolutely level tone, as of a teacher telling his class what to study for the final exam. It is spoken by a drab, ordinary little man whom I have heard read aloud from the Bible words concerning loving one's enemies and turning the other cheek, a man who is considerably older and smaller than the assailant.

Prince looks momentarily confused, as if unable to follow all of the conditional clauses Patrick has laid out. Then he erupts. "Shut up! Just shut up! I don't take orders from no—" And he describes Patrick in the most graphic language, ending with "Maybe I'll just kill you all."

"I don't think you'll do that, Prince." This is spoken by Rachel, very softly. "I don't think you want to kill anybody. You don't want to go to jail." There is a long, silent pause before she adds slowly, "Would you please just put the gun down now? I don't feel very good. You're hurting my neck." She seems to go slack, but her eyes are still alert.

Prince looks distracted.

"Just put it down, Prince," Rachel says, more firmly now. "Mindy's not here." She raises her hand and ever so gently touches his arm, the one that has a stranglehold on her. "You've got to let me go now," she says. "Would you please help me to the floor?" Her words are coming in short, broken gasps.

And slowly she sinks to the floor, aided by Prince still holding the gun.

CHAPTER 24

TRIFLES LIGHT AS AIR

The male marsh wren is fervent in his nest

building, often with a dozen at a time under

construction. During courtship, then, he has

a variety of nests to offer interested females,

thus setting himself up as father of multiple

broods. A competitive bird, he also

plunders nearby nests left unattended.

In the kitchen I hear Patrick's voice. He has eaten his supper and is preparing to leave for his creative writing class. The last step in his preparation each week is to read his assignment aloud to Rachel. As always, the volume and pitch of his voice inform me that he is reading not only to Rachel but also to me.

"'I saw the murderous glint in his eye,'" Patrick reads, "'and I heard the shrill desperation in his voice. He was a monster, and he had my wife by the throat.'" If I didn't know what had happened in the kitchen the day before, I might think my nephew was writing dime-store fiction.

His assignment for tonight was to write a personal experience but to transform it into a fictional scene by altering significant details. After what happened yesterday, he discarded the original paper he had written and dashed off a new one late last night. Patrick's writing professor imposes word limits, a great challenge for Patrick, who thinks the whole world stands with gaping mouths to hear him give expression to each thought that flits across the small, dim screen of his mind. I am grateful to Patrick's professor for the limit of four hundred words on this paper, for his reading of the scene is mercifully brief.

In Patrick's version of yesterday's ides of March incident, which he has titled "Terror in the Afternoon," Prince is holding a knife instead of a gun to Rachel's throat. I am absent from the scene. Mindy, who has turned into Patrick's own daughter, is standing in the hallway, suitcase in hand, instead of sitting in the dentist's office with her mother, as she was yesterday. These are the significant details he has altered.

The truth was that Prince confused the time of Mindy's English tutorial with the time of her dentist's appointment. How messages are transmitted between parties when one is banned from using the telephone and the computer, I do not know, but yesterday's mistake testifies to the unreliability of alternate methods, whatever they may be. None of this figures in Patrick's story, however, only the sudden appearance of the boy bent on "rescuing his girlfriend from the clutches of her overprotective parents."

As I may have predicted, Patrick is the hero of his own story. Arriving home in the nick of time, he finds the boy holding Rachel at knife point so that Mindy can escape to his car, which is waiting by the curb. From there they plan to "flee this one-horse town and head south to the Gulf Coast." Thinking quickly, the courageous, noble, and highly intelligent father in the story composes and delivers a calm but powerful speech to both the boy and Mindy, in which he states and restates a truth that obviously serves as the theme of his paper: True love "hems in," "plants hedges," "builds forts," and so forth "to defend the loved one."

No mention in this version of his threatening to hunt the boy down and make him beg to be put out of his misery for any harm done to Rachel. No mention either of Rachel's slowly slumping to the floor with a surprised Prince struggling to support her weight. No mention of Rachel's reaching out a steady, purposeful hand to knock the gun from his hand, then sweep it underneath the stove. Certainly no mention of the words that came out of Prince's mouth when he found himself suddenly unarmed.

It is an image that will remain with me until I close my eyes in death: Rachel, usually so gentle and guileless, staging a fainting spell.

No mention in Patrick's paper of Rachel's later explanation, that something told her that Prince wouldn't shoot a person who fainted, especially a woman, and that it might distract him enough that she could knock the gun from his hand. She had a glimmer of hope, also, she said, that somewhere under all the layers of meanness Prince might have retained a vestige of the good manners most little boys in the South were taught at some point. So while she could have crumpled to the floor on her own, she was assisted by Prince. So there it is—youth outwitted by age, male by female, strength by weakness, violence by hope. The steel magnolia triumphs once again.

No mention, either, of Prince's subsequent bolting from the

kitchen to the front door, shouting vile imprecations as he fled, and no mention of his backing his car wildly out of the driveway right into the path of a white utility van slowing in front of the mortuary. No mention of the corpse in the van, on its way to the back entrance of the mortuary and the processing mill inside. And no mention of a third vehicle involved in the collision, a red Cadillac coming from the other direction, the driver of which was preparing to turn into the parking lot to pay her respects to Tillie Flower inside the mortuary. Imagine, not even a passing mention of this curious sight: a black Chevrolet sandwiched between a white van and a red Cadillac in front of a funeral home.

It is a wonder to me that Patrick did not include this part, seizing upon the ripe opportunity to make much of the colors black, white, and red—colors his religion elevates as symbols in themselves. It is a wonder also that he did not utilize the stick of butter on the floor. What fun he could have had with it. He could have had Prince slip on it, bang his head on the stove, and lose consciousness. Bent on moralizing, however, he chooses instead to end his piece with a bit of verbal tripe that he does not recognize as such. After the father delivers his persuasive speech from across the room, Patrick writes, "All was quiet for an agonizing moment before the boy, with a look of defeat in his hollow eyes, raised his hands in a gesture of surrender, then clutched fistfuls of his hair and wept bitterly, finally dropping the knife onto the floor." It is a sentence glutted with verbs and emotions.

In the silence that follows Patrick's reading, I wonder if Rachel is contemplating, as I am, the obvious difficulty posed in the final sentence: how one can still hold a knife while clutching handfuls of his hair.

"So how do you like it?" Patrick says. It is clear that he himself likes it very much.

"I guess it's a nicer ending than the real one," Rachel says. "But what happens to Mindy after the boy does that?"

"Well, I couldn't tell everything in four hundred words," Patrick says, "but she'd probably give up, too. She'd understand that what her father said was true, just like the boy did, and she'd know there was no future for the two of them."

What faith my nephew has in the power of mere words, especially his own. To think that two teenagers would be deeply touched and instantly changed by an adult's speech shows no knowledge of humankind.

Rachel makes no reply. I hear the jingle of Patrick's keys as he prepares to leave.

"You'll be okay?" he asks. "You need anything? You have Steve and Teri's number handy." He seems to know he will get no reply, and he rushes on, allowing no time for one. "Well, I better go now. I'll be home around ten, ten-thirty." He pauses. "Oh, and I'll stop and get milk somewhere." He pauses again. "I'm locking the door behind me." And he leaves.

Burglary, assault with intent to kill, kidnapping, and unlawful carrying of a weapon. Besides the traffic violation for the accident he caused, these will be the charges pressed against Prince for yesterday's incident even though he stole nothing, caused no lasting physical injury. I wonder what thoughts go through his mind as he sits in the Greenville County Jail tonight. I wonder what thoughts go through

Mindy's mind as she thinks about him bursting into her neighbors' house with a gun. She offered no words today when she came for her lesson, gave no sign that she felt anything at all when she stepped into the very room where Prince had threatened to kill us all, when she saw the purple bruise on Rachel's neck. During Mindy's lesson she was even quieter than usual, answering only in single syllables or not at all.

Seeing that his car was trapped between two larger vehicles, Prince did what came naturally. He ran from the scene on foot. And he went straight to the person he knew would help him—his mother. She did what comes naturally to mothers. She tried to protect him from the law. The two of them were stopped less than an hour later, in her car headed north on Highway 1.

Have I said that Prince is a black boy? If I have not, let me say it now. Whether his race is the chief cause of Steve and Teri's dislike of him, I cannot say, but in Mississippi, even in the twenty-first century, it must be a factor. As for me, it is his behavior, not his race, that has condemned him in my eyes.

Rachel appears at my door with the tray. "Here's your dessert, Aunt Sophie," she says. She places before me a bowl of chocolate ice cream and two Oreo cookies on a saucer. She begins collecting my supper dishes and putting them on the tray. She is wearing a pair of blue knee-length pants, the kind we used to call pedal pushers, and the orange sweatshirt with OCTOBER BALLOON FESTIVAL printed on the front. She has pushed the sleeves up past her elbows. It is beginning to have the soft, faded look of something much worn and much washed.

"How are you?" I ask her. I want to invite her to sit down, but I don't. She might feel obligated to sit, might try to make polite conversation. Or she might decline, claiming to have other work to do. Or she might sit down, and then neither of us could think of what to say. None of the possibilities is appealing, so I don't ask.

Rachel places a hand against the bruise on her neck. "I'm all right," she says. "It looks worse than it feels." She looks at me. "I hope it didn't upset you too much."

I shake my head. "I don't upset easily," I say. I take a bite of an Oreo cookie and know that what I have just said is untrue. What I mean is that I don't often show outward signs of being upset. What happened yesterday horrified me, both at the time and later. I could not eat more than a few bites of my supper last night, a supper much delayed by the disruption, and when I went to bed I replayed the incident over and over. I imagined how the firing of a gun would sound inside Patrick's kitchen. I imagined Rachel lying in her own blood on the floor. I imagined Prince turning the gun on Patrick, on me, on himself. So many possibilities to alter the outcome. There is no guarantee against terror in the afternoon, even in one's own home.

But the gun didn't fire. The moment is past, and I sit here alive watching Rachel pick up the tray and turn to leave. I stare hard at the colorful hot air balloon across the back of her sweatshirt and wonder if she ever wishes she could climb inside one and be carried to another life in another part of the world. I watch her plod to the door and into the kitchen. I hear her at the sink scraping and rinsing my dirty supper dishes.

I think of Patrick's lunge toward her after she collapsed to the floor, of his falling down on his knees beside her, of his anxious cries. "Rachel! Rachel! Are you okay? Did he hurt you?" All this as Prince escaped through the front door.

"Yes, yes, I'm fine," she said. Patrick held her elbow as she got to her feet, and for the first time since coming here to live, I saw the two of them embrace. It was not a mere courtesy on Rachel's part that she allowed him to pull her close. Indeed, she opened her arms wide and leaned into him. I could not look away. Perhaps some would find it humorous—so slight a man supporting so large a woman—but I did not. He stood straight and firm, and she clung to him as if he were a rock and she a shipwrecked soul.

Two police officers came to the house later to question us and to retrieve the gun. They pulled the stove away from the wall, and one of them picked up the gun and put it into a plastic bag. "Why, look, here's all our leftovers, Rachel," Patrick said, peering behind the stove. "There's some dried peas and rice and a couple of macaroni noodles." To which Rachel said sadly, "Oh dear, I need to vacuum all that out." It was Patrick, though, who got the vacuum cleaner out of the closet and told her to sit down while he cleaned it up.

Wheel of Fortune is on while I eat my dessert. The category is Fictional Character, and the puzzle shows but one letter. __ T __ __ __ __ __ . A young woman with spiked hair guesses the letter *L* and then buys a vowel. She chooses *O*, which turns out to be a wise choice, for now the name of the fictional character is obvious. O T __ __ L L O. She spins again, however, and goes bankrupt, leaving the next contestant, a man wearing a bow tie, to solve the puzzle. See where your greed got you, I want to tell the young woman.

Like Othello, Prince is a jealous boy. I have heard Teri tell Rachel that he is quick to pick fights with other boys, black and white, whom he accuses of flirting with Mindy. He has demanded that Mindy not encourage them, but he always suspects that she does. Since her parents withdrew her from school, he has prowled Edison Street to see if other boys are at her house. He has called on the telephone at all hours just to see if the line was busy. If it was, he was sure she was talking to another boy. And his jealousy extends to her parents, for exerting their will over his, for keeping her within their sight while denying him access. And when his jealousy turned to fury, he came to take Mindy by force, certain that she would do his bidding.

But for now he is in jail awaiting a trial. Unfortunately for him but fortunately for us, Prince turned eighteen a month ago. He will be tried as an adult.

Questions beg to be answered, age-old questions for which there are no answers. Why is a woman attracted to a jealous man? How could a girl like Mindy claim to love a boy like Prince? Perhaps the answers are all too simple. Perhaps they are the same answers as for other questions: How does a woman permit herself to marry an evil man? How could Sophia Langham think she loved Eliot Hess? Love is a problem with no solution. Most often I think of it as a myth, an impossible story that many people believe.

Before his arrest, Prince Cook was a high-scoring basketball player at Greenville High School. A woman may be drawn to a man with celebrity status, even in such a small arena as a local high school. Or the English Department of a small college. Perhaps it was a flattering thing for Mindy at first when Prince was consumed with possessing her. Perhaps she didn't know how dangerous such an obsession could become, how quickly it could turn deadly, how "trifles light as air" could be interpreted by the jealous one as solid proof of faithlessness.

Mindy is not of an age or disposition to endure advice from an old woman. Could I have substituted *Othello* for *Julius Caesar* in her literature book, I would have. Then I could say to her, "Beware of a jealous lover. See here, observe what happened to Desdemona in the end, all for the trifle of a handkerchief." For a jealous man is never satisfied. He will put out the light altogether before he will allow it to shine for another.

And yet a man may seek the light of many women at the same time. A jealous man may demand all from many women, yet not give himself fully to any one of them. There are birds like this, driven by competition to father many broods, to fly from nest to nest, lord to a feathered harem. There are other men who take long solitary flights, who give nothing but their names to the women devoted to serve them.

When Rachel returns for my dessert dishes some time later, I am once again sitting in my recliner. The only light is from the television. *The Beverly Hillbillies* is in progress, but I am not following the plot. The words that Jethro and Elly May exchange mean nothing to me. Having never cared for the program, I usually mute the volume or change the channel, but tonight I want noise to fill up the silence. Rachel picks up the bowl and saucer and wipes the round table with a wet cloth.

"I used to like that program when it first came on," she says to me. It occurs to me that perhaps she wants noise tonight, also.

"You may sit down and watch it with me," I say. But I speak too soon, realizing in her hesitation that she has no desire to watch television reruns with an old woman. To cover up the awkwardness, I say the first thing that comes to my mind. "Did you know he died not too long ago, the man who did this?"

"Who?" Rachel asks. She takes a step toward me, the dishcloth in one hand, the dishes in the other. "The man who did what?"

"The man who created the program. This one, *The Beverly Hillbillies*. He even wrote the theme song."

Rachel cocks her head and says, "How do you know these things, Aunt Sophie? Was that in *Time* magazine, too?"

I nod, for I read it only days ago: "DIED. PAUL HENNING, 93, creator of the long-running 1960s sitcom *The Beverly Hillbillies* (and its spin-off, *Petticoat Junction*); in Burbank, California."

"Maybe I can watch it with you some other night," she says. "I'm going to finish up in the kitchen, then take a hot bath and go to bed early. I feel like I can sleep tonight."

It must be that I fall asleep myself after she leaves, for the next thing I hear is Patrick's key jiggling the lock of the kitchen door. I see him pass by my doorway, then hear his footsteps recede down the hallway as he goes to check on Rachel.

CHAPTER 25

THAT MAKES THESE
ODDS ALL EVEN

Though the eastern phoebe often nests on
cliff ledges, it sometimes chooses more domestic
settings such as porch or shed eaves for its home.
An early springtime arrival, the phoebe frequently
returns to the same nesting site from year
to year, boldly announcing itself by name:
fee-bee, fee-bee, fee-bee!

Three times before today I have awakened in my recliner at Patrick's house and wondered where I was. Each time the answer has come, but the question was disturbing. What if I were to awake one day and have no answer?

One can do nothing to prepare for the quick causes of death such as those of my father and sisters, or of Tillie Flower and Tillie Fowler. But I watch myself for signs of the slow creeping diseases of the mind such as Alzheimer's or dementia. Or the silent onset of certain cancers. Or the mysterious complexity of disorders my mother suffered in her last days. Here is another example of the Principle of Variety for Patrick to exclaim over. Oh, the infinite variety of ways to die!

But for today I have awakened in my recliner, and I know where I am. I have read of birds that return spring after spring to build new nests in the same old places. I suppose someone has tagged these birds to determine that they are the same birds returning and not simply the same species. How much of life is composed of routine, both man and beast coming back time and again to the same pursuits in the same haunts. Here I perch in my recliner in Patrick's house on Edison Street in Greenville, Mississippi. *Soph-ie, Soph-ie, Soph-ie!*

Not only do I know where I am, but I also know what day it is. It is Monday, the day after Easter Sunday. The sky is bright above the treetops. I look at the bird feeder and see it swinging as if lately vacated by a squirrel or a large bird. I find it interesting that certain birds in plentiful numbers in the yard never come to the feeder by my window. Crows and starlings, for example, or doves, robins, blue jays. Perhaps there is a sense of pride in some birds that resists the idea of a handout.

I look at the television screen and ascertain that it is late morning. The sound is muted, but I see Samantha twitch her nose at her refrigerator and stove. Instantly a fully cooked meal appears on the countertop, ready to serve in china bowls and covered platters. She moves to the dining room and twitches her nose to set the table, then returns to the kitchen and begins carrying the dishes of food to the dining room. I wonder why she doesn't twitch her nose again to save herself the extra steps, but I suppose, like anything else, such a gimmick must be used sparingly lest it wear out too soon.

Earlier this morning I saw Ricky and Fred laughing at Lucy and Ethel, who were dressed in funny costumes, but I have slept through *MacGyver* and *Love Boat*. I feel as if I have returned from a long journey, though I know I haven't left my apartment.

And then I suddenly remember what woke me. My daytime dreams are often more vivid than my nighttime ones.

I turn and look toward the bookcase against the wall behind me, for I have just dreamed that someone broke into my apartment and vandalized the books, ripping them apart and scrawling curse words on the covers, strewing them over the floor and nailing loose pages of the Bible at crooked angles on the overturned bookcases. In my dream I grappled with the vandal, a figure in a dark cloak, and when I reached out my hand to pull the pages from the nails, I heard a loud voice in my ear: "Woman, why weepest thou? Whom seekest thou?"

But the bookcase is upright, the books and magazines in order on the shelves. The only voice is Rachel's in the kitchen. The door is partly open. I rise, stand a minute to gain my balance, and then walk slowly toward it. I see that Rachel is on the telephone. She is wearing her brown bathrobe. "I've got my finger on it," she says. Her broad back is bent over, her head nearly in her lap. And then I see that she is reading from a book. I know what book it is.

"'For my thoughts are not your thoughts,'" she reads, "'neither are your ways my ways, saith the Lord.'"

She pauses as if listening. "I know, I know," she says. "I can't explain it. I wish I could. I've been praying so hard. I was—" She breaks off, then begins reading again, slowly. "'For as the heavens are higher than the earth, so are my ways higher than your ways, and my thoughts than your thoughts. For as the rain cometh down, and the snow from heaven ...'" She labors through the words, with many pauses, and it strikes me that she is crying. Rachel can cry and still speak intelligibly. "And here's something else," she says. "I just saw this other verse a little further down. It says you'll 'be led forth with peace.' That's what it says, Teri. And if you're led forth, that means somebody's got you by the hand. He knows your sorrow, Teri. He'll give you comfort." She pauses again. "I know how bad it hurts, Teri. I know." Her voice breaks. "But God is faithful. I know that, too."

And so I am witness to another crisis from this same doorway, another breakdown in the machinery of life. What I have known was coming is here. A vandal has been busy overturning the lives of our neighbors across the street. This is no dream. And this person Rachel has been reading about—the one who claims that his ways and thoughts are higher than ours—has been standing by, watching it all. Now, according to Rachel, he offers to lead them forth with peace.

Perhaps he can be seen in the role of a tour guide after a hurricane or other natural disaster. He takes the dazed victims by the hand and conducts them through the ruins of their home. See, he says to Steve and Teri, here is the wreckage of your daughter Mindy, whose boyfriend wields a deadly gun at innocent people, who is in jail for now but may someday get out and threaten you again. See the girl, once so beautiful, whose mind is now closed to you, who claims that she wants to die, who says words like "I hate you" to those who would lay down their lives for hers.

And see, he says now, moving to another room, here is your other daughter, Veronica, whose mind and body have been wasted from birth, who can do nothing for herself, who can speak no words whatsoever to those who brought her into the world. See her golden hair, her delicate fair skin. See her vacant eyes, her lolling tongue, her convulsions. Now you see her, now you don't.

Two days ago, the day before Easter Sunday, Steve and Teri woke during the night to find Veronica in the grip of a seizure with no beginning and no end. She stopped breathing, and they rushed her to the hospital, where she began breathing again but only faintly and irregularly. A doctor told them that her heart was worn out. Over Resurrection Day Steve and Teri stood at her bedside hoping and praying—yes, Patrick and Rachel had convinced them by now of the efficacy of prayer—that she would stabilize and open her eyes, that a miracle would happen and they would be able to take her home again.

But from Rachel's words on the telephone, it is clear to me that they will not bring her home again. And once more I am flooded with the wonder of a love that finds its joy in ceaseless giving with no earthly hope of receiving, that is overcome with grief when the hours of thankless toil, the daily reminders of empty dreams are suddenly over.

I retreat to my recliner and turn on the sound of the television. I do not want to hear Rachel, a mother bereft of her own children, reading from the Bible to another mother whose heart is broken. My own selfishness appalls me, for here is what fills my own heart. Not sympathy for Teri and Rachel, whose journeys through motherhood have been freighted with such sorrow, but sympathy for myself. Better a journey with a sad ending than no journey at all.

Yesterday, on Easter Sunday, Patrick and Rachel did not go to church. They left early in the morning to spend the day at the hospital with Steve and Teri. I believe they knew that Veronica wouldn't come home. Rachel left bread on the kitchen counter and ham salad in the refrigerator for my lunch. They were gone until late afternoon. "Go lie down," I heard Patrick say to Rachel when they returned. "I'll get together something for us to eat." He came to my door, asked if I had been okay, apologized for lunch. I said nothing, only nodded. There was nothing to say. Perhaps Patrick thought I was upset over lunch, for he apologized again, saying they hated to make me fend for myself and hoped it wouldn't be necessary again.

It was too much trouble to speak of the insult I felt. Evidently Patrick thinks I do not understand that certain things, such as death and neighborly love, change the meaning of *necessary*. Making a ham salad sandwich for Veronica's sake, and for Steve and Teri's, was no hardship, but I did not bother to say this to Patrick.

After that I heard him in the kitchen clattering about for some time, and when he came back to my door, he had a request. "Aunt Sophie, I'm sorry to put you out again, but would you mind coming to the kitchen table to eat tonight? I'm not as good at this as Rachel, and it would help if I could serve it all at once." It was the first time I could remember Patrick's admitting inferiority in any area.

He had found a box of pizza mix in the cupboard, so this was our supper. A Chef Boyardee pepperoni pizza, baked on a rectangular cookie sheet instead of a round pizza pan. Rachel came to the table in her bathrobe. "I hope you like pizza, Aunt Sophie," she said, something Patrick had not thought to ask, of course.

I nodded. The truth was I liked pizza very much. As a younger woman, I could eat a large one by myself, often did so. Patrick had made one for the three of us. The pizza was sitting in the pan in the center of the table, with three plates and forks arranged around it.

Patrick had not thought to set out napkins. Or beverages.

He prayed a long, fervent prayer in which he begged for God's "tender mercies to be poured out on our dear friends and their helpless little girl." He also said this: "And if it be your will to take her up into your presence, to make her whole and well, to serve as one of your choicest angels for all eternity, may it please us to accept this as from your good and wise hand." Evidently Patrick believes in a God who is pleased to create damaged goods only to perfect them later, after their pathetic days on earth are done. Such easy thinking conveniently settles the problem of deformed children. There's nothing like a little trouble on earth to make the idea of eternal bliss more glorious.

After the prayer Patrick said, "Uh-oh," then snapped his fingers and went to the refrigerator. He brought back three cans of 7-Up and set one beside each plate. Then he snapped his fingers again and brought back napkins. These are the kinds of cartoon gestures one might expect to see from a man like Patrick: snapping his fingers, raising one finger and saying, "Ah-ha," hitting his forehead with the heel of his hand. He would not approve of Samantha's nose twitching. No doubt he would consider *Bewitched* a wicked program making light of sorcery, dabbling in the occult.

Meanwhile Rachel was cutting the pizza into squares. She served me first, then Patrick, then herself.

As we ate, Patrick told me that Veronica was "slipping away," that the doctors were not expecting her to "come around this time." They thought she had "gone" at one point while they were there, but then she shuddered and began breathing again, shallow ragged breaths. Mindy was there, too, he said, sitting in a chair by the bed, not saying a word, looking "like death warmed over." It would not occur to Patrick that such an expression was tasteless.

"It was the strangest thing, though," Patrick said. "Mindy reached over one time and started rubbing the back of Veronica's hand, and—You saw it when it happened, didn't you, Rachel?" Rachel nodded and Patrick continued. "And Veronica all of a sudden went stiff and held her breath like she was surprised—" Patrick paused to reenact these details—"and then she turned her hand *over*." He stopped, took another big bite of pizza, and chewed for a while. "Maybe it was just a reflex or something," he said, "but it looked for all the world like she wanted to hold Mindy's hand. Didn't it, Rachel?" Rachel nodded again.

"I never noticed before that she didn't have a thumb on that one hand, did you?" Patrick added. He looked at Rachel, but she gave no response. Perhaps she was thinking, as I was, that a defect of that nature in a child like Veronica was hardly worthy of note.

We ate in silence for a while before Patrick resumed. "Anyway, Mindy put her palm against Veronica's, and she sat there like that for the longest time. And then you know what she said?" It was a stupid question. Of course I didn't know what she said. I was not there.

"She said, 'I felt her *push* against my hand.' She said it real soft, like she was talking to herself, but we all heard her. And Steve said she had probably just jerked a little, and then Mindy got mad and said she knew the difference between a push and a jerk and what she had felt was a push."

I tried to see it from Mindy's perspective. Watching your sister die, you might want to believe something impossible. And Steve's perspective was just as easy to see. With his man's mind, without stopping to think, Steve had merely stated the obvious. A child with such neurological impairment, a child who had never once shown receptivity to human touch or registered recognition of faces or voices, could not be expected to respond to her sister's touch on her deathbed.

Did Veronica press Mindy's hand or not? Who can tell? One believes what he wants to believe. There are mysteries past explaining.

But man seeks explanation. Ambiguity—this is what it is called in literature. An author leaves a matter open for multiple interpretations. It could be this, or it could be that. "Ambiguity of Purpose in *Measure for Measure*." This was a paper of Eliot's rejected for publication many times. It was a paper I typed many times, making minor alterations as instructed. But still it was rejected. It was the cause of many of his black moods. I found it among his things when I destroyed the contents of his desk. And though I burned the paper years ago, I remember well the sentence with which Eliot had ended it, a sentence he retained through each draft. Quoting from, and agreeing with, another Shakespearean scholar named G. B. Harrison, he concluded that *Measure for Measure* was "a flawed play, the soul of which became too great for its body."

Rachel hangs up the telephone in the kitchen and appears at my doorway. "Aunt Sophie? That was Teri calling from the hospital." She speaks loudly, over the closing music of *Bewitched*.

I open my eyes and look at her. Her hair appears not to have been combed this morning, the crest above her brow standing on end as if electrified. "Veronica has died," I say.

Rachel bows her head and presses her hand against her mouth.

"Her soul became too great for her body," I say. The words fall from my lips; I do not mean to be flippant. Rachel raises her eyes and looks at me briefly, then shifts her gaze to the window, her forehead wrinkled. I imagine her later tonight saying to Patrick, "Do you know what Aunt Sophie said when I told her? What do you suppose she meant by that? Or maybe I misunderstood her. The television was on loud."

A soul too great for her body. It is the kind of thing Patrick would latch on to, fitting it to his idea of a transfigured Veronica floating about heaven as one of God's prize angels. I can imagine him volunteering to say a few words at the funeral, then standing, pausing dramatically, lifting a hand as if pronouncing a benediction, and saying solemnly, "We gather today, dear friends, to pay tribute to a precious child whose soul became too great for her body."

"The funeral will be on Wednesday," Rachel says, and then she turns and leaves, wiping her eyes with the loose end of her bathrobe belt. A few minutes later she comes to my door again, wearing her denim jeans and a T-shirt. "I'll be back," she says. "I'm going over to feed Stonewall and let him out for a little while." She dabs at her nose with a tissue.

"Woman, why weepest thou? Whom seekest thou?" These were words I heard Patrick read from the Bible last night. The pizza finished, Patrick dished up bowls of vanilla ice cream drizzled with chocolate syrup. When we were done, he said, "You know, it just doesn't feel like Easter Sunday when you don't go to church. Why don't we read the resurrection story from the Bible?" I rose at once and walked out of the kitchen. I could have closed the door to my apartment, but I didn't. I went to my recliner and sat down. It was growing dark outside by now, but I didn't turn on a light.

Why did I leave my door open, knowing what was to come

through it? And why did I sit in the dark? Why did I accept sound but refuse light? These, too, are ambiguities. Perhaps sound and light are symbols, perhaps not. But this I know. I heard Patrick read the Easter story from the book of John. As before, I could tell his reading was not for Rachel alone but for me, as well. I heard the story in the dark—that Jesus was buried in a borrowed tomb, that the disciples and Mary Magdalene were distressed to find the tomb empty, that Mary recognized the voice but not the face of Jesus in the garden, that she did not answer the questions he asked her, that when she knew he was Jesus she called him Master.

Patrick read until he came to these words: "'But these are written, that ye might believe that Jesus is the Christ, the Son of God; and that believing ye might have life through his name.'" Then he stopped. Unlike Shakespeare in *Measure for Measure*, there is no ambiguity of purpose in John's Gospel.

In *Measure for Measure* the duke disguises himself as a friar and visits Claudio in prison. Life, he says to the convicted man, is not a thing to be counted dearly. Let it go and you will spare yourself the disappointment of seeking things you cannot keep, of growing old yet finding no pleasure in the wealth you have accumulated. This thing called life, says the duke, is greatly overrated. Death—that is the better way, he says, for it is death "that makes these odds all even."

And so I sit in my recliner in the middle of the day, a rich old woman, thinking about Veronica, a poor dead child. I close my eyes and try to imagine her small body fitted with the wings of an angel. I see her lift her arms and spread her hands to fly, hands that now have ten fingers instead of nine.

CHAPTER 26

THE WEB OF OUR LIFE IS OF A MINGLED YARN

*Much of the purple finch's territory is shared by its
cousin the Cassin's finch. Because of their close
resemblance, bird watchers often confuse the two.
An experienced watcher, however, knows that the
back of the male purple finch has a more reddish
cast than that of the Cassin's finch.*

F
or the first time since coming here to live five months ago, I
have left Patrick's house. If spring were to choose a single day
to showcase her beauties, this might be the day. The sun is shining
in a blue sky. The air is mild and fragrant. The occasion is no picnic,
however, no shopping trip, no celebration dinner, but a funeral. Not
the funeral of a family member or close friend but of someone with
whom I never exchanged a word. No need to chronicle the standard
formalities, the funereal trappings, the trite words spoken and sung,

the tears shed, yet I will say that Patrick was indeed asked to take part.

"We want you to read some verses from the Bible," Steve had said to him in the kitchen on Monday night. "You pick them. We don't really have any suggestions. Just read something you think would be good." Steve's voice was weary.

And now I am present to hear what Patrick has chosen. It is from the book of Revelation. This is a book I have read from the red Bible I found on the bookshelf in my apartment. The first twenty chapters of Revelation are not happy ones, nor even comprehensible at times, with their visions of beasts, trumpets, scrolls, and fowls that swoop down to devour the flesh of men great and small.

But Patrick reads from the twenty-first chapter. I suppose these are verses often read at funerals, for they speak of old things passing away—things such as tears and sorrow and pain. And death, of course, although for now death has not passed away. It is all too real for those hearing the sound of Patrick's voice.

Patrick stands on a platform of the small chapel inside Wagner's Mortuary for his reading. He is wearing a dark suit, a white shirt, and a tie with gray and red stripes. His shoes are shined, and his hair, thinning on top, appears to have been treated with some of his grandfather's Magic Hair Tonic and combed wetly to one side. He holds the Bible aloft, a large black one, and speaks importantly, as if addressing the United States Senate. As he reads, I think of another verse in the book of Revelation: "And I heard the voice of harpers harping with their harps."

Perhaps Steve intended for Patrick to read a brief passage. If so, he should have told him. On and on he reads, not bothering to omit parts that offer no comfort. He reads of murderers and whoremongers and idolaters, all of whom "'shall have their part in the lake which burneth with fire.'" He reads of "'seven vials full of the seven last plagues'" and of the length and breadth and height of Jerusalem.

But he also reads of the fountain of the water of life, of twelve gates of twelve pearls, of trees with healing in their leaves. At last he finishes: "'Behold, I come quickly: blessed is he that keepeth the sayings of the prophecy of this book.'" He stops and bows his head, as if preparing to pray, or as if allowing time for others to stifle the urge to applaud, and after a brief silent moment he dismounts the platform and takes his seat beside Rachel and me on the third row.

The funeral ends, the coffin is left behind at the graveyard, and we return to Edison Street, where Rachel and Patrick open the doors of their home to Steve and Teri for a family dinner. It is nearly five o'clock in the afternoon. Besides Teri's parents and Steve's father, the only other out-of-town relatives are Teri's sister and her aunt Helena from Yazoo City, whom I remember from Christmas dinner. Helena's friend Della Boyd, strangely quiet today, is with her. I can't help wondering if the family turnout would have been larger had Veronica been a normal child.

I think about the headstone Steve and Teri have chosen for Veronica's grave. It is "on order," I have heard them say. The one they selected features an engraving of a lamb and the words "A little child shall lead them." I think about the fact that no one will know from looking at the headstone on Veronica's grave that she was deficient in any way. Death equalizes all children in a cemetery. A bystander may see the stone, may take note of her beautiful name, of the four short years of her life, and may think, "How sad—such a sweet young child plucked from the vine, denied a full and fruitful life." He will have no way of knowing that she could not laugh, hold a spoon, or run into her mother's arms. This little child could lead no one. She was denied a full and fruitful life from the day she was born.

A few friends have been invited for the dinner, also—one of Steve's co-workers at the catfish plant, two of the therapists who had worked with Veronica, a former neighbor from the trailer park. Patrick has taken the afternoon off work for Veronica's funeral, and Potts also attends.

Steve and Potts have become friends over the past few months, ever since discovering that they share two interests: guitar and chess. Some nights they get together to play their guitars and sing. For many weeks they have had two running chess games in progress— one at Steve and Teri's house and one at Potts'. I have heard Teri tease Steve about something she read in a magazine. People who play too much chess, she said, often "go off the deep end." She cited a story about a former world chess champion who became convinced that people were trying to frame him for crimes he didn't commit. Walking down the street, he would whirl around and accuse total strangers of following him in hopes of collecting samples of his DNA. I doubt that there will be much singing or many chess games in Steve and Teri's house for some time. I doubt that Teri will be teasing Steve about going off the deep end.

Because Steve and Teri have been visiting the church where Patrick and Rachel are members, the women's Sunday school class has prepared food, many platters and bowls of it, and have brought them to Rachel's kitchen. During the funeral two of the church women came to set up extra folding tables and chairs in the living room, to lay out plates, glasses, silverware, and napkins for fifteen or twenty people.

When we arrive home from the cemetery, all is in readiness. Patrick hurries ahead so he can stand at the front door and direct the guests to gather in the kitchen. Averse to being part of a herd, I prefer to wait in the car until the others have gone in. Rachel waits with me and then accompanies me slowly along the front path marked by large paving stones, which is Patrick's idea of a sidewalk. She is at my elbow as I mount the three steps to the front door.

The food is arranged on the kitchen table. After everyone is assembled in the kitchen, Patrick thanks the church ladies for their help, then announces that after prayer the guests may serve their plates and sit anywhere they like in the dining room or living room.

Instead of the men's clothes she usually wears, Teri is dressed in a black skirt and a pale blue blouse. Whereas the men's clothes hide her body, the skirt and blouse reveal the fact that she has put on weight. The skirt puckers at the waist, is tight around the hips. Steve is solicitous of her, standing behind her like a wall during Patrick's speech and prayer, his large hands on her shoulders. Teri's eyes, void and unfocused, look like the eyes of a blind person.

Mindy stands behind her parents, staring at the floor, a small crease between her eyes. I wonder if her mind is here in Rachel's kitchen or if it is in a cell in the county jail. I wonder how Veronica's death has touched her, if it has drawn her heart to her family. Nothing has been said about the resuming of our daily lessons. I wonder if after this week Teri will take up her duty of guarding Mindy during the day or if she will give it up as a game for which she has forgotten the rules.

When a woman loses a child, does grief sap her love for a remaining child? Or does her love for that child double? And when a woman loses two children at the same time, where does all that love go? These are the thoughts that circle through my mind as Patrick begins his prayer.

Today Mindy wears a short black knit dress that clings to her body, her hip bones visible. Having never been thin, I try to imagine what it would feel like to live inside such a body. Her long blond hair is pulled back in a low ponytail at the nape of her neck, but shorter ragged strands hang loose around her face. She wears no makeup, no jewelry except for a brown leather strap around one wrist. There are hollows under her eyes and cheekbones. Still, she is beautiful.

As Patrick prays, I look at the other people standing in Rachel's kitchen. Teri's parents are standing beside her. She and her mother, who is wearing a childish-looking dress with a large white Pilgrim collar, are holding hands. Her father has a full head of gray hair and a gray beard, which he strokes absentmindedly. His eyes have the hard look of someone brooding over a misfortune. They are not closed.

Teri's aunt Helena is wearing a brown hat on her head. It is an old-fashioned hat with several long brown feathers sprouting from the band on one side. Della Boyd's hair looks as if small animals have been nesting in it, but she is dressed neatly in a dark blue dress with a large, floppy red flower pinned at the neck. Teri's sister has a fleshy cheerful face that looks out of place among a group of mourners. She is wearing a large flowing dress in a floral print and long twisted

strands of turquoise beads. Her eyes have the innocent look of someone not attuned to reality, perhaps of an adult child still dependent
on her parents. But perhaps I am reading too much into people's eyes
today.

I have studied everyone before Patrick has finished praying.
There is not a distinguished-looking person among them. Potts is
wearing the same maroon sport coat he wore when he came for
Christmas dinner. Perhaps he looks at me and says, "Aunt Sophie is
wearing the same sweater and the same bird pin she wore at Christmas dinner." I am wearing a different dress, however, and for the first
time in many months I am wearing shoes instead of bedroom slippers.

But of what importance are the things one wears on his body? I
look at Rachel standing beside me. No denim jeans today, no T-shirt
or sweat shirt, no brown bathrobe. Her dress is of a dark green crinkly
fabric with a high ruffle about the neck, which hides the fading
bruise from the ides of March incident. It is the dress Patrick gave
her for Christmas. Some women would look pretty in such a dress,
but an objective eye would note that Rachel does not. Mine is not
an objective eye, however.

"And so, as we gather ourselves to partake of this food so lovingly
prepared," Patrick says, "we thank you, our wise and loving father,
for being in our midst, for ministering to our grieving hearts with the
salve of your merciful kindness."

There is no telling how long he could go on in this vein, but a
bird interrupts him. It is not a bird I can identify by name. It flies at
the kitchen window over the sink, near where Rachel and I are
standing. It strikes the pane with its long hard bill, then retreats to
the bush beneath the window. Almost immediately it launches a

second attack. The noise is a loud *thunk*, like that of a stone thrown at the window. Several others open their eyes to search out the source of the sound, and even Patrick halts momentarily, as if wondering whether to stop or keep going. After the fourth thump, he closes his prayer. By now everyone else is staring at the window.

Again the bird comes, this time stopping before he collides, raising and spreading his claws before him, fluttering his wings wildly as if in warning. Then once again he charges at the window with his sharp bill. He falls back again, disappearing within the bush, but seconds later he is back at the window.

Della Boyd clucks her tongue and says, "Well, look at that. The poor thing must think his reflection is another bird."

Teri's sister emits a little snort of laughter. "We had a cat once that would paw at hisself in the mirror. Remember, Mama?" Her mother nods sadly.

"Or maybe he's just trying to get our attention," says Patrick. "Maybe he's trying to warn us about something." This is typical of Patrick's attempts at humor, weak and ill-timed. Yes, I want to say, maybe the bird is warning us that there's a fool in our midst.

"Maybe he's telling us the food is getting cold," says Teri's sister. Perhaps she and Patrick will sit at a table together so they can try to match wits. I would guess the two of them to be a close match.

"Come on, everybody, please take a plate and get something to eat." This is from Rachel. She moves up behind Steve and Teri and nudges them to go first. The honor of going first at a dinner like this belongs to those who are hurting most. I think of the habits and instincts that will die hard for Steve and Teri. I think of their eating a meal, turning often to the space between them, ready to wipe a mouth or offer a bite and then remembering that Veronica is gone. I think of Teri waking in the mornings, having no one to bathe and dress, no therapy schedule to keep. I think of her sitting on the edge of her bed for a long time, wondering how to fill all the hours stretched out ahead of her.

Everyone slowly migrates toward the table, but I move closer to the window. I see the bird nestled among the branches of the bush, his eyes darting here and there, alert for danger from above. He looks plump, his gray-brown feathers ruffled from the frightening encounters at the windowpane.

You, sir, are not the most intelligent of your species, I think. Your fears are of your own making. While you fight with a phantom enemy, your little ones might be starving. Come, leave your hiding place and do something useful.

"Aunt Sophie, can I get you a plate of food?" Rachel is beside me again.

No need to tell what food she puts on my plate, where I sit, what I hear. It is a funeral supper. That is enough. When someone dies, the living gather to eat, to keep themselves alive a little longer. This much I will say: As I eat, someone asks, "Did I tell you LaDonna is having *ten* bridesmaids at her wedding?" And someone else says, "I think showy weddings are tacky." I hear someone laugh.

A funeral, a wedding, tears, laughter—a single day may hold them all. "The web of our life is of a mingled yarn, good and ill together." I can quote three lines from *All's Well That Ends Well*, one being these words spoken by an unnamed character and another spoken by Helena as part of a riddle: " 'Tis but the shadow of a wife you see, the name, and not the thing."

I do not agree with Shakespeare's title, that all is made well by a good ending. Suffering cannot be waved aside by a moment of relief. I do agree, however, that our lives are of a mingled yarn. And I know that a wife may be such in name only. The third line I recall from the play is spoken by an old man, who says, "Mine eyes smell onions; I shall weep anon." There is much in life to make one weep, yet with practice one may learn to postpone his tears, sometimes indefinitely.

During the dinner Patrick scampers about refilling glasses, removing empty plates, entreating everyone to go back for seconds, offering desserts. Rachel brings me a plate with a slice of lemon icebox pie on it, and I eat it slowly. Steve's father makes the mistake of asking Patrick what kind of work he does, and Patrick pulls up a chair beside him to deliver a speech of which he never tires: My Life as Manager of the Main Office Supply. Once again I hear the voice of harpers harping with their harps.

At last the meal is finished. The church ladies have packaged the leftovers and washed the dishes. Teri's parents and sister, who live less than an hour away in Rolling Fork, head home, and Steve's father, who is spending the night, walks across the street with Mindy. Helena and Della Boyd get in their car to return to Yazoo City. Everyone is gone except Steve, Teri, and Potts. They are standing by the front door, preparing to leave. It is after seven o'clock and is growing dark outside.

"This time next week it'll still be daylight," Patrick says. "We set our clocks ahead this weekend, you know." This hardly seems like a fitting remark for the end of such a day, but no one points it out. Steve is even polite enough to express his approval of Daylight Savings Time. "I like the extra time after supper," he says. The concept of extra time is a fallacy, but no one points this out, either.

And then Teri and Rachel look at each other. Teri steps away from Steve's side and slowly moves toward Rachel as if drawn by an irresistible force. I watch them come together, two wounded souls bound by more than friendship. I watch Rachel take Teri into her arms as she would comfort a child. Teri sobs against her, saying over and over, "Thank you, thank you, oh, thank you." Imagine, a mother who has just buried her daughter thanking someone.

The men, to their credit, allow them time. They do not try to pry them apart or stanch their weeping. They do not talk loudly to cover the embarrassment of raw emotion. They seem to know this time is as necessary to the women as eating.

At last they move apart, and Rachel and Patrick follow the others outside. I watch them through the screen door. "I'm praying for you, brother." This is spoken by Potts to Steve at the bottom of the steps. It is a curious sight to see two grown men reach out their hands to shake, then simultaneously dismiss the formality and fall into an embrace. They speak no words, but their tears are as genuine as those of the women moments earlier. Two men whose children are beyond their reach, they occupy the same territory. Like the old man in Shakespeare's play, my eyes smell onions. Perhaps I too shall weep anon.

They walk toward the driveway, Potts' hand thrown across Steve's shoulder. At Potts' car, I see them stop and face each other. Potts is talking, with wide eloquent gestures, Steve listening. Almost identical in size, they are hard to tell apart in the dusk.

CHAPTER 27

HOME ART GONE AND TAKEN THY WAGES

The orchard oriole spends most of its time
in Mexico and Central America but migrates
into North America for a few weeks each year
to mate and nest. The male is easy to spot,
for he puts on a flashy territorial display in
early spring, singing so passionately that he
rises several feet off his branch.

I look up from the Milestones page of the *Time* magazine in my lap. It is late April, after supper and before dessert, and Patrick is reading aloud a poem in the kitchen. It is one of several poems that the professor of his literature class has assigned for discussion tonight, a poem that contains the line "Wearing white for Eastertide." It is a poem in which the poet, A. E. Housman, demonstrates his disregard for the rule concerning the misplaced modifier. "It only leaves me fifty more," he writes, speaking of years. It would have been as easy for Mr. Housman to write it correctly: "It leaves me only fifty more." But he didn't.

The misplaced modifier, however, is not what Patrick wants to talk about. He wants to take issue with what he calls "the message" of the poem. It is with amazement that I hear Rachel's reply. "But he has a point," she says. Patrick excitedly counters with "And that's exactly how the world gets its philosophy into the church! It says something that sounds harmless on the surface! And then the average Christian swallows it hook, line, and sinker, not even stopping to think about the long-range implications!" Patrick is fond of the exclamation point, both in his speech and in his writing. He is also fond of nailing down what he considers to be dangerous long-range implications.

"But he does have a point," Rachel says again. Though she is not disagreeing with him outright, I cannot remember a time when she gave such credit to an opposing view. After another flurry of vehemence from Patrick, she says it yet again but this time frames it in a series of questions: "But don't you think he has a point? Don't you love springtime the older you get? I know I do. That's not wrong, is it? Read it again."

She stops him during this reading and asks what the word *Eastertide* means. "It's such a pretty word," she says. Though the explanation could be summarized in a few words as the weeks following Easter Sunday, Patrick chooses, as always, the circuitous route. "As the crow flies" is not a familiar concept to him. He loves the winding roads and scenic lookouts of verbal expression.

He resumes reading the poem, and at the end Rachel says, "Well, fifty years do go by fast. We sure know that, don't we?"

It is easy to tell that Patrick is frustrated and wants to press his point further, but he declares himself out of time. "I want to run by Dr. Germaine's office to mention something to him," he says. I hear the stacking of books and rustling of papers. I pity Dr. Germaine. Instead of a few quiet moments in his office before class, he must listen to Patrick mention something. With Patrick, words like *mention* lose their original meaning.

At the door Patrick says, "Oh, is it okay if Potts comes for supper tomorrow night? I found out it's his birthday." I hear nothing from Rachel. Perhaps she speaks softly or nods. "I can bring something home, though," Patrick adds. "I *don't* want you cooking all day." He speaks as if Rachel must be kept in line. "Oh, here, I forgot about this. I got twenty bucks for that old printer I sold. You can use it for groceries."

He leaves, shutting the door hard, and Rachel sets about clearing the kitchen table. I hear a whistled tune and look at the television to see Opie and Andy walking down a dirt road, carrying fishing poles.

"DIED. BETTY TALMADGE, 81, prominent Washington socialite and entrepreneur who made headlines in the late 1970s when she testified before the Senate Ethics Committee against her estranged husband, Georgia Senator Herman Talmadge." The Milestones page does not spare shameful personal details. The entry for Betty Talmadge relates that she learned via television that her husband planned to divorce her. It also relates that she later blew the whistle on her husband in a courtroom, stating that he kept large stashes of unreported donations in the form of hundred dollar bills in a hall closet.

The detail that convinces me that Betty Talmadge was telling the truth is this: She often went to the coat pocket repository herself, she said under oath, and helped herself to some of the bills when she overspent the fifty-dollar-a-week allowance her husband gave her. This does not strike me as the kind of information one would invent. It smacks of hard reality.

I think of my father's tight clutch on the family purse strings during my years in Methuselah. I recall but once when my mother borrowed from the cache of money Daddy kept at home in an old can. *Borrowed* was her word, but it was not the word he used when he discovered that the money was missing. Apparently Daddy counted the money regularly and kept a running total, something my mother didn't know until she borrowed from it. I was a teenager when this happened, and I heard the discussion through my bedroom wall that night. *Discussion* was also her word, when she asked me the next day if I had heard it. I pretended that I had not.

I think of Eliot's politely confiscatory behavior concerning my money during our thirteen years of marriage. Though I had managed my own finances quite capably during my years as a single teacher, he was of the opinion that no woman really wanted such a responsibility, nor was she adequately equipped to handle it. It is remarkable to me, looking back, that such an outwardly timid, unmanly man, a literary scholar by vocation, was in so many ways fanatically sexist in private. And yet, I must admit, I gave him license to be, for I readily yielded at every turn. I gave over my assets to his husbandly supervision.

Like Herman Talmadge and like my father, Eliot doled out to me a weekly household allowance. I took care to operate within it. That the allowance should be used up before the week ended was a dreadful thought. I knew of no hoard of cash at home from which I could borrow. Therefore, to avoid any show of disapproval were I to ask for more, it was with great caution and deliberation that I made my purchases.

Imagine a leap from total independence to strict accountability for one's expenditures. Yet would anyone believe me if I said that this arrangement did not vex me? I was a married woman now. I had a husband and a home. Weak-willed and nearsighted, I suffered from romantic notions that blinded me to the freedoms I had lost. For thirteen years I believed myself reasonably happy. Even in the absence of children, I clung to the tiny raft of my marriage as the current of life swept me along.

"I want to buy a present for Anita," I said to Eliot one day. It might have been a day not unlike this day. It was in early May, near the end of the spring semester.

Anita McDonald was the only teacher at South Wesleyan whom I counted as a true friend. All the others were merely colleagues, acquaintances of Eliot's who felt obligated to make room for me in their circle. Anita was a single woman, twelve years older than I, whose level of education, like mine, qualified her to teach only freshmen. She had labored in the trenches of Basic Grammar and Composition for twenty-six years but was at last retiring. She was planning to move from Kentucky to Ohio, where her older brother Ernest had a farm. And on this farm old Ernest McDonald had a carriage house he was renovating for his sister's retirement home.

I had typed an article for Eliot that afternoon and had laid it beside his plate at supper. He saw it when he sat down, and it was at that moment, as he reached for it, that I spoke. "I want to buy a present for Anita."

Though his eyes clouded, the prim smile did not vanish. He glanced at me, then down at the paper he was holding. "Fidelity and Cuckoldry in *Cymbeline*" was its title, one with which he was not satisfied. He turned to the first page, where the title appeared again. His smile faded. Without looking at me, he said, "The English Department will give Miss McDonald a parting gift." This was true. A week earlier each faculty member in the department had received a memo asking that a two-dollar contribution be given to the dean's secretary for the purpose of "a retirement remembrance" for Anita. "I have already given our share," he added, "and crossed our names off the list." I did not ask whether he had given two dollars or four.

He leafed through the pages of the paper as I put the food on his plate. I cannot remember what was on the menu that night, but it would be easy to guess. Eliot cared nothing for variety. He had five or six preferences, and I rotated among those. So let us imagine that it was a pork chop that night, with a heaping mound of rice and gravy, perhaps a serving of the large green peas he favored and three rolls with butter. "I want to give her something extra," I said. "Something special. A gift from only me."

He frowned as if he had discovered a typographical error, though I knew he had not. I had proofread the paper three times. The paper was eventually placed in one journal or another, with a different title. I can recall neither journal nor title, nor do I care to. I remember little of the play *Cymbeline*, one of Shakespeare's more obscure comedies, except that, as in *Othello*, a husband was too willing to believe his wife unfaithful.

Eliot sighed. It was a quiet, longsuffering sigh. "Have you money for such a gift, Sophia?" He offered a patient smile.

"I have a few dollars left," I said. "I was hoping to buy strawberries with them." This was a calculated answer, for Eliot loved strawberries.

I filled my own plate and began eating. Eliot set the paper aside and for several minutes gave his attention to his food. He ate quickly, his eyes frequently darting to the paper as if eager to pick it up again.

"Ten," I said at length. I fixed my own eyes pointedly on the typed paper beside his plate. Perhaps I hoped to remind him that my time was surely worth something. Perhaps I only imagined his slight intake of breath, as of surprise. Ten? Ten dollars? So large an amount?

Besides strawberries, banana pudding was another of Eliot's favorites. As he finished his supper, I rose and took a bowl of banana pudding from the refrigerator and set it on the table. I served a liberal portion into a smaller bowl, took away his plate, and placed the dish of pudding in front of him.

He picked up his spoon and ate it. Then he left the table, taking the paper with him. I was at the sink a few minutes later when he returned to the kitchen and then left again. On the table I saw two five-dollar bills. And though so much of that day is erased from my memory, I clearly recall this: As I tucked the money into my apron pocket, I was grateful for his generosity.

The sounds in the kitchen stop, and Rachel appears in my apartment carrying the tray. On it are two saucers, which she sets on the round table. On each saucer is a wedge of something white. She picks up my supper dishes, stacks them on the tray, and takes them back to the kitchen. From my recliner I look at the two saucers on opposite sides of the round table. Has Rachel brought me two servings of dessert, or am I to think that she plans to eat her dessert with me?

On the television Barney Fife is trying to set Andy Taylor up with one of the single women in the town of Mayberry. He is inviting groups of them over to Andy's house in hopes that he will be smitten.

Rachel returns, carrying a saucepan by its handle. She stirs whatever is inside and then slowly spoons something thick and red onto the top of each white wedge. She leaves again and returns with forks and napkins. She sits down at the round table. "May I join you for dessert?" she says. I do not point out the humor of such a question after having made full provision for an affirmative answer. Instead, I nod and make my way to the table.

It is cheesecake with cherry sauce. She did not make the cheesecake, she tells me. One of the cashiers at the Main Office brought it to work today, then told Patrick to take what was left. She did make the cherry sauce, she tells me, but "It's just a can of cherries with some cornstarch and sugar. It's nothing special."

Nothing special tastes very good on top of the cashier's leftover cheesecake. To cover the silence that follows, we both look at the television screen. Barney tells Andy that he needs a wife, that Opie needs a mother. Andy looks exasperated.

"I used to wish he'd get married," Rachel says. "And Barney, too. I used to want him and Thelma Lou to get married on the show."

I say nothing. I never considered that Andy Taylor's domestic life needed to be fixed. With Aunt Bee to cook and keep house, he and Opie were well taken care of. Helen Crump was nice enough, but I liked her as a single schoolteacher.

"Sometimes men change after they're married," I say. Rachel

looks at me, puzzled. "My sisters' husbands took their money, too," I add. My mind suddenly fills with pictures of old boots, coat pockets, tin cans, cardboard boxes behind coal buckets. I see men's hands dispensing small bills as charity, but grudgingly. And then I see my bankbook and the large sum showing my wealth.

There is a song in *Cymbeline*, sung in a forest by one of the king's sons. This one is a short song with a theme: All men come to dust. After the sunshine of youth and the raging winds of old age, "golden lads" and "chimney-sweepers" all come to the same end. Shakespeare employs a job metaphor. After your work is done, he says, you get paid for it. "Home art gone and taken thy wages." This is not necessarily a comforting thought. Where is this home, and what are these wages? I recall a verse from the red Bible, one in which the subject and verb do not agree: "For the wages of sin is death."

"I read once that it is common for women to hide money from their husbands," I say, "but I believe husbands are just as likely to hide money from their wives." Perhaps Rachel thinks I am suffering from the early stages of dementia. If so, my next words surely give her more cause to think so. "Fidelity and cuckoldry may be found on either side of the marriage bed." Rachel appears to be thinking this over. She takes another bite of cheesecake and nods solemnly.

"I had a cousin who took in a baby and raised him as her own," she says. "Her husband told her it was a friend's baby, but a long time later she found out it was her husband's own baby. He had been seeing this other woman all along." If this is Rachel's stab at a relevant response, it is a lucky one.

"The European cuckoo is thought to be a foolish bird," I say. "It makes no nest of its own but lays an egg in the nest of some other unsuspecting bird."

Rachel takes only the smallest of bites. I wonder if life has taught her this: What pleasure there is to be had, take it slowly.

"And then the other bird feeds the little cuckoo when it hatches?" she asks.

I nod. "Yes, some think this is where the word *cuckold* has its origin. Infidelity must be prepared to dispose of the offspring it produces."

If she is not familiar with the word *cuckold*, she does not show it. She puts her head to one side and looks at me. "A person could sure learn a lot from you, Aunt Sophie."

We both turn again to look at the television. Barney is busy disqualifying women right and left from his list of candidates for Andy's wife. He crosses them off for things such as not liking housework or not being able to cook.

"I only knew how to make pancakes when we were married," Rachel says. Like A. E. Housman, she has misplaced her modifier. "Did you know how to cook when you got married?"

I tell her I was forty-two when I married, and though I wasn't a very good cook, I knew my way around in the kitchen.

"Patrick sure ate a lot of pancakes those first few months," she says. "But he never did say a cross word about it." She runs the tip of her fork back and forth through her cherry sauce, then lifts it to her mouth. "I'll never forget how excited he was the day he came home and found out we were having hot dogs for supper."

I glance through the doorway into the kitchen. It comes to me that Rachel and Patrick would have eaten those pancakes and hot dogs within sight of where I now sit. I try to imagine the two of them as newlyweds.

"Where did Patrick take you for a honeymoon?" I ask.

"New Orleans," she says. "He got us a hotel right on the river, and we spent three nights there."

I take note that she speaks of the nights they spent there but not the days. I think of all the collected desire and hope in the word *honeymoon*. I think of the disappointment, also. Often it is disappointment one will not admit. On the television Barney has invited a new group of women to Andy's house, having judged everyone in the first round ineligible.

My cheesecake is disappearing fast. I try to slow down. "There were no honeymoons in Elizabethan times," I say. I tell her what little I know about the wedding celebrations in Shakespeare's day. I tell her of the feast at the bridegroom's house, of the all-day merrymaking, of the bridesmaids leading the bride to the wedding chamber, of their undressing her and putting her into the bed. I tell her of the groom's friends bringing him to the chamber. I tell of their sewing the sheets together with the bride and groom inside and then leaving them alone in the bridal chamber while they went back to finish their party in the adjacent rooms.

"Why, that's amazing," says Rachel. "I didn't know any of that. But I'm glad we have honeymoons today." She smiles. "Patrick told me later that we could've stayed longer in New Orleans but he couldn't wait for me to see the house he'd bought and fixed up." Her eyes make a slow circle around the room. I wonder if this piece of prime real estate was the house she had always dreamed of.

I have no trouble at all imagining Patrick swinging open the front door of 629 Edison Street, announcing joyfully, "Well, here it is!" It is more difficult to conjure up a picture of his carrying her over the threshold, though, knowing Patrick, he surely must have tried. But I can see him leading her by the hand through each room of the mansion, singing out its many charms.

I think of the female cuckoo, which has no nest in which to lay her eggs. I also think of certain orioles of which I have read in my bird book. The female is treated to a showy display by the male: Here it is! See my orchard! See my tree! See my nest! Come, live with me here! Carried away by his ardor, the male often flutters upward off his perch in the rapture of his singing.

CHAPTER 28

TO FEED ON SUCH SWEET HONEY, AND KILL THE BEES

After a winter diet of fruits and berries
in the tropics, the summer tanager is ready
for a change. Braving the risk of stings for
its preferred food, the bird will plunder the
nests of bees and wasps for their larvae and
pupae, its preferred food. Known by its
nickname, "red beebird," the summer tanager
can overtake insects for a quick meal in flight.

Do not ask how it comes to pass that Rachel carries a large porcelain basin of water into my apartment, that she slowly stoops and places it on the floor beside the sofa. She returns with something she calls a loofah in one hand, a bottle in the other, and a white towel over her shoulder. She lays the towel and the loofah, which is a small fibrous sponge, on the table next to the sofa. To the water she adds a capful of solution from the bottle and stirs it in with her fingers. It is a miracle solution Patrick has bought at the health food store. She squints at the printing on the back of the bottle before recapping it, then slowly stirs the water again.

Patrick has become a frequent customer of the health food store, for he believes that the physical difficulties Rachel is undergoing can be eliminated with the right combination of natural herbs and vita-mins. These he avidly researches and brings home for the speedy healing of her body. Patrick's idea of a proper malady is one that spikes and is promptly conquered with medication, not an affliction like Rachel's that comes and goes. "And she said this will help all the swings in body temperature," he said to Rachel after his first visit to the store. "And this is supposed to make you sleep better." I heard the rustle of a paper bag as he extracted his purchases. There were other things in the bag—another pill, a cream, and then a bottle.

"I got this for Aunt Sophie," he said. "The woman said her mother uses it and can't say enough good things about it. She said she used to limp when she walked but now she doesn't." Apparently Patrick believes the woman's story. Imagine, something in a bottle to cure a limp. "She said it's excellent for improving circulation," he added.

"The directions say to soak for thirty minutes, then massage for at least ten," Rachel says now, looking up at me briefly. She touches the loofah. "Five minutes with this and five with the towel. We'll be done before Mindy comes. And I won't be rough, I promise." As if I am worried about Rachel being rough.

I nod and take the bottle from her hand. It is a product called

Feet First, the label of which claims that it is "approved by podia-trists nationwide" and that it will "restore vitality to aching feet." A tag around the neck of the bottle reads, "Going dancing? Pamper your FEET FIRST with a luxuriant foot bath for all-night comfort and ease of movement. Staying in for a quiet, romantic evening? Pre-pare for restful sleep by immersing your FEET FIRST in our won-drously fragrant liquid indulgence. Friends for life, your feet deserve the royal treatment only FEET FIRST can give."

I am not going dancing, nor am I preparing for a romantic eve-ning. Had a foot bath been demanded by Patrick, I would have refused. But Rachel has asked, using the word *please*, as if requesting a special honor, and I have submitted. I sit on the sofa, magazines at hand. Carol Burnett is on the television across the room. Carol Bur-nett is playing the role of an incompetent secretary, smacking gum and polishing her fingernails while Tim Conway, the boss, tries to get her attention over the intercom.

Rachel removes my slippers and socks. Then she gently lifts my friends for life, slides the basin beneath them, and lowers them into the wondrously fragrant liquid indulgence.

Thirty minutes pass, during which I read my magazine and watch Carol Burnett turn into Eunice, whose mother lives with her and her husband, Ed. They play a board game called Sorry, and Mama, Eunice, and Ed end up shouting at one another.

Rachel returns after thirty minutes and begins the massaging phase. She works as if she has long experience in handling the feet of others. While she rubs the sole of one foot with the loofah, she softly and rhythmically kneads the top of the same foot with her other hand.

"Does that hurt?" she says at one point. She lifts my foot to look at the sole. "How long have you had this?" I tell her I don't know, that it hurts more some days than others.

"It looks like a plantar wart to me," she says. "We'll have to get something for that." She moves the loofah between my toes, taking care with the ones that overlap. She gives special attention to my heels. She splashes a little water on the hem of my dress and apologizes, wiping it off quickly. She does not watch the clock, but I do. I am too embarrassed to speak.

The five minutes with the loofah stretches to ten. She moves the basin and sits before me, placing my feet on the towel in her lap. I look down at them as if they are strangers, not friends for life. How is it that such unlovely things have come to be taken into someone's hands and treated gently? I look at the top of Rachel's hair. It is growing longer, losing its crested MacGyver look. I wonder if she is working toward a different style or has simply let it go.

She finishes toweling one of my feet and begins the other. After this the treatment will be finished. Vitality will be restored to my aching feet. I will walk without a limp. Rachel is humming something now, a tune I have heard Patrick singing in the living room of late. Believing that others admire his voice as much as he does, Patrick has volunteered to sing a solo at church. Rachel plays the piano so he can practice it. The two of them give a shaky performance. It is a perfect song for Patrick the Shepherd to sing, for it tells of ninety-nine sheep that are safe in the fold. One shy of an even hundred. But there's one more sheep that has wandered away into the mountains. I recognize the story from one of the parables I have read in the red Bible. Patrick's reedy voice throbs with emotion as he sings, and he labors through many verses before the shepherd finally locates the lost sheep.

Carol Burnett has ended, and Judge Jack is now on the television. A white woman is suing a black woman for emotional distress and two hundred dollars in damages. The white woman has stringy yellow hair and is missing a front tooth. The two women clamor at each other simultaneously, and Judge Jack pounds his gavel. The dispute concerns a hole in a backyard fence, a dog, and the black woman's boyfriend. It is a confusing story, and I do not try hard to follow it.

Rachel cradles my foot in one hand as if it were a small lamb and briskly rubs it with the towel. Perhaps she is thinking of the lost sheep on the mountainside, cold and wet. When she finishes with both feet, she stops humming and looks up at me. "One more thing." She leaves and returns with a pair of nail clippers. Without ado she lifts each foot and trims my toenails. I do not watch her, but I hear the *snick-snick* of the clippers. "There, I'm done," she says at last. A little pile of thick yellowish slivers lies scattered on the tabletop beside the bottle of Feet First.

She reaches for one of my socks and begins folding back the top to slip it onto my foot. Though I could do it myself, I do not stop her. I wonder if the act of putting socks on someone else's feet brings back memories of her babies. "I hope this wasn't a waste of your time," she says. "I hope it does some good."

"All-night comfort, ease of movement, and restful sleep," I say. "Isn't that what the label promises to deliver?"

She gives a half laugh. "The people who write those ads always make things sound so great."

I look down at the magazine in my lap. "Thurl Ravenscroft got a lot of mileage out of that word," I say.

She gives me a quizzical look. "What word is that?"

"*Great,*" I say. "You know, Tony the Tiger."

She glances at the magazine. "Oh. Don't tell me Tony the Tiger died, too," she says.

"In a sense, yes." I hold up the Milestones page and point to the entry.

Rachel reads it aloud. "'DIED. THURL RAVENSCROFT, 91, versatile voice-over specialist whose booming "Gr-r-eat!" made Tony the Tiger, mascot of Kellogg's Frosted Flakes, one of TV's most recognized commercial pitchmen.'" She smiles when she comes to the last sentence, where *Time* magazine reports Thurl Ravenscroft's droll commentary on his fame: "I've made a career out of one word."

I think of how little one generally knows about the person behind a voice.

"And look," she says, pointing to another picture on the page. "Ernest T. Bass died, too. Patrick used to laugh so hard at him." She looks more closely. "Howard Morris, I never knew that was his name." She points again. "And that actor on *Green Acres*, too. Eddie Albert. Why, it says he was ninety-nine years old."

"One shy of an even hundred," I say. I can't help wondering how close Eddie Albert was to his hundredth birthday. I wonder if he was trying to hang on until then or if he was ready for the camera to stop rolling.

Rachel shakes her head. "Well, I guess TV got hit hard last week, didn't it?" She finishes with my other sock and then my slippers. She uses the edge of the sofa to hoist herself to her feet, then sets about returning the basin and other things to the kitchen. On her last trip, after she brushes the pile of nail trimmings into her cupped hand, I speak her name. She stops and looks at me.

"Thank you," I say.

"Oh, you're welcome," she says. "But it's such a little thing."

"It is not a little thing, Rachel," I say, lifting my feet. "Now I can dance all night."

She smiles. "You're funny, Aunt Sophie."

It would be tempting to foist some religious symbolism upon the scene just past, for I have read the Gospel According to John in the red Bible. I have read of Jesus girding himself with a towel and washing the feet of his disciples. I have read the words he spoke to his disciples: "If I then, your Lord and Master, have washed your feet; ye also ought to wash one another's feet. For I have given you an example, that ye should do as I have done to you." Had Patrick been at home to observe, no doubt he would have seized upon the ceremonial nature of Rachel's act. Perhaps he would have written a story about it for his creative writing class. Had he done so, I would have found a way to rip it apart.

And how do I explain what Rachel has done? If I had thought for a moment that she had simply purposed in her heart to obey a commandment, that she set her jaw to the task and humbled herself as an emblem of Christian piety, I would have kicked over the basin and drenched her with the liquid indulgence. No thank you, I would have said, I do not care to be part of a religious reenactment.

I do not dare to say that she washed my feet because she loves me. I am an old woman with no blood ties to her. She will get no more money at my death for having done this deed. In the end I have no explanation that makes sense. It is a mystery.

When Mindy arrives for her lesson, her hair is braided. She is wearing denim shorts from which long frayed strings hang. Her shoes, flimsy affairs, make flipping noises as she walks to the round table. For the month of May my wall calendar features a picture of a river otter with the caption "Learning to Turn Work Into Play." Mindy has not learned the otter's lesson, for she enters my apartment with the air of a slave.

I do not know how the mind of a high school student works. Besides Mindy, my closest contacts have been with two boys who pointed guns at people I loved. When I lived in Carlton, Kentucky, a neighbor boy of sixteen beat his grandfather with a hammer during an argument. The daughter of a colleague at Tri-Community College ran into another car while intoxicated and killed a pregnant woman. I look at Mindy and see a blank wall. Yet sometimes there are small cracks in a wall through which sunlight can filter. Sometimes things can grow behind a wall.

Mindy has had no contact with Prince for over two months. His case has not yet been heard. Steve checks regularly to make sure he is still in jail. So far he is. Steve and Teri hope that Mindy will never see him again. One cannot tell what Mindy hopes, for she rarely talks. In the six weeks since Veronica's death, Teri reports that Mindy has spoken less and less.

One night recently Teri wrote her a letter and slipped it under her door. It was a love letter. "I knew I'd bawl my eyes out," she told Rachel, "if I tried to say it all to her face." The next day she saw the letter in a trash can, torn into small pieces.

The restrictions are still in place. Mindy has no computer, no car keys, no telephone. Though Prince is offstage for now, there are other friends Steve and Teri do not trust. "Bad apples," Teri calls them.

Patrick does not believe in luck, good or bad. I have heard him say this. He gave a talk about it at a cottage prayer meeting, a talk he titled "Luck or the Lord's Will?" He made reference to many things: lottery jackpots, job promotions, Veronica's death, tsunami disasters, disease. He did not mention the kidnapping and murder of his children twenty years ago.

Perhaps it is luck, perhaps not, but the fact is that today's lesson in Mindy's literature book is relevant to her life in a number of ways. Whether she is attuned to the relevance cannot be determined. Perhaps it is luck, perhaps not, but two of the four poems in today's lesson are commentaries about young black men: "We Real Cool" by Gwendolyn Brooks and "Cross" by Langston Hughes. The other two poems are relevant in other ways: "Toads" by Philip Larkin and "Richard Cory" by Edwin Arlington Robinson. Two black poets and two white poets all have something to say to Mindy Lowe in Greenville, Mississippi. Whether she will listen is another matter.

Metaphor and irony are two aspects of figurative language covered in today's lesson. Besides the meaning of these two terms and a rudimentary appreciation for the singing of a skilled poet, I will set down in plain prose what an old woman would wish four poets to tell Mindy in the space of an hour.

Tell her, Gwendolyn Brooks, that youthful follies are deadly. Tell her, Langston Hughes, that the ones who give you life are not to be cursed. Tell her, Philip Larkin, that one can never escape the demands of labor and conscience. Tell her, Edwin Arlington Robinson, that people are not always what they seem to be.

After she takes the quiz over today's assignment, I say, "How did you like the poems you read?" I try to imagine her saying in a Tony the Tiger voice, "They're Gr-r-eat!"

But Mindy's response is a shrug and "Okay, I guess."

Perhaps it is luck, perhaps not, that an incident from my past comes to mind. Perhaps I should pause to question its relevance, but I do not. Instead, I say to Mindy, "Before we start, I want to tell you something." Her eyes, full of suspicion, dart to mine, then back to her book.

I tell her about my father's posting flyers advertising for an assistant at his printshop in Methuselah, Mississippi, in the year 1954. I was teaching in nearby Clarksdale by then. I tell her about four boys who applied for the job. Three were white boys from prominent local families. The fourth was a black boy whose mother did white people's laundry. "This is the boy he hired," I tell her.

No one was surprised, since my father so often used his printing press to speak out against racial injustices in the South, but my mother was worried that the white boys' families would be upset. The Negro boy, whose name was Fillmore Deal, had a speech impediment that made people think he wasn't bright. He had a hard set to his mouth and eyes that said, "Unfair is all I've ever known life to be, and I don't expect anything different from you."

Mindy is picking at a fingernail as I talk. Perhaps she is listening, perhaps she is not. Perhaps she will erupt when I finish, calling me an idiot. Perhaps she will refuse to come to her lesson tomorrow. Perhaps she will tell her parents I do not stick to the literature book but go off on rabbit trails. I know I am taking a chance in departing from the text, especially since I cannot give a clear reason for doing so. But there are times when one must brave dangers. I have read of birds that invade the nests of bees. Sometimes a person must do this, also. He must go forth suddenly and put himself at risk for something he values. I look at the years ahead of Mindy, and I value them for her sake.

"Fillmore was a quick learner," I say. "Somehow between his mother and my father, he avoided the things that a lot of the boys his age got mixed up in. He worked hard and grew up to be a good man. Later on Daddy took him on as a partner, and eventually he ran the whole business. It was Fillmore's idea to start the daily newspaper in Methuselah. He married a nice girl and built a house for his mother next door to his."

I stop. Mindy is still picking her fingernails. The look on her face says, "So what?" And in the silence that follows, I must ask myself the same thing. So what? It is a question for which I have no ready answer. Perhaps I see in this story some suggestion of the four lessons I want the poets to teach Mindy today. Perhaps I want her to see that there are fair-minded adults in the world who want to help teenagers.

I look at Mindy's beautiful hands, her long slim fingers. The same hands that braided her blond hair. The same ones that tore up her mother's letter. I think of the words of Julia in *The Two Gentlemen of Verona*: "Oh hateful hands, to tear such loving words!"

"'Injurious wasps,'" I say to Mindy, "'to feed on such sweet honey and kill the bees that yield it with your stings.'"

She stops picking her fingernails and looks at me with a mixture of astonishment and fear, as if I am a rabid animal and she has not had her tetanus shot.

"Those are lines from Mr. William Shakespeare," I say. "They are spoken by an impetuous young woman who says and does things her own heart warns her against." I lean forward and speak slowly. "I have heard that a drowning man may fight the one who tries to save him. I have seen little children kick and scream when put to bed for the rest they need. Take care, Mindy. Fix your eyes on things of lasting value, things outside yourself. Broaden your mind. There is safety within the gates, where a garden may grow. Sunshine and rain come from above. Those whom you consider to be your jailers desire to set you free."

I have opened my mouth, and nonsense has spilled out. I wonder which of us is more astounded. Surely this is as jumbled a speech as has ever been given. Mindy's lips are parted as if she is about to say, "What the . . . ?" But she says nothing, and her eyes grow suddenly unreadable again. It comes to me that I must sound like Patrick. I have a woeful thought: Perhaps he is rubbing off on me. Were I to keep talking, I wonder what else would pour forth. Perhaps I would speak of hedges and forts, lost sheep, and long-range implications.

"Now then," I say briskly, "let us look at the four poems for today. We have much ground to cover." Mindy glances at the clock and opens her book with a sigh. "Sometimes," I say, "there may appear to be a wall around a poem. But with patience and persistence, we may discover cracks through which to enter."

CHAPTER 29

TO BURN THIS NIGHT
WITH TORCHES

The scientific name of the mockingbird, Mimus
polyglottos, means "mimic of many tongues," a
fitting name for a bird that can imitate dozens of
his feathered friends as well as other creatures
such as crickets and dogs. The mockingbird is a
fearless fighter during nesting season, taking on
larger birds and even cats and snakes.

What do you remember about your early days of teaching when the schools were segregated?" This is the question Potts asks me when the four of us sit down to eat at the kitchen table. It is the twentieth day of May. Here are some of the things I tell him.

In the year 1955, a year after my father hired Fillmore Deal to work in his printshop, I was confronted by the parents of one of my fifth graders in Clarksdale, Mississippi. They both appeared in my classroom after school one day, dressed as if they were going to church. The man held a hat in his hand, and the woman wore one on her head—a little black cloche with a tuft of short red feathers.

Their son's first name was Cameron, but I don't recall the last name. I do remember, however, that Cameron's name bore the Roman numeral IV at the end of it. Though the Supreme Court had passed the landmark decision concerning integration the year before, the public schools in Mississippi were still segregated for years there-after. Where there's a will there's a way, as my father liked to say.

Cameron's parents sat in the two chairs I drew up beside my desk, and the father, Cameron number three, spoke first. He worked at the bank and owned half of the land in Clarksdale. I was seen by some of the parents, he informed me, as too ardent a sympathizer with the American Negro. "We're all for fair treatment around here," he said to me in his deep voice, "but we think you're pushing ideas onto our children that would best be left to their parents to discuss with them."

His wife, clutching her pocketbook with gloved hands, nodded in agreement. "Cameron told us what you said about that Negro boy that died earlier this year."

"Do you mean the boy who was killed by the two white men?" I said.

"The boy who made overtures to a white woman," Cameron number three said.

"The boy who was beaten and mutilated?" I asked.

"The jury acquitted those two men," Cameron's mother said.

"Do you mean the jury of twelve white men?" I asked. "The jury that deliberated for just over an hour? The one that would have returned the verdict sooner if they hadn't stopped to drink some Coca-Colas?"

I could see the pulsing veins in the neck of Cameron the third, just above the starched collar of his white shirt. He was a big man. He could have strangled two boys at the same time by snatching them around the neck, one in each hand.

"Miss Langham, we don't want you trying to brainwash our boys and girls." He leaned forward and looked at me sternly. "Maybe you have your own reasons for saying these things." He stressed the word *reasons* as if to indicate that they were somehow shameful. "But we've come today," he continued, "to let you know that none of us parents like what you're doing, and we're giving you fair warning before we take it further."

I was tempted to ask if their taking it further would include burning crosses and white hoods, but I kept my silence.

His wife glanced at him quickly, deferentially, to see if he was finished. Then she spoke softly but emphatically. "We don't want things to get ugly, Miss Langham, but we've got our reasons, too. We don't want any trouble getting stirred up in Clarksdale. Things are nice and quiet here, and we want them to stay that way." Most likely what she meant was that she wanted to keep her Negro housemaid and cook in their places.

"I have no intention of stirring up trouble," I told her. "But I want to teach my pupils more than reading, writing, and arithmetic. I want them to know the history of their country and the vision of its founders. I want them to understand what the Declaration of Independence and the Constitution of the United States say about the rights of all men."

"Well, Miss Langham, that all sounds real pretty," Cameron the third said, "but you can leave your personal opinions out of the classroom. We don't pay our schoolteachers to undermine what we're teaching at home."

"I am teaching freedom, sir, and respect for all human beings," I said. "Is that different from what you're teaching at home?"

He stood up so fast that the chair almost tipped over backward. His wife stood up, too. "And one more thing," he said. "Cameron tells us you've started reading a new book to the class after recess."

I nodded. I had finished a biography of Booker T. Washington the week before and had started one about Mary McLeod Bethune the next day.

"It looks like to us, Miss Langham, you could find a book about a white person and read that to our children," Cameron the third said. "In fact, we would strongly suggest that you do just that the next time around."

The truth was I was already beginning to wish I had not started Mary Bethune's biography. Hers was a story with far too much religion in it. In the chapter I had read aloud that day, in fact, Mary had announced as a little girl her desire to go to Africa to be a missionary. But no white man, banker or not, was going to tell me what book to read to my class. I would finish the book now even if I had to clench my teeth through phrases such as those I had already encountered: "God was on their side" and "The earth is full of the goodness of the Lord!" and "to take the gospel of Jesus to lost souls." To be sure I would survey my choices more carefully in the future.

At the end of that school year I resigned from the school in Clarksdale and moved to Greenville, where I taught for the next five years. During that time there were no black students at Carrie Stern Elementary School. This was the school where we sang the state song at the end of each weekly assembly program. "Way down south in Mississippi," it ended, "folks are happy they have been born."

My father wrote a piece about the state song around that same time and printed it up on handbills that he distributed and posted around Methuselah. He sent me one through the mail. The title of his article was "Way Down South in Mississippi, Are ALL the Folks Happy They Have Been Born?" Daddy dealt specifically with the various ways Negroes were discouraged from voting in elections. He was fond of using irony, which many of the local readers did not comprehend. He suggested that in lieu of a poll tax Negroes could be made to pay for the privilege of voting by giving up a finger each time. Once their fingers were used up, they could start on their toes.

Though Daddy became morose as he grew older, he never did lose his zeal for speaking the truth through the printed word. He never made much money from his business, at least by his report, but as it was a pastime that kept him away from home, my mother rarely complained. She suspected that he kept the profits a secret, that he had cash hidden somewhere in the shop, but I will say this for my mother: She knew how to keep her tongue. She was not a discontented, fractious woman. She had a boardinghouse to run, and she gave herself to it. It was the only world she knew.

When Daddy died, Fillmore took her to the back room of the printshop and showed her the loose brick behind which Daddy kept a box. She used some of the money to bury Daddy. I never knew what became of the rest of it. She and Fillmore drew up an agreement whereby he could buy the business by means of monthly payments. I do not know where this money went.

In addition to these things, I also backtrack and tell Potts the story I told Mindy the week before, of how my father hired Fillmore over three white boys, how they became in many ways like father and son.

Patrick's eyes are full of admiration when I finish speaking. It is clear that he approves of my standing up to Cameron number three, that he imagines he would have done the same as my father in hiring a Negro boy in the year 1954, that he is amazed and delighted over Fillmore's good character.

"Those would make such interesting experiences to write about!" he exclaims now. I suspect that he is already making plans to do so. In the wake of his creative writing class, he is struggling to write a story, which he hopes will make him famous. I have heard him read various false starts aloud to Rachel, then declare them too "derivative." This is a new word Patrick picked up from his creative writing teacher.

One thing in Patrick's favor: Over the past months he listened to this teacher, who used the word *derivative*, among others, to describe Patrick's story "Terror in the Afternoon." *Wordy* and *contrived* were other words he used. The teacher wrote down a list of stories for Patrick to read and study on his own "to see the power of nuance in realism" and spoke to him at length in his office one night about the "two kinds of simplicity—one producing art and the other banality." All of this Patrick repeated in painstaking detail to Rachel.

Perhaps someday my nephew will write something of worth. Perhaps he never will. Perhaps his great love of words—of his own words—is a handicap he will never overcome. But each time I hear him say to Rachel, "No, no. This won't work. It's too derivative," I am reminded of the miracles I have read about. I envision myself among the multitudes, astonished to witness that the lame can walk and the blind can see.

These are things I have read about the mockingbird: Though known as the King of Song, it is not a composer, only an imitator. It is said that besides other birds, the mockingbird can mimic sounds such as rusty hinges and factory whistles. Though having nothing new to say, it nevertheless gives full-voiced recitals all for the love of song. Perhaps Patrick is destined to be only a mockingbird.

But perhaps he may one day trick some into thinking he is the real thing. And surely this is true: Though derivative, one mockingbird's performance may be superior to another's. One may develop a keener ear than another, produce a finer interpretation of the original piece. Well, we shall wait and see.

Over dessert Potts unburdens his heart. To think that he has reserved this until now, that this has been lodged within him through the consumption of Rachel's brisket, her rice and gravy, her lima beans is a remarkable thing to me. He has asked questions to be answered at some length, has listened to the answers with close attention and asked yet further questions, has waited until this moment when Rachel places before us what she calls chocolate molten lava cups. I cannot help wondering if Rachel feels, as he speaks, that a volcano has indeed begun to rumble.

Perhaps he was wrestling with whether or not to bring up the matter, watching for signs to guide him. Rachel's spoon is halfway to her mouth when he says, "I need your advice on a matter." He glances first at Patrick and me but settles at last on Rachel.

Since my husband shattered my illusions about life and love, I have found few people to like, fewer still to trust. Though an odd time for such a realization, it comes to me in a flash that I am sitting at a table with three people I trust. One of them I do not like very much, and one has served time in prison, but I trust them all. Cicero Potts, whom I both like and trust, holds Rachel's eyes a moment longer and then speaks again. "My brother needs help." I wonder if Rachel hears the difference between "advice" and "help" and if she senses in what is coming that something may be required of her.

She nods as if to encourage him to continue, then lifts the spoon of chocolate molten lava to her mouth. It is a sumptuous dessert, yet one Rachel has pronounced "easy as child's play" to prepare. It is part cake, part pudding. Served warm with a dollop of ice cream, it is altogether satisfying.

Though the word *brother* is one Potts often uses for black and white alike, he speaks now of his real brother. It is his older brother, he tells us, the one who lives here in Greenville in the same apartment building where Potts lives. In the past Mitchell has had trouble keeping a job. "It's not that he lacks intelligence," Potts says, "but he sometimes lacks an understanding of people, especially of the people who hire him." Mitchell wants to reorganize every place he works, wants to tell his bosses better ways to do things. He cannot keep still and wait for opportunities but speaks up immediately, frequently, and loudly. "He makes some good points," Potts says, "but his presentation stinks."

Patrick chuckles and says, "I've known people like that." He obviously doesn't think he is one of them.

"But this isn't the real problem," Cicero says. "Mitchell was living with a girl up until a couple of days ago, and now she's left without a trace." He pauses again, then takes a deep breath and says, "And that isn't the real problem, either. When she left, she didn't take her baby with her."

Again he catches Rachel with another spoonful midway between her plate and mouth. She stops and looks at him. In that instant she must know, as I do, where this is leading. She does not flinch, however, but nods again.

Before Potts can continue, Patrick interjects, "Were they married?" This is typical of the way Patrick's mind works, latching onto details that are neither part of the problem nor the solution.

Potts shakes his head. "No, no. She was barely more than a baby herself, just looking for somebody to fill in a gap until something more interesting turned up. Mitchell wouldn't listen to me, thought she loved him and all that, said this girl was different, this time it was the real thing. Gave her everything she wanted and loved that baby like it was his own. Kept saying he wanted to be a family man now, said he meant to keep his mouth shut and hang onto his job so they could get them a bigger place. Wanted Lawanda—that was the girl's name—to have another baby."

"Where was he working?" Patrick asks. He has been taking bites of his chocolate molten lava in rapid succession so that now his dish is almost empty.

But before Potts can answer, Rachel asks, "What's he doing with the baby?"

"He didn't go in to work today," Potts says. "You can't leave a three-year-old by himself." By this we know that he is using the word *baby* loosely, as women often do, and that the child is a boy.

And then to address Patrick's question, he tells us that Mitchell is working at the Sunnydale Nursing Home, on the custodial crew, that he's held this same job since he took Lawanda in. "But he's scared he'll lose it now," Potts says. "He knows he can't keep calling in sick."

"I could help with the boy," Rachel says.

"Well, we'd need to talk about it," Patrick says. "Rachel's having some health issues," he tells Potts. I am fully prepared for Patrick to enumerate the issues with all the precise terminology, but he does not, most likely because Potts holds up a hand and says quickly, "Oh, by all means I don't want to put any pressure on you, brother. I wouldn't take advantage of our friendship that way."

"But I could at least help out tomorrow, couldn't I?" Rachel asks Patrick. "That way Mitchell could go to work tomorrow, and then we'd have the weekend to talk it over. Wouldn't that be okay?"

"I'm not sure you're up to that," Patrick says. "A whole day with a three-year-old? It would be a lot of work, you know."

"Oh, I know that," Rachel says. She looks at Patrick evenly and repeats, "I know that."

Somehow I hear my own voice. "I'll be here, too." All three of them look at me, but no one is blunt enough to say what they all must be thinking: And how could *you* help with a three-year-old?

Someday perhaps I shall write down a list of all the ways a man or woman may face off the specter of death, especially the tricks a religious person may use to occupy his time in the winter of his life. I will muse over this belief that seems to govern many people's behavior: that what they do in this world will matter in the next. Perhaps I will put this heading at the top of my list: "To Burn This

Night With Torches." From *Antony and Cleopatra* I will borrow the words of Antony as he broods over his falling fortunes, as he thinks about the battle to come, a battle in which he fears he will lose his life. And yet he rallies. The battle is tomorrow. For today, he says, let us eat supper and drown our worries with drink. Let us burn torches to keep the night at bay.

And so, says Rachel by her offer to help, our lives are not ours to keep but to lose. For today let us take care of a child. Let us burn a torch through the night, for who knows how many tomorrows we may have? Let us sow and harvest before the winter comes.

A picture fills my mind as a memory falls upon me like a warm rain. It is a picture of a field of grain. Curiously, the memory is from the biography of Mary McLeod Bethune that I read to my pupils more than fifty years ago. Though Cameron is the only child whose name I can recall from my few years in Clarksdale, Mississippi, I suddenly remember the name of Mary Bethune's grandmother. It was the same as mine—Sophia.

When she was still a child, Sophia was taken from her mother and sold to another slave owner in South Carolina. But she never forgot the stories her mother had told her, stories of Africa. In her old age Sophia sat by the fire and repeated these stories to her children and grandchildren so that they, too, might never forget. She sang songs in a strange language. She told of the village in Africa where her mother lived. She told of the day that everyone in the village was herded onto a slave ship. It was harvest time and the grain was ripe, but there was no one left to reap what had been sown.

CHAPTER 30

STONES HAVE BEEN KNOWN TO MOVE

The gentle eastern bluebird has suffered from competition with house sparrows and starlings for nesting holes. Whereas flocks of bluebirds were once a common sight around orchards and birdbaths, their numbers have greatly declined. Well-placed nest boxes are one way man can help the eastern bluebird population.

I n mid-June my lessons with Mindy come to an end. Having finished the last unit in her literature textbook, I have given her a final exam, on which she scored a respectable 95 percent. She has apparently taken in more than I would have guessed.

Today she comes back to my apartment at one o'clock for the second part of her exam, an essay on a topic of my choosing: "In two paragraphs discuss the form and content of Shakespeare's sonnet 73." I have added this part to the objective exam. It was not included in the teacher's manual. I let Mindy think that every other student completing the homeschool curriculum for twelfth grade English is writing an exam essay.

It is easy to justify such an essay, for the textbook claims as one of its goals to challenge the students in the areas of "critical think-ing and analysis" as well as in "skills of organization and composi-tion." I want to see if Mindy will correctly identify the rhyme and meter of the sonnet, if she will employ the words quatrain and cou-plet, if she will discuss Shakespeare's use of enjambment, image, and metaphor. But more than this, I want to see what a girl like Mindy will write about the content of such a sonnet. Will she say it is a poem about growing old or a poem about love? Or perhaps both? Will she spout standard youthful generalities? Will she make murky unsubstantiated claims? I confess that I do not expect much from her.

It is hard to expect much from a girl who dresses the way Mindy does. Today she is wearing a stretchy yellow T-shirt and white shorts. Her shoes, which are not really shoes at all, are the same ones that snap as she walks. Around one ankle is a slender silver chain. She is also wearing a ball cap, and her hair is in a ponytail, which swings from the back opening of the cap.

After she sits down, I read aloud the sentence of essay instruc-tions to her and then the sonnet. More accurately, I recite the son-net. Mindy is following from a copy I have written out by hand. This is the only poem I remember by heart. When I was newly married, I dreamed of reciting it to Eliot someday when we were both old. I imagined that our love would deepen over the years.

When I come to the last two lines, I say them slowly:

"This thou perceivest, which makes thy love more strong,
To love that well which thou must leave ere long."

I do not give Mindy a time limit but tell her, as I have before, that I am more impressed with quality than quantity. She studies the sonnet at some length and then begins to write. She pauses frequently to look at the poem again. She chews on a knuckle and frowns. She rereads what she has written so far, then resumes writing. She shakes her head, erases something, and writes again. Perhaps she cares more about her grade in twelfth grade English than I thought. It is hard to tell what goes on inside a person. We shall see what comes out.

I go to my recliner to wait for her. I lean forward and see a small brown bird on the ground beneath the feeder. I have seen it before. It does not peck at the feeder but gleans the leftovers. With bright eyes and upturned tail, it hops to and fro in a jerky dance, stirring up dirt and mulch. In this fashion it brings to the surface seeds that have been knocked from the feeder by larger careless birds looking for an easy snack.

I watch the bird closely for several minutes. Perhaps I can find his picture in my bird book and call him by name the next time he comes. For now he is simply a small brown bird, quick and scrappy, content with the leavings of other birds. I think of other birds who take what is left, birds whose names I know. I have read in my book of bluebirds, whose nesting sites have been appropriated by more aggressive birds, who have vacated the eastern orchards and meadows where they once thronged. I think of people, too, who cannot compete with the masses, who stand to the side until others are finished, who step in to clean up or who sometimes simply pack up and leave.

"DIED. HAMILTON NAKI, 78, South African surgical pioneer with no formal training who was a central member of the team, led by Dr. Christiaan Barnard, that performed the first human heart transplant—yet went unrecognized for some three decades because of apartheid restrictions on blacks holding jobs deemed appropriate only for whites; of a heart attack; in Langa, South Africa." I remember much talk about this operation. It was in 1967, the year before I married Eliot. Though Christiaan Barnard became a household name in the weeks that followed, I recall no mention of Hamilton Naki. And now forty years later, after his own heart has expired, I read about him in *Time* magazine.

The entry tells me that many years ago a white doctor operating on a giraffe in Cape Town called on Naki to help. Though officially a gardener, Naki had such fine hands and instincts in surgery that he was soon spending most of his time in laboratories and operating rooms. When he was seventy-six years old, the University of Cape Town awarded him an honorary degree in medicine.

I imagine Patrick reading this and saying, "How wonderful! A black gardener rewarded for his years of service and raised to a position of honor in the field of medicine!" And I could not begin to explain to my nephew the great tragedy of his saying such a thing.

Though there is no picture of Hamilton Naki in *Time* magazine, in my mind I see a tall thin man in a white lab coat, stooped from years of gardening and kowtowing to men who held jobs for which he did not qualify by reason of his skin color. I see his long delicate fingers and his knowing eyes. I see him take his honorary degree in his steady hands, give it a long look, and then put it away in a drawer.

As Mindy writes, I hear the sound of water filling Rachel's washing machine. I hear her close the lid, and then all is quiet again. Perhaps she is folding clothes she has removed from the dryer. Imagine this, a white woman doing a colored man's laundry. For this is something Rachel has taken on. It is not enough for her to keep the boy for Mitchell. She must wash their clothes, also.

For her help Mitchell pays her a small amount. And with this money I have seen her buy things for the child. She and Teri have taken him to McDonald's, they have taken him to the public swimming pool, they have taken him to the park to ride a train, they have taken him to the Humane Pet Shelter to choose a kitten. This animal lives in Patrick's garage, mews at his kitchen door, pounces at little bits of lint and string. He is a black cat with a white face and white paws, or, as Patrick says in an attempt to be witty, a white cat with a black body. The cat's name is Zeego, a name the boy chose for reasons he cannot explain, a name he says quite clearly.

The boy's name is Ahab, a name his mother chose for reasons Mitchell never thought to ask. In the Bible I have read that King Ahab made idols, that he stole a man's vineyard, that he "did more to provoke the Lord God of Israel to anger than all the kings of Israel that were before him." There is another Ahab in literature, a man whose leg was bitten off by a whale, whose life pursuit was to kill the whale. Indeed, it is a sinister name for a child, but one he bears with all cheerful innocence.

Ahab is an active boy, the kind whose naps a mother would anticipate. His young mother must have been exhausted, yet when I look into his eyes and hear him laugh, I cannot imagine how she could have left him behind. Every day I expect to hear that she has returned to fetch him. For over three weeks, however, he has spent every weekday on Edison Street. The four of us—Rachel, Teri, Mindy, and I—join forces to watch him. In truth, this is all we do much of the time, watch him, for there is no keeping up with such a child.

Today while Mindy writes her essay, Teri is keeping Ahab at her house. He likes to play in Teri's backyard, where there are three attractions: a sandbox, a swing set with slide and seesaw, and Stonewall the bulldog. At Rachel's house he has a rope swing, a tricycle, a plastic swimming pool, and Zeego. Inside both houses are toys and books. He likes balls of all sizes and can hit, kick, and throw them with remarkable power and accuracy for so young a child. He eats large quantities of peanut butter, bread, cheese, and fruit. His favorite drink is chocolate milk, which Rachel buys in small glass bottles. This is not a child who suffers from want of attention, provisions, or playthings.

Perhaps I drift off to sleep as Mindy writes. I imagine that I am walking down a dirt road with a tall black doctor. Together we are pulling a wagon that holds dozens of small birdhouses. We stop along the roadside, and he nails a birdhouse to a tree. Then he purses his lips and whistles. A bluebird comes and lights on his finger. "Here," he says, "here's a place for your nest. Rest your weary heart." Then the doctor turns his gentle eyes to me and says, "Now, Sophie, how about your weary heart?"

"I'm done," I hear Mindy say. She is standing in front of me, the pages of her essay in hand. I lift my head and nod, then take the pages from her. "Can I go?" she says. I nod again. She walks toward the door in her flip-flopping shoes and then stops and turns around. "Well, I guess this is . . ." We look at each other across the room. "Okay, then," she says, then half shrugs and adds, "Well, thank you." And she is gone.

As one grows old, losing becomes a way of life. One loses people, possessions, health, and memory. He loses heart. One learns over time to hold things lightly, to quit fighting, to let go easily. And yet as I hear Mindy close the kitchen door, I have a sudden desperate wish to call her back. I have other stories to tell her. The world of literature is vast. We have not yet begun to explore it. I want to keep scratching at the ground, bringing small things to the surface.

I look at the door through which Mindy has disappeared. Through it I can see two of the four new pictures on the kitchen wall. More accurately, they are old pictures in old frames but newly hung. They are pictures from a Bible storybook that once belonged to Rachel's mother, a book in which all the pages have come loose from the binding. There are captions beneath the pictures: "Noah Releases a Dove," "Moses Receives the Ten Commandments," "David Fights the Giant," and "Daniel Faces the Lions." The day Rachel hung them, I asked her what became of the other pictures that used to be in the blue frames, the ones of happy Negroes beside cotton fields. "Oh, I covered them up with these," she said. "I like these better."

"Do you need something?" Rachel asks a few minutes later. She is standing at the door of my apartment with a spray bottle in one hand and a sponge in the other.

"No," I say.

"Oh, I thought I heard you say something."

I shake my head. I do not tell her that it may have been a laugh she heard, a laugh of disbelief. I am reading Mindy's essay, meeting with surprise upon surprise.

"Teri will be bringing Ahab back in a minute," Rachel says. "Shall I close your door so you can read?"

"No," I say.

"You know he'll be in and out of here if I don't," Rachel says.

"I know," I say.

She disappears, and I return to Mindy's essay. As for her discussion of the form of Shakespeare's sonnet, she properly labels the meter as iambic pentameter and the rhyme as that of an English sonnet: *abab cdcd efef gg*. Though she does not mention the use of enjambment, she discusses the imagery and metaphors in some detail. She misspells *metaphor* as metaphore. I did not expect her to take note of the diminishing length of time in the images, moving from months to days to minutes, but she does. I did not expect her to ponder the use of *thy* and *thou* instead of *my* and *I* in the closing lines. This she also does.

Certainly I did not expect her to write the following: "Shakespeare is describing how love does the opposite of what the body does. Just because an old person's body keeps on getting weaker, it doesn't mean his heart can't love anymore. In fact, he's saying love can keep getting stronger the older a person gets." The depth of her insights exceeds her power to express them. Still, it is a better essay by far than most of my college freshmen could have written.

But the most astounding observation is one that has never occurred to me, that most likely never occurred to Shakespeare himself. Mindy strains to illustrate another literary term: *ambiguity*. It is a term we explored in some detail in one of Nathaniel Hawthorne's stories. "*Where late the sweet birds sang,*" she writes, "illustrates ambiguity. It could mean either that the birds used to sing on the bare branches of the tree before they flew away for the winter or else that the best birds aren't afraid of the cold, so they stay late in the year and sing late in the night." To think of a seventeen-year-old girl coming up with something like this. I read the sentence many times to make sure I have not fallen asleep again.

I think of birds I have read about in my book: night-herons, nighthawks, owls. I think of the vesper sparrow that winters in the South and sings plaintively in the quiet of evening. And who can say? Perhaps Shakespeare was thinking of night birds when he wrote the line. Perhaps he was listening to a nightingale.

I hear the sound of Ahab's voice in the kitchen. He bursts in, calling out, "Aunt Wachel! Aunt Wachel!" We are all aunts and uncles except Mitchell, who is Daddy. All of Ahab's *r*'s are *w*'s. Patrick is Unca Patwick, Potts is Unca Cicewo, and Teri is Aunt Tewi. Mitchell has told us that a doctor has used the term *verbal delay* in reference to Ahab, who didn't start talking at all until a couple of months ago. Now it appears that he is making up for lost time.

The boy appears at my door, Rachel and Teri behind him. "Buds?" he asks, which is his word for birds. He is pointing to my bird window and moving across the room at the same time. He runs, wiggles, and flails his arms. This is his customary method of moving. He arrives at the window and squeals, "Bud eating!" A chickadee at the feeder takes flight.

Ahab sees the plastic swimming pool in the backyard and begins cavorting. "Go swim! Go swim!"

"After you lie down a little bit," Rachel says.

"Good luck on that," Teri says. They both laugh, and Teri leaves for home.

"Remember, we always lie down for a little while in the after-noon, and I read you a story," Rachel says to Ahab. She nurses a hope that one of these days he will actually fall asleep. She comes to the window and picks him up. Ahab twists around in her arms and points to me. "Aunt Sophie come wead?" he says.

"No, we'll let Aunt Sophie take a rest, too," Rachel says. "Let's go back to Aunt Rachel's bed. I've already picked out a story for today. You'll like it. It's about a man named Joshua and a big city called Jericho with high walls. And guess what?"

"What?" he shouts.

"Well, you just wait and see," Rachel says. "It's exciting."

I have read this story in the Bible. I have read of the Israelites marching around the walls of Jericho, of the priests blowing their trumpets, of the people shouting with a loud voice. I have read of the walls of Jericho falling flat. Many years ago I heard a Negro choir on the television singing a spiritual: "Joshua Fit the Battle of Jeri-cho." I remember the mighty conclusion of the song, the words and notes falling all over each other. I have read of other miracles in the Bible—of water turning to wine, of a man living in the belly of a great fish, of food falling from heaven, and water gushing from a rock in the desert.

These are stories that religious people like Rachel and Patrick take at face value. Their faith blinks at nothing. If the Bible says a wall fell down or the sun stood still or a man walked through fire or the waters of a sea parted, then the matter is not to be questioned, only repeated endlessly as fact.

Their faith does not stop with Bible stories. They believe that the God of the Bible still works miracles. They believe that walls still come tumbling down. At the supper table one night I heard Patrick read these words: "If ye have faith as a grain of mustard seed, ye shall say unto this mountain, Remove hence to yonder place; and it shall remove; and nothing shall be impossible unto you." Not one of the three of them laughed at this, neither Potts nor Rachel nor Patrick. I have read of another rock being moved: a great stone rolled from the mouth of a sepulcher. And who can say that there are not miracles? Has not the heart of man through the ages wished to think so?

"Stones have been known to move and trees to speak." In his despair Macbeth acknowledged that the reins of the universe were not in the hands of man. He was a guilty man, and he saw visions that made his blood run cold. And do we not all see such visions? Do we not all wish for a miracle to vanquish our guilt?

The same night he read the verse about the mustard seed, I also heard Patrick say to Potts, "Did I ever tell you about the time I won the eighth grade spelling bee?" I have read in the Bible of a donkey speaking like a man. This did not strike me as a miracle of much note, for I have heard such a thing many times since living in my nephew's house.

From the back of the house I hear an outburst of childish laughter. I picture Rachel lying on the bed beside Ahab, a storybook propped on her stomach. I look back at Mindy's essay, and my eyes fall on the meaning she has wrenched from Shakespeare's sonnet:

"The best birds aren't afraid of the cold, so they stay late in the year and sing late in the night." I think of Mindy, so young and so beautiful. Since I am not religious, I have no right to pray for a miracle. But I hope for one.

With the aid of the concordance in the back of the red Bible, I try to find the verse about faith the size of a mustard seed. Instead I find another verse: "Unto what is the kingdom of God like? . . . It is like a grain of mustard seed, which a man took, and cast into his garden; and it grew, and waxed a great tree; and the fowls of the air lodged in the branches of it."

I have noticed something on the Milestones page in *Time* magazine. Starting with the last entry as has been my habit, I have not always made it all the way to the first. More recently I have begun starting with the first entry, and sometimes I do not make it to the end. Sometimes I stop along the way to study a picture or muse over a curious fact: "DIED. FRANK PERDUE, 84, folksy chicken tycoon," who was featured on his company's television ads holding a chicken as if it were a football he was ready to throw and saying gruffly, "It takes a tough man to make a tender chicken."

But here is the thing I have noticed. Sometimes the first entries do not begin with DIED. Sometimes they are still bleak: AILING, PLEADED GUILTY, OUSTED, ARRESTED, CONVICTED. But other times they mark a happy event in someone's life: ACQUITTED, RECOVERING, AWARDED, ELECTED, RELEASED.

CHAPTER 31

THE THREAD OF HIS VERBOSITY

*Even before it hatches from its shell, the
baby killdeer peeps as if trying to converse with
its parents. Once out of its shell, it rests under
its parents' wings until warm and dry. For a
month the adult birds work tirelessly to train
and protect, often pretending to be crippled to
distract enemies away from the chicks.*

The peaches are especially good this year, Patrick tells me as he takes them out of the sack one by one. He begins explaining the cause in his usual long-winded fashion, citing amounts of rainfall and average temperatures throughout the last several months, but I am more concerned with the product itself than the steps that led to its development. I stand at the kitchen counter admiring the shape and color of perfect fruit. There are eighteen beautiful peaches lined up before me when the sack is empty.

Patrick is in the middle of a sentence when I say, "I'm ready to start working now. I can't be talking while I work." What I mean is, I can't be listening to you talk while I work.

"Well, by all means," Patrick says heartily. "Let's get this show on the road!"

"I want to do it by myself," I say. This is a phrase I must have picked up from Ahab, who says it frequently.

It has been longer than I can remember since I last made a peach pie. Perhaps the last one I made was for Eliot almost forty years ago. After he said, "Had I known of your desire for children, I would have relieved you of your false hope before we married," I must have lost my appetite for peach pie.

But Patrick has told me that peach pie is Rachel's favorite, and suddenly I remember my own taste for it. Tomorrow is her birthday, the fifth day of July. It pleases me that we were born the same month. I have laid my plans for her birthday. I will present her with gifts, one tonight and one tomorrow.

Today being July the Fourth, Teri has gotten Rachel out of the house on the pretext of needing her help in preparing for company. It has been three months since "God took Veronica to heaven," which is how Teri speaks of her daughter's death. I have heard her tell Rachel that she still cries during the day when she passes Veronica's room. "I see her empty crib and feel like somebody's knocked the wind out of me," she says. But I have also heard her say that during the night she sometimes awakes with tears of joy after dreaming of "my sweet angel laughing and singing and running through the streets of heaven."

And at long last I have heard Rachel speak of her own children.

One day she placed both hands over her heart and said to Teri and me, "They are always with me, every minute of every day." She remembers their birthdays, their ages. Like Teri, she dreams about them. "Just think," she said to Teri that day, "maybe Toby and Mandy are playing with Veronica right now. Maybe the three of them are walking along holding hands."

It was Steve's idea to have a July Fourth cookout for family and friends, and Teri agreed. She was ready, she said, "to crawl out of my hole." The only family member who accepted their invitation, however, was Teri's aunt Helena in Yazoo City. Not to be discouraged, they went out into the highways and hedges and have now compelled a host of motley guests to come to their cookout.

Then Teri's aunt called back and said she was afraid she and Della Boyd would have to cancel because Della Boyd's brother and his family were coming through Yazoo City on their way to Biloxi and would be at their house over the Fourth. "But I just told her to bring them along, the more the merrier!" Teri told Rachel. "Besides, they have kids Mindy's age, which will be good for her."

And so it is to be another odd combination. Cicero Potts, Mitchell, and Ahab will be coming, also, and two of Steve's friends from the catfish plant. In addition, the vacant house next to Patrick and Rachel has finally been sold to a young couple in their twenties, who have also been invited. They are expecting their first baby sometime in August. Wes and Joanna Lebo may have a tall hedge around their house, but it will do nothing to isolate them from their well-meaning neighbors. You may as well mow the hedge down, I want to tell them, for you will not be left alone, not in this neighborhood.

Every day for the past week I have heard about the details for the party. There will be grilled hot dogs and hamburgers, baked beans, potato salad, and homemade ice cream. Patrick has bought a large watermelon to take over. He and Steve have staked out an area for horseshoes. Teri and Rachel are setting up tables in their backyard with box fans situated so as to keep the air circulating and thus discourage flies and mosquitoes. They are covering the tables with red-and-white-checked tablecloths, and there will be centerpieces of hydrangeas and tiny American flags. Later there will be fireworks at the levee for those who want to go.

But the business at hand for me is a peach pie. It is two o'clock, and the party is scheduled to start at four. I have no time to waste. "Maybe Steve needs help with something," I say to Patrick.

"So you want to get rid of me, huh?" Patrick says. He sticks out his bottom lip as if pouting. "I could peel the peaches, you know."

I consider this. "Very well," I say. "Peel the peaches and then go see if Steve needs help."

Patrick laughs a jovial July Fourth laugh, a day-off-work and the-sun-is-shining kind of laugh. "You tell it like it is, don't you, Aunt Sophie?" He proceeds to peel the peaches and regale me at the same time with a discourse about last year's July the Fourth, which was "a disaster from the word go" since everything had to be canceled because of heavy rain and flooding. "No parade, no picnics, no fireworks," he says. He tells of the postponed church picnic held the following week, of the patriotic musical program, of the games and the greased pig chase. Someone had borrowed the pig from a farmer, he says, but when the chase began, the pig had a heart attack and died. He throws his head back and laughs with gusto. "We had to take up a special collection to pay for the pig," he says.

I want to tell him to stop talking and pay attention to his peeling, but as he is making good progress with the peaches I keep quiet and concentrate on the pie crusts. It will take two pies to feed twenty people. Even then, the pieces will be small. It is my hope that some will eat only ice cream and leave more birthday pie for Rachel. I go slowly, measuring the ingredients into a bowl, cutting in the shortening until it forms small soft pebbles, carefully adding cold water, stirring with a fork.

". . . and said he'd help me remodel the master bath if I'll help him with his kitchen after that," Patrick is saying, "although I'm starting to have second thoughts about it." He goes on to tell me his second, third, and fourth thoughts. I sprinkle flour on the countertop, spread it in a large circle, then roll the first ball of dough through it. "But what it boils down to is this," Patrick says at last. "We could save a lot of money by doing just the floor repair without all the rest of it. We don't really *need* a totally new bathroom."

He is not only peeling the peaches but slicing them, also. I do not object to this, especially when I see that he is slicing them neither too small nor too large. He pops a slice into his mouth, his fingers wet with juice. "These are delectable," he says. "Rachel's going to love the surprise. Maybe I'll let her think I made the pies by myself." He means to be teasing, but I give him no answer. I take Rachel's rolling pin out of the drawer. "Hey, I take it back!" he says. "Don't hit me with that thing! I'll tell her you made them!" He throws up his hands as if to defend himself.

"Watch what you're doing," I say. "You're going to drip juice onto the floor."

"Yes, ma'am," he says. He laughs and goes back to work, turning suddenly serious again. "Especially when I think about all those Christians in Bangladesh and Vietnam and what they're going through every day," he says. I do not have to ask what he is talking about, for I know. He and Rachel subscribe to a magazine called *Martyrs for Jesus* that comes in the mail every month. Patrick reads stories aloud from it after supper. He and Rachel pray for the people in these stories as if they know them personally: Umanu, Trang Chu, Redoy Roy, Giang Phan. If one can believe the stories, these are people who are "persecuted for the cause of Christ," as Patrick likes to say.

"So I have to ask myself whether I really should spend several thousand dollars on a bathroom," he says, "when those people need so much help." On and on he goes, telling now about another man who was beaten in the face and dragged through his village for converting to Christianity. As he slices peaches, he whips himself into a fury of rhetoric over the "lazy, selfish, carnal attitudes of all the comfortable Christians in the western world."

Today is not the first time Patrick has put me in mind of Don Armado, a ridiculous Spanish blowhard, full of affectations and pomposity, from *Love's Labour's Lost*. "He draweth out the thread of his verbosity finer than the staple of his argument." So says the schoolmaster describing Don Armado. Yet today, though the thread of Patrick's verbosity is as lengthy as always, there is something in the staple of his argument that does not rankle as much as usual.

Regrettably, *Love's Labour's Lost* is a misunderstood play, full of obscure references and unintelligible jokes, many of which Eliot tackled in a paper he presented at a conference, a paper I typed for him. I was also in the audience when he read it. I recall wishing that he had addressed the title, another of the play's unintelligible jokes in my opinion. For how could any labor of love be lost?

". . . but he looked them in the eye," Patrick is saying, "and told them he *wouldn't* worship the ghosts of his ancestors any longer! That's when they tied him up and ran a spear through his hand. The next day they did his other hand, and the next day they ran the spear through his heart."

I could remind him that the martyrs, if the stories are true, will have their reward beyond the grave, if his religion is true. "Blessed are they which are persecuted for righteousness' sake," I could say to him, "for theirs is the kingdom of heaven." I could remind him of other words spoken by the apostle Paul, words I have heard Patrick himself read aloud: "Having nothing, and yet possessing all things."

I could also remind him of the large gifts of money he and Rachel have already given to the Martyrs for Jesus organization. I could tell him that the two of them cannot be expected to provide all the funds for all the projects described in the magazine: the children's home, the supply of Bibles for new converts, the vocational training, the food, water, clothing, bicycles. Leave something for others to do, I could tell him. Don't be greedy about your giving. Show some moderation.

But I cannot say this, for I am not supposed to know about the gifts of money. This is information I gathered surreptitiously, by looking in Patrick's checkbook one day while he and Rachel were at church. Imagine, Patrick and Rachel praying and singing hymns while Sophie snoops through their checkbook at home.

"But a new bathroom would be nice for Rachel." This is something I can say. And I remember something else I can say, something

I read in the Bible: Besides, "'ye have the poor always with you.'" I do not look at him, but I imagine his mouth falling open to hear me quote from the gospels.

And he agrees. "Yes, that's true. It really is. I keep thinking of how much Rachel would enjoy it."

An hour later Patrick is watching me take the pies from the oven. He admires them enthusiastically, exclaiming over the design of a flower I have cut into the top crusts. "You ought to go into business, Aunt Sophie!" he says.

Rachel is still across the street helping with the preparations. She has not walked in on the surprise. Teri knows about the secret of the pies. She was also the one who told me about the bathrobe Rachel had admired in a catalog, the bathrobe I will give her on her birth-day. It is a summer robe, pastel green with small yellow flowers stitched along the placket of snaps in the front. Teri has wrapped it for me in white paper and a silver ribbon.

Patrick has a plan. He will come home to get the pies after we have eaten our fill of hamburgers and potato salad. He will present them to Rachel and tell her they are a gift from me. I will cut the slices, and he will serve them. For now he carries the pies to my apartment to cool so that Rachel will not see them if she happens to run home before the party. I do not ask him if he has a plan to remove the smell—the evidence of things not seen. He takes the watermelon and goes across the street to check on the progress of things, promising to come back for me at four o'clock. "You take a little breather now," he says, "and I'll be back to carry you across the street."

"I would like to see that," I say. I know, of course, that he is using the word *carry* as southerners do, to mean accompany or transport by car.

He finds great humor in my remark and is still laughing when he finally closes the door. "You are one funny lady," he says. This is something he has said before.

I go to my recliner to take a breather. From here I can see the two pies sitting on a wire cooling rack on the round table. The Fonz and Richie Cunningham are arguing about a sum of money on the television, so I turn to the Nature Channel, where I hear a man's voice say, "Not everything that looks like a whisker is really a whisker." Imagine this: On July Fourth Sophie sits in her chair and learns about whiskers. She learns that porcupine quills are spiny hairs, not genuine whiskers. She learns that certain birds have bristles around their beaks that look like whiskers but are actually feathers. She learns that the long feelers of catfish are flesh, not whiskers. She learns that human beards cannot accurately be called whiskers, for they are not sensitive to touch.

True to his word, Patrick returns promptly at four to escort me to the cookout. I have put on my shoes and am ready. Several of the other guests have already arrived, he tells me excitedly, and Steve and Teri's backyard looks beautiful. This is the word he uses—*beautiful*. At times Patrick speaks like a girl. He holds out an arm, as if he is an usher at a wedding. I take it, as if I am the grandmother of the bride, and together we make our way across the street. There are three extra cars parked in front of Steve and Teri's house.

And this is how the cookout begins: Patrick takes me into Teri's kitchen by way of the back door. But first we must go through the laundry room. I hear voices before I see people. I hear a woman's voice say, "And she *lives* with you? My word, how old is she?" I hear Rachel's voice: "Yes, she has her own room and bath. She'll turn eighty-one in a couple of weeks." Patrick and I stop. We do not look at each other, and neither of us says a word. Perhaps he is as stunned as I to be stumbling into such a conversation.

"Well, that sure must be a lot of fun, taking care of your husband's *aunt* full time," the other woman says in a tone that means it is no fun at all. "That must be like having a child underfoot."

"Don't forget, Catherine honey, I lived with you and Blake for a while." This is a light, trilling voice I recognize as Helena's friend Della Boyd.

"Yes, but that was different," the other voice says. "You pulled your weight. You cooked and cleaned and did all sorts of things to help out."

And then I hear Rachel's voice again. "Oh, but I love Aunt Sophie. She's a wonderful person. She's part of our family."

And then Della Boyd says, "Oh, watch out, Teri, that pitcher's dribbling. Here, let me wipe it up for you." I hear Teri laugh. "Oh, goodness, I hope it didn't get in the baked beans!" From another room I hear more laughter and other voices, the voices of young people.

Patrick calls out, "Hello! Here we are! Any chance of getting something to eat around here?"

We step into the kitchen, and Rachel smiles at me. "Here, sit down, Aunt Sophie," she says as she pulls a chair from the kitchen table. It is at that moment that I wish I had a thousand peach pies to lay at her feet. I wish I had bought her a new bathrobe for every day of the year. She turns back to the counter, where she is arranging pickles and lettuce on a platter. I stare at her back. She is wearing a white T-shirt with a picture of an American eagle on the back and U.S.A. printed below.

I hear her words echoing in my mind. She used the word *love* and said I was part of the family. She called me a wonderful person. This, I know, is a great exaggeration, yet I feel as if a round of fireworks has quietly exploded within me.

Steve sticks his head in the back door. "Hey, Pat, quit loafing! I could use some help out here at the grill." He waves at me. "Hi, Aunt Sophie. Got any interesting facts to share with us today?" I think of asking him if he knows about catfish whiskers but shake my head instead. Somewhere outside I hear a shriek and then a voice I know well. Ahab has arrived. I hear the sound of Potts' laughter.

"How you doing today, Aunt Sophie?" Teri says. She is carrying a tray of paper cups filled with pink lemonade. "Hey, somebody tell the kids to come on out back," she says. "We're going to get started in a minute." From the other room I hear a Woody Woodpecker laugh, then a girl's voice: "Just ignore him. He's always trying to get attention." I hear a boy's voice: "Trying? You must be kidding. I'm just a magnet when it comes to attention. I could try *not* to attract it, but it would still come. Just like those little iron filings in science class—helpless under power like mine." I hear laughter—a girl's— and I wonder if it could be Mindy.

Minutes later we are gathered in the backyard, a score of disconnected souls. I stand behind Patrick, beside Rachel. I do not like crowds of people. I can sympathize with the greased pig at the church picnic. He looked up, saw a crowd of people, and keeled over from dread and fright.

It is easy to tell which ones among this crowd are parents, for their eyes seek out their children. I see Steve and Teri watching Mindy anxiously for signs that she likes having other young people around. I see Mitchell gazing down at Ahab, who is squatting on the ground digging with a stick. I see another couple I take to be Della Boyd's family, looking across heads and settling on the faces of the other three teenagers. They are good-looking children. The older boy is wearing a sleeveless white T-shirt with a fringed cowboy vest.

I think of all the energy that goes into raising children, the expense of feeding, clothing, and sheltering them, the outpouring of love and labor, none of it lost. Not even on a child like Veronica, not even on a boy like Prince, both gone in different ways. It all counts for something, every act of love, though perhaps not measurable on this earth.

I think of birds about which I've read, birds that go to all lengths to protect their young, those that fight outright though greatly outsized by a predator, those that devise various ruses to draw away the enemy. I think of stories I have read of birds charred in fires, yet underneath their wings their babies survive.

Steve takes his eyes off Mindy's face long enough to ask Patrick to say a blessing over the food. Don Armado takes a step forward and clears his throat. As he begins his prayer, I observe the nineteen people around me. People from all walks and all stages of life. Handsome and plain, tall and short, fat and thin, black and white. I hear Patrick's words rising loftily into the blue Fourth of July sky. I feel Rachel's presence beside me. And here is the thought that comes to me: Oh, the variety of ways to live one's life.

CHAPTER 32

NO OTHER TRIBUTE AT THY HANDS

The American kestrel, with its rust-colored back, smoky blue wings, and distinctive black markings, looks too small and too ornamental to be a predator. One of its favorite times to hunt is after a snowfall. It hovers above the snow, scanning intently for mice holes and smaller birds, then dives feet first to capture its prey.

Having made a presentation speech on my behalf, Patrick is now holding the peach pies on a tray, the same tray that has been used since last October to deliver my meals. Though I have heard Rachel weep when talking on the telephone, this is the first time I have seen her tears. For a certainty, it is the first time I have caused her to cry. I think perhaps it is the first time anyone has ever shed tears over a peach pie.

She looks at me as if I have given her precious gems, and she cries openly and profusely. "Oh, Aunt Sophie, I can't believe you did this for me," she says over and over. Everyone else is sitting in Steve and Teri's backyard observing this display. I expected gratitude, yes, but not this. The look on Patrick's face tells me he is likewise astounded by Rachel's effusive weeping. Teri, sitting beside her, pats her shoulder comfortingly.

"Why is Aunt Wachel cwying?" Ahab says and everyone laughs.

"Maybe she wanted cherry instead." This comes from one of the teenagers related to Della Boyd, the one named Hardy, who is wearing the cowboy vest. There is more laughter.

"Oh no, these are called tears of joy," Potts says.

Della Boyd, in her twittering way, says, "Isn't it an interesting thing how tears can express so many different emotions?"

Another voice, a stage whisper: "Am I missing something? Why all the fuss over a couple of pies?"

"Or maybe she wanted apple," Hardy says. "Or blueberry." Besides the cowboy vest, he is wearing a pair of Bermuda shorts made of squares of colorful madras plaid. On his feet are red high-top canvas sneakers with no shoelaces. If one can overlook his garb, he is a handsome boy. He looks to be eighteen or nineteen. Mindy has been watching him closely, as if trying to figure him out.

And now Rachel rises from her chair and moves around the table toward me like a large shy child, wiping her eyes and smiling uncertainly. "I can't believe you did this for me," she says again. "Why, it's the best birthday present you could have given me, Aunt Sophie. Did you know peach pie is my favorite?" She leans down and puts her arms around me. It is an awkward way to embrace, but she does not hold back. And I do not resist as she pulls me close. My head rests against her heart.

I cannot speak, but Patrick can and does. "I told her how much you liked it," he says proudly. "I brought the peaches home. They're especially good this year!" I expect him to expound upon the favorable weather conditions, to inform everyone that he peeled and sliced the peaches, to boast that it was his idea to present the pies as an early birthday gift at the cookout. But he doesn't. Instead he says briskly, "Okay, we need a count of how many want pie. Aunt Sophie is going to do the slicing. We'll serve it over here next to the ice cream so you can get both at the same time." He carries the tray to a table and sets it down.

And still Rachel holds me. I would not think of pulling away.

In the background I hear Hardy say, "It's what's called a tableau in drama."

At last Rachel lets go and steps back. "Thank you, Aunt Sophie," she says again. "I'll never ever forget this."

I remember something. "Oh, you're welcome," I say, waving a hand in the air, "but it's such a little thing."

"It is not a little thing, Aunt Sophie," she says.

"Oh, watch out, they're going to start arguing now," Hardy says.

Della Boyd laughs merrily. "My, there's just nothing like fresh peach pie in the summertime, is there?" she says. "Isn't this a treat for us all? We're so glad you're having a birthday tomorrow, Rachel." And she starts singing: "Happy birthday to you, happy birthday to you." Others join in. Ahab, out of his chair now, is beside himself with excitement, twirling around in circles.

"Okay now, raise your hands if you want a piece," Patrick says in his manager's voice, and he proceeds to count out loud. "Form a line here, everybody, and we'll get you served. I need you over here, Aunt Sophie. I'll dip the ice cream while you cut the pie."

"Sounds like school," Hardy says. "Raise your hands and get in line." Mindy studies her fingernails. Here is an ambiguity: Perhaps she smiles briefly, or perhaps she winces from a sudden small pain.

Seventeen people want a slice of pie. Joanna Lebo says she's gained too much weight and is trying to stay away from sugar. Mitchell says Ahab will have only ice cream. And Della Boyd's sister-in-law, a petite red-haired woman, publicizes this fact: "I don't really like fruit pie all that much, especially if the crust isn't homemade." Hers was the voice I overheard earlier: "Why all the fuss over a couple of pies?" And even earlier: "Well, that sure must be a lot of fun, taking care of your husband's *aunt* full time."

The red-haired woman reminds me of someone. As I cut slices of peach pie, I can't get her out of my mind. She is beautiful to look at. She wears slim blue pants with a matching blouse and white sandals. Her earrings are silver. Her toenails are painted red. Perhaps she reminds me of another teacher at one of the schools where I taught or a former neighbor, perhaps the mother of a student.

Or perhaps I am thinking of certain birds I have read about, whose appearance conflicts with their actions. There are hunting birds called raptors that are as pretty as songbirds. It is their behavior, not their looks, that settles the matter.

If this woman, Catherine by name, did not open her mouth, one might think her to be as mild and harmless as Rachel. But she is no gentle creature. There appears to be no filter between her thoughts and her tongue, no shut-off valve. Whatever enters her mind drops like a waterfall and flows from her mouth. I try to imagine such a woman as the mother of three teenagers. No doubt sparks have flown in that home.

Perhaps her sharp tongue and her name combine to remind me of Katharina in *The Taming of the Shrew*—the original Katharina, that is, not the tamed one. It was a play of which Eliot was fond. I was not. I did not like Petruchio's methods. I did not like the suggestion that a woman can be manipulated like a child.

But it is hard to imagine anyone taming this Catherine. I can only guess that her husband has had his hands full, as my father liked to say. I cannot imagine her obeying a man's wishes quietly and meekly. I certainly cannot imagine her giving such a speech as Katharina gives at the end of Shakespeare's play, when instructed to tell other women what duty they owe their husbands.

There are names for headstrong women, some of them from the animal kingdom. Barracuda is one that comes to mind. But I do not know her. I have observed her less than two hours. I should not judge. Perhaps this is only her public face. Perhaps she mellows as one gets to know her.

Catherine's husband comes through the line. His name is Blake. I see his hands resting on the edge of the table. They are large, manly hands. If anyone could handle the quick-tongued Catherine, he could. Yet he is a gentleman. "Thank you for sharing this with the rest of us," he says, leaning forward. "It almost looks too good to eat." I do not point out his misplaced modifier.

I glance briefly at his face, his dark eyes, his pleasant smile. During the meal I thought him handsome from a distance of two tables. Now I see that he is the same up close. During the meal I took note of his attentiveness to his wife's needs. I saw the way he turned to her when they talked. He gives no evidence of being dominated by her. I cannot say what system they have devised for their marriage. I see only what I see. One can hear a clock tick, can watch its hands move without comprehending its inner workings. I hear his wife's voice rise in the background now, saying to someone else, "Well, there's no way *that* can be a homemade crust. It looks too perfect!" I cut his piece slightly larger than the others.

Katharina's closing speech in *The Taming of the Shrew* was the subject of a paper Eliot wrote during the mid–1970s—an unlucky bit of timing considering the fervor of the women's movement during that decade. To my secret satisfaction, the paper was never accepted for publication, though Eliot considered it some of his best writing. For so smart a man, he did not understand that the words were out of tune by the standards of a world in which women were no longer securely ensconced at home, whose husbands no longer labored to keep them so.

It surprises me to realize how stirred I still feel at the memory of this paper, titled rather frivolously "Petruchio's Dream Come True." I was not convinced by Katharina's change, so complete and so swift. Imagine a wasp, a wildcat, a devil of a woman being brought within five acts to speak words such as these: "Thy husband is thy lord, thy life, thy keeper, thy head, thy sovereign." And this lord of a husband, the former shrew informs other women, desires "no other tribute at thy hands" except love, beauty, and obedience. Indeed, what more could a man want from a wife than adoration, good looks, and sub-servience? Shakespeare says nothing in the play about what a woman wants from a husband. But Shakespeare, like any other man, was a product of his time. Perhaps his art cannot be faulted for that.

"Rachel, come up here and get your pie!" Patrick calls. She has held back, telling others to go first, occupying herself with Ahab, who has fallen and skinned his knee. She cradles him in her lap as he wails loudly and clings to her. She rises and comes to the table, still holding Ahab. "I think I'll take him in to get a Band-Aid first," she says. The wound on Ahab's knee is barely visible. There is no blood.

"Well, okay," Patrick says, "but come right back. Aunt Sophie has already cut your piece and set it aside." She starts toward the house. "You'll want ice cream, too!" he calls. "The pie is still a little warm." Rachel and Patrick have likewise devised a system for their marriage past my understanding. Perhaps I should say that Patrick has devised a system and Rachel has accepted it. For a moment I try to imagine Patrick married to someone like Catherine. I try to think of her response were he to say, "Catherine, come up here and get your pie!" But the picture does not take shape. I cannot imagine Patrick or Rachel with anyone else.

"He is starting young," I say to Patrick as we watch her carry Ahab inside.

"Starting what?" he says.

"Theatrics for the purpose of arousing a woman's sympathy," I say.

"Hey, I heard that," a voice says, and I turn to see Hardy waiting for the next piece of pie. He suddenly clutches at his stomach and staggers forward, his eyes rolling back in his head, his mouth gaping. He gasps, utters a deep groan, and collapses to the ground but immediately springs to his feet, the fringe on his cowboy vest jiggling wildly. "There, how's that for theatrics?" he says. "Did I arouse your sympathy, huh, did I? Can I have a piece of pie, huh, can I?"

I am tempted to ask Hardy if he has a partner named Laurel, but I refrain. I serve his plate, then say, "There, go sit down, Roy Rogers, and calm yourself."

He takes the plate, throws his head back, and calls, "Hi-ho, Silver!"

"That was the Lone Ranger, not Roy Rogers," I say.

His eyes brighten. "You are right! I was just testing you. Mindy said you were smart, so I had to check it out. Which reminds me. Do you know where the Lone Ranger took all his trash?" And without waiting for me to answer, he sings, "To the dump, to the dump, to the dump, dump, dump."

Patrick can hardly contain his laughter. "Hey, that's *funny*! I'm going to remember that one!" It is just the kind of joke Patrick would love. He is laughing so hard he has trouble landing the scoop of ice cream on Hardy's plate.

"I bet you're wondering how I know about Roy Rogers and the Lone Ranger, huh?" says Hardy.

"No, I am not," I say.

"Well, okay, okay. Don't beg. I'll satisfy your curiosity," he says. "I know you can't tell it from looking at me, but I'm very retro-savvy. I know all about those old TV programs. *Sky King, Sea Hunt, Zorro*, and all the rest. It's a hobby that—"

"Hey, you're holding up the line," his sister says behind him. "She's not interested in hearing about your deviant lifestyle."

"Oh, but she is," Hardy says, leaning forward. "I can see it deep in her *eyes*."

This party is like the train that used to come through Methuselah. The Everlasting Train, we used to call it. You could take a long nap while it rattled by, boxcar after boxcar with no caboose in sight. If you had an appointment on the other side of town, you would miss it.

Dessert done, Patrick supervises the cleanup, scurrying about and shouting directions as if time were running out. It is not yet seven o'clock. When all of the tables are cleared and the trash bags cinched, Patrick begins explaining all the rules of horseshoes, consulting a paper he has printed off the Internet. He goes on and on. When he starts talking about the history of the game, attributing its beginnings to Roman soldiers, Steve breaks in. "Well, maybe that's enough to get us started."

"Okay, any questions so far?" Patrick asks.

"Can you throw overhand?" Hardy asks, to which Patrick replies with great seriousness, "Oh no. You'd never, never want to do that."

"See, I told you," Hardy says to Mindy. To the rest of us he says, "She wanted me to ask."

"I did not!" Mindy says. She acts indignant, but anyone can see it's only an act.

"Any other questions?" Patrick says hopefully.

Hardy speaks up again. "Are there pony shoes instead of horseshoes for really young small children like my little brother here?" His brother, red-haired like their mother and almost as tall as Hardy, gives him a shove.

"No, no. Everyone uses the same size," Patrick says.

These are things I learn about the game of horseshoes: First, I learn that there are innings, foul lines, and a pitcher's box as in baseball. Second, each contestant throws two horseshoes per inning. Third, you can score with points, ringers, or double ringers. And fourth, a tournament can take a long time if twelve people want to play. I find myself hoping that Hardy and his partner, Mitchell, will make a good showing, although it is obvious from the beginning that Hardy is putting more effort into entertaining Mindy than in winning the game. The winning partnerships advance to a playoff round with modified rules, and in the end Wes Lebo and one of Steve's friends are declared the overall champions.

"Rats," says Hardy. "That woulda looked so good in the hometown paper: 'Hardy Biddle Makes Competitors Eat Dust in Game of Horseshoes While Visiting in Mississippi.'"

The party is still young. It is almost seven-thirty when the game is finished and Steve and Potts bring out their guitars. They strum a few chords, and some of the men pull their chairs closer. The rest of us sit around to see what will come of this. Ahab is in the sandbox, burying plastic toys and digging them up again.

"Hey, let's sing something!" Hardy says. This is not something you expect a boy like him to say. But before there is time to consider whether he is joking, a male ensemble somehow organizes itself. Steve and Potts begin singing and playing a solemn song called "Deep River," and Blake, Hardy, Patrick, and Mitchell join in. "My home is over Jordan," the song says, and "I want to cross over into campground." With the other stronger voices, Patrick's tenor sounds less like a trembling reed in the wind.

It is a concert of spirituals that they sing: "Swing Low, Sweet Chariot," "Sometimes I Feel Like a Motherless Child," "Nobody Knows the Trouble I've Seen," "He's Got the Whole World in His Hands," "Poor Wayfaring Stranger." Steve and Potts move easily from one song into another, as if it is a repertoire they rehearse often. They keep going when the others drop out.

I hear the words clearly, words that would sound strange out of their context. In their context, however, everything is right about them: "A band of angels comin' after me," "Sometimes I'm up, sometimes I'm down," "He's got the tiny little baby in his hands," "A-travelin' through this world of woe." The men's voices blend better than one would expect at a backyard cookout.

Potts starts a new song that the others apparently don't know: "The gospel train is comin', / I hear it just at hand." Steve and Potts sing it as though it's their favorite. "Get on board, little children," they sing. This one moves along. Not like the Everlasting Train of Methuselah but like an express train. "I hear that train a-comin'," they sing. "She sure is speedin' fast, / So get your tickets ready, / And ride to heav'n at last!" Then the chorus again, louder and faster this time, then again softer and faster still as if the train has blown through town and is racing against the clock. "Get on board, little children," they sing one last time, slow and easy now as if pulling into the station, "there's room for many a-more."

They stop and there is a moment of silence before Della Boyd says, "Oh my, that was just *wonderful*! You two should make a record! You sure *should*!" She begins clapping her hands and others join in.

I look at the men around me—at Steve and his two friends, at Blake, Wes Lebo, Potts, and Mitchell. Yes, and Patrick, too. And here is what I think: There are good men in this world. I look at the boys—at Hardy and his brother, at Ahab. Yes, there is hope here, also.

Mindy is sitting next to Hardy's sister, the two of them looking like twins with their blond hair and pretty faces. Mindy's eyes are fixed on Hardy. She has not yet learned the tactic used by some women, who take care to appear unaware of a man's presence. Mindy stares openly. I wonder if she has thought of Prince today.

The guitars are put away, but the party is far from over. It is going on nine o'clock, and at last the sky is growing dark. Allowing for no lull, Teri jumps up and announces, "Okay, time for charades. Everybody plays this one!" Steve turns on the floodlights he has rented. Teri has prepared little slips of paper on which are written phrases to be acted out. There will be two teams: men versus women.

It is a silly game but one that everybody seems to like. There is much laughter as the phrases are acted out: "mum's the word," "dressed to the nines," "put up your dukes," "the whole ball of wax," and so forth. Before we know it, the light has faded. Just as Teri's aunt Helena is acting out "close but no cigar," we hear faint popping and whistling noises. Above the treetops large glittery flowers of red and blue fireworks burst open in the sky. "Anybody want to go down to the levee?" Steve asks. "It's only a few blocks. We can take my truck."

"And then it's back here for watermelon!" Patrick announces. "One last fling!"

"Aw, why can't we just eat it instead?" Hardy asks.

Some go and some stay. Another explosion lights the sky, this one green and silver. I can see all I want to see from where I sit.

I hear the sound of Steve's pickup in the driveway. I hear laughter. I hear somebody calling, "Hey, wait for us!" And I hear Hardy singing: "Get on board, little children! / Get on board, little children! / Get on board, little children! / There's room for many a-more!"

CHAPTER 33

MY GRACIOUS SILENCE, HAIL!

*The melancholy coo of the mourning dove is
in truth a sign that all is right with the bird,
for it is the season of mating and nesting.
For nourishment, the babies insert their heads
deep inside the parent's open mouth and feast
on a unique substance rich in fat and
protein, called pigeon's milk.*

I think one more little shim on this end will do it," Patrick says,
then, "Okay now, hand me the level, will you? Let's make sure
she's plumb."

"Plumb what?" Steve asks.

"Plumb level." Patrick laughs robustly at his little joke.

Steve and Patrick are working nights and weekends on Rachel's
new bathroom. Today they have cut through the wall studs in order
to install a new medicine chest. We can hear them quite clearly

through the kitchen wall. Perhaps it is because of the hole they have cut in the bathroom wall, combined with the echo effect now that the old tile and fixtures have been removed. Perhaps it is because they are both using their instructive voices as if talking across stock rooms and warehouses. Perhaps Steve, recently promoted to a supervisory position at the catfish plant, is closely observing Patrick these days to pick up tips on How to Exude Authority.

Patrick, having wrestled with his soul, has decided that the Martyrs for Jesus will not go under because of a single remodeling project. Up until now, he and Steve have done all the work themselves, in preparation for "the tile man," as Patrick calls him, who will be coming next week.

"He sure is going to a lot of trouble for this bathroom," Rachel says to me. She says this while preparing a meal for Joanna Lebo, who is coming home from the hospital today with her new baby. This is a meal that could feed a family of ten.

"That is Patrick's way," I say. I am peeling carrots for Rachel and slicing them into long strips. It is not enough to do them the easy way. For Joanna's meal, Rachel has it in her mind to make something called julienne vegetable medley.

"Bingo, she's right on," we hear Patrick say. "Okay, let's get her in." This is typical of Patrick to use feminine pronouns for inanimate objects. "She's a feisty one," I have heard him say of a thunderstorm and, of a car, "She needs a new radiator hose."

"I tried to tell him I didn't need that big fancy medicine chest," Rachel says. "I was making out okay with just a mirror. But he wouldn't listen." She says this while standing over a skillet with a fork. I look at her standing there. In the August heat she has resorted to wearing shorts and sleeveless T-shirts. Over these she wears an apron. She will not adjust the temperature of the air-conditioning for her own comfort. Besides, she says, her body cannot make up its mind. She is hot one minute and cold the next. She goes barefoot in the house but keeps a sweater handy. Today her hair is pulled back into something called a French braid. It is a style Mindy showed her how to do.

Some would say Rachel does not have a figure for shorts, for she is broad-beamed. Her thighs are dimpled columns. Behind her knees is a purple roadmap of veins. She is browning pieces of sirloin for something called Swiss steak, which will simmer for four hours in a covered dish. I think of the potatoes that are in the oven. It is not enough to bake them once. Rachel means to do them twice.

"Both of you go overboard," I say.

She turns from the skillet and looks at me. "Why, that's not true, Aunt Sophie. What would make you say such a thing?"

I hold her gaze for a moment and then say, "Mitchell, Ahab, Potts, Steve, Teri, Mindy, Wes, Joanna, Lurlene, Prince. Those are some of the reasons I would say such a thing." I could add another name to the list: Sophie.

She shakes her head. "Sometimes you say the funniest things."

"Sometimes you do the funniest things," I say.

Consider, for instance, the case of Lurlene Cook. Imagine telephoning the mother of someone who held you at gunpoint, who threatened to blow you open. Imagine inviting her out to lunch and sitting across the table from her. Imagine ordering from a menu and sharing food with her. Imagine picking up the bill and paying for both meals. This is what Rachel did.

"His mother must be so brokenhearted." This was what I heard Rachel say before this event was set in motion.

I must back up. What set it in motion was something Potts did. He came over one night to talk with Patrick and Steve. His heart was "burdened," he said. "The Lord keeps bringing that boy to my mind." That boy was Prince, who was still in jail, who had in fact gotten into further trouble by being an uncooperative prisoner. After mouthing off repeatedly, he had finally assaulted one of the guards with a fork he had somehow gotten from the kitchen. Things had gone from very bad to a lot worse for that boy.

"He reminds me of myself when I was his age," Potts said to Patrick and Steve that night. "I was headed straight for hell and would probably already be dead and in permanent residence there if I hadn't landed in jail the second time."

Somebody with a Bible came to the jail, talked straight to Potts, and, in his words, "I turned from my wicked ways and gave my heart to Jesus." Hearing this, I wanted to head him off. I knew what was coming. I wanted to cry out, "Don't do it! Don't go down there and try to convert that boy. He's a lost cause. He's bad news. He's a contagion. Stay away from him!"

"And what made Cyrus LeGrande come to the jail that night?" Potts said. "What made him pick out my cell for his little Bible talk? And what made me listen for probably the first time in my life?" He paused for a long time. Perhaps he saw that Steve and Patrick, like me, weren't quite willing to go where he was leading. He finally said, "It was grace, brothers. It was only the grace of Almighty God that let me hear the gospel that night. He worked a miracle in my life."

He gave a laugh. "Old Mr. LeGrande wasn't even a very good

preacher. That man could jumble up more words than you can imagine. But I heard past his words to his message that night, and something told me that what he was saying was the truth."

It didn't take anyone with a Ph.D. to understand what he was suggesting.

"So what are you suggesting?" Patrick said. "Are you going to get Mr. LeGrande to go pay Prince a visit in jail?"

"Cyrus LeGrande is dead," Potts said. "I'm talking about me."

Imagine agreeing to send help to the boy who had walked uninvited into your home with a gun, who had jammed that gun into your wife's neck, who had tried to take your daughter from you. But that is exactly what happened. The three of them prayed over it, and Steve and Patrick gave their blessing to Potts.

So Potts went to the jail. That's when we found out about the other trouble with the guard and the fork. That's when Rachel said, "His mother must be so brokenhearted." I must admit something. My first feeling was not compassion for Prince's mother. It was gladness for us. If Prince had done this thing, surely he would be in jail even longer. Nor was my second feeling any closer to sympathy: Could the jails of our state not be trusted to take the simplest precautions—that is, to keep track of their forks? How could we, the innocent people of Mississippi, have confidence that they would keep track of their inmates?

No miracles happened at the jail when Potts talked to Prince. Prince did not turn from his wicked ways. He did not give his heart to Jesus. "He's closed up tighter than a lockbox," Potts told Patrick. The metaphor was weak, for a lockbox implies something of value inside. But Potts does not mean to give up. When he went the second time, Patrick was with him. And they will go again. Likewise, Rachel will go again to Lurlene. I would not be surprised to learn that she was cleaning the woman's house, hoeing her garden, ironing her clothes.

"I'm glad Joanna and Wes had a boy," Rachel says to me now. "When he's a little older, he can play with Ahab." I imagine the Lebo baby toddling along with his tongue hanging out, trying to keep up with Ahab. Wes and Joanna have named the baby George, after Joanna's father. Imagine two babies named George and Ahab.

I finish the carrots and begin cutting the yellow squash into strips. Rachel covers the meat and starts pulling husks off the ears of corn. No canned corn for this meal. Rachel remembers Wes saying that his favorite vegetable is fresh corn cut off the cob.

"Timothy says those glass tiles run five bucks a piece," Patrick says to Steve. "Did I tell you that already? And the stainless steel ones are even more." Timothy is the tile man who is coming next week. I have heard Patrick call him an "artist," a "perfectionist," a "master craftsman." For this project Patrick has not chosen the lowest bidder.

"So what did you decide?" Steve says. "Did you order a couple hundred of both kinds?" Steve is a person who says, "Ha-ha-ha-ha-ha," while he laughs.

"No, no. I scaled way back," Patrick says. "We're just going to use a few of the glass ones as accents."

"He doesn't need to do that," Rachel says to me. "That's just extra trouble and expense. I could live out the rest of my life happy as can be without those glass tiles." She says this while spending her Saturday to make a meal for her neighbors, while laboring to remove every corn silk so that Wes Lebo can have his favorite vegetable.

"Wes said they were releasing her right after lunch, so they're probably already home," Rachel says.

I glance at my watch. It is a silver one with a stretchy band, a birthday gift from Patrick. It has a large face the size of a quarter and sturdy black hands with arrows on the ends. Like a nurse's watch, it is immensely practical. It tells me that it is a few minutes past two o'clock. Rachel has promised Wes that we will deliver the meal at six.

"Wes said he'd hang a new door for us in here," Patrick says to Steve in the bathroom. "He's so good at it, he can practically do it with his eyes closed. He said it would be payback for wallpapering the nursery."

Steve chuckles. "I guess it's a good thing we decided to do that job last Saturday instead of today."

"Yep," says Patrick. "I guess nobody told the little guy he was supposed to wait another two weeks."

"Joanna sure did fix the nursery up cute, didn't she?" Rachel says. She has taken a brush to the corn and is going after silks in hiding.

"Yes, she did," I say. It is not a subject I wish to pursue. I wonder what it must have done to Rachel's heart to walk into that nursery with its circus motif, its clown curtains and elephant lamp, the posters of the man on stilts and the little dog riding a unicycle. To look at the yellow wallpaper with its border of flipping acrobats, to see the crib, its sheets imprinted with colorful balloons—well, I cannot imagine being Rachel and seeing such a thing.

But it was something she asked for. "May I see the baby's room?" Those were the words she spoke when we went over three days ago to take a gift. It was a blue, pink, and yellow blanket that Rachel made herself. Knitting and crocheting do not come easily for Rachel, but she goes slowly and carefully. She has taught herself from a book. I have seen her at it in the middle of the night, sitting on the sofa in the living room, her head bent close to her work.

Joanna took us back to the nursery that day and laid the blanket on the crib. I could not look at Rachel's face, but I heard her voice: "Oh, what a pretty, cheerful room." Rachel's voice is one I know well by now. It is low and slow. Over the telephone it must sound mournful.

Perhaps it has always sounded so. Or perhaps it was suddenly and irreversibly infused with sorrow one day twenty years ago at the Memphis Zoo. All I know is this: When she said, "Oh, what a pretty, cheerful room" in her low, mournful voice, it was clear that she meant it. One must not judge from sound alone. He must look at all the evidence. I have read in my bird book that the mourning dove is a contented bird in spite of its name and the dark, pensive sound of its coo. I have read in the Bible that the dove is thought to be a symbol of mercy.

I look down at my feet. Imagine slippers made out of purple yarn. I opened them on my birthday after I opened the watch Patrick gave me. At first I thought they were twin drawstring purses until Patrick announced, "Try them on! Rachel made them! The pattern said one size fits any foot, so let's see!" No one would look at them and call them the work of an artist, a perfectionist, a master craftsman, but a thing does not have to be beautiful or perfect to be loved.

"There she is!" Patrick says triumphantly. "Now just a little fill-ing in around the edges, and we're in business." There is a soft thump. "Look at that. Just the least touch and it closes. I bet you could *blow* it closed." There is a pause, during which he must be experimenting. Another soft thump. "See, what did I tell you?" Then, proudly, "You know, it really is true—you get what you pay for!" It is hard to think of a truism that Patrick has not uttered at some time.

"How about the window molding?" Steve says. "Can we get it back up today?" No doubt Steve is thinking this: The sooner we finish Patrick's bathroom, the sooner we can start on my kitchen.

"Yes, but we've got to replace the sill," Patrick says. "Remember, we got a little carried away with the sledge hammer and wrecked it!" He laughs his cheerful home-improvement laugh. He is fudging with the plural pronoun, for it was he himself who hit the edge of the windowsill and broke it off.

"Did you read Patrick's new story yet?" Rachel asks. She is cutting the kernels off one of the ears of corn with a long sharp knife. She goes cautiously, as if shaving hair close to a scalp.

"Yes," I say, "what there is of it." I have finished with both the yellow squash and zucchini and am working on the small red potatoes. The recipe shows a diagram of how to cut them so that some of the red skin shows on each strip. The person who wrote the recipe down must have a lot of time on his hands. He must also fancy himself to be a wit. "To create the most colorful palette for the refined palate," the recipe says.

Patrick has not thought of an ending for his story yet. It is about a July Fourth backyard picnic. One of the characters is a boy named Harley, who shows up wearing white bell-bottom pants and a beanie with a little propeller on top. Another character is a girl named

Melinda who tries not to like him but keeps laughing at the silly things he does. At some point in the story it is revealed that Harley will be a freshman in college in the fall. Furthermore, it is a religious college. The boy's passion for unorthodox clothing is surpassed only by a passion for Christianity.

I try to imagine what a religious college will do with a student like Hardy this fall. For a moment it makes me wish I could teach at that college, that I could have Hardy in my Freshman Composition class and read his papers.

Surprisingly, Patrick's story is not as pushy in its religious tone as one might expect. It does not openly endorse Harley. It plants the reader in Melinda's viewpoint and raises questions about Harley at every turn. If shown this story six months ago, I would never have believed Patrick wrote it. Six months ago, in fact, Patrick could not have written it.

"Teri said Hardy called Mindy again the other night," Rachel says. "He seems to be talking real plain to her, trying to straighten out her thinking. He told Teri he's talking a lot about head problems but also keeps circling back to the heart problem. He said he means to keep at it until he gets through to her." She pauses. "Teri says Hardy is a godsend. Isn't it strange how a young person will listen better to somebody her own age than to her parents?"

I say nothing. The idea of a boy like Hardy trying to address someone else's head problems is baffling. But this is only another mystery past explaining. The world is full of them. There are miracles that refute known laws. I find that I am pulling for Hardy to succeed. I want to see him get through to Mindy. I want to see her straightened out, for I am partial to her. I often hear the words of her essay:

"The best birds aren't afraid of the cold, so they stay late in the year and sing late in the night." I remember the words Hardy said to me: "Mindy said you were smart."

I lift my knife and turn again to look at Rachel. If you want to behold a miracle that refutes known laws, I tell myself, look no further. "As the sun is daily new and old"—from a dusty corner of my memory I hear these words. They are from another sonnet, though I do not recall which one. Shakespeare's sonnet form is generally thought to be the most difficult, for it places a high demand on the closing couplet to contain yet expand the meaning of the previous lines. I think of Rachel as I know her today, containing her past yet expanding upon it. Daily she is both new and old. That she has opened her heart and taken me in is another one of the mysteries of the world past explaining.

"Aunt Sophie," she said to me earlier today, "I wish you'd think about going to church with us one of these Sundays. I wish you would."

"You want to drag me all over town," I said to her.

She knew I was referring to Dr. Robbins. "That didn't hurt you one bit," she said.

"He told me nothing I didn't already know." This is not entirely true. He was Rachel's doctor, a young man in his forties. Behind his thick glasses his eyes were enormous. "Your heart is strong for someone your age," he said to me. I raised my eyebrows. Perhaps he needed a new stethoscope. Perhaps his hearing was as weak as his eyesight. He also said gravely, "*And* for someone your size." He cleared his throat. "I'm sure you know that you would be healthier if you took off some weight."

"No doctor has ever told me this before," I said to him. He did not know what to make of this, and I did not explain that I had avoided doctors my whole life. He looked at the bottom of my foot and told me it looked like it was "responding to the treatment," by which he meant the liquid wart remover. I could have told him that.

"DISCOVERED. A possible NEW PLANET, as yet unnamed; by scientists at Caltech, Yale, and the Gemini Observatory." On the Milestones page I learn that researchers have spied the mass of rock and ice from afar, on the outer fringes of the solar system, and have judged it to be larger than Pluto. Imagine, a thing of that size yet heretofore unknown.

I have come to the brink of a new world, yet it is as old as eternity. "And about the ninth hour Jesus cried with a loud voice, saying, Eli, Eli, lama sabachthani? that is to say, My God, my God, why hast thou forsaken me?" In the red Bible I have sought out this part of the gospel story, to read it for myself. The sacrifice of God's son—it is a plan no man could have devised. This much I know.

These are the things I think about in my recliner on an August afternoon.

There is still much whirring and hammering in the bathroom. Having finished our kitchen work, Rachel and I wait silently for six o'clock to come. She is lying down on the living room sofa, and I am sitting in my recliner. I smell the bread she has baked, the Swiss steak simmering in the oven. After we deliver the meal next door, Patrick has said we will go out for supper. Rachel has requested that it be a quiet place, "not one of those noisy, busy places that's too bright." It will be noisy and busy enough, I want to tell her, with Patrick at the table.

I think of sound and silence, as natural as life itself. Nowhere do I read that God said, "Let there be sound." Having lit up the world, having created the land and sea and sky, having fashioned every living creature, he knew that sound would take care of itself. He made it so that a single voice could carry over many miles.

"My gracious silence, hail!" The words come to me now, words spoken by Coriolanus, a Roman nobleman and warrior, in the play of the same name. Though I do not recall their context, what I do recall is that silence is spoken of as a gracious and welcome thing. To whom the words were spoken I cannot say. Perhaps Coriolanus was addressing his mother, Volumnia, or his wife, Virgilia, or perhaps Virgilia's friend, Valeria. Shakespeare seemed to think all women's names should begin with a V in this play.

I think of the uses of silence, of what grows out of it. I think of the silence of the stars and the planets. I think of long silences broken by praise. I have read of the father of John the Baptist, stricken dumb because he doubted the prophecy of the angel Gabriel. The moment his tongue was loosed, he lifted his voice and said, "Blessed be the Lord God of Israel; for he hath visited and redeemed his people." Through silence one may be educated. And one may be awed. I think of great symphonies fading to silence, confirming the grandeur of what went before.

Though I am no great symphony, one day my life will fade to silence. Perhaps it will awake to praise and awe. Perhaps I shall hear a rush of wings, the singing of a choir. We shall see.

"You want to go with me to Joanna's, don't you?" Rachel stands in the doorway. She has taken her apron off and put on her shoes.

I think of another story I have read in the Bible, a story in the Old Testament about two women not related by blood. Here is what one of them said to the other: "Whither thou goest, I will go; and whither thou lodgest, I will lodge: thy people shall be my people, and thy God my God."

"Yes," I say, and I rise and follow Rachel to the kitchen.

Be the first to know

Want to be the first to know
what's new from
your favorite authors?

Want to know all about
exciting new writers?

Sign up for BethanyHouse newsletters at
www.bethanynewsletters.com
and you'll get regular updates via e-mail.
You can sign up for as many authors or
categories as you want so you get only
the information you really want.

Sign up today